T0035928

NIGHT'S EDGE

NIGHTFIRE

TOR PUBLISHING GROUP

NEW YORK

LIZ KERIN

NIGHT'S
EDGE

NIGHT'S EDGE

Copyright © 2023 by Elizabeth Kerin

A Nightfire Book
Published by Tom Doherty Associates / Tor Publishing Group
120 Broadway
New York, NY 10271

www.tornightfire.com

Nightfire™ is a trademark of Macmillan Publishing Group, LLC.

Library of Congress Cataloging-in-Publication Data

Names: Kerin, Liz, author.
Title: Night's edge / Liz Kerin.
Description: First edition. | New York : Nightfire,
Tor Publishing Group, 2023.
Identifiers: LCCN 2022051661 (print) | LCCN 2022051662 (ebook) |
ISBN 9781250835673 (hardcover) | ISBN 9781250835680 (ebook)
Subjects: LCGFT: Paranormal fiction. | Novels.
Classification: LCC PS3611.E7345 N54 2023 (print) |
LCC PS3611.E7345 (ebook) | DDC 813/.6—dc23/eng/20221130
LC record available at https://lccn.loc.gov/2022051661
LC ebook record available at https://lccn.loc.gov/2022051662

Our books may be purchased in bulk for promotional,
educational, or business use. Please contact your local bookseller
or the Macmillan Corporate and Premium Sales Department
at 1-800-221-7945, extension 5442, or by email at
MacmillanSpecialMarkets@macmillan.com.

First Edition: 2023

Printed in the United States of America

0 9 8 7 6 5 4 3 2 1

For the night bloomers

NIGHT'S
EDGE

2010

SALT LAKE CITY

I'm hungry and it's two in the morning. The fridge is empty. And Mom is dead on the couch.

I know she's not sleeping. Her eyes are open. She's in her bra. Jeans unbuttoned. Her exposed skin is covered in bite marks, yellowing like whey. The couch is stained purple. It used to be blue. Fifth grade started last week. I have a spelling test tomorrow morning.

"I'm sorry. I-I didn't . . . We were just—" Devon stammers from the shadows. I'm too afraid to look at him. I'm just staring at the purple couch that used to be blue.

"We were just messing around and then . . . you know."

I don't. I'm ten.

I grab Mom's cell phone from the coffee table, trying to dial 911. Devon rips it out of my hand, and bends my wrist backward. But I don't feel the pain—not at first. He chases me in circles around the kitchen. My throat goes ragged as I scream in his face. I try to yank a kitchen knife from the butcher block but I can't hold on to it. My wrist is on fire.

"It was a mistake, Mia! I made a *fucking mistake,* okay?" I really don't care. *Leave, I hate you. Leave, I hate you. I hate you, I hate you, I hate you.*

No one's heard of Saratov's syndrome yet. People are still dancing in the dark and feel safe enough walking home at night with a friend. Devon's probably one of the first carriers.

He stops chasing me. We're both gasping for breath, standing on opposite sides of the couch. I wonder if I'll have to live with

Devon now. I hardly know him. Mom hardly knows him. Knew him.

We met him at the Fourth of July festival. He was there by himself and Mom thought he looked lonely. I thought he looked weird. Stringy, unkempt hair the color of dead grass. A tattered tank top that exposed his gangly arms and crude stick-and-pokes.

Mom waved him down and offered him a beer. Later, when we threw away our trash, I realized the can was still full. He'd been pretending to drink it. I thought that was strange and I told Mom, but she had nothing to say about it.

Some nights she doesn't come home. I don't know what they do together. She doesn't go to the store, doesn't buy food. I've never seen Devon eat, and she doesn't get hungry when he's around. Last night I had ketchup and crackers for dinner.

I didn't even know they were here. If she screamed or struggled, I didn't hear anything.

Devon picks up the knife I dropped on the floor. "I can fix this," he whispers.

I back away as he slices across his wrist. I don't want to see any more blood so I look out the window. The night is starless. Clouds suffocate the moon.

He tells me to close my eyes, that he doesn't want me watching. "Just hold her hand, that's all you gotta do. Okay, Mia?"

I take the icy, dead weight of her hand in mine. But I can't close my eyes. Too afraid of what he might do when I'm not looking.

Her body lurches at his touch as he sits down on the couch, like he's radiating some strange electricity. I swallow hard, trying to pretend I didn't notice. He told me not to watch.

He holds his bleeding wrist to her blue lips. As I finally force my eyes shut—

Hers open.

NOW

TUCSON

The needle worms its way into my vein, iron cold, like a key turning a lock. I grit my teeth, realizing I forgot to breathe. I always seem to forget. My eyes rivet to the timer counting down on my phone. Two minutes and thirty-five seconds. That's how long it takes to get a quarter pint. Thirty-four. Thirty-three. Thirty-two . . .

Mom shuffles around the cluttered kitchen in a pair of shabby house shoes the color of Astroturf. The *slip-slap* sound they make on the tile floor is an aggravating constant, like a leaky faucet. Her frizzy red hair is swept into an off-center topknot. She's wearing a pair of my PJ pants—new ones, in fact, that I bought at Target last week, with monkeys and bananas on them. I don't mention it, though. We wear the same size. We're only eight years apart now. She looks so childlike and out of place, like a bewildered ten-foot-tall Alice, accidentally trampling a singing daffodil. Sometimes it feels like she's moving backward through time. But maybe that's just me. Moving forward.

One minute and twenty-four seconds. Twenty-three . . . twenty-two . . .

She always paces and clenches her fists while she's waiting for me to draw, like she's juicing ripe fruit in both her hands. I study her as she leans over the kitchen sink. Her lips have that telltale bluish tint. But that's normal. She tries to distract herself, watering a pot of succulents beside the window she's avoided all day. Only a faint raspberry-sherbet streak of sunlight remains outside. The night-blooming cereus cacti are starting to flower—slowly, imperceptibly. Petal by petal. There's a dead saguaro by the mailbox, blackening to a crisp in the sun. Its bone-dry, lopsided arm still points erect, but barely—like it's exhausted after waving at us all these years, hoping we'll wave back.

Fifty-six seconds. Fifty-five . . . fifty-four . . . fifty-three . . . She starts emptying the dishwasher.

"Mom, I got it." She can't control the shaking while she's waiting for me to draw and always seems to break something.

She grabs a pink plastic tumbler from the dish rack as she approaches. The cup wasn't pink when we bought it. Over time it's turned a weak, unsettling Pepto-Bismol color. But at least we know which cup is hers.

There's a rubber reservoir connected to the needle, gathering the blood. It's almost full, weighing down my forearm. When you see that much blood at once, it's so dark it almost looks black. I used to get a little light-headed during this part and would use it as an excuse to eat a whole sleeve of Oreos. It helps to not stare at the reservoir. Instead, I focus on the cheap wooden plaque above the fridge that reads, IN THIS HOUSE: WE LAUGH. WE GIVE BIG HUGS. WE NEVER GIVE UP. AND WE LOVE ICE CREAM.

Well, one of us, anyway.

Twelve . . . eleven . . . ten—

She's right behind me. My hair stands on end as her labored, humid breath hits the back of my neck. She cranes her head over my shoulder, clutching her pink plastic cup like a vise, watching the countdown with wide, bloodshot eyes. I resist the urge to scratch an itch on my nose. If I so much as flinch in the wrong direction during the last ten seconds, it might spook her. And what she does when she's spooked is out of my hands.

Four . . . three . . . two . . .

A cheerful little jingle. I carefully remove the needle from my arm. Detach the reservoir. Mom presents the cup in her trembling hand and I pour in the blood.

I quickly stand, anxious to toss my needle into the red sharps bin we keep next to the recycling. Type 1 diabetes, if anyone asks. No one ever has. No one comes here.

I don't like to watch when she eats, so I keep my back to her and dig through the freezer for a package of English muffins. I've been on an egg sandwich kick lately.

As I pop one in the microwave to soften it up, I hear a muffled *ping!* from her pocket. Someone's texting her. I notice this, because nobody ever texts her except for me. There's the occasional message from one of her employees at the restaurant, calling in sick. But that's it. I also notice the phone is in her pocket instead of under her pillow or sitting on top of the toilet. Most nights it takes us a good fifteen minutes to find the damn thing before she leaves for work. She's been expecting this message.

I turn and watch her pound a response, one-handed, as she drinks from her cup. I can't imagine something urgent enough to interrupt her dinner. I realize I haven't moved, that I'm anchored to the spot, finger hovering over the DEFROST button on the microwave. She meets my gaze, aggressively sucking her teeth as she drinks to keep them from getting stained. At one point, I got her a fun, curly straw to help with that. But she's always too impatient, unless I remember to grab it for her before I start the draw.

"What's up?" I squint at her, as though I might be able to make out what she's typing.

"Kayla's wondering when the next BevMo shipment is coming." The words rush from her lips. I notice a ruddy glow in her cheeks, but that might just be the color returning to her skin after eating. She places her phone on the table and turns it facedown.

The microwave beeps. I transfer my English muffin to the toaster and negotiate with the janky pilot on our stove. We need to get it fixed, but we'd rather not have anyone come over. The gas belches and feeds the flame. I can feel her eyes on me.

"Anyhoo," she chirps. Nothing shreds her nerves like silence between us. "How was the store today? Did a lot of people come meet that author?"

I nod as I crack an egg into the sizzling pan. "She was kind of a jerk, though. She didn't let us take her picture 'cuz she'd just gotten some gross chemical peel this morning."

Mom's phone pings again. Her spine stiffens and she reflexively reaches for it. But then, she smiles at me and switches it to silent. She knows I know something's off. It's impossible for us to keep secrets from one another. There's a gnawing feeling in my gut. I'm hurt that she'd try to hide something, no matter how innocuous. She promised me, the day Devon left, that she'd never lie to me again. Even then, I knew it was a silly promise. Just a thing you tell a kid. But after thirteen years, I've actually started to believe it.

"Is Kayla melting down 'cuz she drank all the chardonnay?" I offer, trying to loosen the tense snag.

"She's fine." That smile is still frozen on her face, like a glitchy video.

I pop my nightly iron supplements with a tall glass of water, then assemble my sandwich. Sit down at the table, across from her. She nudges the centerpiece aside so she can see me: yellow tulips I bought her a few days ago. She still loves springtime. Flowers. Sunshine.

"That looks good," she lies as I take a bite. She always watches me eat. I don't know if it's because she misses it or if she thinks I shouldn't sit alone. Either way, it's kind of weird. But I've never called her out on it.

"Oh my God, so I read in the newsletter today they're reviving the Main Street Electrical Parade." She smacks her lips, fidgeting excitedly in her chair.

"I don't know what that is."

"Yes you do, it's that parade with all the Christmas lights, re-member? There was Mickey's train and those twinkly snails spin-ning in circles? I showed you the video, I know I did."

Mom gets alerts in her email about all the Disney parks, even the ones in China and Japan. Every couple of days, she'll deliver her remarks on which rides are being rebuilt, which characters are getting makeovers, which limited-edition stuffed animals are be-ing sold where. We were supposed to go to Disneyland over my spring break in the seventh grade. We figured we'd hunker down in the hotel room all day and come out at night to hit the rides and stay till they closed. But that was also the year we had to slash hours at the restaurant and couldn't stay open after dark. Money was tight, so we stayed home. Same thing the following year. By the time we could afford to go, all the parks had installed Sara scanners. She still hasn't unsubscribed from the emails.

I glaze over as she chatters on about the parade. When I think of my mom, I have to think of her as three different people. There's the effervescent art-school dropout, wine-drunk and tie-dyeing T-shirts in the backyard, decorating for Halloween six weeks in advance. Then there's who she was after the turn: Alone. Afraid. Burying emotional land mines so I always had to watch my step. Now, she's both those people combined. Sometimes it feels like she's lost in time: Fantasizing about a trip to Disneyland we never took. Random sobbing in her sleep, dreaming about the night I broke my leg thirteen years ago. I'm not sure if she knows how old I am. I mean, I guess she *knows*. Fundamentally. But human memory builds barriers to separate the weeks, months, and years. Hers are eroding. Time isn't *passing*. It just *is,* like a whirling sphere suspended in space. At least, that's how I think it must feel. She doesn't talk about it.

"Did you put those jalapeño poppers back on the menu? With that funky green cilantro sauce?" I try to engage her on a new topic.

"I think you're the only one who ever ordered them. Luke's trying out some new things. There's gonna be a black bean burger."

"Awesome, I can sample for him tonight." I'm the one who gets to approve the menu at the Fair Shake. For obvious reasons. But Mom frowns when I mention this.

"Oh, you're coming?"

"Of course I am, it's Thursday." Karaoke night at the Fair Shake is my favorite spectator sport. It's become quite the scene since the blood scanners were installed and bars were allowed to reopen. People go out every night of the week now.

Mom cocks her head like she's got water in her ear. "Oh, shit. You're right. It's Thursday."

I shovel the rest of my sandwich into my mouth, but she's

stopped watching me. She gazes into the middle distance, picking at her nail polish—pale mint green, like an Easter egg. I wonder when she did them. We always paint each other's nails. Sometimes we even have this whole elaborate at-home spa night, with masks and hilarious New Age music. Why would she exclude me this time? I feel that gnawing in my gut again.

I almost ask her about it. But before the words crawl up my throat, I stop myself. Not because she's an adult who's entitled to a secret every now and then, but because I remember what she is. My job is to keep things agreeable. We don't fight, because we can't. Because I'll lose.

"You mind if I wear that striped tank dress tonight?" she asks.

"Go nuts." She knows I never wear it. She bought it for me, but it's not my style. I'll be buried in a flannel and cutoffs.

I stand to clear my plate, and she regards me with a tired half smile. She has exactly one wrinkle, a faint frown line beneath the apple of her left cheek. But her eyes always give away her true age. She hates when I bring it up, but I spend a lot of time thinking about my birthday eight years from now, the day she and I will be the same age: thirty-one. She probably thinks I'm dreading it. But I'm not. I've always imagined I'll feel proud on that day. Proud our secret survived for so long. That *we* survived.

☾ ☾ ☾

The Fair Shake is situated just outside Tucson proper, about twenty minutes from our house: a diamond-in-the-rough strip-mall storefront that Mom transformed into a quirky Southwestern gastropub thirteen years ago.

I didn't love the name at first, and I told Mom people would think it was a milkshake place. But she'd already thought long and hard about what to call it. The previous owner not-so-jokingly told her the land it stood on was cursed, and she was determined to pay homage.

According to him, the land had been home to a family of witches who escaped persecution in Salem by traveling west, a century before Lewis and Clark passed through with their covered wagons. The women collaborated with the Indigenous community to create a peaceful little life for themselves in the middle of the desert. When the Spanish arrived and laid claim to their land, the youngest granddaughter, now grown, put a hex on it to protect her family and the Native peoples they'd befriended. If anyone tried to build any kind of structure, it would trigger an earthquake. The hex has obviously expired, if it ever existed. But Mom loved the story. I think she felt connected to these dangerous, powerful women who just couldn't catch a break. Hence, the Fair Shake. Before the restaurant opened, the two of us painted a mural on the adobe wall behind the bar that tells the whole story. It reminds me of ancient cave art: childlike figures scrawled across the craggy surface in rust-colored hues that make you wonder if it was painted with blood.

As we pull into the parking lot, there are already a dozen karaoke enthusiasts waiting to get inside, patiently queueing up under the fairy lights. The bar isn't crowded, it's still a little early for that. They're waiting to get scanned in. Everyone has to wait; waiting is the price you pay to go anywhere after dark. People complained for a couple of months after the scanners got installed, but they shut up once they remembered how good it felt to sip a cocktail in a dimly lit room without worrying that a Sara was trying to seduce them.

There's a thirtysomething woman with bleached, flat-ironed mermaid hair at the front of the line. Our Stetson-sporting bouncer, Rodney, hands her a sanitizing wipe, and she presses her index finger against a small silver panel alongside the door handle. A tiny needle half the size of a thumbtack snaps out of the panel, like a snake lunging from its hole. She flinches as she receives a pinprick and the scanner collects a drop of her blood. Three seconds later—*click!* The door unlocks, and she gains entry. It shuts behind her, and the process begins again. One guest at a time. Even the regulars. Even the employees. But not us.

Mom parks our Jeep in her reserved spot and I follow her toward the back entrance, which leads to her office. The scanners didn't exist the year she bought the restaurant, which is probably why she got such a crazy deal. Nobody was buying nightlife space back then. Whenever there was a Sara attack in the area, the city enforced a curfew till they caught the culprit. We did our best with the spotty regulations, but we almost lost the Fair Shake when I was in junior high and infection rates exploded. We were under curfew for two whole years. When the scanners finally debuted, it was safe for us to open back up at night. Mom was happy to install them. After all, nobody's going to force you to scan in when you own the place.

I've never seen anyone fail a scanner. Most Saras don't try. I'm not entirely sure what happens if you do, but my guess is the cops get alerted and the offending trespasser is referred to the nearest recovery center. I always thought that was funny: "recovery" center. There's no recovering. Once you're at a Sara center, you don't leave. If you could recover, they'd let you go home.

A rush of cool air and a muted, off-key rendition of "Material Girl" greet us as we make our way inside, past the labyrinth of dark adobe storage rooms. It's always reminded me of wandering through an old mine, and when I was younger I liked to come back here with a lantern and a book to get some peace and quiet. We pass the wine cellar, and I squint in the weak fluorescent flicker. The shelves are lined with bottles, at least three deep. About a dozen extra cases that don't fit on the shelves are stacked on the floor. I remember what Mom said about Kayla. Why would she be stressing about another shipment? We're fully stocked.

Mom unlocks her office at the end of the hall. As she grapples with her keys in one hand, her phone lights up in the other. She still has it on silent, but I'm able to glimpse the text as it appears onscreen.

be there in 5

A random number displays above. Not someone in her contacts. She glances at her phone, then me. She blinks twice, in rapid succession, a flash of annoyance I know well. I wonder if she knows I just saw the message. I've always been grateful mind reading isn't one of the side effects, though my awkward gaping might have just given me away.

"Go find Luke and see if he can whip up a few samples for you."

She doesn't give me a chance to argue, let alone answer. She shuts the door and my chest constricts. There's no question she's up to something.

I shift from one foot to the other, wondering what to do. If our roles were reversed, she'd be clawing at my throat, demanding to know who I was talking to. At least, that's what I always assumed. I've never given her a reason to. There are four contacts saved in my phone: the restaurant's main switchboard, the bookstore, my favorite pizza place, and Mom. I don't need any others. I don't get lonely. Loneliness can't exist when two people are lonely together.

I turn and shuffle toward the kitchen, wringing my sweaty hands. *Be there in 5. Who's* going to be here? Why doesn't she want me to know? She's just eaten, so she's not on the hunt. What else could she possibly need? My head rattles with questions like a can of coins. I want to smash it open.

I pass the bar, where a group of guys in polo shirts slur their way through "Don't Look Back in Anger." It's too early for this song and that much Bud Light. I poke my head into the kitchen, where Luke, our barrel-chested chef, dices mushrooms with surgical precision. Flames leap from a frying pan filled with sizzling fajita veggies, and he swoops across the stove to give them a fiery flip. He turns to greet me, adjusting his sweaty red bandana. He smiles and I think I'm smiling back, but I can tell by his sudden grimace that my face is totally blank.

"All good, Fun Size?" He tilts his big, bald globe of a head. "Fun Size Izzy" is the nickname the staff gave me when I was a kid because they thought I looked like a miniature version of Mom— who was, in my opinion, the most gorgeous woman on the planet. I would blush every time someone used it. Nowadays, I'm not so crazy about it. One day last year Kayla declared we were pretty much twins and started grilling Mom about her skin-care regime. She responded with a furtive shrug the way she always does when someone draws attention to her youthful glow, mumbling about SPF 70 and jojoba oil.

I glance at the clock over the stove. Has it been five minutes yet? I should probably go keep an eye on the front door and see who comes in. I realize I haven't responded to Luke.

"Oh uh . . . just wondering about that new black bean burger. I'd love to try it."

"Grab a seat at the bar and I'll bring it on out."

I hear the off-brand Gallagher brothers finish their song to tepid applause. I'm about to head over that way when I'm drawn to a spark of light outside the kitchen window, which overlooks the parking lot. The cherry of a cigarette hovers in the darkness like a red star. A second flicker lights a second cigarette, illuminating Mom's face. Someone else is holding the lighter. But they have their back turned.

I inch behind a corner, hoping she didn't just catch me spying on her. But it's as if everything around her has melted into the darkness except for this stranger lighting her cigarette. Her half-lidded eyes sparkle in the dim light as she takes a luxurious drag. Her lips part with a deliberate pout as she exhales. I strain to hear her conversation. There's the deep, unmistakable rumble of a man's voice. But it's impossible to make anything out.

My heartbeat accelerates and my whole body tingles with fight-or-flight. Mom and I don't talk to men. Not like *that*, anyway. Plus, she quit smoking years ago. She could smoke twelve packs a day and her lungs would stay pretty in pink for the next hundred years. But she stopped the night I asked to bum one from her and she realized I was getting secondhand cravings. That was the last vice to fall. We don't smoke. We don't drink. We don't date—or whatever you'd call what's happening in the parking lot right now. Nausea flares in the pit of my stomach.

"What's up?" Luke approaches, spatula in hand. I jump and turn away from the window.

"Nothing." I can't even begin to explain.

I can hear Mom's musical laughter at my back as I leave the room, like the song of some rare night bird. It feels as if she's mocking me.

I perch at the bar and pick at Luke's black bean burger, scanning the dining room, wondering if Mom and her mystery friend might slip inside. Maybe she'll introduce me to him. Maybe it's all a big misunderstanding. But neither of them show.

I watch Kayla as she vigorously shakes a cocktail behind the bar. She always wiggles her hips in time with the shaker, but I don't know if she knows she's doing it. Everything about her is effortless like that. Clothes and makeup just make sense on her. Tonight, she's woven her pink-streaked black hair into two Heidi braids on top of her head, and her lip gloss matches the ruby grapefruit cocktail she's slowly, seductively dribbling into a coupe glass. I used to tell myself I'd unlock that kind of sexiness once I reached my twenties. But here I am in the same gray flannel I wore to work today, stone-cold sober at the bar picking at a hangnail on my thumb.

Kayla leans over and blows me a little kiss. I half-heartedly pretend to catch it in my fist. "Getcha anything else, Mia? You look tired tonight."

I narrow my eyes, hypnotized by the effervescent fizz in the cocktail glass she's holding. Mom doesn't let me drink, because it taints the blood. But she's already fed tonight. And honestly? Fuck it. If she's allowed to chain-smoke outside with some rando, I'm allowed to sample one of Kayla's signature Snakebites. It's only fair.

"I'd like one of those. Please."

Kayla's mouth hangs open in surprise. It takes her a moment to register what I've just ordered. Because I've never asked for one before.

"Hold up, are you twenty-one?"

"Twenty-three."

"Wait, really? How have we never properly toasted your adulthood? Jesus, I've known you since you were in high school." She snorts as she laughs. "One sec, I'm gonna make you something special."

She skips off to the other end of the bar to serve the grapefruit fizz. I recognize the people sitting there: three of Mom's regulars. Drs. Woo and Abramson, cardiologists at Banner Health whose silhouettes remind me of Bert and Ernie—one squat, one lanky—and Dr. Rodriguez, the lone female of the group, a raven-haired divorcée who's already pounding the cocktail Kayla's just handed her. Twice a week, they sit at the bar, ordering round after round, waiting for Mom to emerge. Saras have this effect on people—pheromones apparently. Everyone who meets Mom wants to fuck her. But for these three, it's become an obsession.

Dr. Rodriguez rarely wears a bra to happy hour and reapplies her lipstick about a hundred times whenever Mom makes the rounds. Woo and Abramson, both married, got into a fight in the parking lot last year when Abramson thought Mom had slipped Woo her phone number and was texting him dirty pictures. He'd made it up, of course, not realizing it would result in a broken nose. Mom was embarrassed at first, when she realized what they were fighting over. But after a while, she decided the whole thing was hilarious. For half a second, I wonder if she was talking to one of them outside. But they look like they're at least two cocktails deep. They've been here a while.

The horny doctors always make me think of the way Mom was when she first met Devon. Totally distracted, unable to perform even the simplest day-to-day tasks. Just waiting for him to call. Waiting for nighttime so he could come pick her up.

Dr. Rodriguez approaches the karaoke stage as the tech cues up Fiona Apple's "Criminal." She refreshes her cranberry lipstick as she takes the mic, shimmying to the tinny piano music. Too bad Mom's nowhere to be found.

The drink Kayla serves me is tangy and sweet, with a smoky, antiseptic aftertaste. I let only the tiniest sip past my lips. Salt rims the glass, and I spin it to get a fresh mouthful with my next taste, enjoying how it neutralizes the hard, cloying flavor.

"It's a mango margarita. The salt is hibiscus-flavored," Kayla announces, studying me as I smack my lips. I take a third, longer sip, and a warm fog rolls in behind my eyes, like my brain is taking a long, hot shower. It seems too soon to feel this way, and I wonder if I'm just imagining it. I gulp from the glass, hoping to make it stick.

Spin, salt, sip. Spin, salt, sip. I'm waiting for the molten anger inside of me to cool. But it doesn't. It's hotter, like the drink is bringing my blood to a boil. Don't people get drunk to feel *better*?

Spin, salt, sip.

This guy, whoever he is . . . what if he's got a family? Kids? At the very least, he probably has a mom and dad. Friends who care about him. After what Mom and I went through, why would she risk doing the same thing to someone else? Is he worth it? It doesn't matter. This isn't how we do things.

This isn't how we do things.

"'Nother round, lady?" Kayla sweeps past to clear my drink.

It's empty? Shit. That was fast. "Um . . . Thanks, but I don't—" I let out a breath. "Kayla, did my mom mention she had like, a meeting tonight?"

"Hm, not sure. Although . . ." She leans toward me and whispers, "I'm hearing a rumor we're gonna be interviewing new barbacks soon. Joey's been slacking. Think he's got a clingy new girlfriend who doesn't like him working nights."

I manage a thin smile. "Y'know what, I think I'll have another round."

"Attagirl." As she gets to work mixing my drink, she flicks her wrist to slide up her sleeve, exposing her forearm. "By the way, did I show you this?"

Kayla has a lot of tattoos. This seems to be a new one: a tiny chain of islands wending its way toward her elbow crease. My spongy, distracted brain takes a second to process the image.

"What is it?"

"It's Ha-*wa*-i'i, ya dork." She pronounces the "wa" with a "v."

"My grandpa was from there. I'm gonna buy a house on Oahu and teach surfing lessons."

"You know how to surf?"

"I mean, I'll learn. And then I'll pay it forward. They've got the lowest rate of transmission in the country. Did you know that? Like, they barely even need scanners."

She garnishes my cocktail. I blink vacantly, waiting for the cold, dewy glass to slide into my hand. "You can come visit if you leave me a nice tip."

I can't think of anything cute to say in return. I go with, "Sounds good," awkwardly ending whatever banter she thought we were having.

She floats away, leaving me to fume in peace.

Spin, salt, sip.

There's still no sign of Mom at the door. God dammit, what the hell does she think she's doing? The rules are there for a reason. They're easy to follow if you know what you're up against. Has she suddenly forgotten everything?

The month we moved to Tucson, a guy who lived down the street from us loaded his semiautomatic with rusted bullets and drove over to his daughter's house after he heard a rumor her husband was a Sara. Rusted metal through the heart can poison all the blood in a Sara's body in about ten seconds, like sepsis on steroids. It's one of the only guaranteed fatalities. A regular bullet won't do you much good. The body mends around it. After the shooting, the medical examiner confirmed the diagnosis and the guy walked. I remember turning on the TV and catching a prime-time news story about it. The buxom spray-tanned anchor beamed as she breathlessly reported, "No jail time for hero dad." Mom huddled in one of her heavy wool blankets, yelling at me to put *Toy Story 2* on instead. I think that was the moment we both understood what we had to do to survive.

Spin, salt, sip.

Holding the world at arm's length was tough at first, especially at school, but I figured out a system. The key, I realized, was calculating the work-to-socialization ratio of any given interaction. I could see people, I could even talk to people. A short conversation about homework was harmless. I never talked to anyone long enough to reveal myself. Teachers scrawled in the margins of my report cards that I was "a shy girl." I didn't like all the things "shy" alluded to: Bitchy. Weird. Socially inept. But "shy" was better than "we know she's hiding something." I could live with shy.

For a couple of years I got my social kicks playing this stupid computer game called Creature Crew, where you'd collaborate with other kids online to build a town for cartoon animals. There was a boy my age from Minnesota who was great at constructing bridges and we became friends and started emailing outside the game. Until the day he sent me a picture of his dick and I realized he was not, in fact, a seventh grader.

Spin, salt, sip. Spin, salt, sip.

During high school I'd spend my lunch periods in the library with a Harry Potter hardcover and a protein bar. Extracurriculars were off the table—I had to be home before dark. When the bell rang at 3 P.M., I'd gather my books at my locker as quickly as possible and vanish without a trace. Sometimes I'd pretend I was the school's resident ghost, roaming the halls in a tattered, translucent ball gown, only making my presence known to tend to "unfinished business." Every time I considered contributing to a conversation or inviting a fellow introvert to lunch—every time I thought about *making a friend*—I forced myself to imagine the nightmarish domino effect. She'd come over for dinner, or she'd need to swing by to borrow a textbook. She'd notice something was *off*. She'd see the sharps dispenser, the blackout curtains, my bruised forearms. She'd tell her parents. Her parents would tell everyone else. And then one day a week later I'd come home to find all our windows shattered and a charred skeleton with its mouth agape in Mom's bed.

If friends were off the table, dating was a nonstarter. Mom was always proud of the way I avoided boys at school. But it was easy. It's always been easy.

If I can do it, why the hell can't she?

I'm not sure how long it's been or when she entered the bar, but Mom is hovering beside me, pulling on her coat as she chats with Kayla. My eyelids are heavy as rocks. I notice Kayla has bused my second empty glass, and I'm thankful for it. I cram a fistful of cold sweet potato fries into my mouth to mask the booze on my breath.

Now we both have a secret.

"Catch ya tomorrow." Mom gives Kayla a dainty little wave.

"Safe home," she replies.

Kayla appears to have comped my drinks, but I have the sense to leave her a good tip. Maybe she'll let me come to Ha-va-i'i.

I place a twenty on the bar, then slide off the stool like a shapeless bag of hot liquid. Laughter bubbles to my lips.

"What's so funny?" Mom cuts me a look. I shrink and stare at my feet, but I can't stop giggling. She rolls her eyes and sails down the dark hallway, toward the back exit. I follow her, letting my hand graze the wall just in case I need support. It feels like my shoes are untied, but I know they're not.

There's a strange smell in the car. Like pine needles and baby powder, mixed with something earthy and metallic. I wrinkle my nose as I buckle my seat belt. It's familiar. Maybe I'm just drunk. Whatever it is, it's making my stomach curl. I crack the window as Mom pulls out onto the road.

"Rhiannon" is playing on the local classic-rock station, and Mom rolls down her window and the moonroof, enjoying the wind in her tangled hair. The engine roars as she speeds up. My gut does a backflip. She starts singing along with the radio.

All your life you've never seen a woman taken by the wind—

She never acts like this. She sticks to the speed limit. Doesn't sing with the windows rolled down. Not anymore, anyway. Over the years, she's made herself small. Doesn't want to attract the wrong kind of attention, or any attention. But tonight she's giddy, lost in some carefree fantasy I haven't been invited to.

A bead of sweat trickles down my brow and I lean my forehead against the cold window with a groan. "Hey, Mom?" She can't hear me. She's belting at the top of her lungs now.

We soar over a dip in the road. I fight the urge to dry-heave and my eyes start to water.

"Mom."

"What?" The corner of her eye glints like a blade in the moonlight.

"I-I don't feel good. Can you pull over?"

"We'll be home soon." She cranks the music even louder. The ethereal chorus swirls around the car as I draw my knees to my chest.

"Mom, I'm serious. Pull over—" I start to gag as sweet, acidic mango lurches up my throat. "*Holy shit*, Mom—"

She glances over at me and notices I've started puking into my hands. She yanks the car to the side of the road and I kick the door open, tumbling to the sandy shoulder. Stevie Nicks keeps warbling from the car.

"Jesus Christ, are you okay?" she calls out, like she just realized I was sick.

"I-I'm . . . uh . . . yep." I hurl again, spitting a wad of sticky half-digested booze. I can feel her watching me as I stagger upright, clutching the car door for leverage. She holds my glassy-eyed stare like she's daring me to look away.

"Mia. Are you drunk?"

But I'm already asking my own question, at the same moment. "Who was that guy?"

I'm surprised because I don't even sound nervous. But the second the words leave my lips, I know I should be.

Her face twists like I've just pelted her with mud. "I knew it. I knew you were fucking wasted—"

I shudder, wilting under her gaze. She doesn't raise her voice like that. Not to me. Not after she's fed. Not when everything's safe. This is new. Something shifts between us. Electric friction in the air.

"Who is he . . . ?" I ask again. Softer this time.

"Get in the car."

"Mom—" Is she upset because I'm drunk or because I'm asking a question she doesn't want to answer?

"There's no guy, Mia. I wasn't talking to anyone. You're obviously shit-faced. I don't know what you think you saw, but it wasn't me."

I want to tell her I saw her *before* I was "obviously shit-faced." I want to raise my hackles and have it out, right here on the side of the road, howling along with the coyotes. But I'm too tired. My head is pounding in time with the stereo. My legs quiver as I crumple back into the car.

She turns off the radio, and I slam the door. Silence coils around us like a chain. Neither of us says a word. I clean my hands with a stack of grease-stained McDonald's napkins in the cupholder and watch the stars streak past the moonroof.

"Make sure you drink a lot of water and don't have any sugar tomorrow morning," she mumbles as we turn onto our street.

"Okay."

We pull into our driveway, but she waits before killing the ignition. She tilts her head in my direction and meets my eye.

"I'm sorry."

I don't know what she's saying sorry for. Lying to me about her little rendezvous? Cursing me out for being drunk? I tear my gaze from her and start picking at my hangnail.

"It's fine."

Of course it's fine. It's always fine. It has to be.

2010

I'm sitting with an ear pressed to Mom's bedroom door. She's started *Beauty and the Beast* over for the fourth time in a row.

Bonjour! Good day! How is your family?

Devon's mumbling on the other side, competing with the movie. *Smack!* The sound of something hitting the wall, but something harmless. A box of tissues, maybe. A slipper. Something she must have thrown at him.

I scurry away from the door as he opens it, but he knows I've been listening. He scowls, then points across the living room. The duct tape holding the edge of the curtain to the wall has started to peel away, allowing a thin crescent of light to slip through.

"Fix that."

I plant my feet. "Let me see her."

"Not time yet."

"It's been two days."

"I told you to wait." He takes a step toward me. I watch his shadow spill across the wall and notice it's somehow darker than mine. "Go fix the curtain, Mia."

His gaze swings to the lethal white sliver on the ground. He doesn't take another step. I don't understand what he's so afraid of or why we had to tape the curtains down. But I *do* understand he's not going to move until I fix it. I hold the power. If only for a few seconds.

"I'm gonna call the cops if you don't let me see her."

"You don't have a phone."

"I'll run next door." I watch him for a response. He sucks his bottom lip and narrows his eyes like two dark flints. That's what I thought.

"Fine. I can't stop you. But here's what's gonna happen if you tell anyone." He gets down to my level, like he's a coach about to deliver an inspiring pep talk. I shudder and try to dodge him, but he seizes my shoulders and forces me back around. I feel that foreign, unstable energy emanating from his hand again, like static electricity but cold—freezing cold.

My mind goes blank, then snaps to a memory of losing my boot in a patch of thin lake ice. The way the frigid water shocked my bare skin. My raw throat as I screamed for Mom when I realized I was stuck.

"If you tell anyone," he goes on. "The cops, the EMTs, whoever they send . . . they're not gonna know what to do with her. They'll kill her in about five seconds if they bring her outside."

"So I'll call them at night." I slowly pronounce each word to keep my trembling voice under control.

"Fine, say they put her in an ambulance. You know what they're gonna do, when she gets to the hospital? They're gonna lock her up somewhere and tell you she's dead." He holds my gaze. "Either way, she's not coming back. The only way she survives is if you do exactly as I say. So please go get some tape. And fix the fucking window."

Rage erupts in my belly and suddenly I'm on all fours, scrambling around his legs, trying to reach Mom's bedroom door. He whirls around to try and grab me but I donkey-kick him in the shin. I know he's faster than me, and stronger too. But I'm so close . . .

There must be more than this provincial life! The movie drones on in Mom's room. I leap to my feet and wrap my sweaty palm around the doorknob. Devon grabs hold of my hair. My vision blurs with pain as I feel a clump of it dislodge. The door swings open.

She slumps over like a doll in a nest of pillows, and she's trying to lift her head but she's not strong enough. Her eyes meet mine, and tears spill down her cheeks. It takes me a second to realize they're not *tears*—not really. They're the color of dark wine, like she's been stabbed through the eye. Grotesque gray and purple lesions cover her face, arms, and hands. And then there's the smell. Worse than our back-alley dumpster in the middle of August. Worse than the night our cat came home after being attacked by a skunk. I can't breathe.

Mom screams and starts scratching at her face. She's gnawed her chipped pink nails into sharp, daggerlike points. I run toward her, arms outstretched. But Devon's still got hold of my hair. He pulls me back and hisses into my ear, "She's gonna *fucking kill you*."

My legs wobble like my whole body's starting to unravel. Maybe it's the stench in the room, sucking out all the oxygen. Maybe it's Devon's touch. Or maybe it's what he's just said—and that somehow, I know it's true.

She lunges for me. Toppling off the bed. Wails when she smacks her forehead against the corner of the nightstand. She sobs and claws her way across the carpet. Blood streaks her ashen face like gruesome war paint, and when she opens her mouth to scream again, her gums retract and her canines look *longer* somehow. I squeeze my eyes shut as Devon lifts me off my feet and shoves me out of the room.

He slams the door and I collapse in the hallway, pressing my hot, tearstained cheek to the cool hardwood. He's still inside, whispering to her, but I can't tell if he's trying to calm her down or if he's cursing at her. She screams again and the wall trembles like the house is made of paper. He turns up the volume on the TV.

Look there she goes, that girl is so peculiar! I wonder if she's feeling well.

I try to stand but my legs are still too weak. I remember all I've eaten these past two days is a heel of Wonder bread and a couple stale, rock-hard Girl Scout cookies from the freezer—the last of the food in our house. I close my eyes and decide I'm just going to lie there. Maybe I'll fall asleep. Maybe I'll die. It'll feel the same either way.

☾ ☾ ☾

A few hours later, I wake up on the couch. The purple couch that used to be blue.

It's nighttime now. Devon's opened the windows to let a little air inside. He must have moved me over here. I can smell the honeysuckle from the garden and a crisp, smoky hint of fall on the breeze. I let myself forget everything for a moment, clinging to the emptiness of sleep as long as I can.

Devon sinks down beside me on the couch with a weary sigh. I curl up my legs, trying to avoid physical contact. He's holding Mom's laptop. A glass of water. Without a word, he offers it to me.

"I'll get my own."

He sets it down on the coffee table within my reach. In case I change my mind.

"How old are you again?"

"Ten."

"Right."

He's quiet, staring out the window. Watching the trees sway in the wind. I wish he'd leave me alone. Why is he sitting here?

"Your mom should be back on her feet by tomorrow night. She'll be okay. She'll be normal, like me."

I cut him a glare. He exhales and rolls his eyes like he knows he's saying all the wrong things, but he doesn't correct himself.

"What's happening to her?" I ask after a moment.

"Well she's uh . . . Have you ever had the flu or anything?"

I nod.

"Human bodies fight back. That's what they're designed to do. When you get sick, you get a fever. That's your body trying to get rid of the virus, or whatever. Her body's doing the same thing. And when it's a real high fever, it can make you a little loopy."

"That didn't look like the flu."

"Yeah well, blood replacement can get pretty gruesome. I told you not to go in there."

"What does that mean?"

"What it sounds like. Her blood has to drain so the new stuff can start circulating. Sometimes it comes up through your skin.

Your nose . . . your eyes. It's all good, though. She'll feel better once that part's over."

"So she's not gonna die?"

"She already did. I saved her."

He looks at me expectantly. Like I'm supposed to know what to say after all that.

"Look, I'm not an expert and you're gonna have a lot of questions. So uh . . ." He opens the laptop and turns the screen to face me.

It's a Facebook page, a private group. Saratov Survivors.

"I invited your mom to join, and when she's up to it she can take a look. But I thought you'd wanna see for yourself."

I cradle the computer in my lap and start scrolling. The group description says only, "Support for The Unspeakable Life." There are 407 members in all.

The first picture on the timeline rolls into view. A baby-faced teenage boy with braces stares into the camera, shirtless, covered in horrific third-degree burns. My mouth goes dry and I taste bile, but I can't look away. The caption says, "Mark was exposed for 3 seconds today when he went to grab a package off the doorstep. Can anyone recommend some at-home remedies?" The comment section is flooded with homeopathic medical advice and links to different products. There's more than one all-caps warning to "STAY AWAY FROM THE HOSPITAL!!!!!" A few people tell the user, probably Mark's mom, that she's "a fucking moron" and "completely insane" to think her kid could withstand three seconds of exposure. An equal number of people defend her. "Omg give her a break. They're learning."

Devon reads over my shoulder and clears his throat. "I started this group last year and it's been a good way to keep everyone informed. You can trust them, they're like a big family. These aren't the only people who have it, though. There are more. A lot more. These are just the ones I know."

A thought materializes, and I stiffen. "*How* do you know them?"

"When you have it, you start to meet each other."

I feel his gaze on me, like he's studying me from some shadowy place, trying to predict my next move. He snatches the laptop and navigates to a different tab on the page. "Anyway, start here. There are a bunch of links and stuff."

He stands and thrusts it back into my hands. But he's still hovering over me. He fidgets, scratching his stringy hair with his nicotine-stained fingernails.

"You gotta promise to stay out of her room for the next twenty-four hours. Okay? She'll lose her shit if she finds out she did anything to you."

It might feel like he's trying to protect me if the whole thing hadn't been his fault. I nod and try to straighten my posture, but the hunger pangs return, leaving me breathless.

"I-I need to eat."

"Oh. Um—" He frowns. Glances over at the kitchen.

"We don't have anything."

Silence. Then, "I guess you can order a pizza."

"Do you have any money?"

He sighs and trudges over to Mom's room.

"She'll have some cash."

He shuts her door and locks it behind him. As I listen to him rummage around in her closet, I glance back at the laptop against my knees. He's pulled up the "Info" section of the page.

There's a grainy photo of a frail, bone-white woman and her black-eyed child wearing mismatched, soiled clothes. They're posed in front of a windowless concrete building lined with rusted barbed wire, under the weak yellow light of a streetlamp. The photo was taken at night. The caption reads, "Larisa and Pyotr Kuznetsov. Saratov, USSR. 1990." I squint and realize their clothes are dirty because they're covered in blood.

I stare at Larisa and Pyotr, scrutinizing each blurry pixel like it contains a secret, coded message. They're holding hands. Larisa's detached gaze floats somewhere beyond the camera. Her mouth hangs slightly agape, like she's left her body behind under that streetlamp. But Pyotr has his eyes locked on the lens. He's young, younger than me. But he doesn't look scared. His teeth are clenched, and I can almost feel how tightly he's gripping Larisa's hand.

The breeze outside rattles the windowpane. It's gotten colder. Darker. I shiver and close the laptop. Pyotr's face burns behind my eyes in faded fragments of blue light. I wonder if he's still alive.

Until I remember he's not. Neither is Devon. And neither is Mom.

NOW

Mom is a heavy sleeper. Right after the turn, she started popping Ambien at sunrise so she wouldn't wake up when the neighborhood kids made their way to the bus stop. But swallowing pills doesn't work for people like her. Her body's only built to digest one thing. She tried snorting them, but she hated the accompanying burn. Best she can do is suck the pills like mints and hope her bloodstream absorbs some of the chemicals before they hit her stomach. But most days she just blasts a military-grade white noise machine and that seems to do the trick.

I need to leave for work in ten minutes, and I've spent all morning looking for her phone. The only place I haven't checked is her room.

The space behind my eyes is throbbing, like someone drove jagged spikes into the back of my head. Tequila is no joke. I know I'll be in even more trouble if she catches me snooping through her phone. But I need to find out who he is.

This isn't the first time I've tiptoed into her room during the day, but I'm always careful not to disturb her. A rude awakening can definitely set her off, especially if she wakes up hungry. Then we have to do an extra feeding to keep her happy and it throws off the whole schedule and I feel like shit after drawing blood twice in one day.

I twist the doorknob slowly and hold it in place so it unlatches without a sound. I make sure to wear socks. Sometimes she can hear the sticky pad of my bare feet. She's wearing her favorite silk mask, embroidered with sexy cartoon bedroom eyes. The blackout curtains stand guard against the oppressive desert sun. A box fan points directly at her head, and the noise machine on the night-stand plays womb sounds. I always thought the "womb" setting was creepy. When I used to sleep in here with her I preferred "summer rain."

My eyes comb the darkness for her phone. It's wedged between two pillows on the bed. She must have been on it before she fell asleep, or she's keeping it close so she'll wake up if she hears it. I loom over her, holding my breath. Reaching, reaching, reaching . . .

I graze the phone's hard, plastic case, encrusted with cracked, iridescent rhinestones. Just a little farther . . .

The phone lights up with a soft *bzzz!* and falls into the crevasse between the two pillows. Mom groans and rolls over. She starts fumbling with her mask, and my heart stutters. I leap across the bedroom on the balls of my feet, light as a feather. *Shit, shit, shit.*

I'm not sure if she hears me shut the door. I'm still clenching my breath as I race toward the kitchen and collapse into a seat at the table. *What do you mean? I've been here the whole time.* I wait for her to hobble into the hallway, for her bleary-eyed glare as she jerks the silk mask up over her bushy hair . . . but she stays put.

What if she's invited this mystery man over to the house while I'm at work? That has to be the person who just texted her.

I catch a glimpse of the microwave clock, glowing neon green against the artificial darkness. I'm going to be late.

I snag the keys to the Jeep, but before I head outside, I duck back into the kitchen. I excavate the pantry until I find what I'm looking for: a can of instant coffee. A few years ago some French scientists figured out Saras can smell you from ten feet away if you've just had a cup of coffee, and they'll typically avoid drinking caffein-ated blood. They'll hurl it back up and have dizzy spells for days. Turns out they're allergic. Mom and I already knew this from the Facebook group. Fucking figures Devon was hunting in Salt Lake City when we met him. Utah's full of Mormons who won't touch the stuff.

I don't drink coffee. But I keep the can of instant in case of emergencies. I tiptoe back to Mom's door and sprinkle a line of it on the floor, a barrier between her room and the rest of the house. When Mom walks out of her room, the stench will knock her off her feet. I hope that will force her to reconsider if she hears someone at the door. It's all I can think of to keep her safe while I'm at work. I can't shove the couch against her door and keep her in her room. She's too strong for that. And I have obviously failed at taking her phone.

I pull a shaky breath and add an extra layer of coffee to the barrier. She'll be upset when she wakes up and finds it there. But if she's guilty, she'll understand why. And eventually, she'll thank me.

(((

It's a short drive to work, only about ten minutes. I could walk or ride my bike, but I never seem to wake up early enough. The Book Bunker occupies one of six charming adobe storefronts, painted in alternating shades of teal and lavender. The townhomes across the street boast spearmint-green trim set against pink stucco. Mom and I call them the Watermelon Towers. The walkways on both sides of the street are lined with antique horseshoes. When I was a kid, I was delighted by all the colors. These days, the vibrancy feels like a sensory assault, as if I'm trapped inside an endless game of Candyland.

The Book Bunker has looked exactly the same for thirteen years. The only thing that changes are the titles on the shelves. A faded cardboard cutout of Arthur still stands in front of the children's section, greeting young shoppers with a wave. The antique houndstooth armchairs in the lounge have never been reupholstered, each with their own uniquely shaped dent to get cozy in. We've been selling the same locally made beeswax candles since 1999, and the spicy cinnamon scent has permanently saturated the walls.

I like the consistency. Sometimes I feel like all I do is watch everything around me change.

I always request the opening morning shift, which guarantees

I'm home before the sun goes down. The days are getting longer now that we're sliding into April, so I have a little more flexibility. But still, I'm pretty strict. Nobody's ever asked me why my schedule is so rigid, why I can never work till close. They just know I'm the girl you don't try to trade shifts with. I sometimes wonder if Sandy, the manager, has an inkling. If she has an opinion about my hours, she's never shared it. I keep my conversations brief, same way I did in school. I show up on time and I stay on task. I make recommendations, wrap Christmas presents, and corral the kids who show up for weekend Story Corner. Every now and then I read to them. Sandy says I do the best voices for *Where the Wild Things Are*.

Mornings at the store are my favorite; it's rare to see more than two customers before 11 A.M. Things usually pick up after lunchtime. Those first two hours are when I do my own reading, poring over new titles we haven't even put on the shelves yet. I take time to decorate my handwritten "Staff Recommendation" card with glitter and gel pens. Sandy often reminds me to limit my recommendations to just one per week, so it doesn't look like the other employees don't read. I told her she should hire people who *actually do*.

This morning, I've nabbed an advance copy of a melodramatic space opera. There's an empress being pursued across the galaxy by this fighter pilot turned assassin, and she has no idea the guy who's been sent to kill her is her childhood best friend, whose mind has been hijacked by alien microbots. I'm totally hooked.

I blame my high school librarian, Mrs. Reyes, for my sci-fi addiction. She knew I never went to the cafeteria for lunch—she noticed me in the library every afternoon and started taking stock of what I was reading, leaving new recommendations for me on my favorite chair before the lunchtime bell. A ragged paperback copy of *1984*. Her own signed, first-edition hardcover of *The Left Hand of Darkness*. I treated that one like gold, always wrapping it in a towel before I slid it into in my backpack.

Last year I saw Mrs. Reyes at Kroger in the ice cream aisle, but I bolted in the other direction before she could make eye contact with me. I didn't want her to ask me about college or anything like that. I still feel bad about it. It would have been nice to talk to her.

I hear the lock click open on the front door. Someone's just scanned in. Most businesses leave their scanners on all day. I want to tell Sandy it's a silly idea, that you definitely don't need them till nighttime. But the general consensus is something like, "All it takes is one exception to the rule." I guess there *could* be that one-in-a-million person who can't be hurt by sunlight. People are always spreading rumors about mutations. I've never seen anything like that, though. Not on our Facebook group. It's got over six thousand members now, and I believe what people post there way more than anything in the news.

I put down my book and stand behind the register, trying to look like I was waiting there all along as the wind chime on the door announces the customer's arrival. But it's only Sandy. I can tell by the clomp of her hiking boots. She's just come from one of her morning adventures in the desert, still wearing her khaki shorts and knee brace with her salt-and-pepper hair in two sweaty pigtails. Her wife is a photographer who gets her up at the crack of dawn to hike to the top of the bluff so they can get good shots of the sun coming up over the saguaros at different times of the year. She's probably got about a thousand of them by now, but I've never heard Sandy complain.

"You're here early," I greet her, then hold up the advance copy of the space opera. "This is awesome, by the way."

"Really? The cover kinda freaks me out. Not sure we can put that on an endcap."

I know what she means. The cover prominently features a very lifelike photo of a brain being ripped apart by tiny robots like a horde of termites, haloed by the phosphorescent glow of an alien planet. I'm not bothered by it, though. I've seen worse.

"Anyway, I forgot it's Taylor's birthday and I'd wanted to do a little surprise for her before she gets in. Here—" She fishes into her canvas tote and hands me a Hallmark card. "Sign this. And then maybe we can grab a gift card from the Starbucks around the corner?"

"How old is she gonna be?" I ask, signing the card with a shimmery blue gel pen.

"Eighteen, I think. Bummer we're gonna lose her in August when she leaves for college." There's always a revolving door of part-time sales associates. That's one thing that does change around here.

"You mind running out now, before it gets busy? I'll watch the front." Sandy removes her knee brace, massaging her puckered, red skin. She's not in the mood to keep walking in the heat and I'm not about to argue.

The sun is murderous this morning, reflecting off the ash-white sand that sprawls in all directions. Mom and I picked the ideal spot to conceal a Sara. If anyone were stupid enough to try to hunt her down, this is probably the last place they'd look.

I forgot my sunglasses, so I keep my eyes pinned to the sidewalk as I shuffle over to the Starbucks down the street. I forget which direction it's in, and I have to turn around after about thirty seconds.

The line's so long I'm barely able to squeeze through the door after I scan in. A colorful chalkboard sign advertises this week's Protection Special: two-for-one nitro cold brews with caramel foam. I'm wedged between the wall and a lady with a baby stroller three toddlers deep. Two of the kids are flicking stray Cheerios into each other's faces, shrieking at the tops of their lungs. I'm not sure if they're playing or having a fight. I don't understand kids. I wonder if they're going through caffeine withdrawal, antsy for their next fix. A lot of parents have started giving babies coffee as a protective measure. I doubt a single pediatrician would recommend it, but a hyperactive, feral toddler is better than a dead one.

The woman's third, youngest child is totally silent and I'm a little put off when she pivots around in the stroller and locks eyes with me. Her single tuft of wheat-colored hair has been secured with a polka-dot bow on top of her head. Her ears have already been pierced with impossibly tiny pearl studs and her socks have little white ruffles on them. She's like a doll. No detail overlooked. I wonder if Mom ever dressed me like that. I don't think she could have, even if she'd wanted to. We were broke back then. It didn't make a difference to me, but eventually I realized how much it embarrassed Mom to dress me in scuffed sneakers and one of her old tank tops, cut and knotted at the waist. She knew how to get creative, though. She painted intricate designs of dragons and horses with colorful puff paint on plain white T-shirts. She shellacked my secondhand Chucks with red glitter, and we called them my ruby slippers. She'd been in her last year of art school in California when she got pregnant with me. My dad was her History of Pop Art instructor, which is one of exactly three things I know about him. She never graduated. But she put her skills to good use.

A delighted squeal at the front of the line pulls the baby's attention from me, much to my relief. I look behind the coffee bar, where a petite, wild-haired barista in a visor is having an absolute meltdown over a customer's puppy. I stare for a full ten seconds before I even notice the marshmallow-shaped dog yipping on the ground.

It feels like I've seen her before, even though I know I haven't.

As I inch closer to the front, I notice plum highlights between her spirals of dark hair, springing crookedly out of her visor like a bird's nest that's just been attacked by some predator. Her name tag reads JADE, and when she smiles I can see she's got a little gap between her two front teeth. She stifles another squeal as the dog chases its tail and her mouth gapes open, like she wants to swallow it whole. Her winged eyeliner is peacock blue, complementing her deep olive complexion, and the points of both cat-eyes are perfectly symmetrical. I wish I could do my makeup like that. My hand always shakes too much. She must have nerves of steel.

I shuffle forward as she toils behind the bar, hitting the blender while she froths a pitcher of soy milk.

"Uh . . . Jermish?" She calls out, screwing up her face as she reads the name scrawled on the cup she's holding. Her voice is deeper than I expected, for someone so small. "Wow sorry, my B. Jeremy?"

She whips her head around and a Slinky-shaped curl flies from the nest. She gives it a gentle tug and I watch it expand and contract.

As she hands the coffee cup to a guy in front of me, she glances my way. The heat of impending eye contact terrifies me. I look down at the baby stroller instead, pretending to be very invested in the ongoing Cheerio battle. Her gaze sweeps over me like a searchlight.

That fight-or-flight tingle surges across my body again, the same feeling I had last night: pins and needles that start in my stomach and spread across my skin, hot and cold at the same time. I draw a breath as I approach the front of the line, trying to expel the fear when I exhale. I understood the feeling last night. Why is it happening now?

"I just wanna grab a twenty-dollar gift card, please."

The gawky cashier rings me up, chewing his lip as he repeatedly taps his monitor, as if he's forgotten which button does what.

As he stalls, Jade whirls around, holding two cotton-candy-pink Frappuccinos, overflowing with whipped cream. "Ooookay, so one of these is for Michelle and the other is uh . . ." She turns in a circle like a spinning bottle, and lands right on me. "For you!"

"Oh, I-I didn't order that," I choke out.

"I know, I made extra. I thought she ordered a venti. My mistake, your treat."

"I um . . . it's cool. I don't really like coffee—" I say as she thrusts the cup in my hand.

"Then you'll love this. It's strawberry."

I feel like a puppet as my fingers wrap around the cold plastic, already dripping with condensation. "That's . . . really nice of you."

I'm desperate to think of something better to say. Something that might, against my better judgment, be the prelude to a longer conversation. I have no idea what would possess me to do that. I'm on the clock, and I don't just *start conversations* with people.

She smiles, and there's a spear of unease in my chest. Something doesn't feel right. I've always had anxiety talking to people I don't know, people who might not be *safe,* but this feels different. I need to leave. Now I stuff the gift card into my pocket and turn on my heel toward the door, squeezing so hard on the cup that the top pops off. I do not say goodbye to her.

Sweltering heat smacks me across the face as I barrel outside. I only realize I'm blocking the door when a customer edges past me. I place a hand over my heart as it pounds. *Danger. Danger. Danger.* I don't understand why. But in that moment, I don't want to understand. I just want to get away.

I consider the melting pink Frappuccino in my hand. The color makes me think of Mom's stained plastic cup.

I hover over the trash can, but I don't throw it away. I don't drink it either. I hold it, letting it liquefy, and stumble back to the Book Bunker.

Later on, I feel stupid. My cheeks burn as I shelve books in the kids' section. I have no idea why I just had a full-blown panic attack over a free drink. I panic over other things, sure. Serious things. Nothing this insignificant. Not only that, I didn't even say thank you or goodbye. This perfectly nice girl probably thinks I'm a complete asshole. But when have I ever cared about something like that? I never have to see her again if I don't want to.

I pause, scissors in hand, about to unbox a carton of coloring books. There was only one other time I cared about something like that. I catch myself chewing that hangnail on my thumb again.

Ninth grade. Two weeks before Christmas. Our Spanish class did a Secret Santa dubbed "Amigo Invisible," and I drew Emily Ramos's name from the cheap polyester red hat my teacher passed around. I remember the thud of my heart as I unfolded the slip of paper to reveal an "EM" . . . then an "ILY" . . . and even though there wasn't another Emily in our class I didn't want to believe it till I saw her full name. I was sure I would throw up, right into my textbook. How was I going to find a Christmas present worthy of Emily fucking Ramos?

Emily and I had orbited each other since fifth grade, when I first moved to Tucson. I was invited to her birthday party that year, but it was during the day, at a roller rink about thirty minutes away. I had no way of getting there and besides, I didn't even know Emily that well and I suspected I only made the cut because her parents forced her to invite the new kid. At school on Monday, Emily told me she was sad I didn't show up. I was the only person who didn't come. My first thought was "Cry me a river, so I ruined the perfect attendance." But later on, I started to wonder if she really *had* wanted me to come. She often picked me first for dodgeball in gym class and always told me how strong I looked when I ran. I thought she was teasing me, like she was saying I had big, meaty man-legs. But her tone wasn't mocking in any way. She seemed to mean it, like an actual compliment. I started to feel bad about missing her party. Maybe I could have taken a bus, or called a cab. Or mustered up the courage to ask someone for a ride. I could have made an effort but I chose not to. It was *safer* not to. I wished I could make her understand. I thought about apologizing, but by then too much time had gone by and she stopped complimenting me during gym class.

By the time we got to high school I was pretty sure she'd forgotten my name. She was friends with everyone, even the upperclassmen. Everyone except for me. Sometimes I'd find myself walking behind her on our way to class, caught in the fog of her peony vanilla body spray. I'd watch her curtain of glossy black hair sway from side to side. It hit her lower back, right above the waistline of her pants so you could still glimpse a sliver of flesh, or maybe even the lacy hint of a thong, if her shirt was short enough. But it wasn't some embarrassing fashion faux pas. She walked like she was aware of it, like she did it so people would notice. That year,

I heard a rumor she'd had sex with an eleventh grader named Rob Garrison. For some reason I couldn't get it out of my head. Every time I saw her, I imagined her on top of this faceless, naked blur of a man, letting him grab fistfuls of her long, shiny hair.

And then Amigo Invisible happened. I panicked that whole week, scouring the mall for the perfect ten-dollar item. I wasn't sure what I wanted to *say* with this gift. I just knew I wanted her to like it. I *needed* her to like it. I never found anything good enough.

The night before the gift exchange, I burst into tears at the kitchen table. Mom asked me what was wrong, if I wanted to talk about it. I remember she seemed pretty shocked, and I was, too. I didn't come home from school with tearjerker stories of being ostracized from the lunch table or getting teased for a bad haircut. I wasn't sure why the hell I was crying. I just knew I couldn't go to school the next day. Couldn't face Emily's reaction when she realized not only was she without a gift, but *I* was supposed to get one for her. I told Mom I felt like I was getting sick and I got my wish. I stayed home.

I haven't thought about Emily in a long time. Don't know why I cared so much about her opinion. But the night before Amigo Invisible felt a whole hell of a lot like this.

I head back to the register to grab my book before punching out for the day. The pink Frappuccino is still on the ledge in a puddle of its own sweat. I pick it up, pop off the dented lid, and pour warm, sticky gobs of it into my mouth. My hands shake from the sugar rush as I drive home.

☾ ☾ ☾

Mom's draw feels eerily normal considering what we fought about the night before. It's as if she purged the entire incident from her memory while she was asleep. She doesn't mention the fortress of coffee grounds in the hallway, either. When I pass her door to use the bathroom, it's gone. She must have held her nose and swept it all up.

She watches the blood bag fill, wearing an unnaturally serene expression. Trying to hide the way she's fidgeting. She even smiles. I immediately notice she's not holding her phone. It's nowhere in sight. I'm not sure if we're going to discuss what happened last night, or even acknowledge it. I start to wonder if I dreamed the whole thing. There's a ringing in my ears and the sudden, bizarre feeling that I'm lost in my own kitchen.

"You okay, babe?" She snaps her fingers in my slack face.

"Uh . . . yeah. Are *you*?"

"Why wouldn't I be?"

Brrriiiing! I pour the blood into her cup. I'm glad to be off the hook, but this feels like a quid pro quo. A pact. She'll pretend my margarita mishap never happened . . . if I act like I never saw her outside with that guy.

She's already decided I've agreed to it. I don't argue, so maybe I have. I pop my supplements without a word.

"So!" She cheerfully smacks the table after she's done drinking. "Here are our options for tonight." She holds up three fingers. I notice her manicure's started chipping—the only sign of wear and tear on her entire body.

It's her night off, and we always spend it together. She pitches the activities. There are always three choices. I get to pick.

She'll usually start by suggesting a movie. Preferably a musical we've seen ten thousand times that we can sing along to. "Watch *The Sound of Music*."

Then there's baking: "Make that blueberry pound cake you were talking about." I appreciate that she always proposes this on my behalf. I can't imagine this is fun for her if she can't eat it.

"Or we can finish the sky in the bathroom." We've been working on a mural, which stretches all the way across the bathroom ceiling.

"Let's paint the sky while the cake is in the oven."

"You mind if I put the movie on while we work?"

Somehow, the decision always seems to combine all three. I don't mind that I don't *really* get to choose. She only gets one night off.

———

Around 1 A.M., I start tottering on the ladder above the shower. I've been sponge-blending the peachy twilit clouds with the cornflower-blue sky, trying to find the perfect texture. I've probably been up here for at least an hour.

I shake out my wrist and glance down at Mom, who's busy shading the golden sand dunes that border the bottom half of the room. When it's done, it'll be a beach landscape with a red and white lighthouse—a re-creation of a town in Cape Cod she once visited as a kid. I've never been, but we looked at hundreds of pictures online to use as a reference. When we're deep into painting, perfecting every blade of grass, every brick, every cloud in the sky . . . it's almost like getting to be there in person.

All the rooms in our house are painted like this. The bathroom was the last blank canvas. We started working on the murals during those dark days and restless nights after we first moved here. We weren't sure what the rules were, whether I should go to school, how often Mom needed to feed, how we would keep each other safe . . . so we stayed inside. When we ran out of canvas and paper, we started using the walls.

"I think I gotta call it a night." I roll my neck in a circle and carefully start to climb down the ladder.

The ceilings in here are nearly ten feet high. Whenever I'm up there I think about Michelangelo at the Sistine Chapel. I'm not scared of the height. I feel powerful. I can see more of everything and see all that everything for what it really is. I can't look down for too long, though, or I get dizzy.

"Aw, come on. You're almost done!" Mom pouts at me from down below.

I feel a yawn coming on and make an extra, exaggerated noise in the back of my throat so she notices it. "I'm pretty tired."

"It's only one o'clock."

"I know. I'm just really wiped for some reason."

I reach the bottom and realize I've stepped into a puddle of white paint on the drop cloth. As I hoist my leg up onto the sink to rinse the bottom of my bare foot, Mom sidles up behind me in the mirror.

"Probably 'cuz of all the tequila you drank last night."

So we *are* going to acknowledge what happened. But only the part where *I* did something wrong. I meet her gaze in the mirror, but her face is a sheet of ice. How does she want me to react? How am I *supposed* to react?

I skitter away, wiping down my foot with a damp, dirty towel. It reeks, earthy with mildew, and I want to gag.

"I said I was sorry," I mutter as my cheeks burn. I ball the rotten towel up in my arms. "I should wash these." I gather a second one from the hook on the wall. A matching set.

"Thanks, babe." She's right beside me, quick as a knife. She seizes my wrist, yanks me close . . . and plants a kiss on top of my head. "I'll finish the ceiling."

She smells bad, like the towels. Or maybe the towels smell like her. She uses all sorts of expensive perfumes and lotions when she goes out. But not when we're at home. It's funny, I haven't noticed the smell of her in years.

I wriggle out of her embrace, like a panicked cat in the arms of some overeager toddler.

"Sleep well." She smiles. I feel like I'm going crazy.

☾ ☾ ☾

I am at the Starbucks. I'm not sure how I got here.

Did I drive? Where's my car?

How late do they stay open, anyway? It's the middle of the night.

I'm the only customer. Jade is alone behind the bar. My heart swells as she greets me in her singsong, unexpected alto. She even says my name. I'm so relieved. I didn't offend her after all. She offers me a cup of coffee.

"My mistake, your treat!"

I glance down into the cup. It's filled with a strange black, viscous ooze. No, I realize. Not black. Red—dark, dark red, darker than wine.

"I don't like coffee," I say, even though I know that's not what it is. I try to hand it back to her. She starts laughing at me.

"I know you don't!" She snorts, doubled over. I'm not sure what's so funny. I don't know what to do, so I start laughing, too. We're both just standing there laughing our asses off. Suddenly, she stops.

"Drink it, I want to watch." She smiles, crinkling her peacock-blue eyeliner.

"I don't like coffee." For some reason that's all I can fucking say.

"Please? For me?"

"I-I don't . . . like coffee . . ."

She's starts laughing again, like I keep delivering the punch line to the world's funniest joke. She steps out from behind the bar and inches toward me. Extends a hand. I jump and slosh the blood in the cup all over my shirt.

A bead of red rolls past the collar of my tank top and down my breast. I watch it, transfixed, and realize I'm paralyzed, like someone's stitched my legs together. Her hand is inches from my face. Every detail is crystal clear. The jewel-toned gleam of her nails. The gold rings on both her index fingers, embellished with rose quartz. She touches my hair, right behind my ear. A jolt of electricity races up my neck and encircles my head like an ice-cold crown. My panicked heart slams against my ribs.

Danger. Danger. Danger.

I snap awake like a whip. I'm frozen on my back, like there's a ghost perched on my chest, covering my mouth with its cold, clammy hand. I want to lift my head and open my eyes, but I can't. I'm soaking wet, and I'm convinced someone's just saved me from drowning till I realize I've sweat through my T-shirt.

Just a dream. A *nightmare*.

I roll over and flick on the bedside lamp. I need to change, I'm drenched. I paw around in my drawers, disoriented and bleary-eyed. I haven't had a dream in years. I started sneaking Mom's Ambien when I was about thirteen. The pills were probably expired, but she never threw them out. She was mad at first, but it was the only way I could get any sleep with her puttering around all night. I have my own prescription now. I don't know how to sleep without it.

I like that I don't dream on Ambien. My subconscious and I have nothing good to say to each other. If I dream at all, it's just quick, nonsensical snippets, like flashes of light catching old-fashioned film stock. This was different. *Real.*

I pull on a new shirt, rubbing sleep from my eyes, but I still feel like my body, my movements, are not my own. I pace the room, too afraid to lie back down. Too afraid to fall asleep and lose control again. Everything about this feels *wrong.* Like I'm under attack.

My breath catches and burns through me. Maybe I am.

I remember the strange quiver in my stomach when Jade handed me my free drink. The way I was so *aware* of her, as if someone had seized my skull and spun my head in her direction. That same someone has infiltrated my dark, dreamless sleep. I don't feel like I'm in control because *I'm not.*

Jade must be a Sara.

The last time I encountered a Sara who wasn't Mom, I would have been too young to be affected by the pheromones. I didn't even know what it meant. I imagined "pheromones" as a swarm of chemical tendrils all reaching out to grab me and choke me to death. Maybe I wasn't too far off. I didn't realize you could still be vulnerable once you were out of range. I wonder if it's more like a parasite that hijacks your psyche. Like how cat people can catch toxoplasmosis. I read about that once. I should have been more careful.

I'm dizzy from all the pacing. I shrivel back into bed and swaddle myself in my blanket.

If this girl is a Sara, how is she out during the day? Working at a coffee shop, of all places?

How is she getting past the scanners?

. . . Why would she target me?

My throat tightens, thick with panic. I stumble across the room to my desk, where my laptop sits dormant. The Facebook group will have the answers. Knowledge is power. Power is control. I'll be back in the driver's seat soon enough.

I don't post anything to the group, because it's linked to Mom's account, not mine, and she doesn't like to draw attention to her case. She's always worried there could be a mole. But if there's been any news about hacked scanners or a mutation, our group would be the first to know. Someone might have posted something.

I scroll through the timeline. I don't even realize I've begun chewing on that fucking hangnail again till I taste blood in my mouth. I'll have to grab a Band-Aid. Open wounds, even tiny ones, drive Mom up a wall.

The most recent post shows a photo of a quaint-looking recovery center in Colorado, designed to look like a rustic ski chalet with a massive black cross stenciled on the wooden façade. The caption reads, "SIGN THIS PETITION TO FORCE SARATOV SALVATION OF BOULDER TO RELEASE THEIR RECORDS!" In the comments, our various cohorts argue with each other.

> » The records are private for a reason. If you were there would you want everyone to know your name?
> » YES YES YES BURN IT DOWN
> » Violates HIPAA it'll never work, you need an investigative journalist to admit themselves
> » Lol ok anyone here an investigative journalist?

I sigh and keep scrolling. Nothing to see here. Our group argues about the Sara centers pretty much every day. These places didn't exist when Mom first got infected. They came along at the same time as the scanners, after those long, dark curfew years. People waited behind locked doors for a cure, for a vaccine, for anything . . . till they finally accepted that the only solution was to try to contain it.

The Sara centers—at least, according to the PSAs on TV—are supposed to be these warm, welcoming places with rose gardens and Christmas parties where patients can get the medical care they need and, in some cases, have their violent records expunged. But the PSAs are all filmed on soundstages with actors. They don't allow cameras inside the actual centers. Mom is convinced it's because they're using the patients as lab rats. I'm not sure what I believe.

I scroll down, down, down, scanning the page for anything useful. Last time I logged in was two weeks ago, and I quickly catch up to the last post I read. I wonder if there's anything older, something I might have missed that's gotten archived. As I start typing "mutation" into the search bar, a red chat bubble flickers in the upper right-hand corner of the screen. Mom has a private message. I ignore it, but then it blinks again. And again.

I don't always read her PMs. I like to stay on top of her safety, but it really depends what kind of mood I'm in. Whether I think she needs me to keep tabs on her. All things considered, tonight feels like an exception.

I open the message, and it's a chain consisting of twelve different people. They're all members of the Survivors group. A few of them have already replied to the first message. I navigate to the top to see what it is.

> » Hi everyone. Pls keep this off the board. My sister and I were visited by the police last night asking if we were still in contact with Devon Shaw. He's been on their radar the past couple months, but they lost his trail somewhere in New Mexico. They believe he might have friends who are sheltering him. I kno you all live in that area and it would make sense for him to try to contact people he's turned, so stay alert. Again, PLEASE keep this off the board. Most of the people in our group were turned by him and a lot of them still think of him as a friend (and prob more ugh).

I slam the laptop shut. I have the sensation that I'm looking down at my body from the ceiling and I'm stuck to it, like Spider-Man. I don't move. Don't even breathe.

Of course. *Of course.*

Mom wouldn't treat a harmless flirtation like a massive secret, even if we both knew it was wrong. She'd show me his lovelorn texts and we'd both laugh about it. She'd never laugh about this. About *him.* I think of her volcanic reaction when I asked about the man in the parking lot. Her lightning-quick, seething deflection.

Mom is the charitable type. Always has been. She left the church when she got pregnant with me, but deep down she's still a good little Mormon girl on a mission. She buys Toys for Tots every Christmas and I always see charges on our joint bank account from places like Amnesty International and the Red Cross. If Devon was desperate and came to her in his hour of need, she wouldn't know how to say no.

I imagine what he must be telling her, flooding those empty chambers of her heart with all the right platitudes. *I never stopped loving you. Let's be a family.*

With a trembling hand, I open the laptop back up and mark all the messages as "Unread." I want her to know that I know, but the conversation has to happen on my terms. If she catches me reading her messages, the argument becomes about me and what *I* did.

I squeeze my head between my knees and rock back and forth in my desk chair. My nightmare about Jade feels ridiculous now. *This* is the nightmare. How could I have missed it? He's been here all along, waiting for me to fall asleep on my watch so he could slither underneath our door. Waiting to steal her away from me again.

2010

There are greasy fingerprints all over Mom's computer screen and keyboard. I've eaten an entire large Domino's pizza by myself over the course of the past six hours as I read every comment and click every link posted to the Facebook group. Behind Mom's door, *Beauty and the Beast* plays for probably the twelfth time. I keep hearing Celine Dion sing over the end credits, and then she'll hit restart. At one point I hear Devon ask if she wants to watch something else, but she doesn't answer.

I'm engrossed in a long, complicated, and predictably graphic comment thread about blood safety. Blood safety as in blood you drink. Blood that Mom now has to drink. If you want to survive, you need to consume a bare minimum of four ounces a day. I jot the number down on a Post-it and underline it. If you skip a day, it's the same as someone like me going without water; after three days, your body starts shutting down. Go four days and you're dead. Someone named Dani tells a story about a time she didn't feed for forty-eight hours and experienced this insane burst of delirium that caused her to chew a hole in the side of her house.

The blood also has to be fresh, people argue. If it's gone cold, especially if you freeze it for later, it can instantly erode your esophagus. I have no idea what this means. A helpful user named Bonnie O. has posted some photos for context. I feel like I'm supposed to scream or gag or slam the laptop shut. But I don't. I just stare at the screen, into the bulging eyes of the woman in the grainy photo, faceup on the floor, neck swollen like a thick, black tire.

Animal blood can also cause a lot of issues. A chatty guy named Robert says drinking from a rabbit gave him the most painful IBS of his life and it never went away. I don't know what that means, either.

I've learned more about Pyotr and Larisa, too. Larisa was arrested after murdering her husband and draining all the blood from his body. She claimed it was an act of self-defense because he got violent with her after discovering she'd had an affair. Patient Zero was the mystery man she'd been sneaking around with, but he disappeared without a trace and they only ever got a first name: Alexei. When the authorities discovered that Larisa not only drained her husband's blood but *drank it,* and also fed it to her eight-year-old son, they threw them both into a Soviet mental institution, where things got even weirder. The doctors tried to force-feed them but they couldn't keep any food down. The average cell couldn't hold them; they could bend the metal bars—which the doctors discovered when they escaped and started eating the orderlies. They moved them to a maximum-security steel and concrete holding chamber. They couldn't be exposed to sunlight, and Pyotr lost a hand while they were experimenting. The Russian scientists declared seven seconds to be the exposure limit, because after seven seconds outside, Larisa perished. That night, Pyotr escaped—nobody knows how. Maybe he had help. A sympathetic nurse or someone on the outside. These aren't official reports, just stories passed down between members of the Facebook group. He was last seen sprinting into the forest, drenched with blood, clutching the still-throbbing heart of the doctor who killed his mother.

After that, the sickness spread north, following the Volga River toward Moscow. According to the Facebook post, the Russians tried to keep a lid on it. But no one suspected the doe-eyed, one-handed eight-year-old until it was too late.

I stop scrolling, gnawing on my last hard pizza crust. If this thing has been spreading since 1990, how come Mom and I never heard of it? When I type "Saratov's syndrome" into Google, all that pops up are creepy conspiracy blogs hosted on buggy old LiveJournals and a lot of stuff in Russian that I can't understand. People don't think it's real.

There were always stories about people like Larisa and Pyotr, rumors of monsters who walked among us. But all stories are true stories, if you look closely.

☾ ☾ ☾

I start dozing off on the couch after the sun comes up. A couple of neighborhood kids walk by the duct-taped window, chattering and bouncing a basketball on their way to the bus stop. I wish I could go to school with them. That this were just another Tuesday.

I wake up a few hours later, and my breath catches when I notice Devon asleep on the love seat right across from me. I bolt upright, but he doesn't budge. I stare at his bare feet poking out of the wool throw blanket. He hugs a pillow to his chest, like he's protecting himself. I hate how normal he looks.

I'm not even trying to be quiet as I make my way to the kitchen for a glass of water. I'm extra loud, in fact, knocking dishes in the sink and slamming the fridge. Devon stirs, but he doesn't say anything. Doesn't scowl or roll his eyes. He just watches me, totally vacant. I wish he'd do something with his face.

"What'd you think of Larisa and Pyotr?" He finally speaks.

I shrug. He sits up and stretches.

"Did you have any questions?"

I wrinkle my nose and cut him a sidelong glance. Why is he being nice all of a sudden?

"Mia, here's the way I see it," he says as he rises. He takes a seat at the breakfast bar, curling his bare toes around the bottom rung of the stool. "We're gonna be a family for a little while. There are things you and your mom need help with—"

"Me and my mom are a family. You're not."

"You're gonna have to make some space."

"Don't you have your own family?"

"Actually, I don't."

"Everyone has parents."

"Yeah well, I just told you. I don't."

His face stiffens as he digs into the back pocket of his jeans and produces a ziplock bag of brown, toasted leaves. He starts hand-rolling a cigarette on the countertop. He doesn't look down as he works. Knows the ritual by touch. I watch his hands so I don't have to maintain eye contact.

"How old are you?" I ask in a small voice. "Did your parents die in like . . . 1920?"

Devon snorts and brings the edge of the translucent rolling paper to his lips to seal it. "I'm twenty-eight."

"No, I mean, *how old are you*? Pyotr never got to be older than eight years old after he . . ." I swallow the words, not sure what to call it.

"I've been like this for the past two years. So . . . Fine. I guess I'm thirty."

"Where are your parents, then? If they're not dead?"

"They are. I think."

"You *think*?" I catch myself sneering, then dial it back. Remembering what he is.

"I asked if you had any questions about the *Facebook page*."

"I don't."

He lights the burner of our stove and hovers over it, cigarette clenched between his lips.

"We're not allowed to smoke in here."

He exhales, slowly. Pale, wispy rivulets escape through his teeth.

"My mom was alone, like yours. But she couldn't take care of me. You're lucky. Your mom loves you. She's not gonna give up on you."

I nod. Hoping that's true.

"Does she still have a fever?"

"Only a little. She'll be okay soon."

I finish my glass of water, but before I head back down the hall, I turn to face him. "Why doesn't anyone think it's real?"

He takes a drag before he answers. "It's still new around here. I don't think anybody wants to believe it. There'll be no more de-nying it once Russia releases their records, though. The Soviets built all these prisons and stuff. And I guess they kept it tight for a while. But there was one person they never caught."

I know he means Pyotr. I inch back into the room, hugging the edge of the door. "When Pyotr was running around Russia all by himself, he had to like . . . kill a lot of people. So he could eat."

"No shit, Sherlock."

"But because the sickness kept spreading, that means he kept bringing people back. Like you did."

Devon nods. Filling the space between us with smoke.

"Why? He knew what it was. He knew it wasn't safe. If he hadn't gone around giving it to people, it never would've spread and if it hadn't spread it never would've come to the United States and we wouldn't be—"

"Think about how you'd feel, if this happened to you." Devon stares me down. "You're just a kid and you're on your own. You scare easy. You're lonely. You need someone to look after you."

"Fine, but then why would he *keep doing it*? If he found some nice lady to be his new mom or something—"

"He didn't want to be alone in the world. At least, that's what I think."

He holds my gaze. I remember what he said two nights ago. *I made a mistake.* Was the whole thing some kind of act? Had he planned to turn Mom the moment he met her?

"Is Pyotr still in Russia?" I ask, if only to fill the silence.

"Nobody knows."

"But all these people on the internet have his picture and talk about him."

"Exactly. Wouldn't you run and hide? If everyone said it was your fault?" He ashes his cigarette in the sink.

And he's gone, back to the darkness of Mom's bedroom. I try to follow him, but he's too quick. The door's already locked. Celine Dion starts singing.

☾ ☾ ☾

I wonder if I'll ever be able to sleep through the night again. The hours tick by. Eight o'clock. Nine o'clock. Before I know it, it's midnight. Then four. I'm still on the couch, hunched over Mom's laptop, when I suddenly realize it's quiet. *Beauty and the Beast* is paused. I hold my breath, slowly shifting to glance at her bedroom door, as though the slightest sound might trigger that seismic, inhuman wail again.

"Isobel, come *on*—" I hear Devon hiss across the hall.

"I said don't touch me." My heart leaps into my throat. It's her, that's her voice. Her *real* voice.

I shut the laptop and sit up straight. Should I go in? She sounds the same, but what does she look like now? What will she do when she sees me?

The door creaks open and I lunge over to flick on the lights. She shambles into the hall, wearing a fresh pair of gray sweatpants and one of Devon's ragged concert tees. She's scrubbed the bloody tearstains from her face and her bottle-green eyes glimmer with renewed health. But she can barely lift her head. She's startlingly thin, like she somehow managed to lose twenty pounds overnight. Devon's T-shirt swallows her, slipping off her shoulder. Her distended collarbone casts a shadow across her milk-white neck like a bruise.

"Dammit Izzy, come to bed—"

She slams the bedroom door and turns to me. It feels like a whole minute she's just standing there, staring. My stomach curdles. Does she not recognize me?

She darts across the room so fast it looks like she might be floating. Wraps her arms around my trembling body. Her embrace is hard and jagged because of the weight she's lost. I can feel her ribs through her shirt, rigid like a picket fence. But her grip is strong, so much stronger than it should be, like she's sealing us up in a tomb together. I should feel safe, being held by someone so strong. Being held by my mom. And I do. But she's different now and denying it won't help her—or me. That's another thing I learned from the Facebook group.

"It's okay, baby. I'm fine. See? Look at me, look at my face. I'm okay, everything's gonna be okay."

My lungs hitch as I spit words through my tears. "N-no it's . . . it's not. I-I read . . . about . . . you'll die if you don't . . . if you don't—" I can't bring myself to say it. *If you don't drink blood.*

"Mia, it's all right." She props me up in her lap and holds my shoulders steady. Like Devon, she has a strange sort of electricity thrumming from her fingertips. But her touch doesn't stun me like his. It shimmers, like slipping between cool, clean sheets. "Devon told me everything. We're gonna be fine. He'll help us."

"No, no, no. He has to leave." I try to twist free, but her grip is too powerful. "He can't . . . he's not here to *help*, he's the one who did this." She doesn't reply. "He hurt you. I saw. Don't you remember?"

"I-I don't. I just kind of fell asleep when he started . . ." She lets out a breath where the words ought to be. "Mia, we need him."

"No, we don't!" I'm screeching now and I'm sure he can hear me. Like I care.

"Just for a little while, okay? We have a lot to figure out, and he knows what to—"

"How long is a little while?"

"I don't know yet, honey."

I manage to wrest my hand free and wipe the snot from my nose. "Promise me he's not gonna live here."

She sighs and hangs her head. When she looks up at me, her eyes are welling. That's good, I think. She's still able to cry. I don't know why I thought she might not.

"I promise, he's not gonna live here."

"And once we 'figure things out' we don't ever have to see him again."

She doesn't answer right away. She takes me back into her arms. Exhales into my hair, warm and heavy.

"Mom?"

"I promise. It'll be you and me. Just like before." Her voice falters and her tears are damp against my scalp. "I'm sorry, Mia."

I peer over her shoulder and realize I never taped down the edge of the curtain like Devon asked. The sun will be up soon. As I inch away and grab a roll of duct tape from the coffee table, her head swoops and she shudders, like someone's just pushed her.

"You okay?"

"Uh . . . I think . . . I should sleep. Just a little longer."

"You're supposed to sleep for the whole day."

"Right . . . right."

I get to work fixing the curtain, making sure it's secured to the wall so no light can get through. The tape's probably going to rip off a lot of paint. Two days ago, Mom would've been pretty mad about that. She'd always yell at me about a security deposit if I put stickers on the wall or spilled something.

As she sways back to her bedroom, I call out to her, "Should I go to school?"

She stops short, rubbing her eyes. "If you want to."

"Okay." I thought I did yesterday. Not anymore.

She turns around and blows me a weak little kiss. "I love you."

I swallow, holding back a fresh wave of tears. "Love you, too."

☾ ☾ ☾

Our orange tabby, Cheddar, runs off the morning of the fourth day. I know Mom and Devon didn't attack him, because I saw him leave. He sprinted like a wildcat out of Mom's bedroom, jumped onto the kitchen windowsill, and tore the curtain from the wall with his claws. All I could do was stare, holding my breath, as he took a running leap toward the window and cannonballed through the glass. For a second he was stuck in the jagged hole, half in half out like a feral Winnie the Pooh, but before I could reach him he wriggled free and sprang out onto the balcony, trailing blood. He never came back.

It shocks me how little things change, though I don't know what I was expecting. Mom and Devon still go out every night, except now they both sleep during the day. She knows I've seen the Facebook group and I know what Saras do at night. But she promises they aren't hurting anyone. Devon knows a guy who works at a funeral home nearby. That's how he's survived all this time. They meet up with him every night. I don't understand why it takes them so long, though. They're always gone till at least 4 A.M.

At dinnertime, Mom leaves me money to order delivery. I don't go hungry again. I should be relieved. But I can't sleep at night when she's not there. I have trouble concentrating and staying awake when I go back to school. I ask Mom to write me sick notes in advance so I can skip as many days as I want. She keeps reminding me that "this isn't forever." She says this about a lot of things.

One afternoon, our doorbell rings. Mom is fast asleep. I haven't been at school for the past two days. I switch off the TV and freeze in the darkness, guarded by our new blackout curtains. Even if she heard it, she's not going to answer. I know I shouldn't, either.

A knock comes next. Just in case the doorbell's broken. Still, I don't move, as though there's a motion-sensing predator outside.

"Izzy? Mia?" a woman's muffled voice calls out. "It's Ruby and Chloe!"

My heart flutters. Chloe is one of my best friends from school. Mom grew up with her parents. They belonged to the same church, before Mom and Gram got kicked out—Mom because she got pregnant, Gram because she stuck by her. Mom lost most of her old friends when I was born, but not the Vaughns. Ruby— Mrs. Vaughn—is a good person. She always sends Chloe to school with extra snacks so she can share with me.

I stand and fidget in the foyer. Holding my breath. I want to trust them. Want to tell them we're in trouble and Mom needs a doctor. But then I think of Pyotr, warning me across time with his steely-eyed stare. I hate it, but I think of Devon, too. *They're gonna lock her up somewhere and tell you she's dead.*

"Mia? Are you home?" That's Chloe. Gentle and poised, just like her mom.

I can't help myself. I fling the door open.

"Hi!" My voice is like a bell. Too bright. I forgot I'm supposed to be home sick. I slide outside and slam the door behind me.

"Hey, sweetie!" Mrs. Vaughn greets me with a grin, but she looks worried.

"We brought you stuff for the science project," Chloe announces, presenting me with a shoebox. "Mrs. Ballard wasn't sure if you were feeling better yet, so she thought it would be good for you to have it 'cuz it's due next week."

"Okay. Thanks." I tuck the box under my arm and pivot to rush back inside. But Mrs. Vaughn puts a hand on my shoulder.

"Is everything okay? I've been calling your mom but—"

"Oh, she's been sick, too." I hear myself and almost gasp. Of all the excuses in the world. I need to escape this conversation. Never should have opened the door.

"That's too bad. I guess there's a bug going around, huh?"

"Um . . . yeah. But we'll be better soon. Thanks for the science box." I try again to leave, but this time Chloe stops me.

"Are you gonna be at the dance recital on Sunday? You didn't pick up your costume."

"Um . . . I dunno. My mom might have to work. I won't have a ride."

"We'll pick you up, it's no problem," Mrs. Vaughn says. "Just have your mom call me, okay?"

"Yup."

I don't even say goodbye. I dart through the door and lock it behind me.

Mom is standing outside her bedroom, protected by a long, spectral shadow.

"Mia? Who was that?"

"Chloe and Mrs. Vaughn."

"Why did you open the door?" Her voice is hoarse. Laced with panic.

"B-because it was Chloe and Mrs. Vaughn?" I hold up the shoebox. "They had stuff from school to give me. We have a science project due next week."

"Well, maybe you should *go back to school* so these nosy assholes stay away from our house."

I bite my lips together. I've never heard her talk about the Vaughns that way.

"What did they say to you?"

"Nothing. Just wanted to know how I was feeling. Chloe asked if I'm coming to the dance recital on Sunday."

"Right . . ." Mom drags her nails across her scalp. "What time is that?"

"I think it's at four." Mom doesn't respond. "It's okay, Mrs. Vaughn said she can come pick me up—"

"No. She's not coming back here. We can't see anyone."

"Not even them?"

"What part of 'can't see anyone' do you not understand, Mia? Jesus Christ."

Mom always gives her curse words extra emphasis, like she's kicking a football with her mouth. I think she enjoys it, after the upbringing she had. But it sounds different this time. There's no thrill. Just fear.

I drift back toward the couch, swallowing to dislodge the lump in my throat.

"I'll help you with your science project once I get a little more sleep. Okay?"

I nod without looking at her. She slinks back into her room.

Later that night, Devon comes over. He comes by every night, but technically Mom kept her promise. He doesn't live here. Mom tells me to be polite because he's "helping us." My version of politeness is to completely ignore him.

But tonight, he's not having it.

Mom's in the shower when he lets himself in through the back door. I grab my half-eaten peanut butter sandwich, about to finish it in my room so I don't have to talk to him. He corners me by the fridge and skewers me with his gaze.

"Heard we had a little problem today."

When he speaks, I can see his gums retract. Only a little bit, but it's enough to stop me in my tracks. I squeeze my sandwich so hard peanut butter oozes out the sides.

"I-I don't know what you're—"

"Your mom said you had a friend over."

"I didn't . . . *invite* her. She came to give me something from school."

"You think I'm a fucking idiot?" He reaches out a hand, but I recoil. Desperate to avoid that ice-cold shock.

"They didn't come inside."

"Well, you must have said something you weren't supposed to, 'cuz now this dumb bitch won't stop calling your mom."

I'm up against the sink and have nowhere else to go. He seizes my arms and I squeal, dropping my sandwich.

"You gotta be better than this. You hear me? Unless of course you're *trying* to get us killed—"

"Let go of me!"

His grip is so strong I'm sure he's going to crush my bones with his fingers. I scream in his face and he screams right back, matching my intensity and volume. My ears ring as tears rise in my eyes. His canines are fully extended now, and he tongues the points.

"Mom! Mom, help me!"

I blink and she's out of the bathroom in a towel, dripping wet. She grabs a plate from the table and hurls it at him.

"Devon, *enough*—"

The plate hits the wall and shatters. He releases me and his hands shoot up in surrender. I race out of the house in my bare feet, stomping on my sandwich on the floor.

"Mia!"

She blocks my exit before I can get past the front porch. I have no choice but to collapse into her embrace.

"He's not gonna hurt you, I promise. He was upset. You understand that, right?"

I raise my tearstained face from her shoulder. Is she defending him? This is all wrong.

"He was gonna . . . Mom, he opened his mouth and—"

"I know he scared you. But that's all he was trying to do."

I pull back from her. She *lets me* pull back. But she's still standing in my way. I'm not allowed to run.

"Mia, he swore to me he would never, *ever*—"

"But he *did*!"

"Did he *bite you*?"

". . . No. But he—"

"Enough, Mia. You scared him, he scared you, and now you're even. I can't believe you think I'd let anything happen to you. Do you know how much that hurts me?" Her voice cracks.

I don't know what to say. Devon watches us from the window, like a hawk in a tree.

"I'll make you hot chocolate before we go out." She tugs on my arm, hauling me back inside, then whispers in my ear, "I need you to trust me, Mia. None of this works if we don't trust each other."

My head wobbles. Something resembling a nod.

☾ ☾ ☾

A few nights later I hear them come home and she's crying. She's not even trying to hide it or stay quiet so she won't wake me up. I wasn't asleep anyway. She sniffles and moans and I hear her say, "I don't want to. I told you, I *keep telling you*. You didn't listen, you *never fucking listen to me,* Devon—"

He mutters something inaudible and I think he's going to storm out, but a moment passes and I don't hear the door. I wonder if he's sitting next to her and letting her cry. Maybe even comforting her. Holding her hand. I hope so. I don't want to imagine her crying alone.

The next night, before Mom goes out, I make another stupid mistake.

She's only given me five dollars for dinner, down from ten last week. She's trying to conserve money. She just lost her job as a docent at the Natural History Museum—where she'd worked since I was born—because of all the shifts she missed. I roll the corners of the five-dollar bill as my anxiety percolates.

I know Gram left us a lot of money when she died two years ago. I think she wanted Mom to buy a house or something. Because of that, Mom says we'll be fine. But still, I keep asking when she's going to start working again. When she'll do something else after dark besides going out with Devon.

I need help. We can't do this forever. There should be another adult involved. Not Devon. Not the Vaughns. A family member. Problem is, I don't know of any. Except one.

"Mom, when was the last time you talked to um . . ." I hesitate, forcing my mouth to shape the words. "My dad?"

She whirls around with a sharp intake of breath. "Why would you—?"

"I just thought . . . and maybe this is dumb. But if we ever needed to ask him for help—"

Her wounded eyes glisten with tears. "What do you mean 'ask him for help'? We don't need him, we've never—"

"N-no, I know we don't. I'm just . . ."

I've never met my dad and I never ask about him. But I'm scared. When you're scared and you're ten years old, you try to find an adult.

Mom turns her back and I hear her sniffle. I hug her from behind, pressing my forehead against her rigid spine.

"I'm sorry, Mom. I didn't mean to talk about him, I know it makes you—"

"Then why did you?" She spins to face me, revealing her misty eyes, really letting me get a good look. Her whole body's shaking. The edges of her gums recede as she goes on. "You want me to call him up after ten years and ask if you can live with him? Instead of me?"

"No! Of course not—" I shrink and stare at my feet.

"I'm serious, I'll try him right now. He'll pretend he's never met me." She picks up her phone, waving it in my face. "Maybe his wife will answer. Want me to put it on speaker, so you can hear?"

"I'm really sorry. I just thought . . . Just in case something bad happens, if there were another grown-up around—"

"The bad thing already *fucking happened*, Mia." All the air leaves my body. This is not a word we use.

She stops crying on a dime. "We don't need 'another grown-up.' I need *you* to be the grown-up, okay?"

I shudder and start inching toward my room. She doesn't take her eyes off me. I expect her to charge after me as I shut my door, but she doesn't. Devon's car has just pulled up the driveway. She stomps outside in her high-heeled boots and a furious *clack clack clack!* echoes across the hall. Later, when I creep out of my room, I count six holes in the hardwood, like bloodless bullet wounds.

When they come back, it's only midnight. I'm wide awake in bed with all the lights on, trying to read but losing my focus. This is how it is now, every night: too nervous to sleep, too exhausted to do anything else.

There's a loud thump outside my window, and I hear Mom laugh. I roll over and pry the blinds open with my fingers. There's a Jacuzzi on our patio we hardly ever use, and Mom is trying to pull the cover off. She's stumbling around in her high heels, howling with laughter. Something about it feels wrong, too big and too loud, like there's a camera rolling nearby. She's not *really* laughing, she's pretending.

She leans on Devon for support, unstrapping her shoes, and when he moves over I notice there's a third person: a fair-haired man who looks like he might be in his twenties, or maybe even an older teenager. It's hard for me to tell exactly how old adults are. He's wearing that missionary uniform I see on all the LDS boys when they go door-to-door: a short-sleeved white button-down tucked into high-waisted black slacks. He doesn't seem like one of them, though. He's looser and more self-assured, although Mom and Devon might be helping him with that.

Mom tosses her heels and peels her shirt up over her head. I snap the blinds shut. Whatever's happening out there, I shouldn't be watching. They think I'm sleeping. Or do they? They'd notice my lights were on if they looked up at my window. They haven't even thought about me. They don't care.

Mom squeals and I peek through the blinds again. She's topless now, and I avert my eyes as though the sight of her breasts might turn me to stone. She starts unbuttoning the boy's white shirt as she pulls him toward the Jacuzzi. Devon lights a cigarette and takes a seat on the rattan deck chair. My skin turns to gooseflesh, like I've just fallen into a freezing cold, slimy puddle of mud. I draw back from the window to the safety of my bed and tug the covers over my head. Bury my face in my pillow. Trying not to listen.

Someone screams. I wish I could pretend I didn't hear it. I wish I could ignore what's happening. I wish I had no idea what any of this means or why they're doing it. I think of the way Mom was crying the other night. She doesn't want this. I need to remind her.

I yank up the blinds and push open the window as fast as I can. I am trying to do this without looking at them. But I can't help it.

Mom and the boy are in the water, and she's pressing her mouth to his, holding him in place. Her hand on the back of his head is like a pale, hungry spider. Blood gushes between their lips. Behind him, Devon sinks his teeth into the back of his neck, still holding his smoldering cigarette.

"Stop!" I make a sound that doesn't feel like it came from my body: a raw, desperate squeak, like a mouse struggling in a trap.

Mom gasps and releases the boy's tongue from her mouth. He slips into the red, frothy water, causing Devon to lose his grip. The boy scrambles out of the tub. I've never seen a naked man before, but there's not much to see. He wears his blood like a dress.

"Fuck, fuck, fuck!" Devon chases after him, quick as a gunshot. He pounces on his back and throws him to the ground, grinding his face against the unforgiving concrete. Mom bursts into tears. Hugs her breasts as she rocks back and forth in the water, roiling with blood. I'm still paralyzed in the window. Neither of them have even looked at me.

"Shit . . ." Devon mutters, studying the boy's limp body. He stands and shoves it with his foot.

Mom hurls herself out of the water like a monster from the deep, dripping wet. I wonder if she's cold. If she feels anything at all. She bends down to turn the boy over, but Devon elbows her away.

"Can't feed if they're dead."

"Wait . . . W-what?"

"Sorry."

"What the fuck, Devon?" She slumps to the ground.

"It's not my fault!"

I clutch the wall for support as the truth washes over me. There's no way they've been getting blood from a funeral home. She lied. But I knew she lied. The Facebook group said the blood has to be fresh. How could it be fresh at a funeral home? People at a funeral home have been dead for days. This boy's been dead less than a minute. I don't mean to, but I gasp aloud. I clamp a hand over my mouth, but it's too late.

Devon's eyes lock on to mine as he pivots toward the house. I'm numb all over, like he's just shot me with a poisoned arrow. He takes off running, and I know I only have seconds till it's my neck in his jaws.

"Devon, no!" Mom screams, but he's already gone.

I meet her gaze, and in that moment I lose all my fear. I crank the window all the way open and kick out the screen. It's not a long drop, I'm on the second floor. I can probably land in the Jacuzzi if my aim is good enough. The blood-spattered concrete is the only alternative.

Devon's footsteps pound outside my door, shaking the framed photos on my wall. I gulp a huge breath of air, as if I'm hoping I can fill myself up and float like a balloon.

"Mia! *Stop*—" I hear Mom cry as I fall.

I hit the Jacuzzi headfirst, and my ankle collides with the hard edge of the pool. Heat surges under my skin and I swear I just heard something crack. My eyes open in shock underwater, and my vision swims with blood. It takes me a second to realize it's not pouring from my own face.

As I raise my head to take a breath, someone's hand forces it back down. Mom yells, muffled by the low hum of the jets. I don't know how he got back down here so fast. I try to kick, to flail my way out of Devon's grasp, but the pain in my leg echoes across my body. I can hardly move. But Mom will help me. She's standing right there. She'll come for me.

She'll come for me. . . .

She'll . . .

Black. Stillness. Only the hum of the jets, getting softer and softer and . . .

He lets go.

I bob to the surface like a blood-soaked cork, choking as I scream and gasp for air at the same time.

Mom has a rusty chunk of chain link in her trembling hand, and there's a hole in the flimsy fence separating the patio from the driveway. She holds Devon from behind, pointing the jagged edge to his throat.

"Get out."

Devon just laughs. She presses the toxic metal to his skin and gives it a threatening twist. This time, he flinches. Enough for her to know he's afraid. But his voice when he speaks is even and calm.

"I thought you were still hungry."

My heart sinks as she sucks her enlarged, bloodstained teeth. Avoiding my gaze. She loosens her grip on him. Drops her weapon. "Mia, go inside and take a shower. I'll be back."

"Mom—"

"You want your mom to die again, you dumb little cunt?" He spits on the ground.

"Please don't talk to her like that," Mom whispers, but doesn't look at him.

Devon scowls and shoves past her. Toward the gate. She seizes his arm. He spins to face her and looks her up and down, taking his time. Like he's driving daggers into every tender part of her naked body. Her lower lip quivers. As though she already knows what he's going to say.

"You're not worth it."

He shakes her free and pushes her toward me. I reach for her, but I'm not sure she sees me. She sobs and collapses to the concrete in a heap.

Devon meets my eye and lights a fresh cigarette, unblinking in the hot firelight. He keeps staring as he eases on his jacket and smooths his hair. Even as he turns his back and stalks past the porch lights into the darkness, it still feels like he's looking at me.

NOW

I don't sleep for the rest of the night. All I can do is rehearse the confrontation in my head: what I'm going to say to her, and how. *When* is also important. I can't wait too long. Around 4 A.M. I hear the TV, and I think about heading out to the living room to bring it up right then. But I can't come in too hot. This can't be a fight. I need a strategy. I should wait until tonight, after she's eaten but before she's left for work. That's usually her most receptive, talkative hour. By the time I decide this, it's 7 A.M. My body is dying for a reprieve after a night of tense, sweaty fidgeting. But my alarm is about to go off.

The car practically drives itself to the bookstore as I run dialogue through my head like rapid-fire lines of binary code.

You know I check the Facebook group sometimes and I always respect your privacy . . .

You can tell me anything, I'm not going to judge you for it . . .

If you're in trouble we can figure something out, you just need to give me the facts . . .

I park and catch a glimpse of myself in the rearview mirror. My bedhead is flecked with blue paint from the ceiling, greasy and in desperate need of a wash. My skin is parched and spiderwebbed with worry lines, and my eyes peer up from the bottom of two dark, sleep-deprived hollows. I don't know when I got to be so old.

I have low standards for workplace appearances, but this is a pretty egregious look. At the very least, I can do something about my hair. As I dig around in the glove compartment for an elastic, a car screams into the lot, vibrating with heavy bass. A moody

New Wave number pulsates from the open windows. Maybe the Smiths, or Joy Division?

I snag a dull pencil and start winding my hair around it to form a messy bun. As I check my reflection, I spot the car in my rearview: a rusty sea-green minivan, covered with tattered bumper stickers. FREE TIBET. COEXIST. LETTUCE TURNIP THE BEET, featuring headbanging cartoon vegetables. A puff of milky vape smoke escapes from the window before the driver hops out.

It's her.

Jade pulls her Starbucks visor over her curls and pops a piece of gum. She's about to pass right by my window. I glance down at my phone, pretending to be deeply engrossed, as my stomach coils into knots. Has she always parked back here? Does she arrive at this time every morning? Or is she doing this specifically to target me?

I keep my eyes glued to the black, vacant screen of my phone, holding my breath as she passes. I don't look up at her, but I know she's seen me. Just like before, her gaze needles at me. The back of my neck prickles. She wants me to see her, and I can feel her willing me to lift my head. But I'm stronger. She needs to know she can't get to me.

I hear her footsteps as she ambles past. Dare to peer over at her as she approaches the Starbucks. I squint at her bare arms in the sunlight, searching for any sign of redness or a blister. But I can't see anything. She walks with a slight, spirited bounce, and it makes me think of a tiny mountain goat, hopping from one foot to the other, never keeping all four hooves on the ground at once. The kind that have a million views on YouTube, frolicking around wearing pajamas. I shake my head, physically forcing the image from my mind. That's exactly what a Sara would want you to think of, when you looked at her. Fucking baby goats in pajamas. But I've won this round. I didn't make eye contact. Maybe she'll give up and move on to someone else.

☾ ☾ ☾

We have a visiting children's author today and I mispronounce his name when I introduce him. He's polite and doesn't correct me, and I mean to apologize after the signing but I forget. It's like I'm ten feet underwater, listening to muffled, distant conversations above me but not understanding anything anyone says. I only have yes or no answers for Sandy when she asks me if I finished that space opera yet and how I'm liking it. She tells me I can head home a little early if I want, that I look sick. I'm relieved, until I remember what I have to do when I get home and I start to feel as sick as I look.

I'm quiet as Mom drinks. She nudges the wilting yellow tulip between sips, trying to perk it up. "How is this thing already dead? Are we watering it too much?"

"We should put it outside, it needs some sun."

I watch the line of red in her cup sink lower and lower. Reciting the lines in my head again.

It's not that I don't trust you . . .

We've worked so hard for what we have. Don't let him ruin it . . .

She studies my face. "You should go buy yourself some nice makeup. You look so tired lately. A little concealer and some vitamin C serum can go a long way."

The suggestion catches me off guard. She never taught me to put on makeup. Back when I was in high school, we decided it made me look too old and might poke holes in our security as I caught up in age. But now I guess I need it.

"That stuff is expensive," I mumble. Trying to get purchase on the conversation again.

She takes another sip. The cup is almost empty, only one or two mouthfuls to go. . . .

"So let me buy you a present. You deserve it."

"You sure it's not gonna turn into *your* present?" I manage a sarcastic smile.

She laughs and downs the rest of the blood. I sit up straight and clear my throat, fighting the thrash of my anxious heart. But before I can begin my impeccably rehearsed monologue, she goes to the sink to rinse her glass. She's not waiting for me to eat. She's got somewhere to be.

"Are you uh . . . heading to the restaurant?" This is not how my speech is supposed to start.

"Yeah, gonna meet Luke early so we can finalize the menu." It's not that I don't believe her. I know she and Luke have been working on the menu all week. And yet . . .

"Mom, we need to talk about the Facebook group," I blurt. Another deviation from the speech. I'd had such a perfectly smooth ascent planned. I was supposed to speak in a slow, calming voice and maybe even reach for her hand.

"Um . . . okay?" She stops in the hallway. I try to read her expression in the dim light. Does she know what I'm getting at? Is she going to play clueless? For how long?

"Sorry, just . . . let me start over." I wish she would come closer. The distance feels wrong. But I keep talking. "I-I love you and our life together is . . ."

Shit. What am I saying. "We've worked really hard to . . . I don't want anything to come between us." There. Okay. Now what?

"You should go to bed. Sandy was right, you seem like you're getting sick—"

"Mom, we need to talk about—"

"The Facebook group, right? Mia, you're not making any—"

"I saw those DMs. About Devon."

Finally, she moves toward me. I slide my hands into the sleeves of my sweatshirt, like I wish I could hide inside of it.

"I-I don't usually check your messages but you *know* I look at the page sometimes when I need information about something and I just happened to—"

"Mia, this has nothing to do with you." She lowers her voice: the calm before a storm. I search her face for that flicker of aggression, a sign I should put up my shield. But she's not here for a fight. Not yet, anyway.

"How can it not? Mom, don't you remember what he—"

"People can change."

"You can't do this! You promised me he was—"

"Stay out of my shit, Mia." *Now* she's ready to fight. Her eyes are like hot coals, dark and smoldering. The color always deepens when she's scared or upset—a Sara side effect caused by stress hormones.

I withdraw and she moves with me like a magnet. Gets right up in my face, trying to use any height difference to her advantage. I'm as tall as she is now, but I still feel a good three inches shorter.

"I'm sorry. I'm just trying to—"

"You don't ever have to see him. Like I said, this doesn't have anything to do with you."

"Mom, you *know* I can't—"

"Don't you trust me?"

I hang my head. *It's not that I don't trust you.* I was supposed to say that at the beginning. I was supposed to do this so differently . . .

"Devon knows things, Mia. Do not forget what he can do." She leans in close, evergreen eyes round with fear. "If the police catch him, he can rat out every person he's ever hunted with."

"Mom . . . are you doing this because you're afraid? Or because you're still in love with him?"

She doesn't answer right away. "What is it that you think I'm *doing*—?"

"Harboring a wanted criminal for starters. Is there more?"

"Either stop running your mouth and have an adult conversation with me, or drop it." I bite down on my lip and keep it clamped there so she can see. "My reasons for doing this are not your business."

"Listen, if you're scared, go to the cops and tell them where to find Devon in exchange for, y'know . . . immunity or something."

She laughs darkly. "Come on, Mia, you're smarter than that. This isn't *Law & Order*. I don't get any kind of immunity unless I surrender to a fucking Sara center."

"They don't have to know you're infected. Call them and report him anonymously—"

"How does that help me when they arrest him and he names me?"

I exhale, still bunching the sleeves of my hoodie in my fists.

"I need to help him. I *want to* help him. And that's the end of this discussion."

"Mom, please. You're not listening to me—"

"No, I'm pretty sure you're not listening to *me*." She spins toward the door, then turns to meet my gaze over her shoulder. She studies me with an upturned lip, like I've just done something obscene. "I don't expect you to understand. You're an uptight, sexless little freak who has *no fucking clue* how these things work."

My heart drops to the floor. She has never spoken to me this way. Ever. She juggles her keys and slams the door behind her. I think about yelling at her back. I think about crying. But I can't do either. I'm completely frozen.

I stare at the drooping tulip, shedding orange pollen from its impotent stamen. My stomach growls but I don't feel hungry. I don't feel anything. After a moment of stillness, I spring to my feet, swiping the tulip off the table. I chuck it into the garbage and grab my sneakers. I don't know where I'm trying to go, but I don't want to stay here. Like I don't want our empty house to watch me cry.

Mom took the Jeep but I have a ten-speed bike in the garage, covered in spiderwebs. I extract it from behind a stack of cardboard boxes filled with old toys and clothes I've outgrown, things we meant to donate. I keep an eye out for scorpions as I dust it off. The headlight strapped to the handlebars still works, but the tires are soft and in desperate need of air. I wheel it out anyway. I'm overwhelmed by the need to move my legs.

I start pedaling, wondering if Devon knows where Mom lives. If he's been to our house. How many times.

I pedal faster, and my thighs cramp against the slow, syrupy tread of the deflated tires. I imagine what it would feel like to plunge a rusted knife right between his lungs. Listen to him gasp for breath, beg me for mercy. Watch his veins protrude and turn black, like they're filled with tar, as his gray flesh shrivels. I realize I shouldn't have left the house without any protection. I didn't even bring coffee. I scan the street for rusty nails as I ride, but quickly give up. It would do me about as much good as trying to weaponize my car keys.

A pack of coyotes yips across the twilight and I slow down, sinking back into my body. Where am I even going? It doesn't matter. I reach an intersection and turn right.

I remember something she said to me thirteen years ago, something I fashioned into a badge of courage I could pin to my heart every morning. *I need you to be an adult.* I did what she asked. Now that I actually *am* one, does she want something else? Would she prefer the ten-year-old who didn't pry when she said she was getting blood from a funeral home every night?

I pedal onward as heat lightning fractures the blackness.

When I stop to catch my breath, I realize I've autopiloted all the way to the bookstore. I sigh and lean over the handlebars, mopping sweat from my brow with my sleeve. My legs are shaking and in the red light of the traffic signal I notice my front tire has gone completely flat.

I wheel my bike across the street and collapse onto a bench outside. It's a few minutes past seven thirty, and Sandy's just closed up shop for the night. The only light she keeps on is a festive paper lantern shaped like a star, hanging over the register. It doesn't matter, though. It's not like I wanted to go inside or talk to Sandy. I don't know what I wanted. I don't know why I'm here, why I rode this way. I do wish I'd taken some water, though. My parched lips crackle in the stagnant heat.

I pull my aching knees to my chest with an exhausted moan, realizing I'm going to have to walk all the way back with my bike. I take a weary glance around the parking lot. The Starbucks sign throws dappled green light across the pavement. I notice Jade's minivan is still parked where she left it this morning. Long day. She must be working a double.

I shut my eyes and press them hard against my knees. Is *that* why I came this way? Did she pull me here across the darkness with an invisible thread? I cough, and my throat feels like it's coated in dust. I want to go inside and ask her for a cup of ice. We don't even have to talk, not really. For some reason, I'm not scared anymore. I'm just tired. Too tired to fight. Too tired, too angry, too *everything*. I know I'm not in control but in this moment, I don't care. This is what I need to feel better right now. Ice.

Just need a cup of ice.

I shuffle toward the store and laugh aloud at my own expense. This is how they get you. Saras know when you're feeling vulnerable. When you're lonely. They can smell your tears. I think of Mom, the night she met Devon. She got upset when she saw some of her old friends at the fireworks and they gave her the cold shoulder. She tried to hide it from me, but I knew she was crying. A few minutes later, there was Devon, standing next to our picnic blanket.

I reach up past the door handle to scan into the Starbucks. I watch the little needle jump out and retract, sucking the blood from my thumb like a mosquito.

The finger prick punches me back to reality. *You have no proof this girl is a Sara.* In fact, the only thing I've proven thus far is that she is *not*. Then why was I pulled here? Why do I feel as though asking her for a cup of ice will solve all my problems?

I leave my bike outside as the door buzzes and unlocks. There are only two other customers. Jade and a ginger-haired boy are wiping down the counters and rinsing the stainless-steel milk carafes. She doesn't notice me right away. I think about turning around, running back out the door. Now's my chance. But the second I consider an exit strategy, the ginger boy waves me over. "C'mon in, we're still open."

Jade perks up from behind the counter. She smiles at me, revealing the gap between her teeth. I catch myself studying her mouth, trying to see if her canines are even the tiniest bit longer than they ought to be. I know there's no point, though. I can't see the difference in Mom's teeth unless she's about to cause drama, and even then it's pretty subtle.

"Hey." Jade quirks her head in my direction. Her dangly earrings catch the light, like clusters of fairy-sized disco balls. "Bookstore girl!"

"Um . . . yeah. Hi."

How the hell does she know I work at the bookstore? *Probably because she's seen you through the window?* I answer myself, and my cheeks start to burn. I'm sure I look as dumb as I feel, hovering six feet away from the counter, sopping with sweat, not saying a word.

"Getcha somethin'? Not a coffee fan, right?"

"I . . . I don't have any money." Wow. This is going *great*. "I mean, can I just get a cup of ice?"

"I can pour some lemonade over it and pretend you asked me to." She leans over the bar with a conspiratorial whisper. Her co-worker rolls his eyes. I wonder how much free stuff she's already given out today.

"Oh, that's nice but you don't have to—"

She plucks a cup from her stack and a Sharpie from underneath her canopy of curls. "Gonna need your name, though."

"Why?" I'm the only person in line. I realize what's happening only after I open my stupid mouth. "Er . . . Mia."

"Is your name Why? Or Mia?"

"Mia."

"Great. Your debts are now paid."

She's quiet as she gets to work. I watch as she scrawls my name on a venti cup and scoops a generous heap of ice cubes into it. I should say something to her. This will be over too fast if I don't.

"I uh . . . I like your blue eyeliner." Sure. Why not. "It's cool, it reminds me of this vintage Barbie doll my grandma once gave me."

Her gaze latches to mine as she pours berry-tinted lemonade into my cup. The corner of her lip curls, and in a gut-wrenching, inscrutable deadpan she says, "You still play with Barbies?"

I laugh, because I have no idea what else to do, and rip my eyes from hers.

"We should have a playdate sometime." She finishes pouring and caps the drink.

I don't say anything. Just keep laughing. All the words I've ever learned are bottlenecking in my throat. It feels just like my nightmare.

She turns her back and does something behind the bar I can't see. When she hands the cup to me, she's kissed it with her magenta lipstick and scribbled "Come on Barbie let's go party xo" in Sharpie next to my name.

"Safe home, okay?" I hear people at the Fair Shake say this to one another when they leave for the night, spoken over friends like an incantation. People don't usually say it to me.

"Thanks. Er . . . you, too." I gape at the kiss mark on my cup, which I've accidentally smudged with my thumb. I rub the sticky pink residue between my fingers. The store is practically empty, but I feel as though I'm being crushed between thousands of bodies, gasping for air. The fear rises from my toes and fills my entire body.

Once again, I forget to say goodbye.

☽ ☽ ☽

I walk my bike up and down the dips in the road, rolling tangy ice cubes between my cheeks. The heat lightning intensifies, splintering the sky with a jagged fist, and the night sizzles with the smell of sulfur.

Jade's not a Sara.

In my tenth-grade bio class, we were taught to keep our reasoning simple, that the purest explanation is often the one we're looking for. Emily Ramos was also in that class. I ignored whatever it was that kept my eyes stuck to that thick curtain of glossy hair all morning. I had bigger problems than trying to find a name for it. I thought everybody felt this way when they longed to make a friend.

I didn't go to the slumber parties where I'd unearth secrets about my girl friends and share a sleeping bag. Never learned the truth when I got my first kiss from a boy. I missed the whole thing. Something in me knew I should feel hurt by that, but I didn't because I never really grasped what I'd lost.

Why is this happening now, tonight? I have no idea who this girl is, I've seen her a total of three times. She could be *anyone*.

Just not a Sara.

I think about the morning I first saw her. I remember the echoes of phantom pain after Mom's betrayal. The sinking feeling I had in my chest all morning. By meeting that man—whose identity I must have known deep down—Mom exposed a crack in our fortress. She shone a light through it, revealing the edges of a different world on the other side.

When she went outside to smoke that cigarette with Devon, it was almost like she gave me permission. But permission to do . . . what? I'm not *doing* anything. I won't, I can't. What kind of hypocrite would I be if I pursued someone while I dragged her for seeing Devon? If I lead by example, eventually she'll remember why things have to be this way.

I'm surprised when I realize I've just turned onto our street. I have no idea how long I've been walking. I pass a neighbor's trash can and toss the Starbucks cup. Can't risk throwing it into our own bin. I stare at the faded raspberry lip stain, and for a second I think about fishing the cup back out. I instantly feel like a creep, imagining where I'd hide it—at the bottom of one of my drawers? I slam the lid shut.

As I round the corner and trudge up another hill, an enormous claw of lightning splits the sky. The earth shudders under my feet as a plume of smoke rises from the other side of the ridge. I force my depleted legs over the hill and come face-to-face with our house. That bone-dry, blackened cactus by our mailbox is on fire. I shield my face with my sleeve as hunks of sharp, spiny ash arc through the air all around me.

I watch the cactus smolder against the night, clotted with

clouds. The sky is black and endless, as if the Earth abandoned its orbit for a forbidden corner of the universe that's never seen stars.

All I can do is stare into the fire. I know I should grab the hose from the garage and put it out before it spreads. There's no hope of saving the plant, though. The withering, charred flesh breaks to pieces and catches the wind.

I reach for a fistful of ash, but it slips between my fingers.

2010

"You're hurt," she whispers.

I'm not sure how long I've been dangling over the side of the bloody Jacuzzi, soaking wet, clutching my leg. I almost wonder if I fell asleep. It was like being asleep, I guess. In the awful quiet I closed my eyes and left my body.

She paws around for her clothes, slowly, like she's coming out of a trance. She keeps her back turned as if she's trying to protect me from her nakedness.

"I-I'm okay," I finally answer. I know I'm not. But we have to deal with the mangled, skinny body lying on the ground between us. I can't stop staring at the boy's rectangular, bony bottom. I might enjoy a squeamish laugh if blood weren't still pouring from the gaping wound on his neck.

I try to turn over and sit on the edge of the pool, but when I straighten my leg it's like someone's holding my ankle over an open flame. I shriek and try to swallow it. I know she's heard, though.

"We gotta take you to the hospital . . ." she murmurs, struggling to step into her underwear.

I grit my teeth through the pain and move around so I'm facing her. "What about him?"

She peers over at the boy and shuts her eyes, like she was hoping if neither of us mentioned him he'd just dissolve into the concrete.

"We'll take him with us."

"What are you gonna do with him?"

She doesn't respond. She's concentrating on turning her shirt right side out. Her eyes are bleary and unfocused and she's swaying back and forth like she's about to lose her balance.

"You should eat something before you drive." *Eat something.* Like I'm talking about half a sandwich.

I start to shiver, that uncontrollable kind of full-body fit that grabs on to every part of you and doesn't let go. I think about inching toward the house to get a towel. I slowly, carefully extend my right leg, dragging the left behind me . . . but before I can put it on the ground she's right next to me. I shiver even harder, still not used to her speed.

"Don't move, honey. You'll make it worse."

The tears finally come. I just want her to pick me up and wrap me in a blanket and put me to bed. I want to wake up tomorrow morning and find her in the kitchen packing my lunch in a brown paper bag, squeezing lemon juice onto my apple slices so they don't get brown. I want her to drop me off at school and kiss me goodbye and live the rest of my life with no memory that any of this ever happened.

"It's your ankle, isn't it? Shh . . . it's okay. I know it hurts—" She thinks that's why I'm crying. She lets me lean on her, taking pressure off my left foot. Once I'm out of the pool, she lifts me up like I weigh as much as the day I was born.

I look up into her face as she carries me over to the car. She's biting her lip so hard she's drawn blood. She sucks it into her mouth with her next breath.

"Mom, I really don't think you should drive. . . ."

"I'll be fine. I ate enough." I'm not sure if she did. I was watching. How much did the Facebook group say was the bare minimum? I wrote it down somewhere. . . .

"Mom—"

"You're okay, babe. I've gotcha."

She eases me into the front seat like she's tucking me into bed and starts the car. Cranks the heat all the way up. I finally get my shivering under control.

"I'll be right back. Try not to move."

She shuts the door, softly, like she's afraid the sound might hurt me. I close my eyes and fold my good leg up against my chest. I know where she's going. I know we'll have to ride with the boy's body in the car. What I don't know is what we're going to do with it.

A few minutes later the trunk opens and in the rearview mirror I catch a glimpse of a long, white lump in Mom's arms, like a faceless, swaddled-up baby. She's wrapped him in a sheet. She accidentally closes the trunk on his foot and I hear a *crack!* followed by Mom's muffled cursing.

"Oh shit, oh fuck . . . I'm sorry." As if she's forgotten he's dead.

We drive for about an hour, maybe more. She's already chewed through half a pack of cinnamon Trident, and her fists quiver as she grips the steering wheel. Her lip is split and stained with blood.

Early on, she makes a comment about how she and her college friends once went a whole week without eating to try to lose weight for spring break. They just drank lemonade with cayenne pepper. I don't think she's really talking to *me*, though. She laughs and says to herself, "Dammit, if I can get through that week, I can get through this night."

She doesn't say anything else after that.

I'm stiff as she drives, not just because I can't move my left leg. I'm trying to be as quiet as possible so she can concentrate. I know she's in pain and we've been driving for a long time. I can't remember when I last saw any streetlights. I don't ask where we're going. *Where* doesn't matter. And there's no point asking what she's going to do when we get there, because I already know.

I can tell she's been here before. She knows exactly when to turn; she's not just driving around aimlessly. We pass a sign that says, PROTECTED WATERFOWL AREA. She makes a sharp left, then turns off her headlights. The dank, heavy stench of wetlands hangs in the air. I know we're near water, but I can't see it. I'm not sure how she can tell where she's going without the lights on. She can probably see in the dark a lot better than I can.

Suddenly, she stops. Turns off the car. Neither of us moves. If it weren't for the shaky rise and fall of her chest I'd swear she was dead again. She's backlit by the shadowy half-moon, like an eclipse.

"Stay here." It's too dark to see her face, but her trembling voice tells me everything I need to know. I was never supposed to see this place.

☾ ☾ ☾

It's another hour in the opposite direction till we reach the hospital. She's run out of gum. She carries me through the revolving door of the emergency room, but this time I can feel her struggling. She's losing strength.

Fluorescent light washes over me and I have to close my eyes. After driving through the dark for so many hours, it's like staring into the sun. I hear the patter of nurses and an elderly patient's dry wheeze from the waiting area. The intercom crackles and a tired, monotone female voice pages "Dr. Hendricks." There are too many people here. Too many distracted, defenseless people.

"Drop me off and go home. I'll call you when they're done," I whisper to her.

"I'm not gonna dump you in the emergency room. Jesus."

She settles me into a chair, then turns to face the reception desk. "I'll be right back, I gotta sign us in—"

"Mom." I pull her sleeve and whisper into her ear. "You can't give them our real names. The Facebook group says—"

"Baby, I got it."

She opens her wallet and flashes her driver's license at me. For a second, I don't understand . . . until I lean in closer and read the text. It's still got her picture and it's from Utah, but our address is different. The name reads "Margaret Cooper."

"Devon made it. He's uh . . . good at that kinda stuff," she mumbles. I can hear a twinge of shame in her voice. She snaps the wallet shut and starts biting her lips again.

"Gotta try to find a vending machine. More gum would be nice."

Moments later, a triage nurse makes her way over to us: hair the color of imitation orange juice and faded blue scrubs that look like they're two sizes too small.

The nurse examines my bruised, twisted ankle, but her focus quickly shifts to Mom. She chews her pen and studies her, saying nothing. Mom is subconsciously mirroring her, grinding her teeth the same way she's gnawing on the pen. My breath catches when I realize there's dried blood spattered on her chest, beneath the collar of her V-neck shirt, just above her bra line.

"Sweetheart, I'm gonna bring you on back so we can take an X-ray of that leg, okay?" The nurse helps me into a wheelchair. Still hasn't taken her eyes off Mom. "We won't be long, ma'am. Stay right there."

Mom shifts her weight and frowns. "I should come with her."

"We don't allow more than one patient at a time in radiology."

"I'm not a patient."

Mom plants herself next to the wheelchair and I crane my neck to face her. There's a tremor in her hand as she grips my shoulder. Something feels wrong. Something in the way the nurse keeps staring at her. I'm pretty sure she saw those bloodstains under her collar.

"We'll bring you to the examination room when the doctor's ready." The nurse starts wheeling me away, but Mom holds tight to my shoulder and nearly tears me out of the chair. I yelp as I try to keep my leg steady.

"Ma'am—" The startled nurse reaches for Mom's hand, but I grab it first. She might snap her wrist in half if she touches her.

"Mom, I'm fine. It's just an X-ray, it won't hurt." I don't actually know if this is true. I've never had an X-ray. But I need her to back down.

"You sure?"

I nod. The nurse looks like she's holding her breath. Finally, Mom lets me go, clenching her hands together to keep them from shaking.

The nurse exhales and skitters down the hall, pushing me along.

Without turning to look back at Mom, she says, "We'll just be a few minutes."

There's a lump in my throat. I feel like I just made a huge mistake.

The nurse wheels me around the corner into an empty exam cubicle and gently shuts the mustard-yellow curtain behind her. She kneels to my level and sticks out her lower lip like a sad, awkward clown.

"So, Annie, how'd that happen to your leg?" This is obviously the name Mom chose for me when she signed us in. I repeat it in my head a few times so I don't forget it. "Looks like it hurt."

"I was jumping into our pool and I hit it on the side." Which is true.

"Your mom lets you swim in the middle of the night?"

"Sometimes?"

"Well don't worry, we'll get it all fixed up for you." She's quiet for a second and makes another weird, exaggerated face, scrunching her nose like she's thinking really hard about something. She inches closer and I can see that the greasy roots of her fake red hair are a completely different color. Not like Mom's.

"Have you noticed anything . . . funny? About your mom lately?"

"No," I answer too quickly.

She widens her mascara-caked eyes to make them look sad and concerned. Like she thinks that will help me trust her.

"Listen honey, I don't know you. And I'm sure your mom tells you not to talk to strangers, but—"

"It's nothing like that," I blurt.

"Nothing like what?"

"Like . . . what you're trying to say." I'm starting to sweat. The lump in my throat thickens.

"What am I trying to say, sweetie?"

"Can you please not call me that? Or honey, or any of those things?" My voice pitches up, like the harder I try to control it the more emotional I sound. I have the sense I'm in trouble, but I'm not sure what I did. All I know is we're wasting time. Mom can't stay here with all those people around.

"I'm sorry. Just trying to help." She stands and smooths her too-tight scrubs. The fabric bunches beneath the bulge of her lower belly. I wonder if she's pregnant. I don't think so. I want to say something mean to her. Hit her over the head with her clipboard.

She takes one last look at me, no longer making that put-upon clown face. Like she wishes I'd say more but knows she can't force me. Finally, she wheels me back out into the hallway. I don't realize I've been squeezing my fists until I release them.

Mom makes it through the hospital visit by chain-smoking in the parking lot with a janitor, who kindly offers her the rest of his pack when she says she's got a kid in the ER. I'm more than a little terrified when she mentions this. Is there any blood on her? Did she hurt him? But she insists she was strong enough to leave him alone.

"We're gonna find another way," she says in a weak, husky whisper once we're in the car. The sun will be up soon, it's nearly 6 A.M. She runs a red light and ignores all the stop signs. The engine roars like a hungry animal. I grip both the armrests.

I've got a clunky boot that itches constantly when I try to walk on it. I'm exhausted and clumsy with the crutch they give me. Mom carries me to her bed and tucks me under the covers. Just like I wanted. I wonder if I should tell her about the nurse. But there's nothing to tell, nothing happened. And we're both so tired.

Mom pops two Ambien, then snuggles in next to me. "Mind over matter," she mumbles into my hair, assuming the big spoon position.

☾ ☾ ☾

The only thing Devon left behind is a dry Zippo lighter on the kitchen counter. Neither of us wants to touch it, as if it somehow has the power to summon him back.

If she misses him, she's too hungry to feel it.

We're sitting in the living room watching *Aladdin* as a tiny sliver of sunset leaks through the edge of one of the curtains. Mom's confused why the sleeping pills didn't work; it's not nighttime yet. She avoids the light on the opposite end of the couch, chewing through her third pack of gum. She's already smoked the cigarettes the janitor gave her at the hospital. I don't know how much longer she can do this. I think about Dani from the Facebook group. After forty-eight hours of starvation, she said, she chewed a hole in her wall. I guess she must have fed eventually. Or she'd have been dead two days later.

I'm hungry too, but I feel bad ordering food or trying to make something in front of her. Even if chicken nuggets won't trigger her cravings. Just doesn't seem nice. Maybe I'll sneak something tomorrow during the day, when she's asleep. If she sleeps.

We need to do some laundry. I'm out of clean underwear and I'm dying to change. The mountain of dirty clothes in the laundry room is starting to smell. I don't want to ask her to do it. She's doubled over on the sofa, clutching a pillow to her chest. She doesn't notice when I limp out of the room, trying to stabilize myself on my crutch.

I balance on my good leg and throw armfuls of ripe laundry into the washer—some of it soiled with still-damp blood. I gag as I catch a whiff, remembering the stench of Mom's room when I snuck in before she'd been fully turned. I glug some soap into the reservoir. Then a little more. Then a *lot*. I don't know what buttons to press, though. Am I supposed to wash it with hot water? How do you clean something that's got blood on it?

"Hey, Mom? How hot should the water be for the laundry?"

No answer. I sigh and prop myself back onto my crutch, hobbling back to the living room.

The TV flickers against the darkness. It's nighttime; that razor-thin remnant of sunlight is gone from the window. And so is she.

My heart punches my ribs as I drop my crutch and spin in a circle. She's left the back door open. A gust of wind blows dry leaves into the kitchen. I grapple with my crutch and race outside as fast as I can. Not fast enough.

"*Mom*—" I shriek as I tumble out the door.

She's still on the stoop. Thank God. I fall down beside her and bury my face against her shoulder. She doesn't even flinch. Just watches the moon rise with sunken eyes, chewing her nails to the quick. She's smeared blood all over her shirt. Her cheekbones jut like jagged cliffs, casting eerie shadows across her skeletal face. Finally, she catches my gaze in her periphery. Her head's so heavy she can't even face me.

"Sorry, baby." She's on her feet before I can react. Stumbling down the steps, weaving toward the Jeep.

"Mom! Stop—" I think I'm forming words but it's just one long, animalistic screech.

She starts the car, shaking like she's about to erupt. Can't seem to grip the steering wheel. If I'm going to stop her, I have to do it now.

There's a bag of gardening tools beneath the bone-dry, neglected window box. I dump it out. Consider my options.

I grab a pair of pruning shears, struggling to hold them as I grip my crutch. Not gonna happen. I ditch the crutch and sprint toward the Jeep, slamming the bottom of the boot against the driveway. My bad leg sticks straight out like a stake. Mom starts the car. Manages to yank it into drive. The tires squeal like wounded dogs.

Snip. Snip snip snip. I gouge a hole in my forearm, shaving off chunks of flesh, letting blood pool in the sinewy crater. I'm dizzy and the ground under my feet feels like thin, crackling ice. I hold up my arm so she can see it in the headlights as she barrels toward me.

She pounds the brakes as my legs buckle. Everything goes white and I hit the gravel face-first. I hear her scream, faint and fuzzy like bad radio reception. Her shadow approaches as my vision clears, and I heave my body right side up to present my butchered arm.

"Are you sure?" I think she asks. It's possible she never did.

But it's how I decide to remember it.

NOW

When I wake up in the morning, there's a shiny black gift bag on the table where the dead tulip was. Mom's stuck a Post-it note on it: "M" scrawled inside of a heart. The bag is from Sephora, filled with the expensive kind of serums and creams I told her not to bother with. There's also a peach-pink lipstick, some eye shadow, and a free sample of mascara. I know she went through a lot of effort to procure this. She must've asked Kayla or one of her other coworkers to go to the mall, pass the scanners, and run the errand for her. She does that sometimes, when she can't wait for an online order—which she couldn't, if she wanted to make up for what she said to me last night.

I dump the contents of the bag out onto the table and stare at them. Does she think I'll be so dazzled by hundred-dollar face cream that I'll forget about the fight we had? That I'll feel special because she knows I know we can't afford it? She does this sometimes. Buys presents instead of apologizing. One night when I was probably like thirteen, I had a headache and couldn't give any more blood because I was too dizzy. She screamed in my face and shoved me to the floor. I knew she only did it because she was hungry. She never apologized, though. Not really. The next day there was an ice cream cake from Baskin-Robbins in the freezer, just for me. That same Post-it was stuck on it, "M" inside of a heart.

I consider sweeping all the makeup into my arms and tossing it in the trash, leaving it on top so she'll see it. But the lipstick catches my eye. I open it and twist the bottom to reveal a silky pink stalk. This one's called Smoked Peach. I wonder what color Jade was

wearing last night, what it was called. Electric Berry. Mad Queen
Magenta. Maybe Furious Fuchsia.

I keep the makeup but throw everything else away. In the car,
I apply eye shadow and mascara in the cracked, yellowing mirror
and smooth Smoked Peach onto my dry lips. It helps to hide the
way they're peeling. I don't think I've ever worn makeup to work. I
don't think *work* is the reason I'm wearing it, though.

☾ ☾ ☾

I head right to the Starbucks on my lunch break. I realize how
desperate I might look, showing up the very next day, wearing
makeup. I slow down, squinting into the sun. I should probably
turn back, this is stupid. But . . . she kissed my cup. Asked for my
name. That can't mean *nothing*.

I'm aware she's just a distraction. I know I should be trying to figure out where Devon is and how to keep Mom away from him. But
this is for *me*. I should be allowed to have something, one silly little
thing, that's just mine. Everything I've ever done has been for her; I
feel a hot stab of guilt as I imagine my younger self hearing me say
this out loud. I'm not going to pursue any kind of relationship with
Jade. This is completely harmless . . . unlike whatever Mom's been
doing with Devon. I just want to catch a glimpse of her. A little shot
of caffeine. A piece of candy you sneak in the middle of the night.

But when I scan in, she's not there. The ginger-haired boy from
last night is behind the coffee bar and a different, older woman is
taking orders and ringing people up. I glance out the window, and
see her van parked behind the building. But I'm not about to ask
for her, or wait for her to come out from the back. I'm not some
kind of stalker. I purse my lips. The Smoked Peach is thin and
sticky on my mouth.

I leave without ordering anything. I'm not even hungry for
lunch. I haven't been hungry at all these past few days. There's
a constant sick swirling in my stomach, like all my emotions are
competing for attention.

When I return to the Book Bunker and take my post at the register, I notice we have a guest in our lounge. They're sitting in one of the chairs that faces the opposite wall, so I can't see who it is. But they've dragged over an antique end table to use as a footrest. They have their dusty checkered Vans propped up on it, feet jiggling and crossed at the ankle. Sandy would not abide by this. Most of the furniture in the store is from her mom's house.

I make my way over, getting ready to use my best "cool older sister who is also an authority figure" voice to tell this rude teen to respect our property.

"Sorry, do you mind moving your—"

The words catch in my throat.

Jade sprawls in the chair, snacking on sunflower seeds, flipping through a bodice ripper with a sexy pirate on the cover who resembles a dollar-store Jack Sparrow.

"Hola." She waves, playing it cool, but it doesn't last long. She pops a sunflower seed and accidentally inhales it. I chew my lip to conceal my laughter but I'm sure I'm doing a terrible job. Her eyes rivet to mine, and I suck my teeth in a panic to make sure I didn't get any lipstick on them. I am way too aware that I'm wearing makeup and suddenly wish I hadn't bothered with it at all.

"Wow, sorry. You were saying?" she chirps between coughs. She smacks herself in the chest and clears her throat, wiping moisture from her eyes. Smiling through the whole thing.

"Um . . . no, it's totally fine. I was just—" It's not fine, her feet are still up on the table. My cheeks burn. I liked this game a lot better when it was me coming into *her* store.

"I'm super glad to see you, actually. I was hoping you could help me find a book."

I give her romance novel a wry side-eye. "*Buried Pleasure* not doin' it for ya?"

She snorts like a kid who's just heard someone belch. "You're funny."

"That's what it's called."

"Oh shit, really?" She flips the book over and giggles. "Kitty B. Castle. You think that's her real name, the lady who wrote this?"

"I mean, sometimes it's a guy."

"Fucking figures."

She offers the book to me, like she wants me to put it back on the shelf for her. Every part of her is in motion; she can't seem to hold still. She grasps a handful of hair and itches her scalp, twitching her nose and rolling her shoulders. I'm reminded of that restless little mountain goat again, wearing pajamas.

"I was actually looking for that Blondie memoir, I think it's called *Face It*? But I couldn't find it."

"We might have it in the back, let me check."

I'm thrilled to have a reason to return to work. Not because I don't want her here, but because I need time to prepare. I wasn't ready, this is *my space*. I feel exposed, like she's digging through my drawers trying to find my diary and when she does she's going to read it out loud.

I head toward the stockroom, then spin back around to face her.

"Could you maybe . . . it's just . . . that table is from my boss's house and she's really—"

"Oh my God, I'm sorry. I'm gross."

She whips her feet away and returns the table to its proper place. "Don't rat me out to your boss, I wanna be allowed back."

My mouth cracks a weak, nauseous smile. I rack my brain for a worthy response, something equally cute and forthcoming to keep the volley going, but I drop the ball.

"Lemme see about that Blondie book," I mumble. I'm clumsy and gooey, like the night I slammed those mango margaritas. I look down and shuffle off.

I already know that if it's not on the shelves, we probably don't have it. Sandy doesn't like to overstock. The "back room" is mostly just holiday decorations and extra photos Sandy's wife took that didn't fit on the walls.

I seize my phone and do a quick Bookshop search, hoping the

algorithm can recommend something edgy and unexpected as an alternative. I want to show I put some thought into this, even if a computer's doing all the work for me. I don't know a whole lot about Blondie, which I'd rather not have to explain to her.

"Got a friend out there lookin' for you," Sandy pipes up from the adjoining break room.

"Oh, she's not my . . . I mean, I saw her."

Sandy cranes her neck around the corner and shoots me her signature side-eye.

"Frenemy?"

"No. I mean, neither. I don't really know her."

She rests her gaze on me with a muted "huh" before she returns to her Subway sandwich. I wonder if Sandy knows about me. If she's known all along, if she ever saw a little of herself in me. If it even works that way. I wonder if *Mom knew*. If everyone knew but me.

I deliver two alternate titles to Jade, rehearsing a cheery elevator pitch in my head. She's torn through her sunflower seeds and started licking the salt off her fingertips. I don't find it off-putting or gross in the least, though I probably should. In a weird way, I admire her; she probably acts the same way in public as she does at home all by herself. I wonder what that's like.

"So, we didn't have the book you were looking for but I grabbed these because I thought . . . because you were into Blondie—"

She shoves her hands into her pockets—probably so she doesn't keep licking them—and I notice pin-sized puncture wounds on two of her fingers from the scanners.

"This first one is by Flea, from the Red Hot Chili Peppers. It's supposed to be pretty cool, it was one of NPR's favorite books the year it came out—" I know this because I just read it on the back cover. I offer it to her. "Um and this one is by the lead singer of Sleater-Kinney—"

Jade's mouth gapes open in an exaggerated *O*.

"I love Sleater-Kinney, I haven't read this one—" I feel like I've just been pummeled in the gut. She pronounced it differently. Like "Slate-r." I said it like "Sleet-er."

My hands freeze around the book even though she's grabbing for it. She frowns.

"What's up?"

"Oh, I just thought . . . all these years I thought it was 'Sleet-er.'" I found out about them five minutes ago.

"I actually think they once said you can say it both ways, they don't really give a shit. But the street the band was named after is pronounced 'Slate-r.'"

"Okay. Cool."

Her smiling eyes rake over me. Once again, my gaze flicks to the ground. My palms tingle, starting to sweat, and I quickly hand the book to her before it spreads.

"Have you uh . . . ever seen them live?" My heart swells as I realize I actually know how to keep the conversation going this time.

"I don't think they really tour anymore. A few years ago there was a rumor they were gonna reunite and do a Cloak and Dagger. Which would've been insane. But it never panned out."

Here's something I *do* know about. During those awful curfew years, before the scanners got introduced, a group of desperate, borderline-insane musicians and their bravest fans created the Cloak and Dagger Festival. It took place in the middle of nowhere, you wouldn't know the exact location till the night of, and you had to be invited. When you bought a ticket, you had to sign a waiver that you'd assume the risk if any Saras came lurking. Now that we have scanners, Cloak and Dagger doesn't have quite the same underground appeal. It's still going strong, though. I always thought it would be cool to experience it, but I never knew anyone who could invite me.

"I'd kill to see that." I tack on a wistful sigh that probably sounds entirely too theatrical.

"Well, you're coming in June, right? Never know who's gonna show up."

"Oh I mean . . . Wait, really? They're doing one here?"

"It's on the fifth, somewhere in the desert outside Tucson. That's actually why I'm out here. I came from Chicago to help put the show together in exchange for an opening slot. Slinging lattes is just a part-time thing to keep the lights on." She excitedly crosses her legs like a pretzel and sits up straight in the cushy chair. "Anyway, if you need an invite I'm your girl."

"That'd be awesome. Thanks." My brain carousels, imagining all the ways this could go wrong. If I've already done the draw and Mom's at work, there's nothing to stop me from going out for a night. There's never been anything stopping me, really. I just didn't have anyone to go with. Although something tells me Mom would be pissed as all get-out. . . .

"So you're in a band or something?" I pour words into the silence.

"Sorta, I mean the lineup changes depending on where I am. I write everything and sing and have a whole show programmed but I'd prefer to play with other people, y'know? My friend Tony who lives near here is hooking me up with some guys from his band for Cloak and Dagger. If we vibe I want to take them on a little tour this summer, but we gotta see." She flashes her gap-toothed grin. "We're called Landshark. I mean . . . *I am*. My act, or whatever. I might want to change it though, I thought it was funny in this kind of ironic way a few years ago but now it just sounds dumb."

"I like it" is all I can say.

"We'll see." She shrugs coyly. "You only just met me."

She hops out of the chair, tucking the book under her arm. "Thanks for the rec."

"I'll uh . . . let you know if we get that other book," I offer, trailing her as she heads to the register, where Sandy's waiting.

"Cool. You know where to find me."

She smiles big and bright, and my heart somersaults into my throat.

☾ ☾ ☾

There's a huge roadblock on the drive home, and I'm stuck in traffic for a good twenty minutes before I find a detour. As I turn off onto a residential dirt road, I spot a black ambulance beyond the flickering flares, parked perpendicular like an ominous barricade. There haven't been too many Sara buses lately. The scanners keep the infected people away from potential prey, and they caught most of the high-volume killers when the centers opened. The black ambulances only come if there's a corpse with a bite, a Sara on the scene, or both. The sun hangs low like ripe fruit in the hazy sky. We're about an hour from twilight. So it's probably a body. Maybe more than one, I think with a shiver, remembering Mom and Devon's boneyard in the wetlands. I want to uproot the thought from my mind like a weed, but it won't budge.

I rush to the bathroom when I get home, knowing I only have a few minutes till Mom wakes up. I wash all the makeup off my face, struggling to scrub mascara stains from underneath my eyes with a soapy washcloth. I'd rather not have her know I used any part of her gift, though my blotchy red skin might give me away.

When I come out, she's already in the kitchen, waiting at the table. We have nothing to say to each other. I grab a clean needle packet from the kitchen cabinet and disinfect my arm. The ritual begins. I yank the tourniquet taut, jab my tender, bruised forearm, and start the timer. I can't help but notice how calm she seems. Usually she's pacing around, doing anything she can to distract herself during those two minutes and thirty-five seconds. But she doesn't seem desperate tonight, and there's a warm, dewy glow to her skin.

"Oracle Road was totally closed off on my drive home. There was a Sara bus, I think they found a body out in the wash."

"That's too bad. It's been quiet lately," she says without looking at me.

I watch the blood bag expand, heavy with black honey. "Where is he staying?"

"If I tell you, will you promise to stop interrogating me and never bring this up again?"

Her eyes bore into mine and I know she's trying to scare me. Trying to make sure I remember what she is, what she could do. But *would* she? She never has. Still, I walk that tightrope, every waking moment.

"Fine. Tell me." I don't break her gaze.

"I found him an Airstream. Out in the desert."

The timer pings and I remove the needle. I slowly pour the blood into her cup. I can't let her stop talking, not when she's finally told me something true—or at least, something that *sounds* true.

"What do you do at night, when you see him?"

"Christ, Mia, what do you think?" Sex? Hunting? Whatever sick combination of both they used to do?

I'm about to hand the cup to her, but I withdraw. Not till she elaborates.

"He's different now, okay? He's been through a lot and he's trying to help other people." She lowers her eyes. "He was in a Sara center. One of the bad ones—"

"They let him out?" I ask, even though I already know the answer. You don't leave unless you run.

"He's got this whole advocacy initiative he's creating. It feels important. It's all about getting our dignity back, taking care of each other—"

"How can he form an 'advocacy initiative' if he's a wanted criminal hiding out in the desert?"

She sighs and digs her fingers into her eyelids, like she wishes she could push them all the way to the back of her skull. "Plenty of revolutionaries were wanted criminals, Mia. Read a book."

"So now he's a revolutionary?"

"*Someone* needs to stand up for us."

I chew the inside of my cheek. "Look, just promise me he won't come here. I don't want to see him, I don't want to talk to him, I don't—"

"If *you* promise this is the last conversation we're going to have about it."

"Fine."

She lunges and yanks the cup from my hand. Blood dribbles across the table then down her chin as she drinks. She snags a paper towel with her free hand to mop up the mess. When she moves to throw it away, she freezes, staring into the garbage. She's just seen the gift she gave me, sitting right on top. She slams the bin shut, downs what's left in her cup like she's slurping from a shot glass, and chucks it into the sink.

Her shattered gaze tells me everything I need to know.

She uses a paper towel like a glove and fishes the bag out of the garbage. Finally, in a tight, choked whisper, she says, "I'll return these. They were expensive."

I feel an apology on my lips, but I hold it in. A different, younger version of me wouldn't have been able to do that. But I'm not about to rescind the upper hand. She grabs her purse and sashays toward the door.

"Bye," I offer.

She shuts it without a word.

☾ ☾ ☾

I spend the night finishing the mural in the bathroom. I'm still bristling with guilt for having thrown her gift in the trash. I can't help but want to make it up to her.

I prop my laptop up on the counter to play some music as I work. My fingers hover over the keyboard. I know what I want to search for but for some reason I'm nervous. What if I hate Jade's songs? What if her voice is terrible and the lyrics are sentimental garbage and I feel like an idiot for obsessing like this? On the other hand, if she's embarrassingly bad that would probably make it easier for me to steer clear.

I search for "Landshark" on Spotify and a sultry black-and-white photo of Jade pops up on the home screen. She's wearing a tattered white tank top that's not much more than a rag, revealing a black leather push-up bra underneath. She's lounging on a rock in the woods somewhere with one long, lean leg dangling over the edge. I'm not sure if those are shorts she's wearing or just her underwear. I have to force myself to look away from the photo, or I'll stare at it for the rest of my life.

Her first song is a propulsive electro-pop number with a hook that sounds like a harp being played underwater. She sings in a low, almost monotone growl, showing off her higher range when the chorus hits. I can't really understand the lyrics, she's mumbling on purpose. Something about meeting ghosts in different cities. Paris. New York. Tokyo. It's strange but infectious. I'm not sure I've heard anything like it, but then again, I don't listen to much music. I make a mental note to play Blondie and Sleater-Kinney next.

There's a link to her Instagram on the Spotify page, and soon enough I'm down the rabbit hole. The first post is a video, an interview at a small college radio station. Jade sits at a shabby desk covered in empty Coke cans, across from a twentysomething DJ in a ragged sweater who looks like he hasn't slept in three weeks. I can almost smell the cigarette smoke hanging in the air. Jade props her shoes up on the desk, just like she did at the bookstore.

"Yeah so just like . . . super curious about how and when you came to songwriting. You're pretty new to the game, right?" There's a forced indifference in the DJ's voice, like he's trying and failing to keep everything cool. Jade's the opposite. She buzzes with passion and enthusiasm, leaning into the mic as she maintains bright, inquisitive eye contact with the DJ.

"Yeah, that's true. I've only been writing for about two years now. I wrote my first song when I was still living at home in Florida. And it was basically just . . . I mean it was shit, you'll literally never hear it, but it was all about how I was ready to *leave Florida* and do my own thing. Which was the first time I'd admitted that to myself, out loud." She glances over at the camera, careful not to exclude the audience. I lock eyes with her image onscreen.

"I hear that. Um . . . In your song 'Windows' we get those same themes coming through. Stuff about like, being ready to leave, knowing you can't stay inside anymore . . . Can you give us a glimpse into where all of that came from?"

"Well, my dad was a . . . I mean, he *is* a bit of a hypochondriac. More than a bit of one actually, he's like . . . I mean, it was intense."

"Shitty thing to be in times like these," the DJ interjects with a wry laugh. But Jade is deadly serious.

"Look, protecting your family isn't *bad*. Just depends how far you take it. You can't control everything. When people in our town started getting infected, people we *knew* . . . He decided we had to stay inside all the time, even during the day. We got homeschooled. Ate a lot of canned goods. You know."

"Oh shit."

"Anyway that's what 'Windows' is all about. I don't like playing it live, though. Kinda feels like a downer."

"Hey, lotta legendary songs are downers. Don't knock it."

Jade smiles and rests her chin on her fist. "Aw, you're all right, Bucky."

The video ends and starts looping from the beginning. I watch again. Scrutinizing Jade's gaze, her posture, the volume of her voice. She shrivels in her seat and breaks eye contact with Bucky the DJ a couple of times as the story intensifies. Anxiously taps her heel against the desk, but quietly, so the mic doesn't pick it up. She's not comfortable talking about this, but she does it anyway. Not only that, but she's put the clip on her Instagram for everyone to see. She wants to share this, even if it hurts. She's felt real pain. Isolation. Like a lot of people. Like me.

I want to know more. I *need* more. All the details and memories, a facsimile of the most important moments in her life. I need a map of her past so I can chart a course for her heart. I put her EP back on. That feels like a good place to start.

I finish shading the sand dunes and touch up the froth on the ocean whitecaps as Jade's music plays on. It feels unseemly at first, like I've brought her into our home without permission. But I ease into it. What would happen if I *did* bring her here? Would she hate our house, would she think the murals were weird and corny? Would she walk into my room and laugh at the ancient glow-in-the-dark star stickers and the cheap fiberboard furniture, covered in glitter paint? Or would she understand and want to stay? What would we do? Would she wear her magenta lipstick and leave a stain on my mouth just like the cup she gave me?

I turn to refresh my paintbrush, and an ice-cold chill surges across my entire body as I look outside.

There's someone standing in the window.

I drop the brush, stumbling against the still-wet wall, smearing paint all over my back. I have no idea how long he's been standing there.

In an instant, he's gone. But I know what I saw.

I know *who* I saw.

I crumple to the ground as I scream.

Jade's EP ends, her silvery voice fading to silence. I listen for the door, for footsteps, for the sound of an intruder. But it's quiet. Nothing but my heart hammering in my ears.

I don't know why he's here. Probably looking for Mom.

He's not here for me.

Not tonight, anyway.

I curl into the smallest shape my body will allow and huddle in the corner. The mural is ruined, and there's paint everywhere. Between my fingers and toes, in my ponytail, all over the back of my shirt.

I should know better than to let my guard down. I am not safe.

I have never been safe.

Not since the night he came into our lives, leaning against that tree as we set up our picnic, watching Mom as she lit up my sparkler and placed a crown of glow sticks on my head.

We have never been safe.

2010

The panic attacks start coming, but I don't know that's what they are at first. All I know is whenever I don't have eyes on Mom, I shake, I sweat, and I feel like I have to pee and throw up at the same time.

One night, she runs in to a gas station for gum and cigarettes and tells me to wait in the car. She's taking too long. Two minutes becomes five. Becomes ten. I watch the clock on the dash, counting the blinks of the blue colon between the hour and minute. I'm short of breath. I feel like my throat's closing up. I think about a girl in my class last year who was allergic to peanuts and described what would happen to her if she ever ate one. I wonder if I'm allergic to something. I might die, right now, all alone in this car. I fidget, trying to get ahold of my shaking, and notice a sudden wetness in my jeans. The edges of everything go black and blurry. All of a sudden I'm in the bloody Jacuzzi again, and Devon is holding my head underwater. I yank the door open, about to bolt toward the convenience store even though I know I won't get far with my giant, clunky boot. There's a muted, electronic *ding-dong* that sounds like a signal from another dimension. Mom emerges from the convenience store, lighting up a Camel.

"Mia, look out!" she screams. She drops her lighter and I watch it fall to the concrete in slow motion, like I'm lost in a dream. An RV, pulling up to the pump twice as fast as it should, crushes the lighter beneath its tire as it barrels toward me.

I'm blind in the headlights, but Mom's already squeezing my arm: the bandaged one I butchered the other night so she could drink from it. My skin is on fire as she drags me back to the Jeep. The guy driving the RV gives her the finger.

☾ ☾ ☾

I've started sleeping during the day, right next to her in the bed so I always know where she is. I haven't been to school in three weeks. Mom can't go outside, so she can't physically force me onto the bus. We fight about it at first, but she gives up after a few days. She's constantly reminding me this is "only for now." But neither of us knows when "now" is going to end.

Chloe and Mrs. Vaughn don't come back, like they smelled the danger from our darkened windows. Nosy people are nosy until they get scared. I miss Chloe, but this is a good thing. They should stay scared.

Mom doesn't want me to give her any more blood, but we don't have much of a choice. She holds out as long as she can, till she's on the razor's edge, chewing her lips to a pulp and banging her head against the door—which we've deadbolted from the outside. I hid the key in a hole in one of my stuffed animals.

We order a phlebotomy kit online, which comes with proper needles, disinfectants, and a reservoir for the blood. But until it arrives, I need to reopen my wound every night. Mom helps me boil water to clean a steak knife, which I use to pry the scab open. I hold my arm over a bowl and wait for a few tablespoons of blood to pool. I'm pretty sure it's less than the minimum amount; it doesn't look like a quarter pint. But it seems to help. After she drinks, she stalks out to the patio to chain-smoke and curb her appetite. I keep asking her if she needs more, but she just shakes her head, lights another Camel, and tells me to not to come outside. She doesn't trust herself, but I know she's not going to hurt me. If she were, she would've done it already.

I'm glad our kit comes when it does. That same night, after we've figured out where to stick my arm and how to use the tourniquet, a breaking-news bulletin interrupts the *Friends* rerun we're watching. A photo flashes across the screen, and I don't recognize who it is at first. But I can tell by the way Mom stares that I should.

"Holy shit . . ."

The picture is of a young man with blond hair and pristine, straight teeth. Mom turns up the volume, and the news anchor says something about "Farmington Bay wetlands." They flash to a second photo and I lose my breath. It's the same boy in his LDS missionary uniform: a short-sleeved white oxford and black tie.

The reporter's voice fades in and out of my ears like static. *Mission to Indonesia. Beloved son. Soon to be married.*

"This is the latest in a series of similar disappearances and subsequent deaths. Residents are advised to take this situation seriously and limit your nighttime activities—"

Mom flicks off the TV and hurls the remote across the room, gouging the wall. I look at her wide, glassy eyes as they darken, awaiting instructions. She must have a plan. Or if she doesn't, she's making one right now. Any second, she'll tell me what it is.

She's motionless, like she was in the car the night we drove to the wetlands. Like an upright corpse.

A minute later, I whisper, "Maybe we should go somewhere."

"Yeah," she says, matching the volume of my voice. Like we're both afraid someone might be listening through the hole in the wall. "We can't make it look like we ran, though. Let's not panic. Pack whatever you need for the next couple days. We'll put the rest of our stuff in storage and tell Jeff we're not gonna renew our lease." I let out a breath and feel the tension melt off my body. She has a plan after all.

"Where are we going?"

"We'll stay at a motel for now. We need to do this piece by piece. No sudden moves. That's how people get caught." She purses her raw lips and heads to the laundry room. Starts empty-ing the dryer, sorting through our clothes. "Grab some stuff and start packing."

☾ ☾ ☾

The goal, she says, is to leave Utah by the end of the week. She wants to figure out what to do with all our stuff. A lot of it belonged to her parents and she's sentimental. She also hasn't decided where we'll go. I know she's wanted to move for a long time, though. Maybe this will be good for us. She's always talked about starting over somewhere else, if she could find a job. She never wanted to move back to Salt Lake with Gram. I know she ended up here because of me.

While we're driving to the motel, she rambles about finding "good public schools," punctuated by the smack of her cinnamon gum. Then she mentions Mexico. "Listen, kids are like sponges. I'll bet we can have you fluent in Spanish in six months." I don't feel like a sponge.

I tape down the curtains in our motel room. Both of us try to sleep, but it's useless. We toss and turn on the stiff, lumpy bed as the hours tick by. I stare at a stain on the cantaloupe-colored carpet, trying to decide if it looks like a cat or Cinderella's castle.

That night, when we draw blood with our kit, I start feeling sick. We only drew a little bit last night, just to test it out. I tell Mom I want to try to get more this time. The needle is stuck in my forearm and I can *feel it,* hard and metallic inside of me, pulling from my vein like a magnet. My stomach churns as I watch my blood pool in the rubber reservoir. I try to pick a focal point on the wall: an amateurish painting of a boy and his black dog over the bed. But everything's already spinning. My eyelids droop. I imagine I'm the Earth, turning on my axis, ushering in the days and nights. I'm *supposed* to spin. This is okay. This is normal.

I'm not sure when I fall or how it happens, but when I open my eyes I'm facedown against that stain on the carpet.

Mom shakes me awake, tears streaking her face. She's removed the needle from my arm. We forgot Band-Aids, so she's keeping her finger pressed against the hole to clot it. The blood bag is empty; she drank before she woke me up.

"We're not doing this anymore," she says in a hoarse whisper, guiding me into her lap. The electric tremor of her touch is different now: a sharp, unsteady flicker.

"N-no, it's fine. I just have to . . . to . . . keep my eyes open—" I stutter, not yet fully awake. "Don't go out."

"I'm not. I-I'm just . . . Oh God, I can't do this." She's crying now. Burying her wet cheeks into the crook of my neck. "*You* . . . you can't. Okay? I don't want you to."

I try to think of something to say, but I'm still not quite sure where I am or what just happened. After a moment, she stands, carrying me over to the bed.

"Mia, I'm gonna go to the hospital." Her voice is calm and even, like a teacher explaining what to do in a fire drill.

"What? Mom, you can't. The Facebook group says not to, they won't help you—"

"Devon created that group. He made all the rules. He knows if someone tells a doctor what happened, someone he hurt, he'll have to answer for it. But there have to be people who know what to do. People who can help us." She twists into her shoes.

I bolt upright, forgetting how dizzy I am. I wince, cradling my head, as I croak, "That's not how it is, you didn't read everything—"

"Honey, Devon is full of shit and so are all his little brainwashed groupies."

"I thought we were leaving. What about Mexico? What about—"

"We're not running away from something we didn't even do." She grabs her jacket.

I stumble out of bed, dragging my boot, as my stomach starts to quiver. "I'm coming with you."

I'm surprised when we pull up to the same emergency room we visited last week. I thought we'd go somewhere new, someplace no one had seen us before. She used her fake driver's license and didn't give them any insurance information. Still, something's gnawing at me. She hops out of the car, but I don't follow.

"Mia, come on. You promised you'd be brave, I don't have time for this tonight." The corner of her lip twitches, like her teeth are shifting underneath.

"We should go somewhere else."

"The other hospital's too far. We've wasted too much nighttime already."

My insides heat up like a volcano. I'm seconds away from exploding. There's no sense trying to talk me down at this point. I've already decided my fears are prophecy. I shouldn't have let her leave the motel. We shouldn't be here.

"We need to go back." I want to say more, but I'm afraid I'll vomit all over the car.

Mom slams her door, then marches around to the other side to open mine. Unbuckles my seat belt and yanks me toward her. I yelp as my boot hits the edge of the door. There's a silver-haired man and woman climbing out of the white Chevy parked next to us. I notice the look they give us—the look they give Mom. She doesn't.

"Mia, that's enough," she hisses. "We're going in. You are not in charge."

Since the night she told me to "be an adult," I've been keeping track of all the times she's contradicted herself. I wonder if being an adult means going along with someone else's plan even if you know it's all wrong. Keeping your damn mouth shut.

We approach the check-in desk, with the man and woman from the parking lot just a few paces behind us. When I turn around the woman is staring right at me. She cocks her head of pewter curls and gives me a tight smile. My cheeks burn as I spin back around.

"Good evening, would you mind signing in?" The nurse on duty has big, round glasses and an unruly black unibrow, like she's channeling an inquisitive storybook owl. I scan the waiting area for the Sunkist-haired woman who helped me the other night, but I don't see her.

The owlish nurse hands Mom a clipboard, and she pauses before jotting down her name. *Margaret Cooper*. She flashes it at me, as though she wants my approval. I reply with a subtle nod.

"Have you been here before, Ms. Cooper?" the nurse asks as she consults the clipboard.

"My daughter Ashley was here last week."

Dread sharpens in my throat. *Annie*. Last week we told them my name was Annie, I'm sure of it.

"She's doing great now, by the way. Thanks for all your help—"

I grab hold of Mom's hand and squeeze it as hard as I can. Why is she saying so much?

"Anyway, I was hoping to speak to a doctor about some uh . . . symptoms I'm having."

The nurse narrows her eyes behind those bottle-cap lenses.

"What kind of symptoms?"

Mom bites her swollen lip and clocks the couple behind us. I'm not sure if they can hear, but I know she doesn't want an audience. I don't either.

"I'd rather discuss it in private with the doctor." Her skittish eyes deepen to that evergreen shade. I wonder if the nurse saw. If she knows what it means. "But it's urgent. I need to see someone tonight."

At that moment, a familiar face rounds the corner, wearing periwinkle scrubs that fit this time. I want to grab Mom's hand and run. I never actually *said anything* to the nurse with the orange hair. But it was the way she asked me those questions. That sad-clown frown. She knew something was wrong. We're here to confirm her suspicions. I wonder if I'll get in trouble because I didn't tell the truth before. I wonder if that's what I'm so afraid of . . . or if it's something else, something worse.

"Annie! How's your leg feeling?" I pretend not to hear her. After all, my name isn't Annie.

"She's doing awesome! Thanks for taking such good care of her." Mom flashes a megawatt grin, like she's auditioning for the role of Loving, Attentive Mother, focusing so hard on reciting her lines that she completely missed the name mix-up. I see what she's doing now. Suddenly understand what I'm so afraid of.

Orange exchanges a pointed glance with the other nurse. They think I don't notice. Why didn't I tell Mom about her before?

I grab Mom's hand and tug on it, hard. "Mom, I need to talk to you—"

"Let's finish checking in first—"

I lower my voice to a thin whisper. "Right now."

Owl picks up her phone. Keeping her eyes glued to us. "Dr. Nolan, I've got a possible Code Seventeen down in the lobby."

The elderly couple from the parking lot withdraws, giving us space. The woman whispers something in the man's ear, and his mouth hangs agape. I wonder if Code 17 means a Sara is here. I wonder if *they* know.

Owl stiffens, then quickly hangs up and moves toward us. "Ms. Cooper, we can bring you upstairs right now. The doctor is available."

Orange swoops behind me, so quiet I didn't even realize she was there. She drapes an arm over my shoulder as Owl takes Mom's hand and slaps a hospital bracelet on her wrist. The second Mom lets go of me, Orange whisks me away.

"Let me go, I'm coming upstairs—" I struggle against Orange's grip, but she's a lot stronger than she looks.

"Shh, it's okay." Mom's eyes meet mine. They're still dark as deepest ocean, but her voice is steady. Owl holds on to her arm, but she doesn't fight her. "I'm going to get better. Like we talked about. I'll be back soon."

"How soon?"

Mom turns to Owl. "Will you bring her upstairs, once I'm settled?"

"Ma'am, our policy is—"

"She's ten years old. She can't be here alone."

Owl pulls a breath, then nods. "Of course."

Orange leads me down the hall, toward an empty examination room. "You want some chocolate milk, honey?" I barely hear her. I'm not sure I could keep it down, anyway.

"Mom—"

She blows me a kiss, heading in the opposite direction, toward the elevators.

"I love you . . ." Her mouth starts to form an "M" to say my name. But she catches herself. "Don't worry. I'm coming back for you."

I try to hold her gaze, but my tears blur everything like wet ink.

The room I'm waiting in doesn't have a clock. I'm not good at telling time when I get like this. Five minutes can feel like an hour, as I learned that night in the car.

True to her word, Orange has left me a paper carton of chocolate milk. The same brand we have in school. I haven't touched it.

I'm sitting on the worn leather exam table, swinging my feet against its hollow metal base, counting the number of times my heel makes contact. One, two, three, four . . . by the time I get to sixty a minute will have passed.

Finally, Orange reenters, carrying a ziplock bag of markers and a stack of computer paper.

"Look what I found. You wanna draw, sweetie?"

"I want to know what time it is."

"It's nine forty-five."

"No, I want to know how long it's been since my mom went upstairs."

Without a reply, she pulls up a chair across from me. I'm still pounding my foot against the exam table, counting. I'll just keep doing this. I don't have to rely on her to tell time.

"What's going on with your arm, Annie?" I don't know what she means at first. She's pointing at the gauze wrapped around the spot where I cut myself with the gardening shears.

"Nothing, I fell."

"Can I see it?"

"It doesn't hurt."

"I just want to make sure it's not infected or anything."

"Why?"

"'Cuz that's . . . kinda my job." She quirks a smile with a disarming chuckle. Reaches out to me.

I snap my arm back.

Orange glances over at the door, as if someone's about to enter. I follow her gaze and stop swinging my foot. The instant I'm distracted, she lunges for my arm and pulls it straight—a stealth effort. They must teach them this in school. There's no way she's smart enough to think of something like that on her own.

I hate her so much.

"Let go!" I shriek, hot and ragged in the back of my throat.

She's totally dropped the sad-clown act. Stone-faced, she grips my arm with one hand and unwraps the gauze with the other.

"Oh honey—" She winces, examining the wound. I know it hasn't healed very well because we had to pry the scab open a few times. I haven't even looked at it for two days, let alone tried to change the bandage.

It looks like it's tripled in size. The scab is a yellow, gooey crater surrounded by a bright red halo—like some sort of inflamed nightmare daisy.

"You ever had a tetanus shot, Annie?" She soaks a cotton ball with a soapy solution the color of strawberry syrup.

"I-I don't know what that is. Please, I don't want a shot. I just want my mom—"

"Deep breath, sweetheart."

". . . What?"

The cotton makes contact with my scab, sending an electric current up my arm and down my spine. All I can do is scream.

"Shhh, it's okay. It's already over. Let me just change that bandage—"

I wrestle my arm away from her, hugging it to my chest. "You can't do this to me without my mom!"

She meets my gaze, but her eyes are like steel. She's done trying to reassure me. "Your mom is very sick. You didn't tell me the truth, last time I saw you."

So I was right. I *am* in trouble for lying. She's torturing me as punishment.

"I need to know your real name, honey. And where you live. We can't help you, or your mom, until you give us that information."

"My name is Annie."

"Sweetheart—"

"Stop it, stop it, stop it! I told you last time, I'm not sweetheart, I'm not honey—"

"Well you're not Annie, either."

Without realizing it, I start to make fists again.

Orange tosses the strawberry-soaked cotton ball into the trash. She's silent as she wraps my arm with a fresh roll of gauze. She's doing it gently, so I don't fight her. There's a tired, quiet emptiness behind her eyes as she works. Not like the sad-clown face. This feels real. Like she's had to do this a lot lately.

There's a knock at the door, and my heart pounds. A statuesque Black woman with closely cropped hair walks in, wearing a wrinkled maroon blazer and two mismatched hoop earrings. Like she got dressed in a hurry. Orange stands to greet her, shoulders tense. She seems important. Is she the doctor? Does she have news about Mom?

"This is Erica," Orange says to me. "She's gonna talk to you for a few minutes while I go get your medicine ready, okay?" Just "Erica"? Not Doctor something?

"I don't need a shot, right?" I say this to Orange first, then look to Erica. Maybe she's the one I should defer to.

"You need a tetanus shot and some antibiotics. Sit tight," Orange replies.

"B-but—"

Orange extracts herself from the room, like she can't leave fast enough. Erica kneels to my level and attempts a smile. She's wearing a perfume that smells a lot like Mom's. Similar spicy floral notes. My racing heart slows as I pull a shaky breath.

"So listen, I just had a chat with your mom." Her voice is warm, almost cozy and familiar. Like peppermint and Christmas carols. I want to trust her, want to unleash my tears. Until I remember she was probably taught to act this way around kids. Just like Orange.

"She's gonna have to stay at a different hospital for a little while, they're coming to pick her up. For tonight, we were thinking you could come with me. I'm a social worker, do you know what that is?" My jaw goes slack. Mom agreed to send me home with a stranger? Not possible.

"I have to talk to my mom."

"I'm sorry, but she's really not feeling well—"

"She's fine, I was just with her—"

"I help kids out all the time, it's what I do. Here, you can see." She fishes a lanyard out of her collar, showing me her hospital ID. "Would you feel comfortable telling me your first name? Same as me?"

I stare right through her, imagining I'm a computer going into low-battery mode. I have nothing to say. No information to offer. I'm closing everything down and dimming the lights. As I try to calculate how long I can stall, the door flies open.

I'm expecting Orange with the dreaded tetanus shot, but it's Owl, accompanied by a burly male EMT. Her scrubs are flecked with blood and his eyes are round as golf balls.

"Erica, can you come out to the loading dock?" she says, breathless. "Might need some help with this."

I shiver, and Erica squeezes my shoulder. I hate myself for wishing she would hug me. She races into the hall behind Owl and the EMT. An earsplitting, robotic howl blares across the building as she shuts the door behind her. A trembling female voice stutters over the loudspeaker, "Lockdown-Code-Seventeen-Lockdown-Code-Seventeen."

Footsteps hammer past, right outside. At first it sounds like just

one person, but more follow. I hear a man cursing as I stagger toward the door, tucking my crutch under my arm. I hold my breath
as I wrap my hand around the doorknob, one finger at a time. If
Mom's out there, I'm safe. I can't say the same for everyone else.
But what if it's not her? They've definitely had Saratov's patients
before. She might not even be the only one here tonight.

I'm not sure what's going to happen if I open that door. But I
know if I don't, I'll have to leave with Erica while Mom goes to "a
different hospital." I think of Larisa and Pyotr in that photo. The
way Pyotr gripped his mother's hand.

I squeeze my eyes shut and twist the door open. Someone seizes
my wrist and drags me out of the room. I try to yell, but they're
already covering my mouth.

I dare myself to open my eyes . . . and it's her. I want to cry out
again. With relief this time. Mom keeps her palm pressed to my
mouth. Electric vibration hums from her fingertips, numbing my
lips.

She snags my crutch and hoists me up onto her shoulder. I feel
wind in my face, like I'm sticking my head out the window of a car.
She sprints toward a stairwell, passing a panicked doctor stumbling
out of the elevator. He's a blur. I wonder if he even saw her. Clearly
these doctors have no clue how to deal with the speed of their "Code
17" patients—if they even knew about that part.

I ball Mom's shirt in my fists to keep myself secure as she runs,
like I'm holding the reins of a runaway horse. That's when I notice
the blood on her. I hadn't seen it before, everything was happening so fast. My heart drops to my feet as she tears down a flight of
stairs. What did I expect? That she just *ran*? That she wouldn't try
anything else? They probably told her the same thing they told me,
that I'd be going home with a stranger, and she'd be going . . . who
knows where. I would have attacked someone too, if I could have.

Right?

Mom kicks open a door and we're in the basement parking garage. I hear footsteps on the stairs above us, but she's got a strong
head start. She bolts between the parked cars and I can feel her

heart thundering. The sweat on her breast. Unless that's blood, too.

We're weaving toward an exit sign at the opposite end of the garage. Mom dashes up a ramp, then soars over the guardrail like an Olympic hurdle jumper.

"Get the keys out of my pocket," she barks as we barrel outside. Our Jeep is in sight, just a few yards away. But there's a second vehicle screaming toward us: a black ambulance awash in flashing red lights, like a welcome wagon at the gates of Hell.

I flail for the back pocket of her worn cutoffs, praying this isn't the pair with all the holes in them. I don't feel anything.

"Other pocket, Mia! Other pocket!"

She slows down, approaching the Jeep, but the Hell wagon is speeding up. I reach into the left side pocket and expel a breath when my fingers brush metal. The ambulance closes in, sirens wailing.

"Keys, Mia!"

But I can't seem to yank them out. The edge of the carabiner is stuck in one of the holes. The harder I pull, the more they tangle with the fraying fabric.

"Give me the fucking keys!"

"I'm trying!"

Mom inhales sharply. Pivots left. Then right. I'm blind in the dizzying red lights of the ambulance, like I'm underwater in the bloody Jacuzzi again. There's Devon's hand on the back of my neck.

Mom makes a noise I've never heard before. A feral roar that sounds like it's splitting her throat in two. Two men jump from the ambulance, racing toward us. I wonder if they have guns. I don't know what she's going to do. If she tries to fight them, she'll have to put me down.

Please don't drop me. Please don't drop me. . . .

She turns around and sprints out of the parking lot; it's like we're airborne. We climb the hill surrounding the building, and I think about Cheddar, cannonballing through the kitchen window, never to be seen again. The sudden burst of strength in his chubby little body. The terror in his eyes.

The freeway borders the other side of the hill. I'm not sure if she knew, if she was even thinking about it. There's a dark, overgrown field just beyond the four lanes of traffic. I can't see anything past it. I know what we're about to do.

"Hang on tight, babe."

She gives herself a runway, gathering speed, fueling the super-human engine hanging in her chest where her heart used to be.

Headlights hurl toward us like comets. I scream again. But I don't shut my eyes.

NOW

I take two shaky laps around the house to secure all the doors and windows. Saras aren't typically known for breaking and entering. It's much easier to hunt outside the home, when their prey is on unfamiliar turf. But either way, I don't want him getting inside.

I pour a line of coffee at both the front and the back entrance, then do my best to scrape the dried paint from my hair. I crawl into bed with a rusty old hammer I found in the bookstore parking lot a few years ago and stashed in my closet. The house is silent as the grave. He must have seen me and run off. But he could always come back once I'm asleep.

There's no point in trying to get Mom to cooperate anymore. Even if she gives me information, even if she agrees to keep Devon out of my sight, she can't control him. The only way to get rid of him is to back-channel. Convince someone else to rat him out. Mom can stay loyal until the bitter end if that's what she wants. In fact, the less she knows, the better. If it's clear she didn't assist in his capture, he won't drag her down with him. I hope.

I cradle my laptop against my knees and log in to Mom's Facebook. The original message about Devon was sent by a woman in Texas named Hannah Smith. While most of the people use aliases, they tend to be honest about their locations. It helps to give people accurate regional advice.

I switch Facebook profiles to message "Hannah" from my account. She might have some wisdom for me. Maybe she'll even call it in. She's already put herself at risk by warning everyone and proven she's brave enough to take a stand. That could easily get back to him.

> Hi Hannah, this is Belle Jones' daughter. I read your message. What should we do if we see Devon or if he reaches out to us? Do you have any advice?

A little blue ellipsis immediately starts dancing across the bottom of the Messenger window. Hannah's online.

> **Has she spoken to him????**
> **Do NOT call the cops**

I'm not sure what I was expecting, but it wasn't this. The ellipses keep dancing. She's still typing. The messages materialize, frantic, one after the other.

> **Your mom should know to keep this to herself**
> **He will def take others down with him**
> **Just ride it out till he gets bored with her**
> **Cuz you know he will**

I sit up straight, rereading her messages, nervously twirling my paint-stiff hair around my index finger. Finally, I start typing a reply.

> Sorry, I don't understand. You were the one who warned us. Don't you think he should be arrested?

The ellipses barely even twitch, she's typing back so fast.

> **Of course**
> **But**
> **We can't screw each other**
> **I messaged everyone as a warning**
> **But that's all it was, a warning**

I wanted to give you all a heads up to avoid him
if you can
Like if he calls you, don't answer. If you see
him, pretend you don't recognize him
That's all we can really do
He will ruin our lives if we try to take him down

My fingers are frozen, hovering over the keys. A second later, she starts typing again:

You didn't answer me before. Has he been in
contact with your mom????

I shut the laptop. She's terrified. I shouldn't have told her.

When all of this started, I acted like it was Mom's fault. But she wasn't in control the night she met Devon and she's not in control now. She's just like Hannah and the rest of them. They're closing ranks. I can't expect any of them to turn him in. They need a neutral party to take action. Someone who can't be roped into this.

Someone like me.

But I can't do anything unless I'm confident Mom won't be blamed for what happened in Salt Lake City; the problem is, I don't *really* know if she's blameless. There are plenty of things she's done without Devon. Things I can't prove. Things we don't discuss.

And then there's the question of what I'm protecting her *from*. If she weren't so afraid of being forced into a Sara center, we could call the police right now and tell them everything we know. We could get Devon off the streets tomorrow and save lives. Mom could get some sort of immunity for her cooperation. But she already said no to this; nothing scares her more than being separated. Being forced to leave her whole life behind—again.

But what if I can prove the Sara centers aren't what she thinks they are? Everything we know, we heard from someone else—who probably got their information the same way. Our Facebook group devours clickbait and spits it right back out. She's never actually researched it or talked to someone who lived there—aside from Devon, of course, who's probably been exaggerating so people feel sorry for him. What if these aren't the secret torture hospitals everyone says they are? Maybe they're safe and comfortable, and I can come visit every night. Maybe Mom can participate in finding a cure. Maybe . . .

It's not a good plan, but if Mom and I stay silent, Devon's going to take her off the grid like some deranged Bonnie and Clyde reenactment. God only knows what the fuck he'll do to *me*.

I place the rusty hammer next to my head on the pillow, keeping one eye trained on the window. Mom comes through the door around three o'clock, and I think about storming down the hall to tell her Devon was here. But it won't change anything. It's not her fault, she was at work. If she'd been with Devon, he wouldn't have come looking for her. I can't yell at her anymore. It won't do either of us any good. Tomorrow, I'll start researching the centers. There's a way out. There has to be.

Eventually, I drift off to sleep. I feel safer when she's here. I'll always feel that way, even if I know it's not really true.

☾ ☾ ☾

I spend the next few nights emailing Sara centers all over the country from a throwaway account, asking if I can speak to one of their patients. I haven't heard back from anyone yet. I spend my days at the bookstore, waiting for Jade.

I treat our visits like a personal reward. I'd happily endure a hundred sleepless nights with a rusty hammer under my pillow if it meant I got to see Jade the next morning.

She doesn't come by every day. So far it's been every other. I wonder what she does on the alternating days. Who she spends lunch with. She comes in just after 2 P.M. and grabs a chair in the lounge, flipping through a magazine or another trashy romance novel till I notice her.

She only gets thirty minutes, so the visits are short. I always feel like I'm hiding something when we see each other—hiding the fact that I know more about her than she thinks. I don't want her to know I've watched all the videos on her Instagram. That I know about her dad and Florida and the meaning behind her songs. Luckily, she likes to chat and always keeps things light. She talks about her prep for Cloak and Dagger and how much she hates the drummer her friend Tony recommended but she has to deal with him because they can't find anyone else. Then she apologizes for just "sitting and bitching the whole time," offers me a handful of Skittles, and asks what people do for fun around here. I tell her I'm not exactly the expert on that stuff.

"Why not? You seem like you've been here a minute."

"What makes me seem like that?"

"You're not fucking snooty like me."

"You're not snooty."

"Oh, just wait till you get to know me better." She smirks. "Chicago spoiled me."

She dumps the rest of her Skittles into her mouth. "Anyway, you should show me around sometime. I need plans. If I have to spend another weekend in Steve's AP Music Theory lecture I'm gonna smother his ass with barbecue sauce and feed him to the wild Saras in the desert."

I pause. I wonder if she's actually seen those Saras in the desert. Like Devon.

"That's the drummer's name. Steve."

"Got it," I laugh, belatedly.

She's back on Monday, at 2 P.M. on the dot. She's brought an extra bag of Skittles this time, and tosses them my way as I sit down in the chair beside her.

"What's your absolute, hands-down favorite book? Like, if the store were burning down and you could only rescue one."

"Well, if the store burned down I'm pretty sure insurance would cover the cost of our stock—"

"Mia. Please make this fun."

I roll my eyes and tear into the bag of Skittles. "I can seriously only choose one? I've worked here awhile so I've read a lot."

"I knew you'd been here a minute." She smiles, like she wants to make sure I don't take it as a judgment. As if I'm afraid of being outed as some burnout desert townie.

"My favorite is actually a kids' book." I choose quickly, eager to stay on topic. "Sort of. I read it a lot when I was younger but if you read it as an adult you'd probably enjoy it, too. It's called *A Wrinkle in Time* and it's about these kids who—"

"Oh, I know that one!"

"Have you read it?"

"Nope."

"Well . . . you should. If you're into that sorta thing."

"What sort of thing?"

"Like, interdimensional travel."

She laughs and tosses her hair over one shoulder. Her exposed ear is pierced all the way up and down. She crisscrosses her legs and leans in close, like the kids at Story Corner.

"Tell me what it's about."

"Well, there's this girl whose father is a renowned scientist studying astral travel, and he goes missing. Nobody knows what happened to him. But one day, she and her kid-genius brother are visited by these mysterious, powerful women from another world who say they know where he is, but the kids have to take this dangerous journey across time and space to bring him back." I purse my lips. "I'm not gonna tell you anything else. Just in case you want to read it."

She rests her chin on her fist with a faraway gaze, absorbing the silence between us. She does this sometimes. She'll indulge in a conversational lapse, like she's tasting wine or a fancy dessert. It scares me. I don't know how to follow her lead when she's quiet.

"I like the way you tell stories."

"I mean, it's not *my* story, I didn't write it."

"That's what I'm saying. I like the way you tell it. Do you, though?"

"Do I what?"

"Write your own stories."

"Oh, nah. I don't think I'd be any good."

What I mean is, I don't think I could keep myself from telling the truth, even if it wasn't a true story. The secrets of my life would seep between the lines and bleed all over the page.

"You never know. I mean, you'll probably suck a little bit at first but that's normal." Warmth radiates from her gap-toothed grin. "I only just started writing songs two years ago."

I almost say, *I know,* but I stop myself.

I'm not sure why she wants to hang out with someone like me. She references movies and bands I've never heard of, and I nod along with an occasional "Oh my God, they're the best." I always have a burgeoning mental catalogue of things I need to Google when I get home. She makes me feel like I'm putting on a costume and reciting lines for her, but I like it. I'm playing dress-up, an exciting game of make-believe. And she's buying it. I think.

On Wednesday, I find her fidgeting in her usual chair. Her cheeks glow and she giggles into her hands as I approach. Says she's "definitely still high" and shouldn't have taken that second Molly at 2 A.M. but it's all fucking Tony's fault because he told her they were going dancing but it was just a bunch of people smoking weed on his couch. She snorts and I laugh along with her, trying to hide my alarm when she whispers, "Can I braid your hair?"

The store's pretty quiet, so I let her plait two lopsided French pigtails on either side of my head. I shiver as her smooth sapphire nails part my hair down the center, gently raking across my scalp. But her jaws are moving a mile a minute, grinding like the gears of a clock. The watery smack of her chewing gum reminds me of Mom. I stand and tell her I need to get back to work, Sandy's gonna shit a brick if I don't finish shelving the latest shipment. She sucks her lip under her teeth as I pull away. My braids unfurl between her outstretched fingers.

"Oh. All right. I'll see ya." Not "See ya tomorrow." Just "See ya." Her eyes leave mine and she rolls out of her chair. She's out the door before I can think of anything else to say.

I spend the rest of the day with a knot in my stomach, afraid I might have upset her, or made her think I was judging her for doing drugs. I don't know how I'd even begin to explain what set me off. I run my hands through my hair, wishing I'd let her finish those braids.

☾ ☾ ☾

Friday morning, the broiling sun casts a steamy, alien halo around the oncoming traffic as I make my way to work. It's the hottest day of the year so far, even though it's only May. The temperature above the gas gauge reads ninety-nine degrees, and it's barely 9 A.M. It's going to be one hell of a summer.

As I switch on the lights and fire up our sound system, it occurs to me that we've never changed our store playlist. The same folksy internet station hums low all day, and while I respect Sandy's love for Joni Mitchell, I've "looked at clouds from both sides now" for five years straight. I start up the computer in the break room, searching for a new station. I'm still worried I might have somehow offended Jade during the hair-braiding incident. Later today, when she walks in, she'll get a subtle, musical hint that I've been thinking of her. Maybe a little *too* subtle, I think, cueing up a station based on Blondie. But I can't risk being direct, or what that might lead to.

There's a pile of cardboard boxes stacked against the back door that I meant to break down the day I went home early. I peel off the tape, then jump on them to get them flat. Crushing something beneath my feet feels good. Like I'm finally awake after a week of sleepwalking. The blood starts flowing as I jump on the next one, stomping in time with the music. Which is when my phone vibrates in my pocket. I pause mid-stomp to pull it out.

A Sara center in California has emailed me back.

> Ms. Jones—
>
> I am the head of nursing here at Saratov Salvation of Mendocino. Before I answer your question re: interviewing a patient here, I'm obligated to inform you that any person infected with Saratov's syndrome who does not self-report is ineligible for our Clean Care program, which expunges certain criminal records when you're admitted. That being said, there is a patient here I can put you in touch with who often counsels our newcomers.
>
> Please let me know if you'd like to schedule a phone call. In order to proceed, we would require a copy of your government-issued ID. This phone call would serve as the beginning of the admittance process for either you or your loved one. For liability reasons, we cannot have a suspected patient go undocumented. I'm sure you understand.
>
> All Best,
>
> Shirley Larsen, Head of Nursing,
> Saratov Salvation of Mendocino

Shit.

I should have known there'd be no way to test the waters or "just chat" with someone without strings attached. Sending that email was dangerous enough. I stare at the screen, squeezing the phone in my trembling fist.

I let out a breath and start jumping on the boxes again. "Heart of Glass" blares from the speakers as I snarl and chuck my phone across the room. The cardboard splinters under my feet, and I imagine it's a pile of bones. Whose, I don't know. Maybe mine.

I don't notice Sandy as she scans in and triggers the wind chime.

"Gettin' your steps in?" she hollers across the room. I yelp and spin to face her. The song ends and a new one begins: a dreamy synth ballad I've never heard before. It reminds me of Jade's song about the ghosts in Tokyo.

Sandy and I just stare at each other for a moment. I wish I could tell her what just happened and explain why I look like I'm on the verge of a nervous breakdown every time she sees me.

I mop sweat from under my bangs and break her gaze to grab my phone.

"Is this new music?" Sandy points up at the ceiling, as though the song is falling down on us like rain.

"Yeah, is that okay?"

"Go nuts. Just turn it down a smidge?"

She smiles—a wry crook of her mouth that's neither warm nor judgmental. Sandy's the vibey type; she can detect—and some-times mirror—anyone's mood in an instant. She doesn't know what to do with whatever she's just sensed in me. Which makes two of us.

Jade's late today. The clock above the register ticks past 2:15. Then 2:20. My heart sinks. I guess I really did offend her. Either that, or she's finally bored with me. She's realized I'm never going to take her out because I never *go anywhere*. As far as she's concerned, I live at the bookstore and I've lived here all my life.

Finally, just before three o'clock, she whirls into the store like a tornado, panicking and pulling at her sailor-striped crop top, and I jolt upright, as though I've been asleep.

"Holy shit, there's a bee in my shirt," she whimpers, approach-ing the register with one hand stuck up the back of her top. "I was just walking over after my shift and I felt something moving around in there and I think it *stung me*."

"How did a bee get in your shirt?"

"Just come to the bathroom and help me, I think I might be allergic."

"Wait, seriously?"

"I mean, maybe? I've never been stung by a bee before so *it's definitely possible.*"

When we're alone in the ladies' room, she rolls up the back of her shirt to her neck, exposing a swollen red bump in the center of an intricate mandala tattooed between her shoulders. Heat surges across my cheeks.

"It doesn't look too bad," I think I say. The words are thick in my throat.

"Here, use this to scrape the stinger out." She plucks a credit card from her wallet. "I studied first aid for a Girl Scouts badge."

I imagine Jade in a kelly-green vest and matching oversized kilt. Still with that gap in her teeth, wild hair trailing all the way down her back like devil's ivy. I disinfect the spot on her back with Purell from the dispenser.

"I always wanted to sell the cookies."

"Huh?"

I rub the Purell into her skin, feeling gooseflesh percolate under my fingers. "Girl Scout cookies."

"Oh, totally. My mom always kept like, six dozen boxes in our deep freeze so I'd crush my sales goals. Which was probably cheating but nobody ever said anything. All moms do stuff like that."

Jade winces as I dig the edge of the credit card into the wound, drawing blood. I pry the jagged black stinger from her flesh with my two sharpest fingernails—the only ones I haven't bitten this week. More Purell. More goose bumps. I wonder if they're contagious, like laughter or yawning. The hair on the back of my neck prickles at the exact same moment as hers.

"I like this song," she murmurs. I'm not sure how long we've been standing there, letting my new playlist fill the silence.

"Same . . ."

"What's it called?"

My breath catches. I have no idea. I was hoping she would tell me.

"I-I'd have to look it up on the computer. This is a new playlist."

She pulls her top back down and faces me, unveiling her smile as she turns. "I thought so."

Danger. Danger. Danger. My heart sounds the alarm.

"We'll have to get you an honorary first aid badge." She reaches for my hand. Her skin brushes mine and everything inside me goes taut. But she's only grabbing her credit card back. She holds my stare for an extra, fleeting second, like she's propping open a door. *Hurry up.*

I know if I follow her, I'll never be able to go back the way I came.

I make a sound that's almost a laugh but more like an awkward, closed-mouth cough as we walk back out into the store.

She twirls her key ring around her finger, studying me as I assume my position behind the register. "Anyway, it's been nice getting to hang with you these past couple weeks. I'll try to swing by again sometime, but it looks like Starbucks is gonna give me the boot pretty soon. Maybe even tomorrow."

"O-oh, that sucks. What happened?"

"My manager gave me a nasty lecture this morning about all the free shit I've been giving away." Her eyes roll to the back of her head. "But how the hell else am I supposed to make friends?"

She smiles, and it's like she's just pushed me over a cliff. She's given me no choice but to say the words that rush from my mouth. "I-I could give you my number, so we can stay in touch?"

Holy shit, holy shit, holy shit . . .

"I'd love that!" As if this were *my idea.* Something she'd never thought of. "Plus I definitely promised I'd get you into Cloak and Dagger next month and I take my promises very seriously."

My body is floating in pieces all around me as she rattles off her number. I flail with my phone, trying to find the perfect emoji for our first official text exchange. "This is Mia" isn't going to cut it. "Mia" plus a heart? Good God, no. A little yellow flower, or the dancing lady in the red dress? Crap . . .

"Got it?"

"Uh . . . yep." I fire off the message. All it says is "Mia."

"Awesome, I'll text you!" She skips toward the door, tossing her curls. Waves at me through the window as she dons a pair of heart-shaped sunglasses.

I'm pretty sure I don't breathe for a full minute. What the hell have I done?

2010

I don't think I've ever seen so many stars. We've been running—Mom's been running—for over an hour. Running *fast*. She'd be impossible to catch on foot, and no cars come this way. We've left the city behind. We're miles off the road, where the marsh melts into the edge of the desert, forming a dry, salty white patchwork.

I think we might have come here to hike once, or maybe for a picnic with Gram. Mammoth towers of rock stand guard on either side, like they're protecting us from whatever's prowling the darkness beyond. I think they're red, but the razor-thin moon doesn't provide much light.

The air is cool but there's no moisture, and the roof of my mouth is like sandpaper. It's getting hard to breathe through my nose, like it's stopped up with dust. I'm pretty sure I'll get a nosebleed if I sneeze. I'm not sure what time it is, how long we have till sunrise. We'll have to find shelter soon. But I don't think we have a destination. She's just running. Running till the night swallows us up.

Mom's chest heaves against mine, and finally her pace starts to slow. I wonder where we are. Where we're supposed to be.

She sets me down but doesn't say anything, wobbling like a puppet with no one to hold the strings as she collapses to the grainy white dirt.

She's breathing hard—too hard. Ragged, squeaky gasps. I crouch beside her. Place a hand on her back.

She stays that way for a long time, panting on the ground in the middle of all that vast, dark nothingness. Like an unmasked astronaut stranded on the surface of the moon.

Finally, she lifts her head, and I swear I hear a weary *creak* as she opens her mouth. "You were right."

I don't know what to say. It's too late, right or wrong doesn't matter now.

I steal a glance at the bloodstains on the upper left corner of her shirt. Just above her heart. Part of me knows I shouldn't ask.

"Is she dead?" I feel my lips form the words, but I barely make a sound.

"Who?"

I don't know. Owl? Orange? Erica? All three of them?

"I didn't kill anyone," she says flatly. "I was trying to get away."

"So you just . . . you hurt them."

She nods.

"Bad?"

"Bad enough."

"Do you think they could be dead *now*? I mean, even if you didn't—"

"I said I didn't kill anyone." She sounds so tired.

"Mom . . ."

"What was I supposed to do, Mia? Let them fucking *take you*?"

She turns from me.

"They never got our names, right? You didn't tell them, when you went upstairs?"

She shakes her head, still not looking at me. I retrace our steps as we ran from the hospital. She left with her keys, and her purse is strapped diagonally across her chest. I can see the shape of her phone and wallet inside. I didn't bring anything. There were probably security cameras, but it was dark when we left and if we change our hair and get some different clothes—

The car. We left the Jeep in the parking lot.

"Mom? What's gonna happen to the car?"

She sits up straight, pulling a sharp inhale that sounds like it hurts.

"Mom . . . ?"

The ground crumbles underneath me. The car will ruin everything. All they have to do is look up the owner.

Mom doesn't react. I watch her face for a flicker of fear, but there's nothing. She starts laughing. Quietly at first, before she doubles over in a full-blown fit. Her eyes well with tears. I have no idea what's happening.

"Oh God . . . thank you." She gazes up at the stars. "Thank you, thank you, thank you, Mommy—"

She's delirious. I try to steady her shoulders and force her to look into my face, but she's too strong.

"Did you hear what I said? About the car? We need to do something about the—"

"It's not our car," she murmurs. "It's Gram's."

"Not anymore, she gave it to us."

"She never transferred the title." She laughs again, from deep in her belly. "We just kept it. She died and we just kept it."

She hugs her knees as tears spill down her cheeks.

"Yeah but . . . Do you think once they figure out she died, they'll look for us?"

"It's enough to give us a head start."

"To where?"

She doesn't answer. I stand, hoping I can encourage her to do the same. But she's still on the ground. She moans and hangs her head.

"Shit. Our stuff. The house . . ."

All I can do is nod. I know we're both picturing our house as we left it, waiting patiently for our return like a dog that doesn't know it's been abandoned yet. I imagine the photos on our walls: Pictures of me as a baby. First Christmas. Me and Mom at the Grand Canyon. The framed charcoal sketches Mom did when she was in college. I think of the nice dishes from Gram's house, stacked in the kitchen cabinets. All the hats and scarves she knit for me. The stuffed animals in my unmade bed.

We were kidding ourselves, when we thought we'd be back to put everything in storage. When we thought we'd have time to do this right. I know Mom is having the exact same thoughts. I know this because she's breathing heavily again, cradling her head between her knees. We'll have to start over, completely.

But starting over is tomorrow's problem.

"We need to find somewhere to stay before the sun comes up." I'm surprised by how calm I sound. The depth of my voice. "Can you look up some hotels or something?"

She struggles to unzip her purse with her shaky fingers. I do it for her and pull her phone out. She stares at the screen. Doesn't type anything.

"Do you have service?"

She nods. But she just keeps studying the picture on her home screen: me onstage at the school spelling bee last year, accepting my first-place trophy. Like our whole life is flashing before her eyes.

I take the phone back from her, gently prying it from her death grip. The internet is weak, but eventually I'm able to load a map.

"Okay, it looks like we're seven miles from this place called . . . Salty Sally's Lodge? They rent out little cabins." I turn the phone around so she can see the Google page. "Would that be okay?"

"For how long?" She swallows hard, unshed tears in her eyes.

"Just for tomorrow. To get out of the sun. We'll figure out what to do once we're inside and we can leave after it gets dark."

"We need another car."

"Maybe we can take a bus or something?"

"At night?"

"Sure, buses run all night." I don't actually know if this is true, but at least we're having a conversation now.

"A bus to where?"

"That's what we're gonna decide at the hotel."

"Salty Sally's Lodge." She crinkles her nose and offers me a weak smile. I can't help but smile back. I have to believe there's a version of this story that has a happy ending.

I tuck the phone into my pocket and extend my hand to her. "We're gonna have to keep walking. It's eleven thirty, so we have a couple hours. Is that okay?"

She nods and stumbles upright. Brushes the white grit from her sweat-drenched thighs. "C'mere, I'll carry you."

"No, I can use the crutch—"

"Not if you want to dance with Salty Sally by the time the sun comes up." She scoops me into her arms, like a kangaroo forcing a joey into her pouch.

"Ow, ow, ow—" I flinch as she grips my forearm, the one the nurse disinfected and re-bandaged. The memory of my inflamed, nightmarish scab flares in my mind. I wonder if it's more painful now that I know what it looks like.

"That still hurts?" She adjusts my weight, slowly putting one foot in front of the other.

"Uh, it's okay. The nurse said I might need some sort of shot but—"

"Shit."

"No, no, no, that's the thing. I don't *actually* need a shot, she just thought—" I clear my throat. "It doesn't hurt that bad. Let's just get to Salty Sally's."

She chuckles as she plods ahead. "Sounds like some kind of dirty sea shanty, doesn't it? Salty Sally."

A muted laugh escapes my lips as I pull the phone back out to make sure we're walking in the right direction. As I zoom in on the map, she starts to sing, improvising on a melody that sounds a lot like the theme to *SpongeBob SquarePants*.

"Ohhh that Sally was a salty lass . . . she never washed her hair. She'd climb the sails and bare her ass—"

I snort, burying my face into the crook of her elbow to muffle the sound.

"And . . . fart into the air?" I finish the rhyme, gasping with laughter. It feels good, like a long drink of water.

☾ ☾ ☾

Our cabin is the size of a walk-in closet, with a flimsy white curtain you can almost see through separating the bathroom from the kitchenette. But there's only one small window, and I can easily cover it with a blanket. Best fifty-nine dollars we ever spent.

Mom collapses onto a rickety bed that's more like a rollaway cot, with a thick, lumpy ridge that hits your lower back.

"Come get some rest, Mia." She pats the space next to her as she closes her eyes. I'm still on my tiptoes at the window, making sure the blanket is secure. The sun will be up in less than an hour. I can't even think about sleep. There's so much we need to do. But she's been running all night and carrying me the whole time.

"You go ahead. I should buy us some stuff. Can you give me a little money?"

"You can't go all by yourself, you don't know this place—"

"I mean, *you* can't go."

She raises her head with a heavy sigh.

"We need a charger for your phone and I have to get something to eat. We'll need to get blood later but we gotta do a better job. We left the needle and everything at the other motel." I pause, racking my brain. "I also think we should get a map and some scissors and maybe some hair dye?"

"Jesus. Okay." She knits her brow and I notice she's looking at my arm. "Get some disinfectant, too. Like hydrogen peroxide or something."

"All right. I don't know how much all that's gonna cost—"

"It's fine. Here." She tosses me her wallet. "My PIN number is 8739, go to an ATM and take out as much cash as you can."

There's a pen on the ancient, coffee-stained night table but nothing to write on. I inscribe the PIN onto my bare arm.

"You're gonna walk?"

I shrug, picking up my crutch. "There's probably some kind of store close by, like a Walgreens or a CVS or something."

"Mia—" I can tell she wants to fight me, but she can barely keep her head up.

"Just go to sleep. I'll call the room from your cell if I need anything." Not like she could come outside to help me if I do. But at least she knows we'll be in touch.

She gazes at me through heavy, half-lidded eyes and slurs, "You're so damn brave."

"I'm just going to Walgreens."

I hobble over to the bed and plant a kiss on her cheek.

"I'm sorry I can't buy cigarettes. But I'll get you some gum."

"Thanks . . . babe." Her mouth goes slack. I've never seen anyone so exhausted.

I slip out of the cabin, quiet as falling snow.

I inch along the shoulder of the town's only main road as the sun rises, leaning on my crutch. A truck pulling a trailer of horses veers to the side, blocking my way forward, and grinds to a stop. The driver leans out the window. He's got a tangled beard that looks like a mess of gnarled tree roots. All the panic I pushed down since we left the hospital comes lurching back up.

"Give ya a lift, sweetie?" He smiles, revealing a mouth of chipped teeth and dark hollows.

"Uh . . . no thanks," I sputter. Frozen to the spot. "I'm on my way to meet my dad."

Something instinctively tells me to say "dad" instead of "mom."

"I could drive you there."

"I'm close." I stare him down, narrowing my stony eyes.

He sniffs with disapproval, and one of the horses he's pulling makes an almost identical sound. He rolls his eyes . . . then his window. He squeals back out onto the road, trailer jostling precariously behind him. The startled horse inside whinnies.

I let out a breath . . . and then a scream. Purging all the fear from my body. *You're so damn brave.* That's what Mom told me. And I am. I really am. The fear I feel is like a compass. If I listen to my gut, trust in my panic, I can use it to protect us. I can turn it into my superpower.

I like that idea. Mom's got her enhanced abilities. Now I have mine.

It only takes an hour to walk to the drugstore, but the trek back is harder. The plastic bag is heavy and my arm is still burning under the bandage. My other arm is occupied by the crutch. I stick the bag under my shirt, which I then tuck into my pants to create a weird, bulging interior fanny pack. I stop halfway back to Salty Sally's to scarf down a protein bar and chug some water. I glance at Mom's phone and realize I have dozens of missed calls from an unfamiliar Utah phone number. The phone was on silent.

My breath seizes as I scramble to turn it off. I don't know who's calling Mom's phone but for some reason I assume if I turn it off nobody can "track" us. I don't even know if phones work that way. I pick up the pace back to Sally's as the hot plastic bag in my shirt fuses to my sweaty stomach like a second skin.

Mom's at the door ready to pounce the second I unlock it.

"Why the hell didn't you answer the phone, what is wrong with you?" She grabs me by the back of my collar, dodging the sunlight as it pours in behind me.

"I didn't . . . Sorry, I thought you were sleeping."

She kicks the door shut. "How could I sleep knowing you were out there all by yourself? I can't believe you did that."

"You told me I could."

"You should've seen I was too tired to make a decision like that! I didn't even hear you leave. You shouldn't have just . . . Jesus fucking Christ—" She slumps down on the bed, face-first. I sit next to her and empty the bag from my shirt. Waiting for her to apologize when she sees I got everything on our list. She doesn't even lift her head.

I grabbed a Greyhound schedule from the lodge concierge. There's a bus we can catch at seven thirty tonight that will take us south, toward Arizona. We'll have to get off and find shelter again when morning comes. Mom still wanted to try for Mexico . . . until she realized she doesn't have a passport. She starts having another meltdown, curling into a ball on the bed, and I have to remind her to take it one step at a time.

"Let's just start heading south," I say.

The most important thing is to keep putting distance between us and that hospital.

I cut off her red ponytail at the nape of her neck, trying to snip it in a straight line but I think that makes it look even worse. She cries when I show it to her, like I'm presenting the head of a beloved dead pet. She cuts mine next. I don't cry. I've always wanted shorter hair.

I've picked out two colors for us. One is a deep walnut brown, almost black. The second one is lighter, with soft, amber undertones. I think the lighter color might look pretty on her, so I let her use that one. Mine turns out a lot darker than I thought it would. I stand in the shower, staring at the black, murky water as it circles the drain, imagining I've just stabbed some fearsome alien creature and I'm watching it bleed out.

While it's Mom's turn in the shower, I switch on the ancient TV sitting on the dresser and flick through a couple of fuzzy channels. There's nothing on, but I linger when I flip to a news network. A husky, anxious man's voice announces, ". . . hospitals are overwhelmed and unable to adapt."

I squint through the snowy interference, trying to catch a glimpse of these "hospitals." Wondering if they'll show a clip of the one we visited. If there's anything particularly gruesome to report.

"Late last night, Russian officials unsealed documents confirming this illness has indeed been circulating since the early 1990s. It also has a name: Saratov's syndrome. Saratov's syndrome, which the former USSR believed to be dormant, is notoriously difficult to research due to the limited number of test subjects. Patients are either reluctant to report their symptoms or violently resist hospitalization. If you know an individual exhibiting the following symptoms, you may report them to our anonymous hotline, which the CDC monitors on an hourly—"

The water stops running and I juggle the remote to switch off the TV. Mom shuffles in a second later, towel-drying her dark, uneven shag. She reminds me of a female rocker from the eighties whose name I don't remember. We had a bunch of her old vinyl records at the house.

"Does that even work?" She points at the TV.

I toss the remote aside. "Nah."

At six o'clock, I break a teacup from the kitchenette against the wall and use a shard of porcelain to cut a second hole in my arm. I let it pool into a paper Dixie cup and tell Mom to come drink when it's half full. Afterward, Mom helps me disinfect both sites in the shower, pouring hydrogen peroxide down my arm. She tells me to bite down on a towel so the people in the next room don't hear me scream.

I watch the sinking sun from an exposed corner of the window, waiting till it's safe to head to the bus station. The days are shorter as September comes to an end, but still, we'll be cutting it close. By seven, we can't wait any longer, even though it's not quite as dark as we need it to be. Mom's covered from head to toe in new clothes, wearing an oversized sweatshirt with the hood pulled up. We call a cab and bolt outside when we hear it roll up to our door. We drape our hotel towels over both back windows to block any residual sunlight. She's already got a pretty nasty sunburn on her nose. Her skin is parched and bright red and starting to blister. The cabdriver cuts us an odd glare in the rearview. I bite my tongue, hoping he doesn't know that hotline by heart.

By seven thirty, it's dark, and we're on time for our bus. Mom squeezes my hand as we climb the stairs, inhaling the thick diesel fumes like summer roses.

I peer over my shoulder at the parking lot and realize the cab hasn't left yet. It's still idling a few yards away. The driver stares into the middle distance, nervously drumming his fingers against the steering wheel.

He catches my eye, then rips his gaze from mine. I start to panic as Mom guides me to a seat.

As the bus chugs away, I keep my eyes pinned to the cab outside our window. We make an impossibly wide turn around the corner, and just before the cab disappears from view, the driver fishes out his phone. Presses it to his ear.

"Mom . . . what do you think he's doing?" I murmur against her shoulder.

"Who?"

"The cabdriver. Do you think he's like . . . calling someone? About us?"

"If he is, it's too late now."

She grips my hand even tighter but doesn't say anything else.

So much for my newfound superpower. My fear can't protect us. *I* can't protect us. Only Mom can do that.

But that's not going to stop me from trying.

NOW

Dinner tonight feels like déjà vu, except this time I'm the one glued to my phone. Mom doesn't seem to notice, though. I usually stare at my phone during the draw, watching the timer till it's over.

Jade said, "I'll text you." But of course, she didn't say when. Or whether we'd be making plans. I'm capable of initiating. I have her number. And I was the one who asked for it. But it feels too soon. That could be the reason *she* hasn't texted *me* yet. There's also a very real chance this entire thing could be completely one-sided. It definitely feels like she's been flirting with me. But that could be how she talks to everyone, and come to think of it I've never actually *been flirted with* so I don't have anything to compare it to.

She might even have a boyfriend.

I don't hear the alarm at first. Mom nudges me across the table.

"Look alive, soldier."

". . . Sorry." I dislodge the needle and start emptying the reservoir.

"Mia, did you ever study *Origin of Species*? In school?"

"Did I ever . . . You mean like, Charles Darwin?" I'm not sure I've heard her correctly.

She nods excitedly, reaching for the pink tumbler. What's this all about? I can't imagine it's related to Disneyland.

"Uh, we talked about it, but we didn't read it. Why, you want to start a book club?" I fill a glass with tap water and reach for my iron supplements.

"There's something I learned last night, something *really* interesting, that I wanted to tell you about."

"Okay?"

My phone buzzes and I nearly choke on my pills.

I try to keep my face blank and casual as I peer down at my messages, like it's just another public safety text from the local bots. But the thud of my heart betrays me.

Hiiiiiiii

And there she is. I open up the message, keeping one eye on Mom.

i'm drunk lol
anyway I got this for you

She's included a photo of a peachy-pink rose quartz in the palm of her hand.

My head's like a balloon, floating away from the rest of my body. She bought me a present? Why? Am I supposed to get her something?

Mom looks at me expectantly, like she wants me to prod her about this "really interesting" thing she just learned. But I'm miles away.

"While Devon was in the Sara center, he was doing a lot of reading and research to pass the time. He started writing this epilogue to *Origin of Species* that talks about the evolution of—"

"Pretty sure you can't write an epilogue to someone else's book."

She bristles, but ignores my arrogant remark.

"It's an epilogue *in spirit*. Anyway, last night he finally finished and told me I could read it. And honestly . . . Mia, think about this: Saras are stronger than any human being has ever been. We live longer, too. Way longer. And this *disease* . . . shit, if you can even call it that . . . you can't inoculate against it. No vaccine, no cure. Because the body *wants it*. Do you get what I'm saying?"

I can't focus. I feel like a computer with too many tabs open.

"Mia, are you even listening?"

I meet her wounded stare. "Of course I'm . . . Yeah. So, Devon wrote this epilogue because . . . ?"

"It's the cornerstone of his entire ethos."

"What, like his whole . . . advocacy-whatever?"

"Mia, this is serious. Saras shouldn't be hiding, or ashamed of what's happened to us. We should be proud. Because we're *evolving*. You get what I'm saying?"

The phone is burning a hole in the table. I try not to look at it, making an effort to give Mom my full attention. But she sounds like one of the adults in a Charlie Brown special.

"We should be allowed to live authentically."

I snap to attention. Something about what she just said. I watch her down the last of the blood in her cup.

"What do you mean?"

"I mean we should be free to live our damn lives."

"So like . . . hunt."

"I didn't say that."

"Does Devon?"

She expels a dramatic sigh and stands from the table.

"I told you, he's different now. God, it's like you don't even . . . Here I am, telling you about this huge thing that's actually made me want to *honor myself* for the first time in years, and—"

I can't fight the derisive snort in my throat. She sounds like some sort of shitty self-help guru. Her face falls.

"What, so this is funny to you?"

As I lower my eyes, my phone buzzes again. I flip it facedown, just in case she's feeling nosy. Which is exactly what she did the night Devon started texting her.

"I'm sorry. Obviously it's not. Funny." My gaze rises to hers. "You deserve to be happy."

That sounds like what she wants me to say.

She stands from the table and wraps her arms around my neck from behind. "Thank you, Mia. That means a lot to me." I don't move an inch.

"Anyway, I'll see ya in the morning!" Her voice is nectar sweet, like Snow White. I half expect to find a swarm of sparrows and chipmunks at the door as she flings it open.

And just like that, she's gone. To work? Devon's? Even if I asked, she probably wouldn't tell me the truth. I stare at the door, listening to the car rumble down the driveway. Every night, the darkness devours another piece of her. I have no way of knowing how much is left.

In the safety of my bedroom, I finally look at my phone. Even though I have the house to myself, I feel better cocooned in my blanket. The glow of the screen between the sheets creates the perfect amniotic tranquility.

> ugh sorry i hope that's not weird
> I thought it was cool cuz it was the exact same
> color as the lipstick you were wearing this
> week haha

Jade's most recent messages appear below the photo of the rose quartz. I'm horrified I haven't replied yet. My heart deflates the same way it did when I thought I offended her while she was braiding my hair.

No not weird at all that's super cool, thank you!

I stare at the screen, not sure if I hit should hit send. This doesn't sound reassuring enough. If she feels the same way I do, if that's the reason she kept coming to the bookstore and bought me this random gift, I need to make her feel safe to express her feelings. Because I'm sure as shit not expressing mine.

Not weird at all I really love it ♥

If I keep second-guessing myself, I won't text her back for another ten years.

yay the witchy lady at the store told me it
purifies the heart and you should sleep with
it on your chest if you can? but that sounds
annoying so do whatever you want with it

I laugh, flipping over onto my stomach, kicking up my heels. Before I can start typing a response, Jade follows up.

Do you work tomorrow?
Nope I'm off
Awesome ok do you wanna come to the desert
for a little jam?

A jam . . . ? I frown as my fingers dance across the keypad.

I dont play an instrument lol
I can give you a tambourine! For real tho itll be
fun you don't have to play if you dont want. just
come hang n have a drink and I can give you
your freaky lipstick crystal

I wonder who else is going to be there. A group setting could be a sign that this is not, in fact, some kind of date. She might have bought me the crystal as a token of our newly minted friendship. I'm sure friends buy friends crystals all the time.

Here's where we'll be, it's Steve's place on this
random ranch

She drops a pin for me. It's far, maybe forty-five minutes east.

come anytime after 4!

Anytime after four. Sunset is 7:24 P.M. I juggle the math in my head. It's approximately ninety minutes there and back, which means I'll have a little under two hours to spend there. It's crazy, but it just might work. Mom will be asleep. If she asks where I went I'll tell her someone called in sick and Sandy needed me to cover. I won't drink. I'll just hang out. And play a tambourine, I guess. If they force me.

I start typing a reply.

> ok! Have to be home before 7:30 but—

My phone rings with an incoming call. For a second I wonder if it's Jade, but FAIR SHAKE flashes across the screen. I groan and sit up to answer.

"Hey, Mom—"

"Er . . . sorry, it's Luke." I'm slow to respond. "Uh, from the restaurant."

"Yeah . . . I mean, hi. Sorry, I didn't—"

"Do you know where your mom's at, actually?"

"She's not there?"

"I hate to call you about this. You don't even work here and I know it's not your—"

"What's going on?" I toss off the sheets and blankets, destroying my peaceful fort.

"Well, Kayla hasn't shown up the past two nights and it's Friday and we're slammed. I can't get ahold of her. And your mom hasn't been in all week. It's a mess here. We need someone to cover bar right away or we're gonna have to close for the night—"

"Wait, she hasn't been there all week?"

"Kayla's been out since Wednesday."

"No, I mean my mom." I pull my knees against my tightening chest. None of this should surprise me. And yet . . .

"Yeah, haven't seen her since last weekend. Just wondering if she's okay and if you can ask her what we should do over here."

I close my eyes, as though that will help me parse it out and find a solution. Clearly, this is Devon's doing. He's insisting she spend her evenings with him—or making it impossible for her to say no.

Either way, she'll tank the restaurant if she keeps skipping work. We're already living paycheck to paycheck. Mom cannot lose the Fair Shake. And then there's Kayla. It's not like her to go dark; she's probably Mom's most responsible employee. She's worked there since I was a teenager.

Luke clears his throat. "Mia?"

"Sorry. Yup. Um . . . let me come by and see if I can help."

"Can you bartend?"

I chew on my thumb. "Maybe it can just be beer and wine tonight?"

"Better than nothing." He sighs. "And you'll talk to your mom, right? She needs to come in and call a staff meeting or something."

"Yes. For sure. She will." She fucking better.

I call Mom twelve consecutive times in the Uber on the way to the restaurant. I resort to texting her, even though I know she's nowhere near her phone—or ignoring it on purpose.

> **MOM**
>
> **You have to come to the restaurant everyone's freaking out**
>
> **I know you haven't been there all week**
>
> **Where is Kayla**

As if she's going to tell me. I shudder in the darkness, gazing up at the full moon as it rises over the wash, turning the saguaros into shadow puppets. She's out there somewhere, knowing I'll cover her tracks. The same way she'll cover Devon's.

☾ ☾ ☾

It's a long night at the Fair Shake. People are not excited to settle for lukewarm beer when they're expecting one of Kayla's margaritas. There's a pang between my ribs the entire time I'm at her post, taking orders from her regulars. I know she's not on vacation, or out sick. I think of the beach in Hawai'i and the surfing lessons she never took—or taught. It's only a matter of time till one of those black ambulances retrieves her body from the desert. The only question is who did it. There could be other Saras lurking around Tucson. But I can't ignore the fact that Kayla works at Mom's restaurant. The red flag is flapping right in my face. It was Devon. Or it was . . .

No.

I can't give Mom a lot, but it's enough. It's always been enough. Hasn't it? I pour and pop bottles, trying to banish the thought from my mind. But it keeps creeping back. Because it's been there all along.

Between orders, I check my phone. Nothing from Mom. It dawns on me that I never actually said yes to Jade's invitation for tomorrow. But I can't think about it right now, as much as I want to. Luke tells me I should take a five-minute break in the back. I guzzle a glass of chilled white wine and make sure I'm alone before I pull up the Sara Facebook group on my phone. I haven't checked it since the night I got the news about Devon. If Kayla's been turned, as opposed to being left for dead, she might have been added to the group. Which means I'll have evidence when I confront Mom about it later.

But before I can search the member database, I'm pulled to the top post on the page. It's from Devon himself. I don't think I've ever seen him post something here. I'm sure he lurks all the time, though, considering he created it.

> » Friends, thank you for supporting one another over the years. As many of you may know, I have created the ADAPT initiative as a means to change hearts and minds across the world. ADAPT stands for Acceptable Deviation and Progressive Transmission, and all my studies have been backed by scientific evidence. Please reach out to me directly if you want to volunteer or make a financial contribution. Saras are strong. Saras are the FUTURE. I look forward to building that future with you.

There are already hundreds of replies, even though Devon only posted a few minutes ago. The first comment is from Robert, a longtime member whose posts I've been reading since Mom's infection. It's long and erratic: the ramblings of a person whose thoughts are pouring out faster than he can type them.

> » Saras ARE th future!!! We are stronger, faster, ad longer lived than any human being has ever been We are BETTER WE ARE EVOLVING WE ARE THE NEXT PHASE OF HUMAN PROGRESS!! The only solution is to bring more Family to ths table nd find strength in numbers. ANYONE WHO RESISTS IS SHOWING U THEY ARE A LESSER BEING!!!!

The rest of the replies build upon Robert's passion, an explosion of support. I don't understand. The guy sounds completely unhinged. I think about what Mom said, about realizing she didn't have to live in shame anymore. No Sara should feel that way, especially if they're trying their best. I get why people would feel seen by Devon's theories. But this feels dangerous. Like they want to create an army or something. And Devon's not saying anything to stop them.

I swallow the rest of my wine.

Luke says I can keep all the tips at the end of the night, but there isn't a lot. I promise him and all the other employees that Mom will be there tomorrow night. I tell them we've been "dealing with a family emergency." People usually don't ask too many follow-up questions when you say that, except maybe "Oh my God, is everything okay?" Which, of course, it's not. Because it's an emergency.

I weave toward my Uber on exhausted legs and scan in, pressing my thumb to the door handle. My phone rings. Mom's finally calling me back.

Ignore. Let her fucking stew.

The hailstorm of texts comes less than a minute later.

> **Where are you???????**
> **Mia?**
> **Do NOT go outside looking for me I am home**
> **It is not safe**

I have to laugh at that last one. *Whose fault is that?* I want to reply. I don't.

By the time I reach our door, I'm itching for a fight. Like I could kick a hole through the house even though I've been on my feet for the past six hours. Mom storms down the driveway as the Uber pulls away, grabbing my wrist to drag me inside.

"Where the hell have you been? You have to be safe around here at night—"

"Yeah, no kidding." I slam the door behind me.

"Excuse me?"

I edge past her and sail down the hall, into the living room. All I want to do is collapse onto the couch, but I risk relinquishing the upper hand if I do. Physical dominance means everything when she gets like this. I stand eye to eye with her, pressing my hands to my hips to keep them from shaking.

"I was at the restaurant. Covering for Kayla."

"So you could come home and guilt-trip me? It's not my fault she hasn't shown up."

"Bullshit." I almost gasp when I hear myself say it.

"I don't appreciate your tone, Mia."

My instinct is to apologize, and I can feel the words on my lips. But if I don't stand up to her, who will? She's going to hurt people. If she hasn't already.

"Where is she?"

"I have no idea! When she's not at work, she's not my problem."

"Mom, I know what Devon's doing."

Her breath catches. "He's not *doing* anything, he's just trying to get people to feel—"

"He wants everyone on the Facebook group to go on some kind of like . . . killing spree."

"That's not what he said."

"Everyone else said it. And he didn't correct them."

"Well, I'm not a part of that."

"Mom, you can't just take the parts of his message you like and ignore the part where he's literally *encouraging mass murder*—"

"It's not so fucking black-and-white, Mia! You don't understand, you've never understood."

I soften my voice but not my resolve. "Look, with or without Kayla, we're gonna lose the restaurant if you keep disappearing like this. After that goes the house. Don't pretend you don't know. He's going to ruin our whole—"

"That's what I was talking about before, when you were too distracted by your phone to listen," she hisses. "The restaurant's the only place I go at night and I'm *sick of it*. I'm done hiding, I can't do this anymore."

"Then you're really gonna hate living in the desert with Devon, running from the cops for the next hundred years."

Tears stand in her eyes. "God, you're so different now. You never used to do this—"

"What?"

"You judge me, I can *feel you* judging me all the time—"

"Mom, you know that's not . . . I don't judge you, your life is hard and I've always—"

"You've never seen me as a whole person." She folds her arms against her chest.

"I-I'm sorry, what does this have to do with—"

"I'm like . . . *a liability* to you. I don't know when it got to be that way, but—"

"How do you know that's how I feel?"

"You think you're supposed to protect people from me—"

"No, you have it backwards. I protect *you*—"

". . . But you don't *see me*."

"Okay, Mom, how would you like to be *seen*?" I'm struggling to remember how this argument started.

"The way *he* sees me."

She wilts to the couch and pulls a pack of cigarettes from the back pocket of her jeans. She hasn't smoked in the house for thirteen years. But I'm quiet as she flicks her lighter. I'm not about to die on that hill.

"I wish you could know what it's like," she chokes between drags.

"I-I'm sorry." And I am. Whenever I stop to consider her neutered existence, how she must feel watching the world turn without her, the empathy is so raw I have to force myself to think of something else. Which ushers in the guilt. Because she can't. And then the cycle repeats.

I watch as she sucks down her cigarette, fighting the urge to open a window. As if any sudden move will be the thing that finally breaks her to pieces. Her shoulders seize as she starts to sob, and I sit down next to her.

"Mom . . . I've been wondering. About the Sara centers—"

". . . Why?"

"Please, just let me explain—"

"Are you crazy, Mia?" She recoils, like I've just revealed I'm carrying a blade in my coat. "They'll try to take you. Just like before. We have to stay together no matter what."

She's stuck in that time warp again. I decide not to remind her I'm twenty-three. Not now.

"Maybe they'll let me come with you—"

She stands, trembling, scanning the room for a place to ash the cigarette tweezered between her fingers. "You force me into a place like that and you're signing my death warrant. They'll experiment on me and call you one day to tell you I killed myself. I can't believe you'd think for a *second* that that's the solution here."

There's an empty mug on the windowsill. Mine from this morning. I watch a tendril of smoke rise from the bottom as she ashes her butt. Mercifully, she cracks the window, then goes for her pack to light up number two.

"I know what the solution is," she says across the darkness.

"What is it?"

She doesn't speak again till she's had a fresh drag.

"I'll tell you soon."

"Mom, what the hell—"

"I'm exhausted. Please, I don't want to do this tonight."

"Do *what*? What are we doing—?"

"Just go to sleep. Thank you for covering Kayla's shift. I'll call Luke tomorrow."

She turns her back to me, blowing smoke out the window. Staring up at the moon. Like she's just turned to stone.

"Mom . . . ?" She's silent. "We have to do something."

"We will." But she doesn't look at me.

☾ ☾ ☾

It's an eerie, rare overcast day. The sun fights the fog and casts a dull, monotone luster over the desert, blurring the line between earth and sky. I sleep later than I mean to, even though it's my day off. I roll over and stare at my phone on the nightstand.

Am I going to see Jade today? If not, why am I staying home? To guard Mom's door all day? Look for clues about her so-called plan that probably doesn't even exist? Nighttime is when I really need to be here. I can't let her go anywhere except the restaurant, and I have to come with her to make sure she does go there. I have to take control. After I'm done using the car, I will hide the keys. Fill her shoes with coffee grounds in case she tries to leave on foot. I will give her extra blood when I draw so I'm absolutely certain she isn't going to have any cravings. Either way, it's going to be a long, ugly night and I know she's going to fight me.

Which is why I should let myself have a nice day before all that.

I finally respond to Jade.

I'll be there!

I spend the entire morning trying to assemble my outfit. It shouldn't seem like I went out of my way to look nice. This is a casual situation. But it's also our first time together outside of work. The first opportunity I have to show her who I *really am*. But none of my clothes tell a story about me. All my life I've tried to blend in. My closet is a gradient of black to gray to white and back to black again. I stand in the mirror in my pilly cotton underwear, craning my neck over my shoulder to get a better view. It doesn't help.

I almost turn around three different times on the drive out. Can't seem to keep a steady grip on the steering wheel. I rehearse my arrival over and over, wondering how many people will be there, how long it will take to find Jade. The social acrobatics I'll have to perform as people stare at me and wonder who I am. I don't know how to do this. But I know I *want to*. As I exit the freeway, the fog starts to lift, allowing a fractured beam of sunlight to pierce the clouds. It looks like it's pointing right at me. I squint and fumble with a pair of sunglasses, passing my last opportunity to exit.

Jade kind of hates Steve, but I see why she keeps him around. The ranch he lives on is a sprawl of white hexagonal warehouses, each with its own lush succulent garden and a heap of macramé décor dangling from the roof. I roll down my window, and a chorus of wind chimes welcomes me. Hammocks hang between each building, inviting neighbors to relax and socialize together. There's a young woman wearing colorful linen pants nestled into one, lazily strumming a guitar. A second girl swings in the adjacent hammock, singing along. Nearby, a wizened man with ropy locks the color of smoke leans over a pottery wheel, swaying to the music playing in his headphones. I have to slow down to soak it all in, struck by this strange, sweet sense of nostalgia for a thing I've never experienced before. I didn't know people could live like this. They seem completely removed from all the panic and danger consuming the rest of the world.

As my car bumps along the dusty dirt road encircling the oddly shaped buildings, I realize Jade never told me which one was Steve's. I don't know where to park. I pump the brakes, anxiously scanning the property. At the end of the road, I hear the faint rumble of bass. As I turn the corner, a makeshift wooden stage emerges, strewn with cables snaking across the sand and through the door of one of the hexagonal houses.

A scruffy twentysomething guy with striped knee socks and aquamarine hair paces around the stage, wiping sweat from between his eyes. It's getting pretty hot, now that the sun's out. As he crouches beside the drum set to adjust the hardware, he looks up and notices my car, creeping toward him. He cocks his head like a confused animal.

"C'I help ya?" I hear him through the open window.

I just blink. My mouth feels dry and dusty.

"You're not supposed to park back here, you a guest on the property?"

"Uh . . . I guess so? Sorry." Am I in trouble? "I was invited by someone. I'm looking for Jade?"

"Of course you are." He rolls his eyes. "Sorry but this is private property and she's not supposed to invite people. She knows that."

It dawns on me that this must be Steve. I peer around the stage, looking for Jade.

"You good? Do you need directions back to the main road?"

"I-I'm just . . . Is Jade here? Can I—?"

"She's probably inside somewhere, I don't know."

My heart pounds and sinks at the same time. Was this some kind of joke? Just to see if I'd drive all the way out here? But why? Guy-who-is-probably-Steve glowers at me from the stage, arms crossed. I don't want to piss him off. I'm not built for this kind of confrontation.

I slowly back up and look for a place to make a K-turn in the red dirt. I should have known I didn't belong in a place like this. I'm the opposite of all these carefree, guitar-strumming desert dwellers. They'll immediately recognize me as an imposter. Better to just get out. Better to . . .

"Hiiiii! You can park back here." I hear Jade's voice behind me, punctuated by the thud of her feet. She's running toward my car from the house, beckoning for me to follow her. I catch a glimpse of Steve in my sideview mirror. He scowls and gets back to tinkering with his drums.

"You're early!" she chirrups. A lump lodges in my throat. Am I?

"It's four, I thought you said anytime after—"

"Oh no it's totally fine, I just meant . . . for me on time kinda means *early* and I get confused when people are *actually* on time, you know?"

Heat creeps across my face.

"Anyway, c'mon back!" Jade waves me on. But I don't hit the gas right away. She pokes her head through the open window, flattening her bushel of curls.

"What's up?"

"That guy over there seemed pretty pissed . . ."

"Oh, the crybaby in the fucking knee socks? That's Steve, by the way." Aha. "He's tired of always having to host everyone but look at this place, how can you not?"

"So it's okay that I'm here?"

"Definitely. Just throw away all your trash and don't toss cigarette butts in Steve's yard."

As Jade guides me off-road toward a parking lot in the sand, my ears start ringing and a thought materializes. Steve was annoyed but not surprised that she was the one who invited me. She must bring people here all the time. As in, I am not a special guest.

I check my makeup in the mirror as my mind races. It's too late to leave now. And I don't want to. I just don't want to be embarrassed. Don't want to have to talk to Steve again. Don't want to know about all the other people Jade's invited. People who might even be here today.

I pretend to be immersed in my phone while I summon the

courage to exit the car. But I don't even have service. Jade raps on my window and, at last, I surrender.

Behind her is a heavyset guy in glasses with a woolly black mustache and colorful sleeve tattoos depicting whimsical scenes from Winnie the Pooh. Tigger stares at me from his elbow crease. I'm nervous about being yelled at again, so I avert my gaze. It takes me a second to realize he's waving at me.

"Tony, this is my new friend Mia." Jade places a hand on the small of my back and guides me toward him. My spine goes electric at her touch. But it's over fast.

"Glad you could make it. What do you play?"

"Oh, I don't really . . . I don't. Play anything." I laugh, still unable to look him in the face.

"She's here to hang. Make her feel at home, Steve already read her the riot act."

She then turns to me and drapes an arm over my shoulders. "I'm so happy you came! C'mon and grab a beer, we're just getting set up."

She leads me over to the stage, still holding me around the shoulders, trailed by Tony. He takes a deep pull from his vape, wrapping us in his opaque white exhale. Neither of us says anything for a good five or ten seconds. I can feel her studying the space where there aren't any words. I steal a glance at her. Her eyes are watery and a little bloodshot, but that perfect, peacock-blue eyeliner doesn't betray her. Nary a smudge. I smell liquor on her breath, smoky and honey sweet. The corner of her mouth quirks a smile, but still, she doesn't speak.

"Do you live here, too?" I think to ask, even though I know she doesn't. I'm so desperate to cut the silence.

"I wish. I've been on Tony's couch these past two months." She peers over her shoulder at him. "He is a deeply generous soul. The ranch here is owned by a bunch of Cloak and Dagger people. Different artists can rent space throughout the year."

"Are there scanners or anything?" Everyone seems so relaxed. It doesn't make sense.

"Nah. There's kinda like . . . this code of trust here, I guess? I don't think we have any Saras but if we did, this crowd is pretty accepting as long as they keep their hands to themselves."

"So they wouldn't call it in?"

"I dunno. That's very Cloak and Dagger, though. Like, if you want to go to a show or work for them and you can get someone to vouch for you, it doesn't matter who you are. Just don't hurt anyone." She turns to me and stops walking, like she wants to make sure I feel the gravity of what she's about to say. "Too many people live their whole lives scared of everyone else. We don't do that here."

I drink in her words. I feel like she's trying to tell me something. Something about *her*.

In the time we've spent together, we've stuck to lighthearted topics. The only *real* things I know about Jade are the things I've sniffed out for myself. Things she put online. Things she's told everyone. But she hasn't told *me* yet.

"Anyway, drinks are in the cooler. I'll be back." She gives my shoulder a squeeze and deposits me under a shaded tent.

Tony takes a seat in my periphery. I was expecting him to follow Jade to the stage but he's right next to me. I know I should say something to him but I'm not sure where to begin. I dig into the cooler instead, hoping to excavate a nonalcoholic beverage, but there aren't any. I crack open a beer and bring my lips to it, but I don't drink. I have to drive home and give blood—probably a lot of it—in less than two hours.

Tony's presence is heavy, though he seems nice enough. I'm not ready for this. Not prepared to navigate small talk with a stranger over a beer I'm not really drinking. I fiddle with the tab on the can, pulling it back and forth till it loosens. Not looking at him.

"So how d'ya know Jade? You from Chicago?"

"No, from here." I pretend to take a sip. "Um, we met at work."

"You're at the Starbucks, too?"

"Er, no. The bookstore down the street."

The tab gives way with a soft *ping*. I pry it off, leaving a jagged edge of aluminum right where my lips meet the can as I feign another drink. I'm focusing very hard on not cutting myself.

"Check, check, check." Jade tests the mic onstage, signaling to Tony. "Let's get it, Tiger. C'mon."

Tony leans over to open the cooler, and his eyes rest on me. Not in a threatening way, like he's mentally undressing me. He's just . . . looking. Longer than I want him to.

"Well, it's nice to meet you . . . uh—" I realize he wants me to remind him of my name.

"Mia." Finally, I peer over at him.

He lopes off, slurping his drink. I taste blood on my lip. Turns out I did cut myself.

I listen to Jade, Tony, and Steve tune up. The woman with the guitar and flowy linen pants has joined them, perched on a stool. She stands and swaps her butter-colored acoustic for a sleek green electric bass that's carved into an elegant S shape, mirroring the curve of her hip. It looks like she's wearing a snake.

Beside me, a trio of girls my age with identical platinum-blond pixie cuts take over Tony's post. They look like they could be in a band together. They probably are. I turn and think about smiling at them, but I miss my window. They're already huddled together like a clique of conspiratorial shorn sheep, whispering among themselves.

The group onstage picks up a chord progression, led by the bassist. Jade bounces on the balls of her feet as she hovers over her keyboard, listening but not joining in. Waiting for inspiration. She waves her hands over the keys with a flourish, like a witch preparing to cast an incantation over her cauldron. In that moment, she meets my gaze. Sticks out her tongue and bugs her eyes.

"*Me-oh, my-oh, Mia, see yaaaaa*—" she croons into the mic, improvising with a self-satisfied cackle. Her fingers finally meet the keys, effortless like skipping stones. A melodic groove thrums from her speakers.

I laugh, sucking my bloody lip. Press the cold can to my cheek to keep myself from turning ten shades of red. The three girls swivel in my direction, staring at me. For an instant I'm convinced I can hear their thoughts: "Do we know her?" in sinister unison.

"*See ya, oooh hey I wanna see yaaaaa*—" Jade holds the last note, and the bassist leans into her own mic. Her birdsong warble emulsifies with Jade's moody growl, creating a dissonant harmony that resolves with their next chord change. I wish I could sing along, or even tap my foot to the beat. But I'm paralyzed under the collective stare of the three wicked pixies to my left.

Finally, one of them speaks, revealing a mouth of huge tombstone teeth. "You play with Jade?"

"Nah, I don't play anything." This question again. I realize I'm gawking at her teeth to avoid looking into her eyes.

"So do you like, live here? Or—?" She's still talking to me.

"Just visiting." I stare at my phone's black screen, knowing I should ask some sort of follow-up question. "Do you? Live here?" I mumble without looking up.

I hate this. I wish Jade would come sit with me. Why did she leave me alone with this White Claw–guzzling Hydra?

"Yeah," the teeth reply. No one says anything else. The music onstage seems louder than before. Bass hammers against my eardrums. I rock to my feet as sweat slides down my armpits and into my shirt.

"Is there a bathroom I could use?"

"Use Steve's, he won't care," one of the other girls pipes up. Obviously this is a trap.

". . . Thanks." I scuttle away.

By now, I am convinced everyone here is telepathically collaborating to murder me. Part of me knows it's ridiculous to be this overwhelmed. But it's too much. I should have known it would be too much..

I wander between the hexagonal buildings but don't dare go inside. An empty hammock behind Steve's house calls to me, and I take refuge there for a moment. Jade's still singing around the corner. They've transitioned into a new song, and a male voice has joined in for a lush three-part harmony. I glance at my phone, hoping it might already be time to head out. Not even close. Maybe it would be best if I just slipped out without saying goodbye. Jade might not even notice I'm gone.

But I want her to notice.

I came here to spend time with her. I'm sure she'll take a break and come sit with me once she's played a couple of songs. I just need to ease into this social setting. Smiling might help. I can make conversation. I can ask people questions about their music, about Cloak and Dagger. It's not hard. I can do this. I breathe in, fortifying my confidence, and head back toward the stage.

Jade has stopped singing. I spot her under the awning, rummaging through the cooler, barricaded by the three pixies. I slow my pace, feeling like an intruder. Wondering if I shouldn't have left the safety of my hammock. I make myself small against one of the many edges of Steve's house.

". . . I mean, she seems cool," one of the pixies says, vapid, as though she's discussing the sand beneath her feet. "I just think we need to be careful."

"Careful of *what*?" Jade cracks open a drink. Catches suds between her lips.

"Saras and stuff."

"It's fucking daytime."

"I know. She's just . . . I dunno, she seems a little off. She won't even look at us."

My stomach clenches.

"Where'd you say you met her?" the girl with the mammoth teeth chimes in.

Jade rolls her eyes and takes a swig from the can.

I bind my arms together and hug myself. I have two options. I can either sneak around the other side of the house to my car and make a break for it. Or I can bravely march right past Jade and the pixies and look them dead in the eye so they know I heard everything they just said. And *then* I'll make a break for it.

But before I can decide, a guy in a tie-dyed tank top barrels out of Steve's house, hoisting a massive bag of ice over his shoulder.

He slams the door behind him, drawing Jade's attention. She turns and meets my gaze, and her face sags with pity.

I wish this place were built on quicksand, that the earth would pull me down like a magnet and suffocate me. I open my mouth but no words come out. All I can do is turn around and stagger toward the parking lot. I reach for my keys, blinking tears from my eyes.

"Hey, where you going?" Jade calls out to me as I weave between the hammocks.

I know she wasn't the one talking about me. She defended me, in fact. But I don't want to discuss it and can't bear to see that pity in her eyes again.

"Um . . . there's an emergency at home. I need to head out."

Against my will, I slow down and let her catch up. Her frown meets mine.

"I'm really sorry, Mia."

"It'll be fine, my mom just needs my help with something—"

"No, I'm sorry about . . . They're fucking vultures. We're not even friends, not really. They fell off a garbage truck from LA and they think they can sing, but all they really do is hang around Steve all day trying to keep other girls away from him." She offers a smile, and then her hand. "Come sit."

She closes the distance between us, reaching out to lace her fingers with mine. I'm sure my hands are sweaty and shaky and embarrassingly unappealing. But she doesn't let go.

"You want another drink?" she asks as she guides me over to the same shaded hammock I was sitting on before.

"I-I kinda can't."

"Oh, I'm sorry. I didn't know you don't—"

"I mean I *do*. I just can't drink right now." It feels good to stop pretending, even about something so trivial.

"Sure, I get it. Long drive home." She sinks against the hammock, pulling me down with her. She maneuvers her body horizontally, lying on her back. Pats the space beside her. "If you're comfy."

I certainly don't look it. My spine is stick straight as I wobble on the edge of the hammock, grinding my heels against the sand. I'm not sure I'm ready to lie next to her. I don't know what's supposed to happen. But she doesn't force me to move or touch me again. She lets me sit there. We're both silent for a moment, listening to the music drifting in on a hot but welcome breeze.

"When Steve got pissed at me for driving onto the property I was kinda . . . I didn't feel like I was supposed to be here and after that I kept feeling weirder and weirder and . . . yeah. I'm sorry—"

"What are you saying sorry for? *Steve* should be sorry." Jade seethes in the direction of the stage. The air between us settles. "I remember when I first moved to Chicago and I barely knew anyone, I was so nervous at the first party I went to I almost turned around and drove back home. Like, *home* home, back to Florida." She picks at the frayed edge of the hammock, unraveling tiny threads. "I didn't drink, I didn't smoke or anything. Not because I didn't want to. I just . . . y'know. I didn't do that at home. I remember being on this guy's rooftop looking down at the city all by myself, feeling like everyone had taken some kind of magical pill except for me. I mean, maybe that wasn't too far off." She laughs. "Anyway. It took time. I didn't feel safe yet."

She looks at me gently; she's propping the door open for me again. Sunlight spills from the other side, warming my face, releasing the tension from my shoulders. With slow, deliberate caution, I pull up my legs and recline onto my back. I leave an inch of space between us, though. My "arm's length" mantra feels like a distant memory, but that knot of fear hasn't come loose yet.

"They said the same shit about me when I first came here, by the way." Jade looks toward the stage, indicating the pixies. "They told Steve and Tony I might be a Sara and they shouldn't play in a band with me."

I scoff, wondering if I'll ever reveal that was exactly what I thought when I first met her.

"They were just being possessive of Steve though. Which is

stupid, considering I don't really do the Steve thing." She narrows her eyes and my breath catches.

"Do you . . . do the Tony thing?" I needle at her, forcing a wry smile.

"Nope. Or the Billy thing or the Tom thing or the . . . Bartholomew thing?" She shrugs innocently.

"Are they also in the band?" I'm only half joking. She replies with a nudge of her elbow.

"I haven't gone out with a lot of guys, either." I don't know why I can't just say it. Can't just *ask her*.

But her smile tells me I've chosen my words wisely. She rolls over onto her side so she's facing me. Extends a hand to straighten my bangs, brushing them across my brow. I shudder. Nobody's ever touched me that way. Such small, intimate care. She holds my gaze, and my heart throbs in every corner of my body. Is this where it happens? Is she going to kiss me? Is she waiting to see if I'll kiss *her*? I break her stare, wooden with terror. My face is on fire.

"I'm gonna go at your speed. Deal?" I don't say anything. She gives my hand a reassuring squeeze. "I used to be really shy, too."

"I'm not shy." I don't mean to sound so defensive. I cushion it with a laugh.

"Fair enough. I mean, you're practically a socialite compared to the way I was two years ago. I used to do this thing where I'd pretend I was face-blind and I didn't recognize people I'd met before."

"Why would you do that?"

Her head comes to rest against my shoulder. The plum highlights in her hair catch the sunlight like rubies, and her curls are tickling me under the chin. But I don't move a muscle.

"Force of habit. My dad was always reminding me and my sisters that Saras usually attack their closest friends. I figured if I never made any close friends, I wouldn't get the life sucked out of me."

She laughs, so I do, too. But there's a shadow behind her eyes. "Fucking tragic. A whole generation taught to be afraid of everyone they've ever met."

"Yeah . . ." I wish I could say so much more. I want to crack myself open and spill my entire life across the sand so she can decode the entrails and determine my future.

"Did you ever know a Sara?" I ask after a moment. "Or . . . did you realize you knew one, later?"

She studies her own silence now instead of mine. "The year after my mom died, I met this guy named Brian at a teen support group at my church. His dad had the same kind of cancer as my mom and we actually went to the same high school, but we barely knew each other before that. We got to be really tight really fast. It was one of those warp-speed friendships that happen in life sometimes. If you're lucky," she adds with a wistful shrug. "We learned to play guitar together on YouTube and had scary-movie nights and stuff and like . . . for a second he was into me and tried to make a move but when I told him that wasn't gonna work for me, he wasn't mad. Or if he was, he never showed it. He was a solid guy. I couldn't have gotten through that year without him."

"What happened to him?" I'm pretty sure I already know.

"He never told me who gave it to him. When he got sick. He was trying to protect that person, whoever they were. He had to leave school, obviously. So everyone knew. His mom didn't let him hang out with his friends anymore. So I didn't see him. He was in prison, basically. And then uh . . . well, a person can only live that way for so long."

"I'm sorry . . ."

"One of our neighbors shot him. I think he might have been on his way to our house. He'd attacked a couple people before that. I don't know what he would've done to me."

"I thought you said he was a solid guy? A good person?"

"Oh, he was. But the way our town treated him, the way his mom kept him locked up . . . that can make even the best people lose their shit." She lifts her head from my shoulder. Stares up into the clouds. "I don't think he would've hurt anyone if he'd been allowed to live a normal life."

The breeze falls still, and her words hang in front of me. I think I agree with her. But the situation isn't quite that simple. I wish I could discuss it with her. Dig deeper. But I can't risk revealing myself.

"And he was the only Sara you ever knew?"

She nods. "You'd think our town was infested with them though, the way my dad reacted. After Brian. He pulled me and my sisters out of school and had us stay inside all the time, even during the day. All our windows were boarded up and we didn't turn our lights on after dark. He thought we'd be safer if we were invisible."

"I get that," I say in a cramped voice.

Since the night I learned about Jade's life in Florida, I've been convinced that shared loneliness would bind us together. But our situations are different. I see that now. Jade wasn't complicit in her isolation. I'm like Brian's mom. I wonder if she bloodlet for him every night, the same way I do. If she knew she couldn't control him.

"What happened to Brian's mom?"

Jade tilts her head with squinty eyes, like she's not sure she heard me right. I realize the question seems a little odd. But if Jade knew me, I mean *really* knew me, she'd understand why I was asking.

"Um, she moved away? I think? God, maybe she died. I dunno. After Brian, I didn't really see much of anyone."

"What about your sisters? Are they still there?"

"Yeah. They're younger. I feel sorry for them, I want to see them but it's just . . . My dad was really mad when I left, he doesn't talk to me anymore. I told my sisters they can come find me when they turn eighteen. That'll be next year." She adds with a faraway smile, "They're twins. The identical kind. It's cute."

"That must have been hard. To leave and not come back like that."

"It wasn't, though. That's why it still feels shitty." She dangles her leg beneath the hammock and starts rocking us back and forth. "There was this girl, Gabi, who I met online through one of my music blogs. When I was feeling really low about everything. She convinced me to come out to Chicago and stay with her. She was friends with all these people who weren't afraid of each other and got together and played music and it was just . . . it looked like everything I wanted."

"Was it? I mean, now you're here."

"Well, Cloak and Dagger made me an offer and it felt like the right thing." She picks her beer can up off the ground and takes a drink before she continues. I watch a drop of condensation roll down her neck, filling the hollow in the center of her collarbone. "Gabi and I were also . . . I dunno. We'd started having some issues and I needed space. We're still on good terms but I'm glad I left."

My thoughts drift to Gabi. Were they a couple or roommates? Something tells me not to ask. It's in the past, it doesn't matter. I'm not brave enough to pry anyway. She might think I'm the jealous type and get uncomfortable. I wonder if I am, though. I have no idea what "type" I am.

She shifts to her side and meets my eye again. Bends her knees and presses them against mine so our legs form a diamond in the middle of the hammock.

"I keep thinking, every time I see you, that it feels like I've known you a really long time. Which doesn't make sense because I don't actually know that much about you." She twirls the ring on her left index finger. "It's almost like we were friends when we were little kids and then we grew apart, but now we're together again and I have to learn who you are now. Sorry, does that sound creepy?"

My mouth shapes the word "No." She pulls the ring off her finger and I hold my breath as she reaches for my hand and slips it onto mine. It's a little tight. Her eyes smile as she traces my palm with her fingertip, and I get the feeling we're about to kiss again. It's now. It's definitely happening right now. And yet . . . she lets go of my hand.

Maybe this really *is* up to me.

My mouth dries up and starts to itch. I'm desperate to escape the intensity. Shatter the moment. Even though it's everything I came here for. I don't know what to do, I feel trapped. I reflexively pull out my phone to check the time. I only have about five minutes till I have to leave. I have no idea where the afternoon went, as if the white-hot sun scorched it all away.

"All good?" Jade clocks my tense posture.

"I just . . . like I said, I kinda can't stay."

"Oh, you were serious?"

"I'm sorry—"

"But you're gonna miss the whole show. Things don't really get going here till after sundown."

"I know, it sucks. My mom's just . . . she's got this thing I have to help her with."

Jade's eyes flash disappointment—maybe even hurt. She's staring at the ring she just slid on my finger. I wonder if she wants to pull it back off.

I know it's my turn to initiate contact. Extend my hand. I'm icy with certainty that if I don't, this is over. Whatever *this* was.

"I can stay a couple more minutes."

I focus on her hairline framed by thin, springy baby curls instead of looking into her eyes as I twine my arms around her waist, clasping my hands behind her lower back. I feel her body stiffen and I start to withdraw, boiling with embarrassment. What the hell did I just do? This was wrong. Too much. How could I have misread everything so tragically?

But before I pull away, she locks my arms in place with her own and slides her knee up between my legs. Presses the spot where my fly meets the long, thick seam on the inside of my jeans. Where the seam meets my skin. The pressure echoes across my hips and surges through my body. She rocks her knee back and forth with gentle determination. Stroking my bare arm with the back of her smooth, almond-shaped nail.

"Is this okay?"

I think I nod. I've forgotten every word I've ever known.

We still don't kiss. That is, I don't kiss her. If she wants me to, if that's what she's waiting for, I can't. I'm completely paralyzed by the rhythm of her leg as it sweeps over me like a warm, heavy pendulum. Back and forth, back and forth. I feel my breath coming in hiccups. She laughs into my ear. Her soft, sticky lips brush the back of my neck.

The hammock swings in time with her knee. In time with my body. Like she's weaving me and everything around us into a song. I don't know where I am or how I got here. Whether it's been hours or just a few seconds.

She digs her knee in harder. Harder still. Everything burns and aches and the sudden sunburst of pleasure takes me by surprise. I gasp so loud she snorts with laughter.

"Shhh, be cool, babe." She tousles my hair, then gently, deliberately starts the dance over again.

But I'm all too aware of where I am. How I got here. What I don't remember is how long it's been.

I sit up, light-headed and too quickly, nearly flipping the hammock. Jade snags the edges to steady it.

"You okay?"

"Yeah, it's not . . . I'm just—"

I dig the phone out of my back pocket, sick with self-loathing.

7:03 P.M. Forty-five minutes back, and that's with no traffic. The earliest I'll walk through the door is 7:48.

"I-I really need to go. I'm sorry."

I'm on my feet before Jade can say anything, racing behind Steve's house to my car, trailed by my spindly shadow.

"Mia! Hang on!" She's chasing me again. I want to yell in her face. Make her understand. *You can't follow me.* "I forgot to give you your present."

I sigh, squeezing my phone in my fist. "We can get together this week and you can give it to me then—"

"I'll be two seconds, don't move!" She ignores me, clambering through Steve's back door. Shit.

I pace in a circle as the day collapses behind the mountains, painting the desert with menacing strokes of sepia. She asked for two seconds. I'll give her ten. But that's it.

Ten . . . nine . . . eight—

I can text her and explain later.

Seven . . . six . . . five—

Explain *what*, though?

Four . . . three . . . two . . .

Fine. Twenty seconds.

I can't leave before she comes back.

Not after what we just . . .

I don't know how I could be so stupid. Just letting this happen. Nobody's fault but mine. Whatever's waiting for me at home, I deserve it.

Thirty seconds.

Nope, that's it. Time to go. I can't wait any longer.

I pivot from Steve's door as Jade flails outside, presenting the rose quartz like a treasure hunter who's just absconded with the Holy Grail.

"Oh my God, I was so worried someone stole it!" She hurtles toward me, trying to decode my agonized, vacant stare. "Sorry, I meant to say yes, let's hang this week. I just didn't want you to leave without this."

She smiles wide, thinking she's just assuaged my fears. If only it were that easy. She presses the quartz into my palm and squeezes all five of my fingers around it like a promise. I realize I'm still wearing her ring.

"Thanks. I'll see you this week," I choke. Last chance for a goodbye kiss. I blow it, of course. All I can offer are shifty eyes and an awkward wave as I swoop into the car. I swallow bile as I turn the ignition. Tuck the quartz into the passenger seat with one hand as I spin the wheel with the other.

Jade vanishes in a cyclone of dust as I screech out of the parking lot. Bass thuds in the distance, arrhythmic to my thundering heart.

7:08 P.M.

Sixteen minutes till sundown. Forty-five minutes from home.

2010

It's impossible to get comfortable on the bus. It's the bus and it's my arm. The lancing pain from the infected wound creeps past my shoulder, wringing my neck like a choke hold. I doused it with hydrogen peroxide just a few hours ago, but I think I made it worse somehow. I'm too scared to look at it and I don't say anything to Mom.

I'm desperate to distract myself. Should've at least bought a magazine or something at the drugstore. All we have is Mom's phone, but we need to save the battery. I play the license plate game in my head to pass the time. So far I've got Utah, Colorado, Arizona, California, and, for double points, Maine.

Around 4 A.M., the bus will make a stop in Flagstaff, Arizona. That's where we'll get off and find shelter for the day. When the sun goes down, we'll board another bus. Whichever one is headed south. We'll do this as many nights in a row as we can. Mom's hoping we can reach the border and post up in a hotel while we try to get new passports. I've never even visited another country. I'm not sure I want to move to one. But I'll do whatever Mom thinks is best. I'm good with the day-to-day stuff: hair dye and bus schedules. But she's better with long-term planning and knows more about traveling than I do.

I spend the first couple of hours convinced we're about to be pulled over after that cabbie supposedly called the Sara hotline. But the driver only stops for bathroom breaks and nobody bothers us. There's only one other passenger: a lone young man with a face of dull, craterous acne scars, carrying a duffel bag and an acoustic guitar. When we make a stop at St. George, a teenage couple boards: a girl with a torn T-shirt and no baggage, followed by a boy with a swollen nose, crusted with blood, gripping her hand. Mom goes taut in her seat. Her eyes rivet to the boy's broken nose as he passes. The bloody tissue poking out of his back pocket. She peers over at me, realizing I've caught her staring.

"I'm fine," she says in a thin voice. Grinding her teeth.

We disembark at Flagstaff, following the map on Mom's phone to a Days Inn just a couple of miles down the road. So far, so good. The process begins again. We check in, tape down the curtains. Crawl into bed. Try to sleep.

I watch the rise and fall of Mom's chest as she drifts off, aligning my breath with hers. But it doesn't work. No matter what position I shift to, my arm keeps burning. Not just my arm. My whole body's on fire now. I'm clammy with sweat and my face is so hot I have to get up and soak a washcloth with cold tap water so I can drape it over my face. But it doesn't help. All it does is dampen the scratchy sheets and stiff pillow, making me even more uncomfortable.

At five o'clock, Mom's phone starts to make a horrible screeching sound. I slowly, painfully pull myself upright, shaking the fog of whatever half sleep I managed. Mom gropes for the phone with an irritated grimace.

"I thought we were getting up at six thirty," I mumble, wincing as I bend my elbow too fast.

"It's not the alarm. . . ."

Her face pales as she reads the text onscreen.

"There's a curfew here."

"Where?"

"I mean here in Arizona."

"Since when? Was there one last night?"

"Maybe it's new." She places the phone facedown on the bed and covers it with a pillow, like she's afraid it's going to start shrieking again.

"Does that mean we can't get on another bus?"

"I'm not sure. All it says is everyone has to be inside by eight."

"Or what?"

She shakes her head. Her guess is as good as mine.

"But like . . . a bus is inside. Right?"

"I'll have to call them. I don't know."

I watch her pace the perimeter of our dingy, dimly lit room with the phone pressed to her ear. Dialing all the automated prompts. Intermittently yelling "Operator!" or "Agent!" to no avail.

"Don't any fucking humans work for you?" she howls into the mouthpiece before chucking the phone onto the bed.

After Mom's fed and the sun goes down, we decide to check out and start walking back to the bus station. Mom thinks it's better if we try to keep moving. I'm thankful that my crutch goes under my good arm, but still, I know she wishes I were faster. The streets empty out as the stars reveal themselves. Thirty minutes till this so-called curfew and only a smattering of cars remain on the road.

A traffic light turns green at an empty intersection. "I don't think the bus is coming."

Mom cuts me a glare. "If it doesn't come, we walk." She thaws a bit. "You need me to carry you again?"

"No, that's not what I . . . What if someone sees us?" A wave of panic crashes over me.

"We'll stay off the main road."

"Mom, I keep having a bad feeling and you keep not listening to me—"

She stops walking and spins to face me. "This is different, this isn't like the hospital. We don't have a choice."

She narrows her eyes and studies my arm. The way I'm awkwardly bending my elbow to keep it still. "What's wrong?"

"With what?"

"With *that*."

I withdraw with a muted squeal as she reaches out for me. She clenches her eyes shut and exhales through her nose, framing her face with her hands the way she does when I don't clean my room or I get a bad report card.

"Mia, I thought you cleaned it—"

"I did!" My voice cracks.

"Let me see."

"On the bus, you can." I relent. Because there's not going to be any bus.

"Please just let me carry you—"

"No! I'm fine." I forge on ahead of her to prove it.

A moment passes before she follows, drawing her lips into a tight line. I fight to keep my arm steady as fever flares across my skin.

We're the only people sitting on the bench at the bus depot. The ticketing vestibule is dark and chained shut with a heavy padlock. We both know what we have to do, but neither of us wants to move. I can tell Mom is dreading another night on her feet, and I can't ignore the way I'm burning up. But if I make a big deal of it, if I tell her how bad it really is, she's going to want to take me to a doctor. And we can't do that. Especially now, when we're supposed to be inside. Maybe we can go back to the Days Inn for one more night and disinfect my arm again. I'll take some Tylenol and get some sleep . . .

"Someone's coming." Mom points down the road at a set of distant headlights. I freeze, hoping it's not the bus. All I want to do is crawl back into that stiff, scratchy bed.

A flash of red and blue cuts the night. It's a squad car. Not just one. A second, then a third emerges behind it, all three silently whirling their lights. No sirens. Somehow that's even more unsettling. I hold my breath as they cross the double yellow line and form an ominous V shape to sweep the empty street.

"Get down," Mom hisses, pulling me under the bench. I wail as she tugs on my arm.

"Shhhh!"

"I-I'm sorry . . ." Tears burn down my feverish face.

She turns in a circle and we both spot it at the same time: an outdoor restroom marked by a triangular, supposedly female-shaped, silhouette.

She jerks her head toward the door, careful not to touch me again. We stay low to the ground, slithering across the filthy pavement. I hold tight to my crutch, dragging it along.

Mom shoves the door with her shoulder and I brace myself, knowing it's probably locked. But it swings open. We tumble inside as red and blue floods the parking lot. I can't tell whether they're pulling up to the bus station. They might just be passing through. But we're not about to take any chances.

It's not particularly dirty, as far as public restrooms go. Smells like the plumbing works. I'm thankful, if we're going to have to hide out here for a while. But it's stuffy inside, like a box that's been baking in the sun all day. Unless that's just my body temperature peaking to new heights.

The motion-sensing fluorescent lights blink on as we enter. Mom clutches the sink to steady herself, staring at her reflection in the crooked mirror that's less like a sheet of glass and more like a warped piece of reflective metal. I slump against the wall, pressing my cheek to the rough concrete, hoping it might be cool to the touch and offer some relief. It's not, and it doesn't.

Mom lets loose a defeated laugh, rubbing her bleary eyes. "Any bright ideas?"

"I don't wanna walk," I mutter into the wall.

She sidles up next to me, turning my chin so she can get a good look at my face. "Jesus Christ, you're burning up."

"No, no, no, I'm okay, I just don't want to—"

"I need to see your arm now."

"Please don't touch it. . . ."

"Does it hurt really bad?"

A sob crawls up my throat but I push it down.

"No, it's fine. I-I just . . ." I sink to the floor, pressing my face against my palms. "I just wanna go back to the hotel—"

"Shhhh." Mom squeezes my shoulder with sudden urgency. "You hear that?"

Her hearing is a lot better than mine now. I bite my lips together, still trying to hold my tears inside. Trying to listen.

"I don't . . ."

She yanks me upright by my collar and pulls me over to the handicap stall at the other end of the bathroom. Slams the flimsy partition behind her and latches it. As she kicks down the toilet seat so we can stand on it and hide, the door to the bathroom creaks open. She carefully hoists me up by the waist and hugs me against her chest. Locking me in place.

Through the slender gap between the door and the wall, I see a woman with an overstuffed backpack shuffle into the bathroom. She has a long, matted blond braid dangling down her back and blistered, sun-seared skin the color of terra-cotta. She's wearing a pair of dusty denim shorts sunken to the widest part of her hips, hanging loosely around her flat bottom and gangly, emaciated thighs. I wonder if they used to fit her.

I exchange an uncertain glance with Mom after we've both had a moment to inspect our guest. I'm woozy and nauseous and my legs are starting to cramp. But Mom doesn't move an inch. Doesn't let me go. She reminds me of a cat stuck in a tree, rigid between two feeble branches as her pupils dilate, realizing she can't climb any farther but can't get back down.

The woman turns on the sink, splashes her face with water, then digs into her backpack to retrieve a palm-sized battery-operated radio. She flicks it on and sets it at her feet. It's caught between two stations: one playing an old Shakira song I once did a gymnastics routine to, and another blaring a commercial advertising Oscar Mayer hot dogs. She doesn't fix the dial. Just lets it play on, filling the hollow silence with scratchy nonsense.

The woman pulls a bar of soap from the front pocket of her backpack. She removes her shirt and starts scrubbing it in the sink as she hums along to the radio. She's not wearing a bra. She has a tattoo of a daffodil on her left shoulder and the words "Jeremiah

29:11" on the right in fussy calligraphy. I can count enough of her ribs to know she's thinner than she should be.

I watch her reflection in the crooked chrome mirror. For some reason I thought she'd be older. The back of her looks so weathered and frail. But she's got wide, youthful eyes and full lips—though they're as parched and blistered as the rest of her.

When she's done washing her shirt, she attacks her armpits with the bar of soap, contorting herself into a painful-looking pretzel so she can properly rinse.

There were people living on the streets in Salt Lake City. Not a lot, but we'd sometimes see them making camp under a freeway overpass when we'd drive downtown. Mom always told me not to stare. She'd often roll down her window and offer a couple of dollars, or a bottle of water if it was a hot day. But we never stayed long. Never really said anything. Sometimes they'd say, "God bless you," and she'd say, "You, too." I'm not sure if Mom believes in God anymore. But she says we need to respect people who do. Sometimes I wonder what it would be like to believe in something—someone?—like that. I never understood how the praying part of it worked, though. Why some people got their prayers answered and other people didn't. Whether there was some secret riddle you had to answer once you had God on the line.

Gram used to pray. I never knew what she asked for. If she ever got it.

I try to extend my good leg to stretch it, but Mom pinches me and forces me back into position. I'm wobbly and short of breath. I don't think I'll be able to stay like this for much longer. Everything feels too tight and too hot, ready to explode.

The bathroom door swings open a second time. Mom's arms tense around me. I wonder if our mystery lady has invited a friend. But her raw, stricken yelp tells me otherwise.

"Stop fucking following me! I told you, I got nothin'." She recoils, knocking over the radio. The dial turns. Shrill, empty static fills the air.

I strain my neck, but I can't see the person she's talking to.

They're standing in the doorway, too far from our vantage point. I meet Mom's eye. She shakes her head. We have to stay put. No matter what happens out there. The woman yelps again and I squeeze my eyes shut, wishing I could make the same sound.

"No! Don't you fucking . . . *No!* I told you, I don't . . ." Her words decompose into a ragged shriek. She heaves and struggles for breath; a terrifying, guts-deep gurgle. *Smack!* A body hits the ground. Probably hers. A freezing-cold tremor rockets through me.

"Don't move," Mom whispers into my ear, rising to her feet. She picks me up and sets me back down on the toilet seat, posed like a trembling frog.

I grab for her sleeve, but she's already gone. In two swift steps she's out of the stall, looming over the sink. The partition rocks on its hinges from the force of her shove.

A tall, bearded man in a black leather jacket has the thin, petrified woman in a choke hold, pinning her to the ground. The fringe on his sleeves quivers as he tightens his grip. He's facedown on top of her and doesn't notice Mom's already right next to him. I don't know if she's strong enough to fight him if he's a Sara.

If he's not . . .

Mom slams her heel down on the base of his spine. I hear a sickening *crunch* as he goes small on himself with a howl that cuts right through me. He tries to flip over but he's too weak, flailing around like a fish that's just been plucked from the water. He releases the woman, who skitters out from underneath him, gulping air as she claws her bruised neck. She yanks on her wet shirt, hugging her arms over her shriveled breasts.

From the safety of the toilet seat, I watch Mom push the man's greasy, shoulder-length hair aside, examining his neck. Her breath comes in shallow, reverent gasps as her whole body starts to chatter. I can feel her thoughts from across the room, vibrating on the same wavelength as the dim fluorescent light. *This one's bad. This one deserves it. I deserve it.*

"Fuck, fuck, fuck, fuck, fuck me." The brittle woman takes

cover underneath the sink, shivering so hard it looks like she's having some kind of seizure. Mom's got her back facing me, but if I
had to guess she's probably just exposed her teeth.

"Holy-Mary-Mother-of-God-pray-for-us-sinners-now-and-at-
the-hour-of-our-death-amen," the woman spits like a tongue twister.

"You shut your fucking mouth," Mom hisses at her. "How
would you feel if I prayed over you like a babbling psycho every
time you shot junk up your arm?"

"I-I don't . . . I'm not a—"

"Sure." Mom's eyes are like shards of glass. "You're welcome,
by the way."

The man on the ground starts weeping—out of fear or because
of the pain, I don't know.

"I'm sorry, I'm sorry, I'm sorry, I was just . . . I w-w-wanted—"

Mom flips him over like a pancake, with one hand. He screams
and I cover my ears.

She stares into his face for a tense, wrenching moment . . . then
bolts upright. Clarity strikes us both between the eyes at the exact
same moment: These two people just saw everything. Well, maybe
not *everything*, she hasn't killed him. But if she does . . .

"Mia, c'mon out."

I don't move. I need a second to worm my way into her mind.
Figure out what her aim is.

"Mia." Deeper now. The monster's voice.

I creep out of the bathroom stall, staring at my feet so I don't
have to look at either of Mom's trembling would-be victims.

"I can't stop you, either of you, if you want to tell someone what
you saw." She addresses the two of them, still in her thick, throaty
growl. "But this is my daughter. She's been through hell and I'm
all she's got. If you send the police after me, if you call one of those
hotlines . . . it's over for her. So think about that. Before you pick
up the phone."

She snags my hand in hers and pulls me toward the door.

"Fucking-cocksucker-cunt-bitch-*shit*!" the man screeches, using all the breath left in his lungs. When he draws another, he screams in agony, letting it right back out. The cycle continues, over and over, as he wheezes helplessly on the floor.

Soothing, cool night air rushes my lungs as we race outside. But relief doesn't last long.

I steady myself against Mom's hip as the world starts to capsize, like one of those old-timey cartoons where the final image spirals into blackness. *Th-th-th-th-that's all folks!*

"Yo! Wait! Don't . . . Hang on!" the blond woman calls out.

I blink my vision back into focus, squinting in the hazy moonlight. She stumbles out of the bathroom, struggling to strap on her backpack and zip it up at the same time. A few items come loose, and she doubles back to pick them up.

"I'm sorry for what I . . . I mean, I just kinda panicked and—"

Mom spins to meet her eye as she sheepishly shoves a pair of socks into her bag.

"You need to go."

"I am, believe me. Going, going, gone. More miles I can put between my ass and that lunatic, the better—"

"No, I mean . . . I don't want to do anything. To you." Mom's gaze softens. "You seem okay."

"Nah, I trust you."

Mom makes a sound like she's just swallowed water with her nose.

"You're not gonna do any of that stuff in front of your kid." The woman beams like she's just cracked some kind of clairvoyant code. "I can tell. I sense these things about people. I've always kinda . . . What I mean is, when you had Tate on the ground like that? If you were really gonna . . . y'know. I think you would've just . . . *done it*. Wouldn't've said anything at all." She shudders. "And after that you would've done it to me, too."

"Still might."

"What's your name?"

Mom's mouth doesn't move. The woman's inquisitive eyes skate to mine. I peer over at Mom and copy her face exactly.

Mom glances over at the bathroom as we walk on. "Who was he?" She's not inviting the woman to join us, but she's not discouraging her, either.

"Tate. Met him at a shelter outside Vegas last week. They wouldn't let him in 'cuz it was just for women and kids, but he asked me if I could go in and try to score for him. He even tried to give me money but I was like . . . Nuh-uh, dude. This train don't stop there no more. You know?"

Mom nods, but slowly. It's not clear if this was a rhetorical question.

"Next morning, he's waiting for me at the door. Follows me all the way to the train yard. Hops the boxcar right behind mine. And I'm thinking . . . what's this guy sniffing around me for? He knows I'm not holdin'. I mean . . . he *should*—"

She collects herself with an anxious laugh.

"Point being, that's one scary-ass dude you do *not* want stalking you across state lines. Tell ya what, when he walked into that bathroom . . . I was all, 'Hoooo, Magda! Your number's up, ya dumb bitch.' God, if you hadn't been there . . .'"

Relief crackles across Magda's weathered face, and she smiles. Her teeth are pearly and fake-looking, straight as a fence. They seem new. Like they don't match the rest of her.

"Anyway, I was hoping I could hang with you for a minute. If that's okay."

Mom releases a strangled-sounding sigh. But Magda's still chattering on.

"I'm trying to get to Tucson, to my cousin's house, but I'll go wherever you're headed for the time being. Just till I feel safe again. You know?"

I think this time she's expecting an answer.

As I watch Mom's face for a response, the dizziness comes roaring back and I lose my footing. I bury my face between her breasts, groaning like a kid half my age on the verge of a tantrum.

"Mia, what's wrong with you?" I can't tell if she's upset or scared. She sounds like she's shouting from the top of a mountain.

I've only just now realized that my arm is completely numb.

"She okay?" That's Magda, but I can barely hear her either.

Mom picks me up. My sweaty skin fuses to hers, sticky like glue.

Her chest vibrates and I can tell she's saying something to Magda, but I don't know what. A second later, we're on the move. I'm not sure where we're headed, or if Magda's still with us. Whether I'm awake or asleep. I cling to the smell of Mom's shampoo like a tether. Hoping I'll be able to find my way back.

☾ ☾ ☾

When I wake up, we're back at the Days Inn. Or is it? It's not the same room as before. We could be anywhere. Or maybe . . . *is* this the same room? I don't know. I feel like I'm hanging upside down like a bat as all my blood pools into my skull.

A bitter, chocolaty smell mixes with the stale breeze blowing from the air-conditioning. Coffee? Who's drinking coffee? Not Mom. Even the smell of it is too much for her now.

I roll onto my back, careful not to disturb my arm, rubbing my parched, prickly eyes with my good hand.

A voice. Soft and low, like dark velvet. Female. Mom?

No . . .

". . . Right, well that's the issue with the fucking shelters. They don't trust anyone anymore. Can't say I blame 'em. But still."

Magda's still here.

Magda's drinking coffee.

Mom made coffee for Magda.

I try to shimmy to a seated position, cradling my heavy head. She needs to leave. What does she think is going to happen when Mom gets hungry again? She thinks she knows what we're all about. Thinks we're the exception to the rule. Or that maybe *she's* the exception—if she's nice enough.

"Sorry, that's rough," Mom replies.

"Tucson'll be good, though. My cousin has this ostrich farm, where the kids can go pet 'em and see their giant eggs and stuff like that? He says I can work there if I want, which is great actually because I've been thinking about enrolling in veterinary school after I—"

"Mia." Mom springs to her feet as I try to crawl out of bed. She looks a little green, probably from the nauseating smell of Magda's coffee.

I point a feeble finger in Magda's direction. "She needs to go."

"Magda's fine. We're just talking—"

I shout over Mom's shoulder as my eyes lock on to Magda's. "She's not your friend. You're just food. You know that, right?"

"Mia, please—"

"You're stupid. She's tricking you. You need to leave—"

Mom shoves a thermometer into my mouth, shutting me up. She clamps my jaws around it. I don't know where she got a thermometer. Did they go to a store? What time is it? How long have I been asleep?

The thermometer beeps and Mom yanks it out from under my tongue.

"Do you want to *die*?" I plead with Magda as soon as I have control over my mouth again. God, maybe she does. Considering what she's probably been through. You don't get to be that skinny if you've had a good life.

"How now?" Magda asks Mom, ignoring me.

"One oh three."

"That's no good, honey." I'm not sure who she's calling "honey," me or Mom.

Mom massages her temples, sinking down beside me on the bed.

"Mia, here's what's gonna happen."

I hate when she starts sentences like this. She's letting me know, right out of the gate, that I don't have a say in anything.

"Magda's going to take you to see a doctor."

"What? No. Mom, you don't even know her—" I stammer. "And what are you gonna do when it's time to eat? If I'm not here? You're . . . you can't—"

"She's helping us with everything. You don't need to worry."

"What do you mean she's helping?"

"This isn't a debate, Mia. You're sick. Magda's taking you to get your arm looked at, and I'm staying here."

"How do you know she'll bring me back when I'm done?"

"I'm in debt to your mom," Magda interjects. "Gotta close that loop."

"And she only gets paid once you're back."

Magda responds with a furtive shrug.

"How much?" I ask.

"None of your business." Mom thrusts my left sneaker into my hand.

When it's clear I'm too stiff and woozy to tie the shoe myself, she gets on her knees and does it for me.

"Ask them to take a look at her leg, too," Mom says to Magda. "See when she can stop wearing this damn boot."

"They're gonna ask how she broke it."

"Make something up."

"No but like . . . how *did she*? Break it? They might need to know in order to—"

"It's a long story."

Magda swallows and I can sense her unease. I wonder if she's starting to doubt her first impression. If she's going to change her mind and leave me at the hospital and call the hotline instead of bringing me back to Mom.

"You can't make me go."

"Your mom's being sweet 'cuz she doesn't want to scare you," Magda chimes in. "I had a friend back home whose arm got infected like that after she . . . I mean, it doesn't matter—"

"Magda . . ." Mom shoots her a warning glance.

"I want to hear," I snap.

"Anyway, my girl was in bad shape, she had a fever and everything, just like you, and by the time her boyfriend brought her to the hospital she was nearly brain-dead and they had to amputate her arm." Magda studies me for a reaction. "That's when they have to—"

"I know what 'amputate' means."

"Take my phone. Call me when you get there." Mom hands me her cell and a scrap of hotel stationery with the phone number on it.

"Mom, I can't just go with a stranger. I—"

"She's not a stranger. I know her now. You'll get to know her, too." Mom meets Magda's gaze. "She's a mom. She can handle it."

"If she's a mom then where are her kids?" I hear the cold sass in my voice, but I don't care until I catch a glimpse of Magda's face. Her downcast eyes. Her pink, burning cheeks.

"Mia, I've made some bad choices lately," Mom says without looking at me. "I need to stay out of this. For you. We'll be together again after this is over. I promise."

She doesn't wait for me to nod or indicate any kind of agreement. She makes a deliberate show of opening Magda's ragged backpack and placing a thick envelope inside. She slowly zips it up, but doesn't give it back to her.

"When you're back and she's safe."

Magda replies with a dutiful nod and heads for the door. Mom makes her way around the corner and into the bathroom to avoid the light.

"Mom—" I whimper. She shakes her head.

"Call me as soon as you get there."

Click. She locks the bathroom door. I hobble toward it, but Magda pulls me back.

"My friend only had a couple hours after the fever spiked till she lost that arm. We need to go."

I'm too weak to fight her, but she's not strong enough to carry me. We struggle in the doorway till my vision starts to swim and a fresh wave of sweat weeps from my forehead. I meet Magda's gaze.

"I don't want to walk."

"Good, me neither."

Magda and I wait for our cab on a bench outside the Days Inn. The sun screams in my face. I chip chunks of flaking green paint from the bench, trying to keep my aching head down. Magda produces a pack of cigarettes from her threadbare shorts.

"D'ya mind?"

I shrug. She sticks a smoke to her bottom lip and flicks her lighter, then sighs and puts it back.

"I can wait."

"I don't care." I really don't. I just want to get this over with.

"Your mom told me what happened last time you two tried to go to a hospital. That's fu— . . . messed up. Really messed up." I don't reply. She takes this as a cue to continue. "I told her she was lucky you guys were in Utah, though. When it happened. Rate of infection is pretty low there, so they aren't making everyone take blood tests yet. They can't prove she had it so hopefully they'll just—"

"What blood tests?" I glance up at her, shielding my eyes from the light.

"They've started doing 'em in California and Nevada. Making everyone give blood the second they walk into a hospital or a doctor's office or any place like that. Just to be safe. All the prisons, too. As soon as you get cuffed. Anyway. I passed out in the lobby whenever I had to check in for group. Every time I see my own blood like that I just . . . *oop*. The nurses started leaving a fainting couch out there for me. Literally, that's what they called it." Magda exhales with a muted laugh.

"Wait, just California and Nevada? Is Arizona making people give blood?"

"That's the thing, that's why we gotta do it this way. You and me. I told your mom we had curfew in California about a week before the blood tests started popping up, so she thought it would be better if we didn't take any chances. You don't want these people having you on record. You don't know what they're gonna do, with all that info. Know what I'm saying?"

I don't, exactly. But Magda's pinched, anxious frown tells me I'm lucky I don't.

"Your mom seems like a good person. I'd hate to see this thing follow her around for the rest of her life."

"You keep saying that."

"Saying what?"

"That my mom seems like a good person."

"Do you not think she is?"

"I-I'm not . . . I didn't say that—"

"Do you think this thing is her fault?"

"I know it's not." But there's uncertainty lurking behind my eyes. And I know Magda's seen it.

"Sometimes, in life . . . hell, I'll say it—in a *girl's life* . . . you get tangled up with people who want to control you because they've lost control of everything else. People who make you feel safe when you're not. Your mom ever know someone like that?"

The name is rancid in my mouth. All I can do is nod.

"I had someone like that, too."

"Is that where your kids are?" I immediately know I've said the wrong thing. Magda's face sags as she picks at her brittle, jaundiced fingernails.

"Nah, thank God. My aunt has them. That's why I'm going to see my cousin after this. That's his mom. Thinkin' if I can show him I've turned things around . . . Anyway."

She flashes an artificial grin, deflecting. There's the gleam of those teeth again, polished like pearls.

"You have a pretty smile," I offer in a small voice.

"Oh, thank you! That's so sweet. These weren't cheap. Full disclosure, that's part of why I've gotta make my way to my cousin's. Sometimes you gotta choose between your rent and some primo chompers. Way my teeth looked before, I couldn't even talk to the friggin' garbage man, let alone get a job interview. Kinda had no choice except to splurge. Couldn't have paid my rent much longer anyway, not without a new job—"

A checkered black and yellow cab pulls up with its muffler hanging half off. Magda's tone instantly deepens, but she doesn't stop talking, not even to draw a breath.

"Okay, here we go, here's what we do. You ready? I'm your mom and we don't have insurance and we've been on the street for about a month. You hurt your arm when a dog bit you and you broke your leg skateboarding."

"I don't know how to skateboard—"

"They're not gonna quiz you."

She rises and offers a hand to me. I don't want to take it. But I feel too faint to stand on my own.

In the cab, we're both totally silent. I'm surprised Magda knows how and when to keep her mouth shut, but she's got more self-awareness than I thought. If you can't help but spill your guts every time someone addresses you, it's probably best to say nothing at all.

I glaze over with terror when we roll up our sleeves for the blood test, just inside the hospital's revolving front entryway. Could being close to Mom have tainted my blood in some way? Hugging her? Touching her sweat?

Magda sinks to the floor after they draw her blood, getting dizzy. There's no fainting couch ready for her at this hospital. I bend over to offer my hand, but she waves me off.

"Don't worry. Someone'll bring me some crackers once we pass the test."

The technician takes our small red vials to an analysis machine behind the reception desk. I grit my teeth as the seconds tick by. Is it taking longer than usual? Is this how it always is?

I meet Magda's gaze, but she's got a smile plastered to her wan face. *Everything's gonna be fine.* How the hell does she know? What makes her think she's got all the answers?

"All right, ladies. C'mon in. How can we help you today?"

"She needs a doctor. I need a cracker," Magda says from the ground.

I call Mom before the nurse takes me back to the examination room. She answers on the first ring. "Any problems?"

"Nope."

"Have you seen a doctor yet?"

"Soon."

"Okay. I love you. Get off the phone and sit next to Magda. Try and act like you like her."

She hangs up before I can say "I love you" back.

The nurse has to give me a shot in my arm to make it numb so she can clean the wound. Magda tells me to turn my head, not to watch. She distracts me by playing cat videos on Mom's phone, holding it up so I can see. They're glitchy and load too slowly, but I'm grateful.

"Am I gonna need a tetanus shot, too?" I meekly ask the nurse, still turned away from her.

"Already done. Told ya you wouldn't feel anything."

She re-bandages my arm with fresh, clean gauze, then rises and beckons for Magda to follow her. The two of them hover in the doorway, speaking in low, grim-sounding voices. I suck in air as the bottom drops out of my stomach. We were too late. They're going to amputate. Just like Magda's stupid friend. I should've said something sooner. Should have told Mom to drop me off at a hospital somewhere and let me fend for myself.

"Oh, baby girl." Magda rushes toward me as tears spill down my cheeks. Throws her arms around my neck. "You're gonna be fine—"

"We're going to keep you here for twenty-four hours so we can get you some fluids and antibiotics." The nurse crouches down to my level. She's wearing lotion that smells like lemons. "Is that okay?"

I start crying even harder.

"I-I thought we were gonna have to . . . to . . . my arm—" I hiccup.

"No way, José." Magda kisses my wet cheek. "You're leavin' with all the same parts you walked in with."

Magda calls Mom from the hallway to give her an update. Later, after I've been admitted and I'm lying comfortably in my bed with *Oprah* flickering in the background on mute, she lets me call her, too.

"What do we do when it gets dark out?" I whisper to Mom.

"Don't be talking about that, please."

"There's nobody here, only Magda."

She's seated in a chair by the window, flipping through a rumpled, five-year-old *People* magazine. A coffee-stained Lindsay Lohan graces the cover.

"She's coming back to help me."

"Does *she* know that?"

"I told you, Mia. We worked everything out."

"But Magda passes out when she sees blood." Magda perks up at the mention of her name. Cuts me a warning glare. *Don't talk about blood.*

"She'll be fine. I promise."

I stare at Magda, nervously rolling the magazine into a tube shape, like she's about to get up and swat a fly.

"Please be nice to her. Don't . . . do anything," I whisper to Mom.

"Trust me, she's safe. She's the only way I'm getting you back, right?"

I nod, even though I know Mom can't see.

"Put her on for a sec?"

It feels like Magda's been gone for hours, and when I glance at the clock, I realize she has. The IV in my arm has started itching, and I can't find a comfortable position. Dinner is a sad attempt at a knockoff kids' Happy Meal: soggy, underdone chicken nuggets, oversalted fries, and a fruit cup that's mostly honeydew melon and one solitary grape. I wish I could eat; I haven't had a proper meal in days. But I'm too nervous about Magda. I play the scene in my head, over and over. She enters the hotel room and Mom is waiting on the other side of the door. She pounces, unable to control herself. The carpet is soaked with blood and Mom leaves red footprints all over the bathroom when she goes to take a shower after it's all over.

The nurses take my dinner tray away and change my IV bag. I switch off the TV when the news comes on. There's only one thing they talk about now.

I watch the sun sink low behind the trees in the parking lot. Almost time for curfew. What if Magda tries to make her way back and gets arrested? What if nobody comes for me and I get abandoned at the hospital and someone calls Erica and I have to live in a foster home where I have to sleep on the floor with six other kids and a nasty old woman makes us split a single can of beans for dinner?

Finally, about ten minutes after the nurse turns on my bedside lamp, Magda emerges in the doorway. Holding a tray of drinks from McDonald's.

"Hospital food sucks, so I thought I'd bail you out," she says, presenting the tray to me. "I wasn't sure if you liked chocolate or vanilla, though. I bought both."

My voice squeezes through grateful tears. "I like both."

"Then they're both for you."

"No, it's okay. I'll take the chocolate—"

"I already had one on the way over. Had to get my strength back after . . . well, you know." She nestles at the foot of my bed with a self-deprecating chuckle.

"Did you pass out?"

"Is the pope Catholic?" She hands me the chocolate milkshake first. "I don't know how you do it. Every night."

"We haven't been doing it that long." I pound the straw on the armrest of my hospital bed.

"Still."

I nurse the milkshake, enjoying the way it cools my raw throat.

"I'm not gonna tell anyone. I know you're worried. Your mom is, too," Magda whispers. "Please let her know she's safe."

"What if someone offered you money?" I say with the straw between my teeth, matching the low volume of Magda's voice. Just in case the doctor swoops in unannounced.

Magda snorts. "Like a bounty? What is this, some kinda Western shoot-'em-up?"

"I'm serious."

"I don't need that kind of money."

"What if they said they'd give you . . . something else?" She meets my probing stare. Gets a look like she's just tasted something rotten.

"I don't think I like your tone, baby girl."

"Sorry."

We're silent for a moment, except for the slurp of my straw.

"What happened to your friend? The one with the arm?" I nudge the subject in a new direction. "Did she learn how to do everything with her other hand, or—?"

"She's okay. Surviving. You know."

The corner of Magda's mouth sags.

"It was you, wasn't it?"

She shrugs.

"You've still got both your arms. You lied."

"Got you out the door, didn't it?" She reaches for the other milkshake. "Everything else was true, though. I could've died that day, easy."

"But . . . how? I don't get it."

Magda sighs. Relinquishes the milkshake to me after indulging in a single sip.

"C'mon, honey." She taps the crease of her bony elbow with two fingers.

She's having trouble looking me in the face. There's an extra straw on the drink tray. I stick it into my boot to scratch an unreachable itch.

"I still don't know why you're helping us. I mean . . . I know the money part. But the stuff they say on the news . . . all of it's true, you know—"

"You don't have to be some kinda saint to save someone."

I'm quiet as I mull it over. I nod, conceding. "I still think you should be careful, though."

She raises her milkshake like a glass of champagne. "Right back atcha, honey."

I'm released the next morning. Magda stays at the hotel that night, and Mom orders us a mountain of Chinese takeout for dinner. We watch *Titanic* on the TV, which takes over five hours with commercials. I fall asleep but Mom and Magda stay awake to finish the whole thing, whispering to each other and laughing into pillows.

I sleep through the night for the first time in weeks.

The following evening, Magda's cousin Rich picks us up in a sputtery old SUV to take us all to Tucson. He sticks to a windy, pitch-dark desert back road to avoid the cops. He says the police aren't nearly as strict about curfew if you're in your car, but if they see you drive past, they *do* have to pull you over. I don't think Magda's told him about Mom. I wonder if he can guess, though, considering Magda's insistence that he come pick us up at night. Mom chews her nails to the quick on the ride south.

At one point, Rich pulls over without a word. It's dead silent, aside from the distant call of a coyote and Magda's gentle snore up front. I hold my breath as his feet crunch against the gravelly sand. Mom grasps my hand as terror pulses behind her dark eyes. What is he doing? Is he going to kill us? Sell us? Is *he* a Sara, too?

"Aw, suck a sack o' dicks . . ." Rich mutters as he kicks one of the tires. He pops the trunk, and Mom whirls around to face him. I hope she hasn't just shown him her teeth.

"Oh, shit. Sorry to wake ya," Rich whispers as he snags a tire iron and a spare. "I'll just be a sec."

Mom lets out a breath and rests her head on my shoulder. I take her hand, damp against mine. I wonder if we'll ever trust anyone again.

☾ ☾ ☾

We decide to stop running. Forget Mexico. The curfew's not going to let up anytime soon. It's safer to stay put, and Tucson doesn't seem so bad. A couple of months after we've settled in, I ask Mom if we can go visit Magda at the ostrich farm.

"I don't think that's a good idea," she says.

"I miss her. You should call her and see what she's up to."

"I said no, Mia."

I wait to ask again, the following night. This time, Mom gets angry. She pounds the table and stalks around the kitchen like a tiger in a cage.

"We can't see Magda. She's not here anymore. Please stop asking."

"What do you mean she's *not here*? Did she move? Has she been talking to you?"

She doesn't say anything else.

"Is she dead?"

"She had a lot of problems. You know that."

"Why didn't you tell me?" Still, she doesn't say anything. "You should have told me. I can't believe you didn't—"

"I didn't want to make you sad."

She rinses her bloodstained tumbler in the sink and closes the door to her room.

I think about it every day for the rest of that year. How she died. When. Where. Whether she was alone. I can't stop wondering.

I also know, deep down, that I don't need to.

NOW

I don't know why there's so much traffic. It's a Saturday. Where are all these people going on a goddamn Saturday?

I squirm in my seat, making crescent-shaped dents with my fingernails in the leather steering wheel. Every time the car inches forward, I check my phone for service. But there's nothing. I don't know how else to get ahold of her, to tell her I'm on my way, that I'm all right. That she doesn't need to go outside.

A fire truck wails past, then an ambulance. But not a black one. This is a regular accident. A traffic cop stands in the middle of the freeway, waving our stop-and-go daisy chain over to the left. The right lane is closed.

Another couple of inches. Check the phone. Nothing.

I don't know how I thought I'd pull this off. I should have known I couldn't trust myself to leave on time. I thought if I didn't drink or smoke weed or anything like that, I'd be all right. But what I did instead could hardly be described as sober. My throat is dry and scratchy as scorching-hot shame lurches from my belly.

I cut my wheel and weave around the traffic cop. Check the phone. There's one bar.

I jump out of my skin and dial out. CONNECTING flashes across the screen. Connecting . . . connecting . . .

I'm surprised when my lights flick on automatically. It takes me a second to realize they're programmed to do this the moment it starts to get dark out. I've always been home by now.

Connecting . . . connecting . . .

The cars in front of me start to accelerate. But the Subaru I'm trailing is too busy rubbernecking at the accident: an SUV that's rear-ended a Prius.

I lean on my horn, enjoying the way the obnoxious moan reverberates between my ears.

The call connects, and the other end rings. I don't hear it right away, because I'm still ramming my elbow into the steering wheel.

"H-h-h . . . M-Mia?" She's answered, but the sound is completely garbled.

"Mom. I'm sorry. I'm on my way, okay?" Words rush from my mouth in double time. "I got called in to work and I just left but there's an accident. I'll be home soon. Twenty minutes at the most. Maybe less."

Twenty minutes if I fucking floor it.

"Mom?"

"M-m . . . You need . . . I-I . . . S-s—"

The call disconnects.

I drift to the right, tear past the Subaru, and swerve back in front of it, spitting sand from my wheels. The speedometer climbs past eighty. Eighty-five. Ninety. Ninety-five. . . .

She's inconsolable when I burst through the door, gasping for air and prowling the shadowy foyer as she watches the driveway for my headlights. I've never seen her skin so pale. Not since those first few unbearable nights after Devon left, with the chewing gum and the sleeping pills.

I sprint right past her, toward the kitchen, ripping off my jacket. But she's already seized a fistful of my hair. I yelp as it catches and she drags me back toward her. My tiptoes graze the floor, just barely.

"Where the hell were you?"

My body goes rigid, like I'm reflexively playing possum.

"Mom, I promise I'll do it fast. Just let me go so I can—"

I feel as though I'm watching myself through a pane of frosted glass, like I'm not really here. I always knew she could do this. Whether she *would* . . .

She whips me around by the neck, so I'm facing her. "What is this, are you *testing me*?" Her spittle clings to my eyelashes. "Do you *want me* to go out there? I'm only doing this for you, you know. I don't have to—"

"No, no, I know. And thank you. For waiting. I just—"

She grips my hair tighter and twists it between her fingers. My scalp prickles and burns.

"Where. Were you."

"I-I had to work. I told you, on the phone. Sandy called me this morning and asked if—"

She breaks my gaze and relief courses through me. But not for long. Something else has pulled her focus—to the floor. To my jacket on the floor—the *rose quartz* on the floor, which was in my pocket.

She arches her brow with a disapproving sniff, as though she's can smell where it's been. Where *I've* been.

I ramble, desperate to distract. "Anyway, I had to cover for someone at the store and I *told* Sandy I couldn't stay till close but then she left and she had the keys and there was nobody else to—"

Her eyes are still stuck to the stone. She doesn't even blink.

I'm not sure if I should comment on it. Come up with some story about where it came from. Or if that might make things worse. She's pulled my hair so tight I can feel blood pooling in the follicles.

"You're wearing *makeup*."

"You bought it for me."

"Who was texting you last night?"

Her free hand moves to my neck and she wraps her fingers around my throat, one at a time. But she doesn't squeeze. Not yet.

"Who is he?"

"Nobody! I promise you, cross my fucking heart, Mom. There's *no guy*."

She gouges me with her gaze. But I think she believes me. Because it's true.

At last, she releases me. I want to collapse into a heap on the floor, but I can't show her how much she just scared me.

I race to get the draw started, pawing around for the needle and disinfectant from the pantry. While my back is turned, she bends over and picks up the rose quartz. I spin to face her and lose my breath, watching as she rolls it around in her palm.

"I'm trying so hard not to let you down, Mia."

I wince as I stick myself with the needle. The tourniquet wasn't tight enough. I almost missed the vein.

"You haven't. I promise. You being here is proof of that." And yet, I can't look at her.

Blood starts flowing into the reservoir. I've forgotten to set a timer. But I can eyeball it. I'll give extra tonight. That was my plan, anyway. Before all this.

"But if you want things to stay the way they are, if you want us to be *safe*, you need to stick to the rules. No exceptions. Ever."

I'm silent. Watching the blood bag swell. She paces in circles around the table, hunched over with her arms crossed like a shield against her hunger. Still clutching Jade's quartz.

A hundred different vicious insults burn in the back of my throat. It's not safe to say anything till she's fed, though. I can't talk back and tell her what a hypocrite she is, that none of this would have happened if *she* hadn't broken the rules first.

I wonder what that's like, to know someone can't fight back. To take their silence as concession.

"Y'know, you were right," she says. I lift my head with a curious frown. She must have known that would get my attention. "I thought about what you said. Last night. I don't want to lose the house. Or the restaurant. Or you."

"Okay . . ." I'm getting dizzy. I wonder how much blood is in that bag. I've started to lose my grip on time.

"If it comes down to it . . . I choose *you*, okay? Every time."

"Yeah . . . me, too," I mumble.

"Then why is this happening to us?" She buries her face in her hands. "Everything feels so different. *You*, you're different—"

"I'm sorry. I don't think I'm different. I feel the same—"

"You need to be here for me, Mia."

"I'm here! I'm right here and I promise I'll never be late for you again."

She raises her head. Her lips are like two bruise-colored slices of plum as she squeezes the quartz in her fist. A crack starts to form, a jagged fissure right through the center like a vein about to burst.

I notice she's looking at my hands. I'm not sure why . . . till I glimpse Jade's ring on my finger.

"Please just tell me where you were. I swear I won't get mad."

"Mom, I was at work. I'm not lying to you." I hide my hands in my lap.

Neither of us says anything. No sound except the cold clink of the leaky faucet against one of my dirty bowls in the sink.

"Where's the cup . . ." She stands and starts throwing open the cupboards.

"I forgot to do the dishes. Sorry. I'll do them after I—"

"It's fine."

Mom grabs the reservoir off the table. I hardly have enough time to dislodge the needle myself before she tears it from my arm.

She drinks directly from the bag, squeezing it like one of those watered-down portable yogurts she used to pack in my school lunch.

I stagger upright, clinging to the countertop for support. I knock a jar of peanut butter from the pantry shelf and plunge in a spoon, desperate for sugar. Lick it clean.

Mom sits, still guzzling from the bag. She sighs, posture loosening, and releases the quartz from her fist. It rolls out onto the table in three separate, craggy pieces.

I stare at it from across the room, waiting for her to apologize or acknowledge it at all. I turn toward the sink so she doesn't see the tears welling.

"Do you want to do some painting? Before I go to work?" she pipes up in a hoarse whisper.

"I-I'm . . . kinda—" My words are thick and sluggish, like they're stuck to the roof of my mouth with all that peanut butter. My gaze rests on an engorged water droplet hanging from the faucet. It comes apart and tumbles into the dirty cereal bowl as a new one forms.

"We could watch a movie. Or binge some old *Jeopardy!* episodes—"

Finally, I glance over at her. She's sucking her teeth like she always does, filling the silence with a strained, wet squeak. She catches me staring and smiles.

"I don't feel good." I shove my shaky hands into my sleeves as I slouch toward the bathroom. I realize I forgot to take my iron supplements, but I can't bring myself to go back the way I came.

Clumps of hair circle the shower drain as I gently shampoo my bloody scalp, biting my lip through the sting. I steady myself against the slick tile wall, studying the peaches-and-cream clouds on the ceiling through a veil of steam. I start to dry-heave and sink to the bottom of the tub, letting the high-pressure water assault my spine.

Mom is right. Things are different.

But not the way she thinks.

She's the one who's started changing. All I'm doing is changing in response. Adapting.

I lace my fingers between my toes and rest my chin on top of my knees. Watch my hair congeal in the drain like bloody gristle.

She hurt me because she's sick.

Right?

Because I was late and she was starving. Because she's sick.

Right?

A knock at the door. Mom enters without waiting for me to respond.

I watch her shadow dance from the other side of the shower curtain. I shiver at the bottom of the tub and draw my knees toward my breasts, into an egg shape.

"I'm going to work, Mia," she says. So soft I can barely hear her over the thudding water. "You can call Luke and ask him. I'm gonna be there."

"Good." I squeeze my egg shape even smaller.

"I'm sorry we had a fight."

Is that what she thinks happened? That *we* had a fight? She pulled my hair out of my head.

But I started it. Didn't I? I was late. I was supposed to be here.

"Mia?"

"Me, too. I'm sorry, too."

She draws back the curtain and I jump. I can't help it. She frowns at me, huddled on the floor of the tub.

"You okay?"

How am I supposed to answer? Can't she see all the blood in the water?

"Yeah."

"Aren't you cold?"

"I'm fine."

She just stares at me.

Finally, she pulls the curtain shut. I smell perfume in the air as she spritzes herself before she leaves. It mixes with the steam, making me gag.

Danger. Danger. Danger. There goes my heart again, throbbing against my thighs.

I tuck into bed with my wet, stringy hair wrapped tight in a towel to clot the bleeding.

For some reason I can't stop thinking about Jade's friend Brian. A "solid guy." A person whose goodness Jade believed in no matter what. She still believes in it.

But I'm not so sure.

We need to believe that everyone we give our love to is a good person. But if they change . . . and if that change hurts us . . . what then? Are they still good, deep down? Because they "weren't always like this"?

When I shuffle through the memories, when everything is quiet and I dare to think back on that first harrowing year we spent together after the turn . . . I wonder how many signs I missed. I believed she'd never hurt me. But I saw her hurt other people. I saw what would happen if someone threatened us.

Does she think I'm that someone now?

Am I?

I sit up and seize my prescription bottle from the nightstand. I crunch two Ambien, then settle back in, slowly, painfully unwinding the towel from my hair. What's left of it.

I want to talk to Jade. Want to ask her how she did what she did. How long she planned, how she made sure her family would be okay. Granted, she had less to worry about. Nobody in her family was infected. Then again, maybe that means she worried even more.

I wonder where she went first. She mentioned Chicago, someone named Gabi. How much money did it cost to get there? Did she have a car? Did she make a plan or did she just disappear on foot one night with a backpack full of clothes and a toothbrush?

I know I couldn't do it that way. If I even dreamed of doing it. Whatever "it" means. I'd have to make one hell of a plan. I'd have to start moving money from our joint bank account, slowly. Maybe request a paycheck advance from the Book Bunker and pick up extra shifts. I couldn't take the car because Mom could report it as stolen. I'd have to hop on a bus or a train or something.

But all of that is possible. I *could* do all those things. I tell myself I won't, but it's the fact that I *could*. I've never thought about "could" before.

I pull the blankets over me. There's a faint shimmer in my chest, like an ember warming my body with every breath I take. Maybe it's just the pills. But maybe it's hope.

The night I saw Jade's video on Instagram, when I heard about her escape from Florida, I knew it meant something—knew *she* meant something. That invisible thread pulling us closer wasn't wrapped around *her* finger. It was around mine. When I learned the truth about her, I decided right then that we had to be together. No matter what "together" meant. This is why Jade is here. She's going to show me the way out.

I pull out my phone. I'll ask her right now, while I'm feeling brave. It rings four times, then goes to voicemail. She's probably still jamming outside. I'm sure she'll try me when she sees my missed call.

Then again, maybe she should know this isn't an ordinary situation. I'm not just calling to say good night. Or ask when we're going to see each other. We should try to see each other as soon as possible, though. Tomorrow. I should definitely see if she's free tomorrow.

I opt for a follow-up text, which feels a little shameless but the drugs help with that. I know she'll get it once I tell her what's happening.

I pause, fingers hovering over the keypad. What *am* I going to tell her, though? The whole truth? No, just enough so she knows it's serious. I'll tell her I'm worried I can't stay here anymore. That the reason I've been so shy is because I know if I fall headfirst into whatever this is, I'll have to blow my whole life up. But I think I'm ready. Even if I'm not ready, I *want to be*. I'm ready to be ready.

I type way more than I should, and the wispy clouds in my head are at least partially to blame. But I've said everything I want to say.

> My life is an absolute catastrophe but that doesn't mean I don't want to see you. Since we met I've started wondering if it's time to make some big changes. I'm inspired by how you left home and everything. It would be awesome to see you tomorrow, if you're around. I have a lot of questions and I would really love to spend some time together. Thanks for a great day today. I'll be thinking about it for a long time. Xx

I've never signed a text, or any kind of correspondence, with kisses before. Again, I blame the Ambien. I don't even reread it. Just hit send.

Mom wakes me a few hours later, home from work, watching *West Side Story* out in the living room. I can hear her humming along.

Good night, good night. Sleep well and when you dream, dream of me—

I can't get back to sleep, because I'm checking my phone every five minutes. Jade still hasn't replied.

I bury my face into my pillow, groaning as I bump my bald spot the wrong way. Of course she's not going to write back. She's drinking and smoking and singing her heart out with her friends under the stars. I'm not a part of that. I'd do anything for some sort of "unsend" button. I'm already ashamed of rereading it in our text chain next time she replies, probably about something completely unrelated two weeks from now.

I feel stupid for letting myself have these thoughts about running away. For giving myself permission to feel like this. I know Mom is still awake. I wonder what it would be like to talk to her about Jade. About anything that didn't have to do with her.

I turn on a lamp and try to read. I realize I haven't finished a book in weeks—a lifetime for me. But my vision is blurry from the medication. The words melt together on the page. All I can do is stare at the ceiling, at those weak green glow-in-the-dark star stickers. My childlike, sloppy attempt at the Big Dipper.

Sunlight staggers through the curtains. I have no idea if I've been sleeping, but it feels like waking up when my phone buzzes between my sheets.

She texted me back. I open it, and a wave of relief hits me as I read. I imagine her saying the words aloud.

I am SO sorry I missed this. I hope you slept
ok. Are you around tonight/at the bookstore? I
have to go to Sbux later to pick up my shit (did
I mention I was officially fired lolol). Lemme
know. ♥

Finally, I close my eyes, and my body succumbs to a dreamless sleep.

☾ ☾ ☾

Relief doesn't last long. I drive to work with a beanie over my patchy hair and a sharp kernel of guilt inside me. If I meet Jade tonight, she'll expect me to reveal myself and what's been troubling me. I won't tell her *everything*. But to give voice to it, even the smallest part of it, to speak my ache for freedom into existence . . . Last night I wanted to embrace it, but in the light of day it all feels wrong. It *is* wrong. Even if I don't say the words "My mom is a Sara," I'm telling the secret by telling someone how the secret makes me feel.

I catch myself bargaining again as I ring up customers and watch the clock: It's okay to be with her. It's even okay if I tell her what's really happening with me. I can say how I feel. *But I don't have to act on it*. I don't have to leave home, even if I think I want to. It's not like I've promised someone I'm going to do it. I haven't made a commitment or signed some sort of contract.

The plan is to meet her at eight. After I've done the draw. After Mom's gone to work. I assume she actually showed last night and hopefully she'll go back again tonight. She needs to keep things relatively stable if I'm going to make a plan. Even though I'm not making a plan. Because I'm not actually acting on any of this.

I get home after work with plenty of time to spare. If I want to go out again later, nothing can derail the ritual. This needs to feel like a normal night.

We sit across from each other, both of us knowing we should probably say something.

She stares out the window instead of at me or the blood bag. I trace the scuff marks on the dirty linoleum floor with my bare toe. An owl outside announces the moonrise.

I wonder when we'll do this for the last time. Whether one of us will sit down at the table, but the other won't show. I wonder if she thought last night was the end. I imagine her pacing the hall like a soon-to-be widow on the beach, wringing her hands, fearing the worst. I feel sad for her, almost forgive her for the way she reacted.

The timer pierces the silence, and she drinks. I remembered to give her the straw this time. I am so thoughtful. So good. Finally, she casts me a thin, pursed smile.

She rinses her cup, then squeezes my shoulder as she passes the table. Everything inside me tenses. But it's a gentle touch. Her lips graze the top of my head, like I'm still six inches shorter than she is.

"Thanks, baby," she says into my hair. "I love you."

"You, too." I always seem to respond that way now.

Every time I say it, I have that feeling again like I'm watching myself through a foggy window. Not really here.

☾ ☾ ☾

I'm leaning against Jade's green minivan parked between the Starbucks and the bookstore, watching her rummage around in her tote for her vape so she can take a pre-dinner hit. She offered to pick me up, but I thought it might be better if I took an Uber to meet her. As though I feared she might sense what was going on inside my house by looking at the outside of it.

"Are margaritas okay? Tacos?"

I'm relieved she has suggested the one drink I have some experience with—even though the results were mixed.

"Sounds great."

She unearths the vape from her bag and tugs from it. Then offers it to me.

"Oh, I'm not . . . What's in it?"

"Just tobacco, no weed. It's orange flavored."

I shrug and pluck it from between her fingers. Why not. She smiles and I'm not sure why, till I notice she's looking down at my hand. I'm still wearing her ring.

"Sorry, I didn't . . . Do you want it back?"

"Why would I want it back?" She moves my hair behind my back, exposing my bare shoulder. Runs the ridge of her nail between my goose bumps.

I pull from the vape, but I get the sense I didn't do it right. I think I'm supposed to inhale deeper. The sweet, sticky smoke tastes good, though. I breathe it out through my nostrils as I hand the vape back to her, letting it tickle my sinuses. Working very hard not to cough.

Jade takes my hand, curling her fingers around mine. Swings our arms back and forth like two kids skipping outside together for recess. I don't ever want to let go.

We bullshit our way through the first round of margaritas and guacamole. We rehash Steve's nastiness. We discuss her wardrobe for Cloak and Dagger and a secret cover song she wants to add to the set list, a song Tony hates that I've never heard of called "Heaven or Las Vegas." Someone has a birthday and a mariachi band appears seemingly out of nowhere to serenade them with a slice of cake. They're loud and we have to stop talking for a minute. My ears burn as I wonder if it's time for me to pivot the conversation.

When our second round arrives, Jade raises her glass to me. Narrows her blue-rimmed eyes with utmost seriousness.

"Here's to you," she says, and clears her throat like she's about to launch into some sort of monologue. I'm not sure whether to cringe or swoon.

". . . For?"

"Being brave as shit. Texting me last night and telling me all that stuff."

I feel naked under her gaze. Not in a good way. I wish she would stop.

"It took me *years* to open up to people about my whole deal. Nobody knew how me and my sisters were living. But as soon as I said something to someone . . . good things started to happen. So—" She bumps her glass higher. "Hear, hear."

I meet her salt-rimmed glass in the middle of the table. We clink, and tears well in my eyes. Before I can get a grip, before I can push them down, they come pouring down my face. Horrified, I take a long drink to hide my sudden, uncontrollable sniffling. But I'm sure she's noticed.

She doesn't say anything. Just sips her margarita with a calm, reassuring tilt of her head. Like she's already listening and all I have to do is start speaking.

When I still don't, she reaches across the table for my hand. Gently places her own on top of it like a warm blanket.

A response finally stumbles from my mouth. "Thanks. Um . . . sorry. I just . . . What I was trying to say last night was that . . . I mean, I-I guess you've gone through something like this before and I had a feeling you might—"

The table starts vibrating and cuts me off. It's coming from Jade's phone, sitting on the other side of her plate. She seizes it, seething, as the ringtone kicks in.

"I swear to God . . ." She hits ignore, but for an instant I'm able to see **Gabi** flashing across the screen.

"I'm sorry. Keep going. You had a feeling I might—?" She fixes her eyes to mine, making sure I know I've got her full attention.

"You might know how to . . . I mean, not that I'm *actually* gonna go anywhere—"

"But you've thought about it."

I gulp my drink, then nod.

"I thought about it for a long time, too," she says. "Like, probably at least a year. My mom always used to say, 'If you don't know what to do yet, don't do anything.' So I waited till I knew exactly what I was going to do."

Our dinner arrives, and we pause till the server clears the way. Jade heaps sour cream onto her tacos as she elaborates.

"There's always a moment, always that one *really fucking terrible day* when you just know you're done. I don't know if you've had yours yet or if you know yours is coming. But if you're here talking to me about it, I'm guessing it's one or the other."

"Last night was pretty bad," I mumble.

"So what's the deal? It's your mom, right?"

I nod. Stabbing black beans with my fork one at a time but not eating them.

"She seems kind of intense with your schedule."

I nod again. Maybe we can do this like a game of Twenty Questions.

"Was she upset when you came out?"

I swallow in the wrong direction and cough.

"Oh, she doesn't . . . I haven't . . . We don't talk about that stuff."

"So she's not the weird religious heebie-jeebie type."

"No, we're not like that. I-I mean, she used to be Mormon. As a kid. But then she got kicked out and my gram left with her because my grandpa was dead and he was the only thing keeping her there and she hated everyone anyway, so . . ." Shit. I'm rambling. "Anyway. It's not that."

She probes me with her blue-winged gaze. As though to say, *Then what is it?*

"My mom is just . . . I think she's sick." That's as much as I think I can muster. "I mean, she is. And I have to take care of her. But she doesn't listen to me. She picks fights all the time. She doesn't let me do anything or go anywhere or—"

"How old are you?" Jade asks.

"Twenty-three—"

"Did you ever go to college?"

I shake my head.

"Did you want to?"

"I don't really know. Maybe? I always knew I probably couldn't, so I was never like, dreaming about what I was gonna major in or anything."

Jade nods. "I could tell you'd been here for a while."

I take another long drink from my glass, sucking grains of salt from my lips. I'm glad I didn't drive here. There's a good chance I'm going to want another.

"So . . . okay. You say she's sick." Jade untangles my explanation as she chews. "Sick with what? Is it like, a mental thing?"

I nod, going along with it. Thank God she didn't just say what I thought she was going to say.

"So, if you tried to have a rational discussion about moving out and doing your own thing, that would probably send her into a tailspin, yeah?"

I nod.

Jade leans in, lowering her voice. "Has she ever like . . . hurt you? Physically?"

The scabs on my scalp prickle underneath my beanie and I fight the urge to scratch them. I should be careful about how I answer this one.

Thankfully, Jade's phone saves me. Three shrill chimes ring in succession. Even the notification sounds pissed off.

"Wow, I'm really sorry. Lemme put it on silent—"

Jade pounds out a curt reply. I can't help but try to sneak a subtle peek.

"I stupidly told Gabi I'd swing through Chicago on the tour which made her think I was moving back for some reason and now it's like . . . this whole thing."

"Oh . . . The tour's happening?" There's a hollow in my chest, and not just because of Gabi. Will Jade come back to Arizona, after it's over? Probably not. It's not like she's from here.

"Yeah, we're gonna get going after Cloak and Dagger. It's a

small thing. Small venues. But it'll be good. I want to keep up the momentum after the festival."

She tucks her phone into her bag, then studies me.

"I meant to talk to you about it. Tonight, actually. Obviously this is all just . . . it's weird timing. Our whole . . . yeah."

"Yeah."

"But anyway, here's what I propose. If you're looking for an out, and if you think you can get your shit together within the next couple weeks . . . you can come with us."

"Come with you like . . . on the tour?"

"I mean it would just be you, me, and Tony in the van for a few months. Probably a lot of crappy hotels. Nothing glamorous. But if you need a breather from what's going on here—"

I don't say anything for a moment. Jade flings a jumble of words into the silence. Almost sounds embarrassed.

"I-I mean obviously if you're not ready to . . . I know it feels really fast. It's just, when you texted me last night and said you were thinking of leaving home, this kinda felt like the perfect . . . I want to help if I can. The way somebody once helped me. But—"

"Gabi?"

"Yeah. She was that person for me." She takes my hand again, this time under the table. "I was hoping maybe I could be that person for you."

I stare at our joined hands. Something feels off.

"But you don't talk to Gabi anymore."

"Sure I do. I was just talking to her earlier. Which is why she's so mad."

"You know what I mean."

Jade lifts her hand from mine and I get the sense I've done something wrong. I blame the tequila for my sudden courage to prod this particular topic.

"She just . . . she got weird. She thought I was going to stay in Chicago forever. Every time I traveled somewhere, or even *talked* about it, she just kinda . . . yeah. And I'd say to her like, 'You of all people should know this is literally why I left home.' But she just kept doing it. So now . . . yeah. I'm not gonna come back after this. Not for good, anyway. Just gonna swing through and grab some of my stuff."

"Right."

"I'm sorry. Is that okay?"

"Is what okay?"

"That she's . . . y'know. A *presence*." She sips her drink then quickly adds, "For now."

I have no idea what she means by that. A presence. As if we're in a creaky old house filled with cold spots. But the qualifier calms my nerves. They're not together. She's shedding her. I decide not to ask any more questions. I don't need to. She's here with me, toasting me like it's my birthday, holding my hand. I remind myself nothing new can start unless something old ends. If she needs to talk about it, I'm prepared to listen. I can hold up my end of this relationship. I smile at her, and she scrunches her nose in reply. I'll never get tired of seeing her make that face.

We huddle in our corner booth for the next two hours as the restaurant empties out. Twining our legs under the table, nursing ice water with lemon between our margaritas. Jade has laid out a whole plan for me and I've been more than happy to listen. I haven't agreed to it. Not in the least bit. But I'm enjoying the fantasy. We'll kick things off in Vegas, then make our way to LA, where we'll splurge on a fancy beachside rental for a night. Then we'll drive up the Pacific coast and camp among the redwoods somewhere. I've never been camping before, with a tent and a fire and all that. After that, Portland and Seattle. Then east, through Chicago, where we'll eat deep-dish pizza and avoid Gabi. New York is the final stop. Neither of us has ever been there.

"Maybe we could just stay," she wonders aloud, licking the salt from the rim of her glass. Too drunk to be subtle about it. I wonder what would happen if I reached across the table right now, grabbed her by the collar, and pressed my mouth to hers. I squint like I'm deep in concentration, as though there's a way I might telepathically convey the image to her.

"I have a friend who just opened this recording studio in Queens and keeps trying to offer me a job," she goes on. Definitely didn't receive my telepathic message. "It could be cool. I dunno."

"I wanna see the Rockettes," I slur with a faraway sigh.

"I'll bet ya do." She waggles her eyebrows and tosses a tortilla-chip shard at me. I try to catch it between my lips but it's not even close.

I'm almost angry at myself for my impatience. The way I flail for our first kiss like an amateur thief, grabby and anxious, as though I'm terrified the opportunity will slip through my fingers.

That's not to say it is a bad kiss.

I might be bad.

But the kiss, in and of itself, lives up to its promise.

As soon as we're out in the parking lot, I make my move. Leaning on the hood of her minivan for support. My legs betray me as I seize her wrist and pull her toward me. It's less of a kiss and more of an offering. An invitation. I'm not even sure my lips make contact with hers at first. They just hover there. She sucks in air, as surprised as I am, and we're so close I can feel the fine hair beneath her nose quiver as she exhales.

She opens her mouth. I have to remind myself it's time to close my eyes. She's a good two inches shorter than I am, which I hadn't noticed before. She winds her arms behind my neck, balancing on her toes. Her tongue is salty as it finds its way to mine, and I imagine I've just been pulled beneath the waves by a terrifying and beautiful mermaid, lungs full of seawater.

She slides her knee between my legs again. Yes. This. I've been aching for this. But then . . . My hat. She starts pulling my hat off my head. I claw for her hands behind my head and tear my lips from hers.

"What's up?" Her eyes are bleary, like I've just woken her from a deep sleep.

"I . . . nothing. I-I just wanna—"

I yank the cap back on. What's left of my hair flickers with static electricity.

"It's fine, never mind."

"You don't seem fine."

"Can you please not worry about it?" I snap, instantly regretful.

Her eyes scrape over me and I'm not sure if she feels sorry for me or put out. Either way, it's not how she was looking at me a minute ago.

I ease back toward her, slipping my arms around her waist. Hoping we can sail past it. But she's tense now. She peers over her shoulder, gnawing on her lip.

"Hang on. Do you feel like someone's creeping on us?"

There are a couple of stray cars at the opposite end of the lot: stragglers hitting the Starbucks before it closes at eleven. Otherwise, we're alone.

"Um . . . I don't see anyone. But it's okay if you want to—" She must be saying that because she wants to stop and doesn't want to be rude. I know this is all my fault.

"I'm serious. Shhh."

She scans the area. It's perfectly silent, like we're sealed in a chamber with a star-studded ceiling. Even the coyotes have gone quiet.

At that moment, a cop car winds around the corner, making slow, deliberate circles around the lot. Just doing a regular patrol. Who knows how long those pervs were watching us, though. My skin crawls, and Jade rolls her eyes.

"C'mon, I'll give you a ride home," she says as the squad car peels off in the opposite direction.

"It's fine, I'll get an Uber." I fumble for my phone without looking at her and request a ride.

"Please come with me?"

"Look it's just . . . it's my house, okay? I don't think you should come to my house."

"Okay," she says, letting out a sigh. "I'm glad you told me that, Mia."

She unlocks her car but doesn't get in right away. Her stare burns through me.

"After Cloak and Dagger, we can do this, all right? I'm here for you."

She opens her arms to me. I shuffle forward and fall into them as my eyes sting with the threat of tears.

"You're pretty drunk, maybe you shouldn't drive."

"Nah, my tolerance is solid." She winks. The only person I've ever known who doesn't look completely moronic when they do that. "I probably just seem that way."

She braids her fingers between mine and kisses me.

I feel my pocket vibrate. My ride is approaching.

"Sorry . . ."

"Call me this week. We'll make plans for the night of the show."

"Can't wait." And I mean it. Now that I've had this, now that I've tasted her, I don't think I can subsist on the simple things that used to give me joy. I'm going to starve this week.

I head across the parking lot, back toward the restaurant, overwhelmed by a sudden urge to twirl around on my tiptoes. *Not now,* I laugh to myself. *At least wait till she's gone, you idiot.*

I catch her wave from the corner of my eye. I really hope she's okay to drive. I have no idea what it means to have "solid" tolerance.

I can already smell the campfire we'll build among the redwoods. We'll drive up the slate-blue coast and I'll prop my feet up on the dash of the minivan, cracking the window for a breath of cold, pine-soaked air. We'll string a hammock between the trees and when it gets dark we'll curl together like two vines and watch the stars come out. We'll—

"She's getting away, you know."

The voice is like a fist down my throat, punching toward my heart.

I know who's behind me. I'm totally disoriented, lost in time. I am ten years old. A hundred. Not even born yet. . . .

"You're incredibly shitty at this. Didn't your mom show you how?"

My ride is right around the corner. I should run. Not even turn around to look at him.

Devon materializes in front of me. Blocking my way forward. I should have known I'd fuck myself by hesitating. His stormy eyes flick to mine and I have to bite my tongue to keep the nausea down. He's the same, exactly the same. But of course he is. I don't know why I was expecting someone older, someone with thinning hair and atrophied muscles. Someone I could escape from or even fight. He's the same person I watched from my window that night in Salt Lake City, stomping on that broken body with his blood-soaked boot.

"Stop following me." I deepen my voice and square my shoulders. He laughs in my face.

"Calm down. Jesus. I wasn't. Explicitly."

"How long have you been—?"

"I like to try and poach from that Starbucks over there. Before people go in. Which is what I assumed *you* were doing. Till I realized what you were . . . y'know. Doing." That wolfish grin, followed by an innocent shrug.

My mouth goes dry as the taste of fear creeps across my tongue. Bitter, like iron.

"Anyway, when I saw you, I thought . . . okay, let's see how this goes. And, predictably, you're a fucking mess."

"See how *what* goes?" He replies with a blank stare. "What did you just say? About my mom?"

"She told me she was gonna pull the trigger Friday night, so I figured I'd give you two some space while you . . . y'know . . ." He waves a dismissive hand in front of my face. "*Adjusted.*"

I fight for breath, drowning in his words.

"Actually, you look *great* for forty-eight hours." He wets his lips as his eyes sweep over me. "Really great." I clench my clammy fists inside my sleeves.

My mind races as the pieces interlock. Mom said she had a plan. Wouldn't tell me what it was. Devon thinks I'm a Sara. Fucking shit. *Did Mom tell Devon she was going to turn me into a Sara?*

"Thanks, I guess," I mumble, tight with panic. I need to play along. If Devon realizes I haven't been turned yet, he might try to do it himself.

My phone vibrates inside my sleeve, and I wriggle it out for a quick glance. *Your driver has departed.* Shit. I didn't make it back to the restaurant in time.

I give the parking lot a panicked once-over. Someone's turned off the lights at the Starbucks, and the last customers are gone. I hope that squad car will make another circle. But I don't see it anywhere. We're alone.

"Do you want to make this work, Mia?" He reclaims my attention with a stern glare, like he's playing the role of a disappointed teacher. Folds his arms across his chest. I glimpse those faded stick-and-pokes bordering his sleeve, green like old bruises.

"I-I don't . . . I mean, yeah. Of course I do—" I'm not sure where he's going with this.

To my surprise, his face softens. "Look, you've had a hard time. With your mom and everything. You shouldn't have had to deal with all that. I hope you know she did this to help you. She wanted to change your life."

His words slice straight through me. "I-I know."

I'm woozy, as if I just downed another stiff drink. Nobody's ever put it that way. He's not wrong. Being like Mom *would* change my life.

My rigid body loosens as I picture a day that doesn't revolve around counting the hours and watching the sun. Watching *her*. What would I do with all that freedom? Who could I become?

I could let him do it. Right now. God, it would be so easy. . . .

I blink and fight to straighten my posture. What the hell is wrong with me? He gets on my level for all of two seconds and *this* is how I react? I understand it now, this power he holds over Mom, over everyone he's ever met. But not me. Not tonight.

He sneers and exhales loudly through his nose, taking my silence as ungrateful stubbornness. Which I'm happy to play along with.

"I agreed to let you into the group as a favor to your mom. You need to look to her as an example. You take one look at her and you say, 'Hell yeah, sign me up.' You know? She's special, and you have that same potential. But we have rules. If you don't pull your weight, that's not gonna work for me. You *had her,* that girl was right where you . . . I don't understand why the fuck you didn't—"

"I got nervous, okay?" Then, I add, "She could've screamed."

"Not if you've done your job right." Devon frowns, chewing the underside of his lip. "Look, it's fun to dick around before you make your move. But you can't let them leave. Not without you. Follow them to the next location. Trust me. They *want you* to follow them."

I'm flush with furious heat. "Was that how you hunted my mom?"

He flinches, like I've struck him somewhere soft and vulnerable. He lets out a breath and shoves his hands into his pockets. Stares at the pavement.

"I wasn't *hunting* her. I bit her." He fumbles in his pocket for a pack of cigarettes and lifts his gaze to mine.

"What's the difference?"

"Huge." He pinches a smoke between his lips and lights it. Looks at me like he's about to offer me one but changed his mind. "Someday you'll know what I'm talking about."

There's a lapse between us as he sucks from his cigarette and I survey the parking lot for an exit strategy. I'm not going to be able to keep up the ruse much longer, and I don't think those cops are coming back.

The bookstore. I have the key to the store. If I can make it over there and get inside, Devon won't be able to follow me. He can't pass the scanner. I'll be safe. I can hide out and sift through everything I've just learned. Make a plan.

But if I scan in, he'll know I'm not a Sara.

I need to lose him before I unlock that door. He's blocking my way forward, but the store is behind me, on the other side of the horseshoe-shaped shopping center.

I slowly pivot on my heel, getting ready to turn. "I gotta go, Mom gets pissed if I'm still out by the time she gets home."

I face the bookstore, and for a second I think he's going to let me go. But he's already beside me, quick as light racing across the room when you flick the switch.

"I'll drive you. I need to talk to her."

"Oh um . . . I have the car. So I'll just . . . meet you there. I guess."

He follows my panicked gaze across the deserted parking lot. We both realize I've just said the wrong thing. The Jeep is nowhere in sight. I shiver. He smiles.

I don't know what to do except keep moving toward the store. Just need to get inside. Need to be fast. *But how?* He's so much faster. . . .

"You're gonna have to get used to me, girlie." He drapes an arm over my shoulders, latched to my side as we walk. There's that old crackle of cold electricity emanating from his hand. I lurch at his touch.

He shoots me a puzzled glance and slows down. I study his flinty eyes as they pore over my face and my hands and my feet and my—

"Step into the light." All the pretense melts from his voice. He knows.

Something in how I reacted when he touched me. I shouldn't have . . . I couldn't help it—

We're less than ten paces from the bookstore. I try to keep walking, but his grip on my arm tightens, strangling my circulation.

He yanks me under a streetlamp and aligns his face with mine. So close I swear he's about to kiss me. He breathes stale smoke into my eyes as he examines them. Searching for that telltale dark shadow. But I'm even closer to the bookstore now. A running leap with my keys in hand and I just might make it. There's the matter of the scanner, of course. But . . .

A car pulls into the lot, headlights blazing like two golden halos. In the darkness, I spot the red cherry on top. The squad car is back.

I struggle against Devon's grip, but he's not looking at me anymore. He's riveted to the cruiser, locked in the crosshairs of the driver's gaze.

He drops my arm and spins away from the light.

His whisper cuts the darkness. "Don't. Fucking. Move."

But I'm already reaching into my bag, curling my fingers around my keys one by one so they don't jingle.

I spring toward the door, half blind in the approaching headlights. I've got the keys in my right hand as I ready my left to press against the scanner. Devon sees me make my move but hesitates before he grapples for my arm. His fingers brush mine, but there's nothing to lock on to. As long as the cops have him in their sights, he's not going to go full speed or bare his teeth.

"Mia—" he snarls under his breath.

Click. Twist. I simultaneously scan in and unlock the door, stomach churning. Devon laughs as I gain entry. His suspicions confirmed.

"Fine, Fun Size. Run home. See how that turns out for you."

He spits on the ground as I slam the door behind me. Frantic, dissonant wind chimes echo across the parking lot.

I crouch behind a chair in the shadowy lounge, watching him through the window. He sparks up another cigarette, pacing back and forth like he's guarding the place. He pauses in front of the door and stares, like he's trying to burn a hole with his eyes. I'll bet he wants me to think he can actually do that. As if I don't know better. As if he weren't the one who taught me everything.

I chew my cuticle and force myself to inhale deeply, but it feels more like hiccups. Devon is right. Every part of me hates it, but I know I can't go home. She's been thinking about doing this. All the pieces fit. She would never agree to any kind of solution that might separate us. This solves every problem we've ever had. Except for the fact that I'd be a Sara. Which she obviously doesn't see as a problem.

But if she actually *meant it,* wouldn't she have done it already?

Did she just say this to Devon to get him off her back?

Or is Devon just saying this to get *me* off *hers*? So I'll run away and he can finally have her all to himself?

I can't rule anything out. He always finds a way to get what he wants.

"Oh my God—Mia?"

I scramble between two bookcases with a muffled yelp. Dim light peeks through the stacks. Sandy's silhouette calls out to me again.

"What are you doing here?"

For a second, I want to cry. So relieved to see Sandy and not someone else.

My throat tightens as I reply, "I'm sorry. I didn't mean to. I was just . . . Um—"

"Are you okay?"

She approaches and flicks on the overhead fluorescents. I squint and shield my eyes, but I don't come out from behind the bookcase. My legs are wooden.

"Um . . . yeah there's some guy out there. I was at dinner and waiting for my Uber and he was kinda . . ."

She leans against the endcap with a sigh, closing the distance between us. "Shit, honey. I'm sorry. Should we call someone?"

"No, no. He'll leave. Eventually."

"You sure?"

I swallow a shard of terror as I collapse into one of the lumpy old chairs: the one Jade always sits in.

"Please be careful, when you go home," I whisper. "Maybe like . . . wait till morning?"

Sandy's face stiffens with understanding. She sinks into the seat beside mine.

"Mia, if he's a Sara, we need to call it in."

There's a cold spear in my chest. What about Mom?

"I mean I don't actually *know* if he was. A Sara. He just kinda seemed . . . yeah." I've said too much. I wish I could take it back. I'm trying to protect so many people at once all my threads are getting tangled.

"Either way, we should call the police. Better to play it safe."

"No. Please don't do that."

"Mia, we have to—"

"Just *don't*, okay?"

I drag my legs to my chest and hang my head.

"Do you know this guy?"

I'm all out of ideas. My brain's been working overtime cobbling cover stories and I don't have any material left.

"Mia . . . look, I don't know what's going on. With you. But—"

"I'm sorry. I didn't mean to bother you, I didn't think anyone was here. And I'm sorry for slacking at work lately it's just been a really crazy—"

"That's not what I . . . I mean, in a way maybe it is. I can tell you haven't been feeling . . . It just seems like you're kinda—" She exhales with a thoughtful frown. "I don't want to pry. And we don't have to call the cops if you don't want to. But I want you to know you can come to me if you're in trouble. Okay?"

I nod, just barely. Raising my head to stare into the middle distance.

"That girl who's been hanging out here . . . If this has to do with her, if things at home aren't—"

"It's not about that." Why does everyone think *that's* the cause of all my problems? Probably because it's easier to imagine. Because I've gotten so good at hiding the truth. Nobody looks at me and thinks, *She's definitely been harboring a Sara for the past thirteen years.*

"Sorry. I just . . . I need to think. About what I'm gonna do," I croak.

All of a sudden Jade's plan to steal away in the minivan doesn't seem as crazy as it did an hour ago. But she can't leave till Cloak and Dagger is over. And I can't leave until . . . what? Until I've made a safe plan for Mom? There isn't one. Nothing she'd agree to. Am I waiting to see if Devon was telling the truth? How do I do that without putting myself in danger?

"Lemme get you some tea," Sandy whispers, rising from her chair.

Sandy makes me a cup of Earl Grey, which I know is caffeinated. I drink the whole thing. It should clear my system by the time I give blood again. Hopefully. All things considered, it's a risk I'm willing to take. Sandy calls her wife to let her know she won't be home till morning. That there's some "black van activity" outside the store. She falls asleep about an hour later in the lounge, curled up around her wiry legs like a kitten in a basket. Her featherlight snoring is the only sound. We've switched off the lights.

I tiptoe through the labyrinth of shadowy stacks toward the break room and shut the door. Wedge myself between a pile of cardboard boxes and a dusty Christmas tree. Artificial pine needles jab the side of my face as I slide to the floor.

The phone rings three times on the other end. Then four. I don't think Mom's going to pick up. I thought she was back at work but she could be anywhere, really.

"What's going on?" she answers, barbed and breathless. I know what it means when she picks up the phone like this: *I'm putting out a fire over here, if you tell me there's another one I'm gonna wring your fucking neck.*

"Hi. Um . . . sorry. You sound busy. Are you at work?"

"Of course I'm at work. We're training the new hire. Although we might need a *new* new hire by tomorrow."

I don't say anything. I'm having trouble swallowing. I have no idea where to start. What I'm going to ask her first. It feels wrong to do this over the phone, but I can't go home till I know the truth. Till I know I'm safe. . . .

"Is something wrong?" She softens. I can hear her moving to a quieter area. Shutting a door. Probably her office. "Mia?"

"Devon followed me tonight. He came up to me in the parking lot when I was—" Quickly, I add, "I-I went out. Sorry. I had to run back to the store, I forgot some books I bought in the break room—"

"Oh, that's . . . it doesn't matter. Are you okay?"

This isn't the response I was expecting. I bring my cuticle to my lips.

"He promised he wasn't gonna bother you."

"That isn't . . . it's not . . ." I squeeze my eyes shut as though she's standing right in front of me. "He cornered me outside the store and . . . he said . . . he thought . . ."

"Mia—" Like she knows what I'm about to say.

"He thought I was a Sara. Because you told him you were gonna do it."

"I tell Devon a lot of things I don't mean. He does the same to me." She answers quickly. She wants this conversation to end. That harried edge returns to her voice.

"Why would you tell him that?"

"Because he kept harassing me about it. He wants to head up to Montana with the group, they're all gonna live on this ranch together—"

"Group? What *group*?"

"You know. The people he's working with. He wants me to be there. I told him that wasn't possible. Not without you. Which was when he suggested it."

Dead air between us. I suck my bleeding finger.

"So it was his idea?"

"I said I was gonna do it this week so I could go back to work and get my shit sorted out. After you and me had that . . . conversation. I told him I needed some space and that was my excuse."

"But now he knows you lied and he's coming after me." I heave an exhausted sob, but no tears come. My heart's been pounding for so many hours my ribs ache.

"He won't hurt you. He knows I'll never speak to him again if he lays a hand on you."

"You really think he cares about that?"

She sighs, distorting the connection. I know I've just touched a nerve.

"Are you gonna go to Montana with him?"

"I told you, Mia. I chose you. That's what I meant."

"So like . . . that whole plan you were talking about. That was your out? Montana?"

A moment passes before she speaks again. "Where are you right now?"

"At the store." There's a tremor inside me that makes me feel like I shouldn't have told her.

"I'll come get you."

I don't know whether that cup of tea was strong enough to protect me. I scrounge around in the storage room till I find an old piece of rusted rebar the contractor left behind after we remodeled the bathroom last year.

I stick a Post-it to Sandy's knee as she sleeps. *Thanks for the tea. Please stay safe.*

The Jeep pulls up outside and I stare at it through the window for a moment. I wish I didn't need her to save me. She drums the steering wheel as she waits for me. I watch her across the distance.

She might hurt me. In other ways. But her teeth on my skin is the holiest threshold. A line she would never cross. She is still my protector and terrified to lose me. I hate that the best defense I have against a Sara is another Sara. But in that car, in that house,

I'm safer than I'll ever be out here. She's safer than Devon. I know that much.

Gripping the jagged piece of rebar in my fist, I bolt toward the Jeep, scanning the darkness to the right, left, and behind me. I feel like someone's just thrown me out of an airplane and I'm waiting for my parachute to billow out behind me. Wondering if there even is one.

I clamber into the car and Mom grabs the back of my shirt like a dog seizing its pup by the scruff, pulling me all the way in.

"You're okay. He's gone. It's gonna be all right . . ." she whispers, kissing the top of my head. Her tears soak through my beanie.

I am transported. We're on the couch again, the purple couch that used to be blue in Salt Lake City. I have just seen her for the first time since she died. She's promising me nothing will change. Promising she'll always be there for me. I do not yet know how any of this is going to turn out. In this moment, I am safe. Naïve. Naïve but safe. You can't have one without the other.

She lets me go and peels out of the parking lot.

"He called a few minutes ago," she whispers. Less to me and more to the darkness.

My heart stammers. I hadn't thought of it earlier, during that avalanche of terror and confusion, but Devon saw me kissing Jade. He knows I snuck out with a girl tonight. He might have told Mom.

"What did he . . . ?"

"He just got nasty the way he always does."

"Did he say anything about me?"

She bites her lips together. "Like I said. Just the usual nasty shit."

I'm too afraid to pry. If he tried to rat me out, she's decided not to believe him. All these two ever do is lie to each other. I guess sometimes that works to my benefit.

"We're locking things down now. Okay, Mia?"

"What do you—?"

"I mean we're not answering our phones. You're not leaving the house after dark unless I'm with you. You're not staying there alone, either. We stick together. We don't let Devon come near us.

Eventually, he'll give up. He has his group now. People who can protect him. Plenty of girls, too. He'll move on."

Will you? I want to say.

"We survived this long for a reason," she goes on, quieter. "We seal everything up and nobody gets in. That's the only way this thing works."

I think I nod.

I want to survive.

Survive for *what,* though?

Is this it? Me and Mom and the house and the Fair Shake till I'm a hundred years old? Opening my frail blue veins every night, puncturing my tissue-paper skin as I squint through a pair of bi-focals? No one will touch me. Kiss me. Buy me gemstones, toast to my success, slide their knee between my legs. Just me. Mom. The house. The Fair Shake. Survival.

The pale threat of dawn seeps between the Tortolitas. Mom stomps on the gas as I watch the fading stars flash past the moon-roof. They flutter, like exhausted eyes fighting to stay open. Same as mine.

2010

Mom buys the house sight unseen. There are a couple of pictures online, but the real estate agent won't show it to her at night because of the curfew, even though she insists she doesn't have any daytime availability with her work schedule. She doesn't have a job yet. She pays for the house in cash; I know this because I have a panic attack in our motel room one night when I become convinced we're going to wind up homeless. "We're gonna be like Magda and have to wash our armpits in the bathroom at the bus stop," I stutter through tears. She calmly shows me her bank statement and tells me she has enough money to buy a decent place for us to live.

We also buy a used Jeep, the exact same year as the one we left at the hospital. It's a different color. Gram's was white. This one is a light khaki green. But the interior is familiar. We both feel at home the first time we sit in it. We've stopped worrying someone's going to track us because of the one we left behind. Saratov's cases have exploded and hospitals are underwater. They're so focused on the patients they have that they don't have time to deal with the ones who got away. At least, that's what we hope.

A guy from the dealership drops the new car off in our driveway one morning and I'm giddy as I stare at it through the window, anxious for sunset so Mom can take us for a spin. Once again, Mom pays for it sight unseen and emails all the paperwork. This is how she does everything now.

Our house looks just like the one next to it, which looks just like the one next to that. Almost like camouflaging. It smells new, like wet paint and freshly sanded wood. Mom keeps complaining about it. She used to say our place in Salt Lake had "strong old bones" and that she could feel the vibrations of everyone who'd ever lived there when she caressed the bumpy, uneven walls. We're the first people to live in this house. But I like the newness. It's completely empty the night we arrive, but Mom has made sure there are a couple of boxes from Ikea waiting for us on the front stoop. We spend the evening assembling our beds with an Allen wrench as I eat pizza off an upside-down cardboard box. I remember how fun it is to have an activity. A relaxing night at home.

The day after we move in marks six weeks since I broke my ankle, so I can finally stop wearing the boot. I've only ever taken it off in the shower, and my skin underneath is pale and puckered, with a shrunken calf that looks like it belongs to a kid half my age. Mom starts giving me ballet exercises to do in our new kitchen, using the shimmery faux-quartz countertop as a barre support. We do them together every night while we watch TV.

I'm not ready to start at a new school and Mom doesn't force it. I'm on her schedule now. We go to bed at 5 A.M. and wake up around four in the afternoon. At sunset, I draw—with a clean new phlebotomy kit and a fresh needle every day. Then she cooks me dinner, even though I know the smell makes her stomach turn. I've started learning to do more of it myself. I can easily pop chicken nuggets in the oven and I know how to boil water for spaghetti. Microwaved burritos are good, too. After dinner we watch TV and do our ballet exercises, and then she takes her classes online. She's getting a degree in hospitality so she can manage a restaurant or a hotel or something like that. A job she can do at night. We're both hoping the curfew won't last too long. She insists it can't go on forever. They'll have to try to reopen things eventually; the country will lose too much money if they don't. I ask why the president can't just print more money and give it to people. She rolls her eyes and makes a sound that's almost a laugh but more like a sigh, patting me on the head.

We find new ways to fill our evenings. Mom orders paint and a few canvases from an art store online. She does a lot of landscapes, old places she used to know. There are never any people in them.

One night, I find her sketching on one of the bare white walls in the living room. I'm startled at first. She would always yell at me for stuff like that at our old place. But she tells me we own this house and we can do whatever we want with it. Excitement swells up inside me for the first time in weeks. To paint on the walls feels so deliciously disobedient. We spend the rest of the night plotting our mural and every night after perfecting it. We play show tunes on the stereo and sing along. I do the big broad strokes with the roller and she adds all the shading and detail. Our first mural is an abstract desert sunset, a gradient of carnation pink and tangerine, framed by sharp, geometric mountains that look like stalagmites in a cave. It feels like we're outside and underground at the same time.

((((((

I turn eleven on October 22. Mom always comments that I was supposed to be a Scorpio like her, but I dodged my fate by a day. Instead, I'm a Libra. According to her, that makes me balanced, organized, and generous. Had I been a Scorpio, she says, I would have been ambitious, secretive, and "very sexy." It feels like she says this as a way to compliment herself. Or maybe she's hinting that I won't be, when I grow up. Either way, whenever she mentions it, my cheeks burn up.

My birthday is nice. We make a Funfetti cake and she gets me a giant stuffed panda bear to snuggle with at night so I feel comfortable sleeping in my own bed.

And that's not the only cause for celebration. There's an announcement on the news that night that the curfew is being suspended with some "strict personal safety guidelines." They say it's okay for people to go out after dark, but strongly discourage socializing with strangers. Safety in numbers is the name of the game. If you go home with someone you've just met, you're accepting all the risks that come with it. Mom snorts, "Sure, just add booze and a hundred single twentysomethings. What could go wrong?" They go on to report that far fewer cases have been documented these past two weeks, and the situation appears to be "under control." Mom and I know this is only because Saras have stopped going to doctors and hospitals.

We're excited, though. Our town might be allowed to have Halloween, and we haven't had a chance to explore our new neighborhood. For once, Mom's condition feels like a good thing. She can protect us. I declare, apropos of nothing, that I want to dress up as an Oreo cookie. Mom says she can make a costume for me with the empty Ikea boxes and some polyester stuffing.

"You should go with me as a glass of milk," I say.

She wrinkles her nose and laughs. "Yeah but like, if someone sees me standing by myself, without the cookie, I'm *just a glass of milk* for Halloween."

The following evening, Mom is slow to come out of her room for the nightly draw. I'm worried. Something doesn't feel right. She slouches across the house with a weary sigh and sinks into her seat at our newly built table. Tears stand in her eyes as she helps me tighten my tourniquet and prep the needle.

"Mom . . . are you—?"

"It's fine. It's not . . . it's something I gotta just—" She swallows hard and her hands form a steeple over her lips. "Y'know how a while back, you and me talked about what happens to women once a month, when their body is ready to have a baby?"

I squirm in my seat and my eyes leave hers. I'd rather look at the needle in my arm than talk about this. But I nod.

"That's stopped happening to me. Usually, that means you're pregnant—"

My gaze snaps back and my blood runs cold. *No.* Not this. Anything but this. If she's pregnant, he'll have to come back. To "take care of us" again. She might marry him. Or I'll have to give blood to the baby. Or both. Or . . .

Mom sees the terror blaze across my face and reaches out for me, careful not to disturb the needle. She grabs my free hand.

"Honey, it's okay. What I'm saying is I'm *not* pregnant. People like me . . . they can't have babies anymore. That's why this happened. I just double-checked on the Facebook group."

We just stare at each other for a moment. She rubs the valleys between my fingers.

"Did you want to have more kids?" I finally whisper.

"Maybe. I mean . . . yeah," she concedes. "Would've been great to give you brothers and sisters. I never had any and everyone else did. I didn't want you to grow up lonely like me."

"I'm not lonely."

She brings my hand to her lips and gives it a kiss.

That Friday night, I start getting sleepy in the middle of our painting session. My nose is running like a faucet and my throat has that dry, scratchy feeling it gets before full-on fiery soreness takes hold. Mom says I'm probably getting a cold, and sends me to bed early with my panda. After a couple of hours, I wake up thirsty. I call out to her, but there's no answer. The lights are still on in the hallway, but I don't hear any footsteps or the sticky sound of the paint roller. Maybe she's at the computer with her headphones on. I slide out of bed, swallowing a wad of mucus.

She's not in the kitchen or the living room. Her bedroom door hangs open and her computer screen is dark.

I burst outside, surveying the driveway and front stoop. The car is gone.

I sprint around the yard in my bare feet. I don't know why. It's not as though I'm going to find her in the rock garden, tending our succulents in the middle of the night. She took the car. I flick on all the porch lights. But of course nobody's there.

Infomercials flash across the TV screen as I assume the fetal position on our stiff new Ikea couch. We don't have a landline here; she's got our only phone. And she's taken it with her. All I can do is wait.

Panic flares inside me, and I run to the bathroom twice to vomit. I don't know if it's because I'm sick or because she's left me alone. She didn't even leave a note.

I wonder if Devon knows we're here. If she *told him*. I imagine the blood of a hundred helpless strangers saturating the pristine new Astroturf in our backyard. The sound of Mom's artificial laughter, keeping me awake at night. The stench of Devon's cigarettes.

I throw up a third time.

I stare at the clock on the cable box so I know exactly how many minutes have passed. Forty-seven. Forty-eight. Feels like I've been sitting here for hours.

Finally, at 1:36, there's the crunch of tires on gravel outside. I make myself small on the couch, afraid she might not be alone, and wipe my nose on my sleeve.

She doesn't see me at first. She removes her shoes—high-heeled peep-toe pumps I didn't even know she'd bought—and quietly shuts the door behind her. She's by herself.

I spring from the couch and she gasps, clutching her chest. "Oh my God, Mia. You scared the shit out of—"

"Where did you go?" I'm already sobbing.

She races toward me, arms outstretched. Tears well in her eyes, triggered by mine.

"It was stupid. I'm sorry, Mia. I shouldn't have left—"

I dodge her embrace, firmly crossing my arms.

"Where. Were you?"

"I was just . . . There's this wine bar downtown and I thought it'd be nice to—"

"You didn't tell me!"

"I-I know. I'm sorry. It was a spur-of-the-moment thing, I didn't think you'd wake up, I figured you were safe—"

"*You can't even drink wine!*" My throat is really starting to hurt now.

"You're right. I . . . I just wanted to go out and meet people."

"We're not allowed to do that! The guy on the news said if you go out you can't talk to anyone you don't—"

"Please don't yell at me," she whispers, wounded. Eyes pinned to the floor. "I'm just lonely, okay? It sucks. This whole thing just sucks so much. . . ."

I take her in, piece by piece, head to toe. Wet black mascara rings her eyes. She looks a little like my panda bear. She's styled her hair into soft, luxurious waves and pinned half of it back with a pretty, feminine twist. Her legs, long and lean like a dancer's, glisten with baby oil underneath her distressed denim miniskirt. She's achingly beautiful, even with makeup smeared all over her face. She knows it, too. Knows she deserves to be admired by someone. Adored, even. But she's all alone.

"I'm sorry." I squeeze the words between sniffles.

"No. *I'm* sorry. For leaving like that. I don't know why I . . . I just felt so—"

"It's okay."

She meets my gaze. Knows I'm lying. I know it, too.

She swings her purse around to her hip and tears it open. From her wallet, she produces a business card and holds it up to me. I strain to read what it says in the weak light of the TV.

"There was a guy I was talking to. Pete. He gave me this."

She rips it into four tiny pieces and spins to face the trash bin.

"You don't have to do that. . . ." Not that I want her to call Pete. But this isn't about him, or any other person who might slip her their number. It's about how I felt when I realized she was gone.

"May as well, can't say my taste in guys typically yields the best results," she mutters, then glances my way and softens. "Well, except for that one time."

She folds me into her embrace, and I close my eyes and breathe her in. She's wearing perfume. Light and floral, like rose petals. But there's still that strange, sickly sweetness just beneath it. The smell of what's become of her. I wish I didn't know what it meant.

"I was so scared when I-I looked outside and . . . your car

was—" A dam breaks inside me as the tears rush back to my eyes. "I thought m-maybe he knew where we were and—"

"Shhh, don't worry. He's not coming back. Ever."

She crouches to my level and wipes my face with the bottom of her silk blouse. The fabric is cool and smooth against my hot face.

"And I promise, I will never leave this house again without telling you. You will *always* know where to find me, okay?"

"Promise?"

I hold up my pinky. She nods and locks her little finger around mine.

"Okay. Then I promise, too."

NOW

I'm home for dinner.

I am the only one who's home for dinner.

I'm paralyzed in the hallway, staring at the empty table. I fight for breath, like there's an icy rime hardening around my lungs.

She wasn't in her room. Or the shower. Or the garage. She's nowhere.

I had the car at work. Someone must have come to get her. Someone who was *just here*. The sun has only just dipped below the horizon. It's barely safe enough.

I play back the week we spent together, combing our interactions for a sliver of a clue. We've been strict. As soon as the sun goes down, she doesn't let me out of her sight. I'm grateful for her protection. I've gone to the restaurant with her every night. There's been no sign of Devon since our encounter in the parking lot, and I haven't heard Mom talking to him on the phone. In fact, she took out her SIM card. We both did—although I stealthily put mine back in the next morning so I could text Jade. She sent me my ticket to Cloak and Dagger, and the show is tomorrow night. I still haven't decided if I feel safe enough to go or if I'm coming with her after it's over. I haven't decided a damn thing. All I've done this week is hide from Devon and use Mom as my shield.

But now she's gone.

I call her phone, and my heart drops to my feet when I hear it jingle in the bathroom. I dig it out from underneath a towel and survey the mess she's left. The curling iron has been left on. The faint scent of her perfume hangs in the air. Maybe she wasn't snatched. She was planning to go out. I grab her phone, hoping there might be some evidence of her whereabouts. She must have snuck her SIM card back in, like me. But the passcode isn't working. The device scolds me with a hard, curt vibration. I try again. Nope.

Her passcode's been the same for years. I wonder how long ago she changed it. I shouldn't have been so quick to trust her. Just because she's protecting me doesn't mean she's stopped going behind my back. I fucking hate myself for being so trusting.

I microwave a brick of frozen mac and cheese, but it's like glue in my mouth. I sit at the table by myself. Six o'clock becomes seven. Finally, I stand and open all the curtains. I plant my feet at the big picture window in the living room, staring out at the driveway as though I can will headlights to crest the hill.

My phone rings and I bolt toward the kitchen counter.

It's Jade.

"What's goin' on?" I try to brighten my voice to disguise my unease, but I sound like I'm hosting a kid's birthday party.

"Uh . . . what's goin' on with *you*?" There's an unsettled tickle in her voice, almost a laugh but not quite. "You okay?"

"Totally. Why?"

"You didn't answer my text this morning. About confirming your ticket. They need to have all the codes claimed by midnight so they can send everyone the location. If you don't do it now, you're gonna lose your spot."

"Okay. Yeah. I'll do it."

I didn't answer her because I still haven't decided if I'm going. I know she'll be hurt if I miss it. But if Devon tries to follow me, if anything were to happen . . .

"Mia?"

"Yeah, I'm still here."

"Do you promise you'll do it tonight? I don't want you to—"

"For sure, I'm on it. Thank you for reminding me."

There's an uncomfortable hiatus. She's sensed a shift in me. In fact, this whole week I've been so dodgy I'm surprised she still cares.

"You okay, babe?"

I don't like when she calls me that. Mom says "babe."

"Um . . . Yeah it's fine. It's just been a weird week—"

"I know we talked about some heavy shit on Sunday. It's okay if you need a sec to like, process it. But I really want you to be there tomorrow. It's gonna be amazing."

"Yeah. I can't wait." I sink into the couch, pulling a pillow over my thundering heart. I can't help myself. I'm aching to open up to her. She's the only one who *almost* knows the truth. "My mom is missing."

"Oh my God, what? Why didn't you tell me right away?" Before I can answer, she cuts back in. "Wait, missing as in like . . . she's a *missing person*?"

"I don't know if it's . . . it's not like a kidnapping or anything—"

"You said she had some stuff going on, right? Mentally, I mean."

"Um . . . yeah it's sorta like that."

"Do you think she's safe?"

I don't say anything.

"Did you call the police?"

"She hasn't been gone that long. I should probably wait. She might come back."

Jade sighs on the other end. "I can come over and wait with you. If you want."

My spine stiffens, "yes" on my lips. But she can't come here, can't see the inside of our house. The murals. The blackout curtains. The biohazard disposal. The pathetic, shut-in life I've been living.

"I'll be okay. But thank you. That means a lot."

"Babe, I wish you'd told me. This whole week I've been worried you weren't—"

"Everything's really crazy here. I'm sorry." I clench the pillow underneath my chin and start to rock back and forth. Glad she can't see me like this.

"It's okay. You'll get a break from it tomorrow. But listen, if you decide you don't want to go, if you need to hang out and wait for your mom to get back, I totally—"

"Let's just . . . We'll talk tomorrow. I'll let you know what's happening."

"I hope it's a yes."

"Me, too."

"Confirm your ticket either way, though. Okay?"

I nod with a thousand-yard stare. A moment passes before I remember to use my voice.

"Yep."

Seven o'clock becomes eight. Becomes nine. I could go out and look for her. But maybe that's what she wants. Maybe this whole thing is a trap to get me out of the house by myself. Devon and his freaky little family could be right outside the garage, waiting to grab me on my way to the car. I fold a fleece blanket around my shivering body like a burrito . . . then bolt upright.

The Facebook group. I'll find clues there for sure.

But when I log in to Mom's account, the tab for the Saratov Survivors group is gone. I type it into the search bar. No results. What the hell? I click open her messages. The inbox is empty. No new DMs, and all the old ones have been deleted.

I shudder and collapse into my desk chair. The group's gone dark. Devon deleted it for some reason. And Mom must be involved. She's erased her entire history. She's gone.

She's not coming back.

She didn't say goodbye.

Didn't even leave a note.

I scream, grab a heavy hardcover book from the corner of my desk, and furiously chuck it across the room. It smacks the window but doesn't leave a mark. I wish I'd shattered it.

I only let myself cry for a few minutes. Fuck it. Fuck her, fuck *every single thing*. After all I've done, all I've given up. I hope she comes back someday, expecting me to be here. All she'll find are stacks of unpaid bills in the mailbox and rats in the kitchen. I won't leave a trace. Just like her.

I never took any steps to execute my plan-that-was-not-a-plan. Didn't move any money around or ask for an advance. The best I can do is withdraw a heap of cash before I climb into Jade's van. Release the bits and pieces of my life to the wind as we drive. I can figure it out. If I want this, I'll have to.

But first, there's the matter of tomorrow night. The show. *Jade's* show. I can't miss it, not if I care about her. I won't.

I dry my eyes on my sleeve and pull up her email to access my ticket.

There's a lot of fine print attached to this thing. I doubt anyone reads it. If you've made it this far, if you've sought an invitation and secured your spot, you're not losing sleep over the potential risks.

> Ticket holders acknowledge this is an open-air venue and blood scanners have not been installed. Security is present at the event. Please report any suspicious activity by texting "3035." Personal protection is permitted.
>
> By confirming your ticket, you hereby release and discharge Cloak and Dagger Events from any and all claims, damages, demands, actions, causes of actions or suits of any kind resulting from injury or subsequent death while on the grounds.

It's what I expected, more or less. "We won't exclude anyone but feel free to bring a rusty machete. Don't sue the shit out of us. See ya there!"

My cursor hovers over the CONFIRM button. I've never willingly put myself at risk like this. But that was before I knew I could feel this way. Before I knew anyone like Jade, who made me feel so brave and so capable because that's who *she* was. Tomorrow could be the first night of my new life. I don't want to spy on her world through the window anymore. I want to be inside.

And as for risk? My entire life up until this point has been one supermassive, jaw-clenching clusterfuck of risk. Living here with Mom, that ever-present shiver running down my spine, reminding me what she is. What she could do to me. The way I hold my breath when she wraps her arms just a little too tightly around my waist. The same thing that might kill me out in the desert could kill me at the kitchen table.

Confirm. It's done. Every sunset since I was ten years old has been for her. This one's for me.

(((

I'm almost glad she's not home by morning. I check every corner of the house anyway, heart in my throat. But there's no sign of her.

There's still a chance she'll be home later tonight. Part of me wonders if I should try to wait for her. Give her something to eat before I go. But she denied me last night, like a slap in the face. Who knows where she fed. *Who* she fed on. No, I'm not going to wait.

I'm off from work today, which almost makes matters worse because all I do is agonize over my closet. What do people even wear to Cloak and Dagger? I Google a couple of photos and my stomach does a backflip. The people in the pictures are slathered in glitter-saturated body paint. Maybe those people are performers; pants will still be permitted for someone like me. The next photo doesn't make me feel a whole lot better. Sure, this girl is wearing pants, they just happen to be made of metallic blue leather, reflecting the neon lights like a radioactive swimming pool. Her hair is a wild mane of orange and black, like tiger stripes. She holds up a big handmade sign that reads, I'M ALIVE, MOM, mouth hung open like she's singing along to her favorite song.

Why didn't I do my research sooner? I need a literal costume for this thing.

I tiptoe into Mom's room, like I'm afraid she's passed out under the blankets with the fan and white-noise machine cranked to eleven. I don't think it's ever been so quiet in here.

My fingertips dance across the dresses hanging in her closet.

Velvet, silk, and lace. So feminine and delicate. The smell of her wafts toward me as I pull one out. Chanel and decay.

I feel like she's watching me.

The dress I choose is short, but I can wear leggings underneath it. I think it's black crushed velvet, but in the light I can see it's actually the color of cabernet. The color of something else I don't want to think about. I return it to the rack and choose a wrap top instead, made of translucent black lace. There's a small V-shaped opening in the front that exposes the navel. I'm not sure if I've ever seen her wear this. This isn't an outfit for work. There's a strange, delicious twinge between my legs as I imagine myself in it. As I imagine Jade seeing me in it.

I don't have a black bra, so I have to borrow that from Mom, too. I hate wearing her clothes, and I hate that we're the same size.

I picture the scene playing out in an alternate dimension. A place where everything is normal. As in, she's normal and she's helping me get dressed for a big date. She offers me sophisticated alternatives from her own closet after I panic about not having anything to wear. She tells me to have fun as I leave the house, but not *too* much fun, and to call if I've had too much to drink. She waits up for me. Gives me a hug if it went well. An even bigger one if it didn't.

I strap on the bra and slam off the lights.

Just before Jade is due to arrive, I burst into the kitchen, assembling the phlebotomy kit with shaking hands. Old habits die hard. If Mom comes home in the next few minutes, it might still be fine to drink, if a little foul tasting. I cinch the tourniquet, hissing air between my clenched teeth. It doesn't seem like she's coming back. But if I don't leave her something, if I break tradition, I'm going to panic about it all night and not be able to think of anything else.

A text from Jade: **We're outside!!!!**

I start to get light-headed, and not because of the blood.

I text back slowly with my free hand. **Cool 1 min**

Timer's just about done.

Sweat seeps through the holes in Mom's lacy, revealing shirt.

I pour the blood into Mom's cup and carefully wipe it down. As I choke down my supplements, I place it at her spot with a note that says, "Drawn at 7:32." She'll know if it's too cold by the time she gets home. If she gets home. I expect the cup to be completely full when I get back.

I stare at it as I reach for my keys.

She escaped first.

She left nothing for me.

At least I've left her this.

It's not Jade's car outside, but a sleek black fifteen-passenger van. Party-bus vibes. I refresh my lipstick in the hallway mirror and spot that jagged piece of rebar from the bookstore, sitting on the end table. I tuck it into my jacket, even though I know it won't do me much good. Might as well. Personal protection *is* permitted.

Jade rolls down the window and pushes her sunglasses to the tip of her nose, giving me a theatrical, saucy once-over. Her eyeliner is extra bright and thick tonight, loaning her the exaggerated look of a smoldering cartoon temptress.

"Well, excuse you," she says, letting out a high-pitched whistle. I feel her eyes on my exposed navel, and my entire body blushes.

Tony's driving, chugging an extra-large iced coffee. Jade's in the front seat. She clambers into the back so we can sit together. "What am I, your fucking chauffeur?" he mutters, deadpan.

There are two other people in the van, seated toward the middle: a young woman with bleached hair and marmalade freckles and a guy in a vintage basketball jersey, bare arms covered in glitter. They cuddle, passing a vape back and forth. I haven't seen them before.

"Mia, this is Tallie and Morrison. Buddies of mine from Chicago."

Muted "hi"s between puffs from the vape. The girl, Tallie, has her lip pierced. She pokes the stud with her tongue and sucks it back in as she speaks.

"We used to be neighbors. It's basically a family reunion." Jade smiles and ruffles Morrison's hair as she weaves her way toward the last row of seats, all the way in the back. I follow her.

"All we're missing is Gabi," Tallie points out, an edge to her voice.

Jade stiffens and grits her teeth. "Yeah. Sucks."

She gives my shoulder a tight, reassuring squeeze, guiding me into the seat beside her. Tony backs out of the driveway as I buckle in. I wring my hands with a sharp intake of breath as we round the corner.

Jade peers over at me, as though she feels my tension. But she doesn't understand it.

"Gabi's not coming. I promise," she whispers, lips brushing my ear. "She's sitting in Chicago all by herself being a jealous little hermit."

"Jealous?" A wave of gooseflesh crashes over me. But that might just be her lips, moving down to my neck.

"Well, wouldn't you be?" A cynical chuckle escapes her lips, vibrating against my skin. She traces the edges of my lacy shirt, bordering my exposed midriff. I should feel something. I should feel *everything*. But there's only the dark, suffocating fog of guilt, obscuring everything but the image of our house as it vanishes in the rearview.

"Your makeup looks pretty." Her fingers move to my bangs to straighten them.

"Yours looks better." I try to smile, swimming upstream through my dread as we merge onto the freeway.

"You want me to do yours?"

"O-oh I mean, you don't have to—"

She digs into her backpack on the floor and produces a makeup palette the size of a hardcover textbook. Opens it across my lap.

"Pick a color."

———

Jade gently brushes gold-flecked eye shadow on my lids, like other-worldly pollen. We stop to pick up a few more people on our way to the desert. I glance at my reflection in the darkened window as we wait outside Steve's compound. But Jade quickly redirects my gaze. We're not done yet.

"Just a little black in the creases to make it pop," she murmurs, sending a soft tingle from my ear down my spine. "Close your eyes like, halfway?"

Jade flicks a little extra mascara onto my lashes, then presses a small compact mirror into my palm.

"Thoughts?"

I glance at my reflection and catch my breath. I feel magical, like I've just stepped out of a dream. Maybe hers. I close the space between us, angling my lips toward hers. But she withdraws.

My heart twists. Jade subtly cocks her head at Tallie and Morrison. I hadn't noticed before, I was so absorbed in what Jade was doing, but Tallie's sharp gaze is hooked to me. I've stormed into the middle of an awkward, delicate dance without knowing any of the steps. It's all to do with Gabi somehow. Tallie and Gabi are friends. I don't see why her feelings are so important, though. She's not even here.

"Later. I promise," Jade whispers in my ear with a shadow of a smile.

At that moment, Steve and the pixies tumble into the car. They smell like they've been drinking since lunchtime.

"Hiiii-ee!" The pixie with the big square teeth waves at me. As if we became friends last time we saw each other. Maybe she thinks I'm someone else.

"Buckle up, kids," Tony shouts from the front. "Our set's at nine thirty, we gotta fucking punch it."

He revs the engine and Jade grabs for my hand with an exhilarated squeal. Under the seat. Where the others can't see.

———

There's a narrow dirt road snaking off the freeway exit, winding through the saguaros and into the darkness. We follow it, and for a few minutes it's completely silent. I wonder if this is part of the ritual somehow. Or some sort of safety precaution. Maybe a little bit of both.

After exactly five minutes of zigzagging across the dust, my suspicions are confirmed. The instant the clock hits 8:48, Tony rolls down all the windows and cranks the stereo. Bass rattles my bones and everyone in the car cheers at the tops of their lungs. Jade takes off her seat belt and dances in the aisle.

A moment later, we catch up to an ancient Volkswagen bus with streamers trailing from the windows and hot pink LEDs where its brake lights should be. The turn signals are purple. A bumblebee-yellow convertible blasting ethereal trance music emerges behind us. Four young women sit side by side, their long Day-Glo hair tangling and fusing together in the wind like a neon rainbow. They honk to greet us. The VW bus does the same. We travel together in a cluster, like three merging flocks of migrating birds. It takes me a moment to realize we're all listening to the same song.

An enormous archway made of blanched bison skulls, lit by flickering blue strobes, marks the entrance. The skulls look too big to be real, but it's hard to tell in the flashing light. The sound of distant instruments tuning up sends a tremor across the earth as I climb out of the van. The stage sits on a hill overlooking the desert like a space-age acropolis, casting dappled neon across the sand below. Jade hops up and down, clutching both my hands in hers. Tony hands me a laminated badge on a lanyard.

"Here, you can come backstage and hang with us. They'll kick everyone out and make us dance with the plebes after our set, but it's better than nothing."

"Thanks." I beam, hanging the lanyard around my neck. Cinderella at the ball at the end of the world.

Tallie and Morrison walk ahead of the group, under the archway of skulls, not-so-discreetly unfurling a ziplock bag of pills. "Anyone need?" Tallie turns around and offers.

"What are they?" I whisper to Jade.

"Caffeine pills."

"Oh. Cool—"

"But it's always laced with a lot of other shit. You never know where Morrison gets this stuff. I'd stick to coffee."

As soon as Tallie and Morrison are out of sight, Jade seizes my waist and locks her mouth to mine. Finally. The taste of her is sharp and tart, like sour apple. She nudges a piece of hard candy into my mouth with her tongue, laughing.

"Here, you finish it."

I clench the candy in my cheek, savoring the artificial syrup as she pulls away.

☾ ☾ ☾

Jade, Tony, and Steve run a quick warm-up before their set. I wait for her backstage with Tallie, Morrison, and the pixies, whose names I've now discovered are Gina, Bethany, and Fiona. Now that they know I'm not going to threaten their quest to possess Steve, they've started sending some warmer weather my way. I'm still on edge, though. This time, it's Tallie and Morrison giving me the cold shoulder. They cuddle on a couch at the opposite end of the backstage bar, jaws fidgeting as the pills they've swallowed start to take effect. Whispering as they intermittently steal a glance at me. They think I don't notice. They're not exactly being subtle about it, though.

Gina pours shots for everyone. She calls them "Redheaded Sluts," then turns to me with a coy chuckle and says, "No offense. I'll give you an extra one for your trouble."

I never actually considered my hair to be red. Mom's hair is that vibrant, enviable shade of auburn. Mine's more like a watered-down version of that.

"It's so pretty, by the way." Gina approaches with two shot glasses. She hands one to me, then, uninvited, strokes my hair. "Is it natural?"

"Uh, yeah." I throw back the shot, but I can't get it all down in one gulp. My eyes water as I sputter, trying for a seamless second swig.

"So jealous, oh my God," she whispers, then hands me the second glass. She smiles and raises her to mine. "To fucking Landshark, right?"

"Yeah," I reply weakly, still feeling the first Redheaded Slut burn through my chest. Gina clinks her glass to mine and tosses back her shot, but I refrain. For now.

I wonder what I'm waiting for. Why I'm trying to pace myself. I'm free, aren't I?

I stare at the shot in my hand, watching the viscous, under-mixed booze swirl in the dim light like a cranberry-red oil slick. I suck it down. All at once this time.

Landshark is on first, and Jade is starting to get nervous. She paces the backstage area, nursing a beer. Keeps peeking outside to see how many people are here.

"Nobody comes this early, it's okay," she mumbles as I sidle up beside her. "Nobody" looks like a pretty decent crowd, though. There have to be at least two hundred people flocking to the stage. But two hundred is probably pennies on the dollar compared to how big the crowds are for the headliners.

The shots are swimming around in my head, but I somehow feel equipped to offer some wisdom. "Well, how big were the venues you played a year ago?"

"Oh, like practically closets," she snorts, and pulls from her beer.

"This is a hell of a lot bigger than a closet."

"It is at that." She hangs an arm around my shoulder and squeezes me against her. "I'm really glad you're here, babe."

She offers me a sip of her beer. I don't mean to, but I finish it.

Jade's set begins five minutes later. I give her a stealthy kiss for good luck while Tallie and Morrison have their backs turned. A jittery guy in a headset comes to fetch our backstage gang and leads us to a roped-off platform toward the front of the stage, right behind the lighting techs. They ignore our tipsy whispers, busily prepping cues on their tablets. Gina has swiped a bottle of Jameson from the backstage bar and cuts it with Coke for a protective caffeine boost. She passes it around, and I take a generous swallow as the stage darkens. The modest but eager crowd erupts with excitement.

"Friends, please give a warm welcome to your Cloak and Dagger opener—all the way from the Windy City—Landshark!" a disembodied godlike voice booms.

Blue-tinted black light floods the stage as Jade, Tony, and Steve enter. Jade's wearing elegant evening gloves made of white fishnet, with the fingers cut off. They glow under the black light like the outstretched hands of a spirit materializing from the wall. There's a camera pointed right at Jade's keyboard so the audience can see her hands from the massive projector screen hanging above the stage. The effect is mesmerizing.

We all scream at the tops of our lungs as she pounds a few propulsive opening chords. I don't think I've ever screamed this loud for fun. Because I wanted to.

She kicks things off with her song about ghost hunting in different cities. Says, "This is for all the friends I've made on my way here tonight," before the beat drops. The song takes on a new meaning, now that I know her.

There's a fan strategically placed beneath her keyboard, blowing her hair up around her face like she's staring down a storm. Her makeup gives her an alien effect in the black light: dramatic colors highlighting the sharp angles of her face. She's more than beautiful, more than the embodiment of everything I never knew I wanted. She's an echo from another world, calling me to join her on the other side.

As Jade's set progresses, more and more bodies fill the crowd, drawn to her moody Siren's soundscape. I close my eyes and sway to the thundering bass, enjoying the way it vibrates across my skull. For half a second, I wonder if I'm a stupid-looking dancer. I've never had anyone I could dance next to, someone whose moves I could copy. I crack an eye open and glance over at the three pixies, clumsily rolling their bodies and tripping over each other, trying not to spill what's left of their drinks.

At that moment, a passing face in the crowd pulls my attention from Jade. At first, I'm not sure why. It's a woman, worming through the writhing bodies. She's alone, not dancing with any group. I can't stop staring at the black-and-pink Heidi braids pinned on top of her head. *Kayla?*

Relief shoots through me. She's alive. Maybe this is why she's been missing work. Maybe she got a job with the festival, or started following one of the acts on tour. She might have just quit with no notice—after all, she talked about running away to Hawai'i. I guess I can relate. I raise my hand to wave at her. See if she wants to come dance with us.

But she's gone in the next flash of light. Like I imagined her.

"I've had a beautiful time here in Arizona, you've all been so good to me." Jade holds her arms out to the crowd like an embrace. Her final song comes to a close. Steve plays an embellished, drawn-out fill from the drums behind her. "I hope you all have the most unforgettable night of your fucking lives!"

The audience, which has now tripled in size, shrieks in reply. The sound ripples across the sea of bodies, washing over me.

"Thank you, Cloak and Dagger!"

She exits the stage, and everyone cheers.

Somewhere in the crowd, I think I hear someone scream. The wrong kind of scream.

☾ ☾ ☾

Jade beelines toward me as she makes her way out of the artists' tent. It's situated in the center of a garden of LED tulips, pulsing alternate colors in time with the music blaring from the stage. It reminds me of the garden scene from *Alice in Wonderland,* if all the flowers had been controlled by robots. Jade reaches me and grabs both my hands, twirling me in a circle.

"Oh my God, did you see all those people?"

"Yeah! It was amazing!" I wrap her into a hug, bouncing up

and down. Absorbing her sweat and her glitter and all her sweet, infectious adrenaline.

"C'mon, follow me." She pulls me by the wrist back toward the artists' tent.

I glance back at the others, still catching up on the other side of the twinkling tulip field. She shakes her head.

"I just want it to be you."

We're finally alone together, sharing a small velvet sofa in a dim corner of the tent, keeping our distance from the clamoring friends-of-friends and top-dollar ticket holders. We stick two straws into a single fruity tiki drink. I remove the decorative orchid and tuck it behind her ear. The music is too loud to talk. So we don't.

I'm not entirely comfortable kissing her like this in front of people, even though Tallie, Morrison, and the rest of them are nowhere in sight. But there's no way in hell I'm about to stop her. I'm heavy and molten as she coils both her legs around my waist, turning sideways on the couch to face me.

I feel her tickle my exposed midriff as she fumbles with the button of my jeans. I tense, my hand instinctively flying to hers. I want this. I want this and I'm almost drunk enough to let her do it. But I don't think I could ever be so drunk that I'd literally let someone into my pants in a room full of strangers. God, would she be trying to do this if she were sober? I wish we were home alone in my bed. Or . . . maybe not *my* bed, I guess. Somewhere else, somewhere better . . .

"Sorry," she whispers with a furtive laugh. "We can stop."

My body reluctantly cools as she grabs for the neglected drink on the table without looking at me. I'm quick to intercept her.

"Is there somewhere else we could go?"

Jade finds Tony at the bar and snags the van keys from him. "Yo, Morrison's pissed at you for leaving him outside." He eyes us. But doesn't say anything else.

We cling to each other, laughing as we navigate the field of tulips, careful not to step on any of them. Every few paces, Jade grabs my face and kisses me. This time carefully avoiding my beanie as she clutches the back of my head.

"C'mon, at this rate we'll never get to the car," I giggle into her mouth.

"Then kiss me while you walk."

Someone sprints past us, knocking into Jade. Her teeth hit mine and she whirls around with a scowl.

"Hey, watch where you're—"

I open my eyes and notice everyone around us is frozen mid-step. Girls stop dancing in line for merch. A guy on his way to the stage with a beer stops. The bouncers in front of the artists' tent are rigid and shifty-eyed. It's like some sort of *National Geographic* show where a burrow of rabbits all rise to their hind legs at once, all smelling the same imminent danger on the wind. The sudden stillness is terrifying.

Jade's sensed it, too. The air is unstable, like we're caught in a cloud of invisible toxins that could explode at any second. We exchange a glance and I study her face, etched with worry I've never seen before.

The music from the stage cuts, as though someone's just unplugged the whole sound system. Scattered protests rise from the audience, but for the most part, it's quiet. A crescendo of harrowing silence. Jade grips my hand and when she shudders, I do too.

"What's happening . . . ?" I ask under my breath. As if she'd know better than me. Like it might be part of the show somehow.

She opens her mouth to reply, but a swell of screams swallows her words. It's coming from the stage. The people who were frozen seconds ago start bolting past us. I'm not sure what the hell we're supposed to do, but I know we can't stay here. My fingers calcify around hers.

"The van. We need to get to the van." I stumble, pulling her along with me. Drunk and unsteady. But she's not doing much better. "We gotta run, Jade."

But everybody else seems to have the same idea. Running. All in the same direction.

The crowd surges past, jostling us left and right. Jade trips and I yank her upright before she hits the ground. I have the feeling if either of us falls, we won't be getting back up.

Another scream, this one closer and deeper, a bloodcurdling baritone. Male. Someone large, someone strong. Not strong enough.

"What the hell is going on?" Jade whimpers. To me. To everyone.

I wish I could answer her. It has to be Saras. I can't think of anything else that would make people panic like this. But why would Saras try to feed here? Most people in the audience are protectively caffeinated, they can't drink from them.

Black and blue tears streak Jade's face as she runs. I never imagined seeing her this scared. I keep pulling her along as she shivers against me.

In the distance, I spot the archway of skulls, silhouetted by those flickering blue strobe lights. "Just keep your eyes up there." I point to the arch, then lock my arm around her waist so she can lean on me as she runs. She's shaking so violently I'm not sure how long she can stay on her feet. "That's where we gotta go. We're not far, we'll make it."

A deafening *pop* cuts the night. It's close, entirely too fucking close. Then another. *Pop, pop, pop.* Someone's shooting . . .

"Get down!" Jade screeches.

But we can't. We'll be trampled.

I survey the area as we try to keep pace, swept along by the crowd. Slowing down could get us killed. There's a barricade of sandbags to the left, dividing the loading dock from the ticketing booth. We can reach it if we cut across the crowd. If we can carefully start weaving to the side . . .

Pop! Pop pop pop!

A body hits the dust behind us. Jade covers her ears and howls, "Fuck, fuck, fuck, why do so many people have fucking guns?!"

Open-carry state. No blood scanners. Not hard to do the math.

Cloak and Dagger literally said "personal protection" was permitted. I clutch her collar in my fist, pulling her toward the fringes of
the crowd. Toward safety.

I elbow a barrel-chested guy in the ribs as we squeeze through
the bodies, just a few yards from the barricade now. Jade yelps and
crumples against me, transferring all her weight to her other foot.
Shit.

"You hurt?"

I don't even wait for her to nod. With an out-of-body burst of
energy, I drag her up onto my back and fasten her legs around me
like a belt. Plowing people out of our way with a ragged growl. I
don't care who else I'm hurting in the process. Not like I can do
much real damage, compared to those rusted bullets. I breathe
blood into my mouth and realize my nose is bleeding. I don't know
how that happened. Not sure who hit me, or when.

I climb the fortress of sandbags, hauling Jade along with me.
She's not able to put any pressure on her left foot, but she's man-
aging okay with the other, relying on her upper body. More people
break off from the crowd to scale the barricade behind us. It better
not fucking collapse.

Pop! Pop!

We tumble down the other side, breathless, bracing each other's
fall.

Jade sobs against my breast as we lie in a tangle on the ground,
just holding each other. I'm not sure if she's rocking me back and
forth or if I'm the one doing it to her.

"Nathan?" A woman beside us spins in desperate circles. "Oh
my God . . . *Nathan where are you?*"

A girl stumbles down the barricade. Bare, bone-white shoulders painted with blood. She's been shot. Her eyes roll back as she
clutches her butchered neck, convulsing until she topples face-first
into the sandbags. I swallow a wave of hot nausea. That's not blood
pouring from her bullet wound. It's a thick, syrupy ooze, black as
tar. The bruise on her neck darkens and her entire body bloats

with dark purple, as though all her veins just burst at once. I shut my eyes.

"Don't look behind you," I whisper to Jade. Which of course, she does immediately.

"Jesus Christ . . ." She buries her face into my hair. I feel her hyperventilate and I try to steady my breathing so she'll fall in line. "Fuck, she's a Sara, isn't she?"

"I mean, she was."

She looked young. Younger than us. I wonder if she was one of Devon's.

People are still screaming on the other side of the barricade, punctuating the dull roar of the stampede. The gunshots continue. One after another, after another. My ears ring and everything sounds like it's underwater.

It's not over. That girl wasn't here alone.

The cold, jagged edge of a thought sticks in the back of my mind. It's been there since we started running. These Saras didn't come here to feed. This was a recruiting mission gone wrong.

I know I saw Kayla in the audience. Alive.

And if Mom's been gone all day . . .

Jade pulls me in closer, hugging me tight.

"Shhh, it's okay. I'm here, we're gonna make it."

I didn't even realize I was crying.

☾ ☾ ☾

Helicopters start circling. It feels like we've been on the ground for hours, but I could be wrong. Everything's a nightmarish blur. We hear sirens next. Help is on the way, but it wasn't fast enough. But how could it be, when we were hidden on purpose?

Jade and I are still lying wedged between two sandbags. Haven't moved an inch since we climbed down to safety. I peer through my fingers at the surrounding carnage. People are bleeding, trying to put pressure on their wounds with torn pieces of clothing. It's hard to tell who's been bitten and who's been shot, though.

The helicopter churns up air. Chills hiss across my bruised body.

"We should try to get to the van," I say in a frayed whisper. "Let them focus on the people who are really hurt."

Jade nods, unfurling her shaky limbs. "Maybe Tony and Steve and the rest of them are waiting for us."

"Yeah. That's probably where they'd go."

I help her to her feet, letting her put weight on me to avoid her bad ankle.

"It's probably just twisted," she assures me, hobbling along. "We can put some ice on it when we get home."

Jade grits her teeth and forges ahead toward the parking lot. Which is where the emergency crew seems to be corralling us anyway. "Please *walk*, do not run, to the designated parking area," a gruff, militaristic voice barks into a megaphone. "Clear the grounds. I repeat, *walk*. Do not run."

We reach the van, but nobody else is there. We decide to climb inside and wait, huddled together in the back seat, listening to the staccato of helicopters overhead. Neither of us says anything. After a few minutes, Jade turns the ignition and cranks up the heat. I'm grateful.

"Thank God I was with you . . ." she breathes. Braids her fingers with mine. "You knew exactly what to do."

"I don't always." I close my eyes, remembering all the times I panicked in the face of a crisis, the moments I froze when I should have fought back.

"You do when it fucking counts." She rests her head against my chest.

Someone raps on the window and my body goes taut, convinced it's another gunshot. My breath steadies when I spot a tuft of turquoise hair. I never thought I'd be so relieved to see Steve.

Jade scrambles to unlock the door and dives into his arms. Tony is close behind. The three of them embrace—actually it's more like

Tony and Steve forming a protective circle around Jade, squeezing her from every side. Tears spill down Tony's cheeks.

"Get in here." He calls me over in a husky voice, drawing me into the group hug.

I feel more bodies join as Bethany, Fiona, and Gina link up with us. They tremble and it's contagious, reverberating across the group. One of them is wet with blood, pressed up against my back. Not hers, I sense. Someone else's.

"Where's Tallie and Morrison?" A tiny whisper from Jade, to no one in particular.

"Tallie wanted to stay behind with him when the EMTs came," Steve replies with a grave frown, breaking up the hug.

"Is he gonna be—?"

"Don't know yet."

A gulf of silence.

"We should head to my place. We have scanners on the doors," Tony says, a fissure in his voice. "Tallie said she'd meet us there."

"Traffic is gonna be a fucking mess at the main gate with all the cops, but we can try to sneak out the artist gate," Steve offers, clapping Tony on the shoulder. "Let me drive."

☾ ☾ ☾

We listen to the news on the radio. Desperate for facts, as though that might help us make sense of what we just saw. As though that were possible.

I'm listening for information about arrests. Names. But none have come yet.

What they do seem to know, so far, is that the vast majority of the wounded were struck by bullets. The reporter on the ground calls the whole thing a "devastating knee-jerk reaction."

That's not to say there weren't a couple of Saras in the mix, instigating the whole thing. But maybe not as many as everyone thought.

Maybe Mom wasn't even there.

Maybe this had nothing to do with her.

We reach Tony and Jade's apartment a little after 2 A.M. Each of us scans in to enter the building. The sting of the finger prick is like a reassuring kiss.

Jade expands the pull-out couch in the living room. We all climb in together and crawl under a pile of blankets, trying to warm up. But the shivering doesn't stop. Gina tries to turn on the TV so we can watch the news, but Bethany and Steve get upset and say they don't want to anymore.

Around three, Fiona's dad pulls up on his motorcycle outside. The *put put put* of the exhaust rattles the windowpane, breaking our trance. I watch her through the window as she wilts into his arms and he folds her up in his thick leather jacket.

A few minutes later, Tallie calls Jade. Morrison didn't make it through surgery. He'd already lost too much blood. Not a bite wound. He was shot.

Tony rises with a bone-weary sigh and lumbers over to the cluttered kitchen. I hear the clink of cups and silverware as he rinses dirty items in the sink. When he reemerges, he's holding an armful of shot glasses and a bottle of tequila. Eyes red and swollen.

Without a word he assembles the glasses in a circle on the coffee table and fills each one to the brim. "Don't have any limes." He finally speaks. "But . . . y'know. Take what you need."

"Can I just have a cigarette?" Jade murmurs.

There's a tingling sensation against my leg, under the blanket. It takes me a second to realize it's my phone. I dig it out and stare as Tony lights a cigarette in his mouth and passes it to Jade.

Mom's calling. Emotion blazes through me, like I can feel her magnetic pulse across the distance.

"I-I'll uh . . . be back in a second." I fumble my way toward the bathroom.

I close the door and stuff a damp towel along the bottom to muffle my voice. Just in case. I swipe ANSWER, but when I open my mouth, nothing comes out but a puff of air.

"Mia . . . ?" Someone croaks on the other end. It has to be her.

But her voice is weak, laced with fear and uncertainty. Almost sounds like a different person. "Where are you, babe?"

"Where am *I*?" I hiss. "Where have *you* been? You just . . . you *left*. Without even—"

"Mia, something . . . happened. I need help. Please come home." She fights to keep her voice steady.

I hug my arms around my chest, pacing back and forth across the icy tile floor.

"So you're home now," I finally say.

"Please just come back. I need you."

"What do you mean 'something happened'? *What* happened?" She sniffles but doesn't answer. "Where's Devon?"

"He had to go. Mia, please. I'm scared . . ."

"Go where?"

She breaks down, sobbing into the phone. I have to pull it away from my ear, but the sound has already burrowed under my skin.

"Please, Mia—"

"If I come home and you're not there I swear to God I will never—"

"How soon can you be here?"

"I dunno, I gotta get a ride—"

She stops crying, like the flip of a switch. "A ride from who?"

"Just stay there. Don't move." I hang up before she can say anything else.

I stagger back to the couch and settle in next to Jade. Squeezing my phone between my damp palms. She gently nudges me with her elbow.

"What's up?"

"My mom called."

"Oh my God. Did she come home?"

"I guess."

"Is she . . . okay?" Jade narrows her eyes.

"Would you be able to give me a ride?"

☾ ☾ ☾

Jade steers the minivan one-handed, holding my hand with the other. It's about twenty minutes to my house, but we don't say much. I examine the mascara-stained hollows in her tired face under the glow of the traffic lights. I wish I could spill my guts to her. Tell her how scared I am, how angry, and why. If Mom was at Cloak and Dagger, how can I ever forgive her? Even if she got hurt there, even if something went wrong or the group abandoned her . . .

There's no reason I can't tell Jade the truth. Everything keeping the secret together has begun to fray; what difference would it make now? But something's holding me back. I don't know what.

"Pull up down the block," I whisper as Jade turns onto our street.

"Look, if things get weird again . . ."

"I'll be okay—"

"Call me. I'll turn around and come right back."

The van crawls to a stop alongside the curb. She faces me, steely eyed, as she puts it in park. "I owe you so fucking big, Mia."

I throw my arms around her, keeping us fused together for a good minute or two.

"I'll call you tomorrow," I breathe into her ear. Slowly easing myself from the embrace.

"You better."

I watch Jade's headlights disappear over the ridge as I walk up to the house. Anxiety roils in the pit of my stomach as I reach for my keys and unlock the door. I have no idea what's waiting for me on the other side. Is she hurt? Dead? Is the whole thing some kind of trap, should I turn around?

Mom's sprawled on the couch in a pair of pink underwear, her bare leg bruised and black with bloodstains. It reminds me a little too much of the night I first found her.

"Mia, thank God . . . we need to clean this up, it hurts so bad—"

She struggles to a sitting position, clutching her hip. All I can do is stare.

There's a dark, dime-sized hole in her thigh. A bullet wound.

A layer of dust covers her hair and clothes.

But I knew. Didn't I?

I close the door and approach her slowly.

"That a rusted bullet?" I point at the wound, playing dumb.

She nods with a guttural moan, cradling her head. "Devon pulled it out pretty quick so it's not gonna spread but holy fucking shit it hurts so bad—"

"Where is he now?"

"He said he'd come back to check on me tomorrow. There were other people he needed to help," she mumbles, distracted by the pain.

"Other people he turned?"

Her lips curl, exposing her teeth. I inch back. I've already said too much.

"We should clean the wound." I stagger to the kitchen to grab the first aid kit I keep with my blood-draw supplies. Trying and failing to catch my breath. I almost wish she'd just gone to Montana.

"What are you wearing?" She appears behind me. Still limping, holding her thigh at the source of her pain. But her eyes are wide and alert, like she's suddenly tapped a new well of strength.

Before I can answer, she pulls the collar of my dusty black top. "This is mine."

I flinch, then plant my feet with a sharp intake of breath. No sudden moves. "Mom, please sit back down so I can clean you up. You're gonna make it worse—"

"And what's all over your face?" As though she couldn't see me before. It was darker in the living room. Shit, I should have just stayed in there.

"What do you mean what's all over my—"

She extends a hand, wiping glitter from my brow bone with her fingertip. Still, I don't move an inch.

"Where were you tonight?"

Where were you? I stand there mute, staring at the wall.

"All you do is lie to me now. Do you know how that makes me feel?" Tears gather in her eyes. She's still holding on to me. "Don't you trust me, Mia?"

"No." The word jumps from my mouth all on its own.

She grips my arm and yanks me in close. Her eyes flash to darkness, deeper than I've ever seen. I wonder how quickly I could grab that rusty rebar from inside my jacket. Just to get her to back down. But my arm's twisted in the wrong direction.

"I don't know who you are anymore," she says in a trembling whisper. Froth forms at the corners of her lips. "You're not my baby girl."

I take a desperate glance around the kitchen. The can of instant coffee is up on the shelf behind her. Maybe I could try to knock her into it and see if it falls? Somehow spin her around for a split-second distraction?

"When did you get to be this way, Mia?" She pushes my bangs off my sweaty forehead, not looking into my eyes but right past them. "We should've done this a long time ago. Before you got to be this way."

"Should've done what, Mom?"

But I already know. Devon was telling the truth. She wanted to. She's *always* wanted to.

It's the only way we'll always be together.

She clamps her hands around my shoulders, and my whole body quakes at her touch. I don't even have time to struggle.

Her gums retract and I'm paralyzed by the thrum of her fingertips and ice-cold terror. I close my eyes as her hot breath hits my neck.

But as she leans forward, she buckles. She's put too much weight on her injured leg. In the second she takes to regain her balance, I knee her in the thigh, making direct contact with the bullet wound. She screeches into my ear. The sound sends shock waves across my skull as she stumbles backward and I collapse on top of her. She snags my foot and sinks her teeth into my calf, right through my jeans. It should hurt more than this. A lot more. But that's a

Sara bite: instant, numb submission. Which is somehow even more terrifying. I don't scream, though. Don't have time. I heave myself forward with all my strength and jab two fingers into her bullet hole, twisting them around and around till she releases me.

Her eyes roll back as she wails, a hellish groan from deep in her belly. And then . . . silence. She goes pale as a sheet and topples over, thick black lashes fluttering above the whites of her eyes as she twitches. I slide across the floor, holding my throbbing calf as blood pools inside my jeans, trickling down my leg. She's stopped twitching now. Completely motionless. I feel her wrist for a pulse. She's still alive. Just passed out from the pain. I hate how relieved I am.

I hobble toward the bathroom, already halfway out of my pants. I need to clean the bite with hot water and bandage it as fast as I can. This one won't kill me. But if she wakes up and smells what she's done, she's going to want to keep going.

We used to read stories about kids who bit their own parents, or vice versa. Accidents, always accidents. That's what they'd say, anyway. We'd look at each other in tacit agreement that we'd never need the advice they posted in the aftermath.

Not us. Never us.

Finally, in the bathroom, I let myself cry. I keep my mouth closed so there isn't any sound.

We don't have any gauze, so I tear a clean towel into strips and wrap them around my calf after I've slathered the wound with Neosporin. I'll go to the pharmacy tomorrow morning.

Tomorrow. How the hell are we going to face each other tomorrow?

I sink down on the couch, picking glitter from underneath my fingernails. Mom's still supine on the cold kitchen floor. I slide a sheet underneath her and roll her onto it to drag her to bed. I can't carry her. As I pull her unconscious body toward her bedroom, her eyes blink halfway open.

"M-M . . ." Like she's trying to say my name.

I ignore her.

She tries to lift her head and looks up at me. Eyes fully open now.

"Mia. I'm sorry."

I don't answer. We round the corner, into her bedroom.

She curls into the fetal position on the sheet, starting to sniffle. Hides her face from me.

"Please forgive me, baby. I'm so, so sorry. I-I didn't mean to . . ." She slurs like she's drunk. The crying gets louder. More dramatic. Reminds me of that night I heard her laughing outside my window with Devon.

"Can you stand up?" I mumble. We've reached the edge of her bed. I just need to get her into it.

She nods and grabs hold of the headboard to pull herself up, avoiding her blackened leg. I wonder if the bruise will ever heal. Every other time she's had an injury—a broken toenail or a scrape on her knee—it's completely healed by morning, like it never happened. But this one's different. I feel a fleeting pang of sympathy until I remember how she got hurt in the first place.

She winces and hoists herself into bed.

"Please say something. Didn't you hear me? I'm so sorry."

She rocks her way onto her side to face me. I show her my back.

"I love you. So much. I didn't mean to—"

I make my way out of the room. Her sobs get even louder, more embellished, like she's gasping for air. The door is heavy as an old iron gate as I pull it shut.

I have no idea how I'm going to sleep tonight.

I surround my bed with a circle of coffee grounds and climb in, gripping my phone in one hand and my rusty hammer in the other.

What the hell am I doing?

Is this how it's going to be from now on? Up all night in a cold sweat, waiting for her to creep into my room and finish the job?

My memory flickers. No, it won't be. Because before all this happened, I decided I was leaving. It's time.

I rub my swollen calf, adjusting the makeshift bandage. Nudge the hammer aside and unlock my phone.

> Something really fucked just happened

I stare at the message before I hit send.

I don't know if I'm brave enough for what comes after this. But the person who survived that stampede, who saved Jade, who defended herself when a Sara sank its teeth into her skin . . . that person was me.

> Whoa hang on you ok?

I shut my eyes and center myself before I continue typing.

> I haven't been totally honest with you
> My mom is a Sara. She was at the show tonight.
> I think she's gonna kill me

There. It's done. I clench my head between my knees as the room starts spinning.

Jade calls me and I immediately flick the phone to silent and hit ignore. My breath scorches my chest as I hold it there. But there's no sound from Mom's room.

> don't call she might still be up
> shit ok yeah I'm sorry
> Mia wtf I wish you'd told me. This is serious.
> yea
> Did she hurt you?
> yea
> Are you ok???

im fine

Ok you need to leave your house I'm coming
back over

No no no. Not till tomorrow morning. While
she's asleep. There's a lot I have to do before
I go.

MIA

please don't come here I'm serious wait till
morning

are you sure?

Yes. Keep your phone near you I'll let you know
what's happening.

TODAY

It's just past 5 A.M. The sun will be up in about an hour. I'm laser focused now, able to shove my doubt to the sidelines and do what needs to be done.

The closest Sara center is in Phoenix, about two hours from where we are. There's a twenty-four-hour hotline, but I can't call until I'm sure Mom's asleep. If they can come get her, I'm free to go. I don't want to be here when they take her, though. Too scared I might change my mind when her tearful protest starts. Jade says she'll come get me before they arrive. I need to pack for the tour. For *everything*. But I can't make any noise till the sun comes up. I'm stiff as a board in my bed with the hammer back in my hand, concealed under the blanket. Nothing's stopping me now that I've made my decision. I'm getting out of here alive.

I tiptoe outside and down the driveway in my bare feet as early light creeps between the cracks in the blackout curtains. She can't follow me out here. I can place the call safely.

The nurse who answers the phone has a saccharine Southern accent. I'm not sure if it's the sound of her voice or the blinding sun or all the alcohol I drank last night, but my head is pounding. She tells me it's a five-hundred-dollar fee to come pick her up. The rest is covered, though. CDC takes care of all that. Technically this is a self-surrender, so she should be eligible for immunity. It's more than she deserves. But she can have it. I still want her to have it.

The nurse starts grilling me once she's established what we're doing. Next of kin? *Me.* Anyone else? Spouse? *I just told you. There's nobody else*. Does she have a bloodletter? *Me*. Will you be coming to the center to bloodlet for the patient? *No*. Is there a forwarding address for you? *Not right now*.

There's a pregnant pause each time I answer, and I feel like I'm wearing a too-tight T-shirt that keeps shrinking. The nurse's breathy drawl is thick with judgment that seeps through the phone like hot tar, making my ears burn.

She's just some do-gooder. She thinks she knows how to handle this thing, but I doubt she's ever had to threaten someone she loves with a sharp piece of rusted metal.

I pull open my dresser drawers, covered in scratch-and-sniff stickers I applied to the unfinished fiberboard in an attempt to make it look more cheerful thirteen years ago. I lay piles of clothes on the bed. I consider my worn, stuffed panda, its fuzzy black spots sunbleached with age. I haven't slept without it since I was eleven. But it's not coming with me.

I put half the clothes back. I need to pack light. Jade and I are going to be living out of her van until we get to New York. At least, I think that's still the plan. We never *really* talked about it, never actually laid out the schedule and the stops. We don't have a concrete plan for the end of the tour, either. But she mentioned a friend who offered her a job in New York, and I'm sure I could find something to do there. We can share a little studio apartment and furnish it with eclectic stuff from funky thrift shops. Drink coffee on the fire escape in the mornings. Wine at night. It would be nice to live near a park. It doesn't even have to be one of the nice parks. Just some green space with a few trees, where we can have picnics and watch kids play in the snow when it gets cold. I haven't seen snow in years.

I wrestle with a dusty purple suitcase wedged all the way at the back of the closet. I've never actually used it. Mom bought it for me the year we thought we'd be going to Disneyland. As I dislodge the suitcase and topple a stack of ancient paperbacks, I spot a dozen tiny yellow flowers painted on the wall, faded beneath layers of dust. A cold lump thickens in my throat.

My fantasy and the swell of hope it brings both vanish as I turn on the overhead light. Against my better judgment, I brush away the dust, revealing the mural.

This one is a scene from *The Princess Bride*, one of our early favorites. Mom painted an expanse of expertly textured green grass across the bottom of the wall, where Westley and Buttercup lie in each other's arms. I contributed the little yellow flowers surrounding them. Up above in the powder-blue sky, I inscribed the magic words in my haphazard, childlike penmanship: *As You Wish.*

I withdraw and shut the closet door with more force than I mean to. I feel that awful, snakelike squeeze around my chest again. I fight against my body, pressurizing my tears. This is going to happen, I tell myself. You'll hear a song from *The Sound of Music*, or smell someone's Chanel perfume on the bus. Someone will say something that isn't *exactly* a thing she'd say but your brain will bridge the gap and whisk you back in time. *This is going to happen.*

I get dressed robotically, forcing myself to gulp deep breaths to slow my racing heart. As I pad toward the darkened kitchen, I pause in front of Mom's room and stare at her closed door. For half an instant, I think about opening it. Not to wake her, not to say goodbye. Just to see her. But I talk myself out of it. It's better this way.

I ask Jade to pull up down the block again so Mom doesn't hear a car in the driveway. I don't want to take any chances. I sink down at the kitchen table. Probably for the last time. No, not probably. Definitely. I'm leaving, aren't I?

There's a smear of dried blood on the floor, over by the fridge. Red. Mine. It feels wrong to leave it. I should go clean it up. But I stop myself. Let her see it as they carry her out. Let her remember.

Ok I'm outside

My legs wobble as I shuffle toward the door, pulling the purple suitcase behind me. I open it carefully so the hinges don't squeak, leaving it unlocked so the transport nurses from the Sara center can get in. I feel like I should glance over my shoulder and take it all in, one last time. But I don't want to. I can't.

Jade waves at me from down the street. She's changed her clothes from the night before, styled her hair, and even managed to re-apply her signature blue eyeliner. Warmth blooms inside me as I approach. That's the thing about Jade. You try to knock her down, the next morning she gets right back up, puts on her makeup, and greets you with that supernova smile. She's still limping a bit, though. We should probably see a doctor about her ankle. She's playing it cool, but I know it's got to hurt.

"Here you are." She beams at me, holding out her arms.

"Here I am."

She opens the sliding door of the minivan and takes my suitcase, then opens my door in the front and guides me into my seat. Like I'm a very important passenger going on a very important journey.

"We'll head back to Tony's place for tonight so we can pack. Sound good?"

I nod, but there's a thorn of disbelief in my side. This is it. I'm in the car. I'm never coming back.

"You okay?" She pushes her sunglasses to the tip of her nose and studies me. I nod again.

She settles into the driver's seat beside me but doesn't pull onto the road right away. She drums her nails on the steering wheel and flutters air between her lips, like she's thinking hard about something. Now it's my turn to wonder if *she's* okay.

"We probably shouldn't stay parked here," I say after a moment.

"I know. Um . . . there's just one quick thing I wanted to talk to you about. Before we . . . y'know. This is a big deal, what you're doing. And I'm really glad I'm able to help."

"Okay . . . ?"

"On the tour, though. Or like, I guess before the tour starts. We're gonna have to uh . . . I mean, *I'm* gonna have to swing through Chicago first. For a minute."

"That's fine." I think so, anyway.

"And I know I told you I'm in this like . . . very weird situation. With Gabi."

I don't say anything. She doesn't wait for me to nod.

"I need to uh . . . First of all, my stuff is still at her place. My cat, too. I have a cat I left there. Matilda. You'll like her, she's great."

"Okay?"

"And the thing is, you're gonna be *with me* so I can't put this off any longer. I don't *want to* put it off—"

"Jade . . . what are you—?" My stomach snarls.

"I'll tell her, I can't *not* tell her. And I'll do it right away. I promise. But I just . . ."

"Tell her *what*?"

"I-I mean, about you. I'm gonna tell her about you."

"Is she still your girlfriend?"

Jade doesn't answer. But of course she is. Yet another thing I already knew. I think of how she made sure not to kiss me in front of Tallie and Morrison last night. She's still protecting Gabi. Still cares about her.

"This whole thing with you and me . . . It happened *really* fast." Jade stares at her hands as she talks. "I'm happy, it's been amazing. And I think it needed to happen. For both of us. But it's not fair if I don't tell you the whole truth. If you're coming with me."

Neither of us speaks. The air between us hardens like ice.

"Jade, why didn't you—"

"Look, at the end of the day, none of this matters. Not really. I'm here for you. We're doing this. I want to help you."

"I . . . I don't want *help*, Jade. I want—"

"I know, babe."

"Please stop calling me that."

"It's gonna be okay, Mia. I promise."

She reaches out to embrace me. I let her, but my arms hang at my sides. I don't hug her back. All of a sudden I don't know what the fuck to do. This was never going to be easy or feel good, but five minutes ago at least it felt *right*.

Humiliating heat prickles across my skin, rushing up into my cheeks. Jade and I have hung out exactly three times outside of work. We haven't had sex, haven't taken off our clothes. I look into her eyes, at her perfect peacock-blue liner, and realize I've never even seen her without makeup. We don't know each other. *We don't know each other.*

I force myself away from her and get out of the car.

"Hang on. Mia—"

I yank my suitcase from the back seat and start trudging back toward the driveway, dragging it behind me. I'm not sure what's worse, letting her see me cry or crying alone inside the house.

"Mia! Wait! Please don't—"

I'd kill to be able to slam the door.

I retreat to my room as my eyes readjust to the darkness, blurred with tears. I slump down on the bed, forcing myself to sift through the wreckage. I should still allow the van from the Sara center to come. No matter what, I'm not safe. This needs to happen. Of course, I'll be here by myself, after that. The last thing I ever wanted. But maybe it's better than tagging along as Jade and Gabi's third wheel. Who knows how long it'll take her to end things. If she does at all. At least if I stay in the area, I can eventually try to visit Mom at the Sara center. Maybe she'll get some sort of treatment there and we can make amends someday. We can see each other at Christmas and on our birthdays. Maybe . . .

Creeaaaak.

My breath catches and I whirl around, expecting to see Mom in the doorway. But nobody's there. I hold still and wait for the sound a second time. Nothing.

"Mia . . . ?" Jade timidly calls out.

Oh fuck me.

I race down the hallway, cursing myself for leaving the door unlocked. She stands in the living room, her posture meek and resigned. A bead of blue falls down her cheek.

"I'm so sorry. Please, just come with me. It's over between me and Gabi, I promise. I'm ready—"

And that's when I notice it. The door to Mom's bedroom, which was closed just a moment ago, hangs wide open.

"Leave," I whisper, trying and failing to keep my voice steady. "Now."

"I'm not leaving without you—"

"*Jade*—"

Creeeeaak. Mom emerges from the bathroom, unleashing a predatory, inhuman shriek. She only has to take two lightning-quick strides to reach the place where Jade stands. I'm not sure her feet even touch the ground. If she's still got pain from her gunshot wound, she's decided she doesn't feel it.

Smash! Jade tries to flee, but she crashes into the coffee table, knocking a lamp to the floor. Mom seizes her ankle, the same one she twisted last night, and drags her in like a fish on a hook, facedown. My shaky legs are limp and heavy as I bolt toward them, like I'm a rag doll filled with wet sawdust. Everything feels like it's happening at half speed, like in a dream. Because it must be a dream. This can't be real.

Jade claws at the carpet with bloody hands amid the pieces of the broken lamp. "Mia!" she screeches. The dream speeds up. Fast, faster, too fast.

"Mom, please just let her go and we'll talk." I sound about as steely as a mouse.

Mom glances at me with those eyes like hot coals, but she says nothing. She pins both of Jade's legs to the ground, about to pounce on top of her from behind.

I throw myself onto Mom's back and wrap my elbow around her throat. But my choke hold is barely an inconvenience to someone as strong as her. I won't be able to hang on much longer. Jade writhes underneath us, trying desperately to free herself. My eyes dart around the room. How can I save her, what can I do?

Mom wrenches my arm free and head-butts me from behind. Blood pools in my nostrils as my vision goes gray.

I roll onto my back with a groan and realize I'm staring up at the big picture window, covered by its heavy blackout curtain. I could open it just a little bit, just to scare her. Just long enough to get her to drop Jade. . . .

I grapple for the edge of the curtain and ball it up in my fist, forcibly yanking it to the side. There's a loud *crack* as the strained curtain rod snaps free and tilts downward at a terrifying angle. *No, no, no.* All the air leaves my body as lethal white light pours into the room, like I've just opened a mortal wound.

My scream becomes Mom's scream. We're howling together at the exact same frequency and it thrums between my ears like we're singing in some unholy chorus.

I flail with the broken curtain rod, even though I know I won't be fast enough. We know this from the Facebook group. Seven seconds is all you have.

Seven . . . six . . . five—

The burn is quick and ruthless, splitting the skin with blistered, bloody fault lines. Mom curls into the fetal position, trying to shield her face from the light. Jade rolls out of harm's way, gasping like someone's been holding her head underwater. But I hardly notice.

"Oh God, Mia . . ." She wails on the ground.

"Shut up and fucking help me!"

The curtain rod slips between my shaky hands as Jade limps over. Even on tiptoe, neither of us is tall enough to hang it back up. Jade collapses as her ankle gives way.

"Cover her up if you can't cover the window!" She reaches for a quilt on the couch. But it's too late.

Mom's scream resolves into a horrific gag, wet and viscous. The burn has ravaged its way inside of her.

Four . . . three . . . two—

The hooks slide off the rod and spill to the ground, taking the heavy curtain down with it. I follow, slumping to the floor. A savage moan escapes from the deepest part of my body.

One.

Silence rings in my ears. I dare to peer over at Mom, or at least . . . the spot where she was.

Years ago, there was a photo someone posted to the Facebook group, a photo Mom hadn't let me see. But I snuck onto the computer later that night and pulled it up. I had no idea what I was looking at. It reminded me of a blueberry crumble Mom once made at Thanksgiving that burned to a molten, syrupy crisp when she set the oven to 450 instead of 350. I lost my appetite for two whole days.

I avert my gaze from the carnage as bile congeals in my throat. The dry heaving starts, and I turn in a circle. There's Jade, silhouetted in the window, panting and massaging her swollen ankle as tears stream down her face.

"Mia, I'm so sorry—"

"Get out," I hear myself say.

"We should call someone. Right? We should—"

"Please just go."

"I-I just . . . Oh, Mia, I'm so—"

"What did I just say?" I pick up the curtain rod as though I'm about to strike her. Like I can use it to sweep her outside like a rat. "You shouldn't be here, *you never should've fucking been here.*"

She hobbles toward the door, clutching the wall for support.

"I-I really am sorry, Mia," she whispers, choking back a sob. I say nothing.

The door creaks open, then softly shuts. She's gone.

Everything is gone.

☾ ☾ ☾

I sit at the kitchen table, motionless. Hypnotized by the second hand on the clock above the sink. Tick, tick, tick, tick, tick . . .

I don't know what the rules are, when something like this

happens. Don't know who takes the blame. Part of me wonders if I should let the people from the Sara center find me here and accept whatever punishment I deserve for what happened in the living room.

And then there's Devon. Mom said he was coming back for her. Tonight. What will he do when he finds her like this? What will he do to *me*?

I can't stay here. I have to go somewhere. Not to Jade. I don't know. I don't have anyone. And that was on purpose. There's nobody. But that's the way it was supposed to be all along. Before this happened. Before *I made this* happen. . . .

I can't think in here. I need to get outside.

But there's something I have to do first.

I make my way toward the living room, crunching broken glass beneath my socks. It punctures the soles of my feet as I tamp down the tears. Guilt rises from my stomach, hot and corrosive, but I push that down, too.

I heave the blackout curtain over my shoulder and, gently as I can, lay it across her remains. I stare at the shapeless mass underneath. *Seven seconds.* At least it was fast. There's no comfort in it now. Maybe someday. Whatever "someday" means. I can't seem to picture it.

I step outside and crumple to the ground in a sudden fit of vertigo on the front steps. Cradle my spinning head. I'm aching to run. I was *supposed to* run. But my body is leaden.

The sun starts to warm my back, like a reassuring squeeze. Finally, I breathe. Slow and deep. I am alive. *In, out.* Alive. *In, out.* Alive . . .

I don't know where I'm supposed to go. What I should do, how I survive this. Everything is bare and colorless, a raw void of suffocating uncertainty. I know only one thing: I need to be gone by the time Devon comes back here.

Good. Okay. Let's start there. *In, out.* Still alive.

There's a weak glimmer in my chest; maybe now they can finally catch him. *Yes*. The trap has been set. But I need to go to the police right away so they can make a plan. We don't have much time.

In, out. Still alive. Very much alive.

When they see what happened inside, what happened to Mom . . . if I tell them it was an accident, that wouldn't be a lie. Jade would back me up. I won't be in trouble. Especially if I can help them catch Devon.

In, out.

The hot flagstone stoop starts singeing my bare legs. I'm going to need to stand soon.

But what happens after that? After I stand?

Figure it out once you're on your feet.

I rise and let myself be still. Everything is so, so still. There's no wind. The dusty street is silent. I realize why my body won't obey my urge to run. I am not meant to disrupt this. I'm meant to let it wash over me.

So, this is it. The world without my mother.

That liminal hush, my bated breath, as I wait for the universe to shuffle its cards and deal me a new fate.

At last, a breeze. I brush the hair from my eyes.

In, out.

Okay.

The police station. I'm going to go to the police station now. To tell them about Devon. That's as far as I've gotten, but it's far enough.

I feel myself start to move forward, like I'm dancing with someone older and stronger, balancing on their feet. One step, two steps, three. Now I'm in the driveway. Clutching the keys to the Jeep. I meet the vacant stare of its dark windshield. As though I'm asking permission.

I realize I've left the front door open. Daylight bleeds across the foyer, splitting apart the shadows, burning through the darkness.

I should go back and close it. But I don't.

ACKNOWLEDGMENTS

I'd like to start by thanking my parents. I love you. Thank you for your encouragement and always allowing me the space to create, heal, and find myself again and again through my writing. To Sam, for all of the above, as well as all the brilliant, early-days suggestions when I first set out to write this book. Thank you for being my flashlight during a dark and winding year. For talking to me about blood and coffee during hundreds of long dog walks. For spinning me around when there was something to celebrate. And for the quiet, necessary company when there wasn't.

None of you would be reading this without the faith and support of two very important people: my friend Hilary, and my agent Liz Parker. Three years ago, I wrote a short story to get some *stuff* out of my system. Didn't know how it was going to evolve or what it meant. But these two did. Hilary, thank you for letting me send you twenty-five pages a month throughout the pandemic when motivation was such a scarce commodity, and for so many nights spent on your couch throwing books at each other and wondering where all the wine went. Liz: your unflinching belief in this story has meant more to me than you'll ever know. Thank you for seeing these characters—for seeing *me*—and being our champion. How lucky I am that we came into each other's lives exactly when we did.

Huge gratitude also goes out to my brilliant, sensitive friends who beta read for me, as well as those who read the original short story. To Christina Brosman, who has patiently allowed me to ramble about these characters for three whole years and offers the kind of enthusiastic wisdom that actually makes a person excited to sit down and rewrite. To Ana and Gautham, my chosen siblings, for letting me scream secret, exciting news into their ears and helping me steer the ship when things got stormy. Thank you also to Abby, for patiently mending my heart. To my mother-in-law, Sallie, for always making me feel safe and celebrated, and the Kirsch family for letting us borrow Tucson whenever we needed it. What a gift it was to experience that world, night after night. To my Verve family, as well as Merideth Bajaña, who lifted this project to heights I never could have imagined. Melissa Darman in particular deserves her own standing ovation. To my editor, Kelly Lonesome, who knew *exactly* what I was trying to say and why I was saying it, every step of the way. I'm so honored to be a member of the Nightfire Coven. To Jac Schaeffer, Laura Monti (who was the first person on the team to read and shout about it), and Leslye Headland, for seeing all the breathless possibility in the world beyond this book. Can't wait to see what the future has in store for us.

Of course, I'd be remiss if I didn't thank every single person who bought my first book, told a friend, tagged me on Instagram, and made me feel like I could *really* do this. I'm endlessly grateful for all your rowdy cheerleading. Thanks for your patience as I wrote something new and (hopefully) worthy of your love.

Finally, I'd like to thank Sydney and Avery. Sydney and Avery were dogs. They were the best friends I ever had. The year I wrote the first draft of this book, Sydney's health started declining. Every morning, she'd wake me up around 5 A.M. because she wasn't feeling well, and I would stay awake with her till she fell asleep again. That's when I wrote most of this book, between the hours of 4 and 7 A.M., on the "night's edge," with Sydney snoring in my lap. The following year, during the edit, Avery started showing signs that she was ready to leave us, too. Thus, we repeated the night's edge writing vigil. I miss them with my whole heart, every day. But because you are reading this, my sweetest little friends live on. So thank *you,* as well.